P9-CEO-510

House Divided

Also by Mike Lawson

The Inside Ring

The Second Perimeter

House Rules

House Secrets

House Justice

House Divided

A Joe DeMarco Thriller

MIKE LAWSON

Atlantic Monthly Press
New York

Published simultaneously in Canada
Printed in the United States of America

FIRST EDITION

ISBN: 978-0-8021-1978-0

Atlantic Monthly Press
an imprint of Grove/Atlantic, Inc.
841 Broadway
New York, NY 10003

Distributed by Publishers Group West

www.groveatlantic.com

11 12 13 14 10 9 8 7 6 5 4 3 2 1

For my brother Steve, for taking care of Mom and Dad

1

A satellite orbits a blue planet, huge solar panels extended like wings.

Alpha, do you have Carrier?
Negative. Monument blocking.
Bravo, do you have Carrier?
Roger that. I have him clear.
Very well. Stand by.

Nothing more was recorded for eight minutes and forty-eight seconds. Time was irrelevant to the machines.

I think Messenger has arrived. Stand by.

Confirmed. It's Messenger. Messenger is approaching Carrier. Alpha, do you have Messenger?

Roger that.

Bravo, do you still have Carrier?

Roger that.

Very well. Stand by. Transport, move into position.

Four point three seconds of silence followed.

Transport. Acknowledge.

A second later:

Transport. Acknowledge.

Four point nine seconds passed.

Alpha, do you have Messenger?
Roger that.
Bravo, do you have Carrier?
Roger that.
You have my green. I repeat. You have my green.

Three heartbeats later:

Transport, Transport. Respond.

There was no response.

I'll transport in my vehicle. Maintain positions. Keep me advised.

Nothing more was recorded for six minutes and sixteen seconds.

This is Alpha. Two males approaching from the north. I have them clear.

Alpha, take no action. Do I have time to retrieve Carrier?
Negative.
Very well. Stand by.

One minute and forty three seconds later:

This is Alpha. The two males have stopped. They may have sighted Carrier. They have sighted Carrier. They're approaching Carrier. I have them clear.

Alpha, take no action. Transport acknowledge.

Two point four seconds of silence.

Return to jump-off. I repeat. Return to jump-off.

After thirty-five minutes elapsed, a program dictated that the transmission was complete and the recording was compressed and sent in a single microsecond burst to a computer, where, in the space of nanoseconds, it was analyzed to determine if it met certain parameters. The computer concluded the recording did indeed meet those parameters, and at the speed of light it was routed through a fiber-optic cable and deposited in a server, where it would reside until a human being made a decision.

2

Jack Glazer was getting too old for this shit.

It was two in the morning, rain was drizzling down on his head because he'd forgotten to bring a hat, and he was drinking 7-Eleven coffee that had been burning in the pot for six hours before he'd poured the cup.

And there was a dead guy lying thirty yards from him.

"Has the ME been here?" he asked the kid, some newbie who'd been on the force maybe six months and looked about sixteen years old—but then all the new guys looked absurdly young to him. And naturally the kid was totally jacked up, this being the first homicide he'd ever caught.

"Been and gone," the kid said. "Forensics sent one guy; he searched the vic, ID'd him from his wallet, and said he'd be back in a couple hours with his crew. They got another—"

"So who's the victim?"

"The name on his driver's license is Paul Russo. He was a nurse."

"How do you know that?" Glazer asked.

"He had a card in his wallet, some kind of nurses' association he belonged to. He also had the name of an emergency contact, some guy named—"

"Did you write down the contact's name?" Glazer asked.

"Yeah."

"Then you can give it to me later."

"The thing is, sir, this guy has cash in his wallet and he still has his credit cards and his watch. So I don't think we got a mugging here. I'm thinking drugs. I'm thinking this guy, this nurse, was pedaling shit. You know, Oxy, Vicodin, something, and he gets popped."

"Could be," Glazer said. "But now this is really important, uh . . ." Glazer squinted at the kid's name tag. "Officer Hale. Where's the body, Hale?"

Hale, of course, was confused by the question, because the body was clearly visible.

So Glazer clarified. "Hale, is the body in the park or out of the park?"

"Oh. Well, that's kind of a tough call," Hale said. "The head's on the sidewalk but the feet are on the grass. I guess it's kinda half in and half out."

"Yeah, I think you're right. So why don't you grab his heels and pull him all the way into the park."

The kid immediately went all big-eyed on Glazer.

"I'm kidding, Hale," Glazer said, but he was thinking, *Shit. Why couldn't the body have been in the park, or at least three-quarters in the park?*

Paul Russo had been shot near the Iwo Jima Memorial, and the memorial was located in a park operated by the National Parks Service. This meant the park was federal property—technically, not part of Arlington County and out of Jack Glazer's jurisdiction. If the guy had been shot in the park, Glazer would have pawned the case off on the feds without hesitation. He was already dealing with three unsolved homicides and he didn't need another.

"Where are the two witnesses?" Glazer said.

"In the back of my squad car."

"Did they see anything?"

"No. They're dishwashers. They work at a Chinese restaurant over in Rosslyn and were on their way home. All they saw was a body on the ground and called it in."

Great.

Glazer walked over to look at the body: a short-haired, slimly built man in his thirties with no distinguishing features. Just your average white guy. He was wearing a tan jacket over a green polo shirt, jeans, and running shoes. He was clean and healthy-looking—except for the small, red-black hole in his left temple.

Glazer noticed there was no exit wound from the bullet. This surprised him because it made him think that if Russo had been shot at close range, which he most likely was, the shooter might have used a .22 or .25—and that was unusual. Most folks who bought handguns these days, particularly men, didn't normally buy small-caliber weapons. Everybody wanted hand cannons—big-bore automatics with sixteen-round magazines.

He took his flashlight and shined it around the area but didn't see anything—no shell casings, no footprints, no dropped business cards from Murder, Inc. He looked again at the position of the body. Just like Hale had said: it was almost exactly half on the sidewalk—which Glazer was positive belonged to Arlington County—and half inside the park. Goddammit. It was going to be a real tussle to get the feds to take the case.

"Hi there."

Glazer turned. A man was walking toward him, a handsome dark-haired guy in his early forties dressed in a blue suit, white shirt, no tie, holding an umbrella over his head.

"Sir, this is a crime scene," Glazer said. "Get back behind the tape."

Glazer glared over at Hale, wondering why the damn rookie had let a civilian into the area. Then he found out.

The guy took a badge case out of the inside pocket of his suit coat and flipped it open. "Hopper, FBI," he said. "I think this one's ours." He smiled at Glazer then, and he had a great smile—charming, disarming, all these even white teeth just gleaming in the dark. "I mean, I'd love to let you have it," he said, "but my boss says we gotta take this one."

What the hell?

"How did you know about the victim?" Glazer said.

"Beats me," Hopper said. "They just told me to get my ass over here. One of our guys must have picked it up on the scanner and heard you folks talking about it. I don't know. What difference does it make?"

The difference it made was that there was no way an FBI agent would have hustled over here at two in the morning to take over the case. Maybe when it was daylight, but not at two A.M.—and not for an apparent nobody like Paul Russo. And this agent. He wasn't some low-level Louie; Glazer could tell just by looking at him. This guy had weight.

"The body's on the sidewalk," Glazer said. "My sidewalk."

Hopper looked down at the body. "It's half on the sidewalk. And the rule is—"

"Rule? What fuckin' rule?"

"The rule is like football. Wherever the runner's knee goes down is where they spot the ball. His knee went down in the park."

"I've never heard of any—"

"Come on, Glazer. I'm tr—"

"How do you know my name?"

Irritation flicked across Hopper's face. "They gave it to me when they called me. Probably got if off the scanner, too. Why are you giving me a hard time here? I'm doing you a favor. This is one less murder on Arlington's books. It's one less case you have to clear. You oughta be thanking me, not arguing with me."

Glazer already knew he was going to lose this fight—and anybody looking at the scene, not knowing a single thing about criminal jurisdictions, would know he was going to lose it, too. In one corner you had this confident six-foot-two, handsome as Mel-fucking-Gibson federal movie star. In the other corner you had Jack Glazer: five-ten, a stocky, strong-looking guy, a guy tough enough to have maybe played linebacker for a small college team but not big enough or fast enough for a big-name school. It was the neighborhood mutt squaring off against the government's Rin Tin Tin—and nobody would have put their money on the mutt.

But still—even knowing the feds were going to win this jurisdictional tug-of-war—this guy pissed him off. And something was seriously out of whack.

"Yeah, well, we'll have to settle this later, when it's daylight," Glazer said, shifting his position slightly, blocking off Hopper's path to the body. "I need to check with my boss. But for now—"

Glazer's cell phone rang. He looked at the caller ID. *What the hell?*

"Glazer," he said into his phone. He listened for a few seconds, said, "Yes, sir," and hung up.

Glazer looked at Hopper for a moment and then slowly nodded his head. "That was my boss. He said this is your case."

3

Gilbert swiped his badge through the bar-code reader, punched in a six-digit security code, and pressed his thumb against the pad. When the annex door lock clicked, he pulled the door open, nodded to the no-neck security guy who had a small desk on the other side of the door, and went to his cubicle. He tossed his backpack on the floor, spent ten minutes bullshitting with another technician about how his new cell phone was a piece of shit, then proceeded to the coffee mess, where he poured the first of a dozen cups he would drink that day.

Back in his cubicle, he booted up all the machines, spent fifteen minutes on one of them looking at e-mail, then turned to the machine that provided him with an annotated description of transmissions intercepted in his sector in the past twelve hours. He tapped the SCROLL DOWN key as he studied the screen, sipping his coffee, then stopped. "What the hell?" he muttered.

He tapped on a keyboard, routed the transmission he'd selected to a program that would deencrypt it, and for forty-five minutes did other work. Then he put on his headphones.

Alpha, do you have Carrier?
Negative. Monument blocking.

Bravo, do you have Carrier?
Roger that. I have him clear.
Very well. Stand by.

When the recording stopped, Gilbert muttered "Holy shit," played it again to be sure, then copied the transmission to a CD.

The label on the CD said NATIONAL SECURITY AGENCY. There were a lot of other words printed on the label as well and, when taken collectively, these words indicated the CD was classified at the highest level and whoever listened to it would rot in a federal prison until their teeth fell out if they didn't have the proper clearance. There was nothing unique about the label, however. Every CD in the annex, including the one that contained forms for purchasing office supplies, had the same label.

CD in hand, he walked through a maze of cubicles, nodding to folks he passed, but didn't stop until he reached her office. She was sitting at her desk, head down, reading something, and when he knocked on the doorframe to let her know he was standing there, she looked up with those frosty eyes of hers.

"Yes," she said.

No *good morning, how-are-you, how's-it-going?* It was always business with her, never a moment wasted on mundane social interactions.

"I think you need to hear this," Gilbert said, holding up the CD. "I think two guys got killed last night."

Other than a slight elevation of one blonde eyebrow, she showed no emotion. She took the CD from him and slipped it into one of the three computer towers beneath her desk.

"Password?" she said.

She wasn't asking if the disc was password-protected; of course it was. She was asking for the password because if she tried to open the CD without it everything on it would turn to gibberish.

"Grassyknoll, lower case, one word," Gilbert said.

She typed the password and listened to the recording with her eyes closed, giving Gilbert a chance to study her. She was at least ten years his senior, getting close to forty, he guessed, but she had a good long-legged body, a narrow face with a model's cheekbones, and those incredible scary blue eyes. He couldn't understand why such a good-looking woman didn't have a husband or a lover, but since she worked about sixteen hours a day and was the least approachable person he'd ever met, maybe that wasn't so surprising.

"When did this take place?" she asked.

"About one A.M."

"Where were they?"

"I don't know, exactly. Somewhere in the District or Northern Virginia. For some reason, that's best location we could get. I need to take a look at the software to see if it's got some kind of glitch, but it could have been the com gear these guys were using."

She didn't say anything for a moment. She just sat there staring at him like it was his fault the fucking software didn't work, but then she nodded and he exhaled in relief.

Claire Whiting scared the hell out him. She scared everyone. Well, maybe not Dillon, but everyone else.

Dillon Crane was on the phone when Claire entered his office.

Dillon was sixty-three years old, tall and slender—and the subject of infinite office speculation. His short white hair was trimmed each week by the same barber the president used, and his suits were handmade by a Milanese tailor who now resided in Baltimore. The suit he wore today was light gray in color, and his shirt was also gray, a darker gray than the suit. Claire had no name for the color of his tie—something with maroon and charcoal black and dark blue all swirled together—but whatever the color, it matched the suit and shirt perfectly.

Dillon never wore white shirts and simple ties to work. He'd remarked once that a white shirt, accompanied inevitably by the ubiquitous striped tie, was the uniform of a bureaucrat, and even though he was one he refused to dress like one. And since the hundred and fifty thousand dollars a year he earned from the National Security Agency was a pittance compared to the annual income from his trust fund, he could afford to dress however he pleased.

He smiled when he saw Claire in his doorway—that annoying ain't-life-droll smile of his—but continued with his phone call. "Clark," he was saying, "all I can do is relay to you what we intercepted. It *appears*—and I can't be any more definitive—that a certain opium-growing warlord is about to assassinate an Afghani politician who has grown contrary of late."

Claire realized Dillon was talking to Clark Palmer, deputy to the president's national security advisor. Dillon, on one occasion, had said to her, "Clark's a rock—only not so smart."

He listened for a moment, rolled his eyes for Claire's benefit, and said into the phone, "No, Clark, I won't send you a memo. The entire conversation was two sentences long, and I've just given you the NSA's translation and interpretation of those sentences. Have a nice day."

Dillon hung up the phone and smiled at Claire again. "You look lovely today," he said.

She ignored the compliment as she always did.

"We picked up something that could be important."

"I'm sure it's important, Claire, or you wouldn't be here. But is it interesting?"

Dillon, as she well knew, was easily bored. And she knew exactly what he meant by *interesting*. A White House lackey leaking a memo to the *Post;* a colonel at the Pentagon whispering bid specs to a contractor; an undersecretary at State calling her lover at the Israeli embassy—those things could be important and they often were—but they weren't interesting. They were business as usual.

The CD in Claire's hand was not business as usual.

"Yes, Dillon," she said, "it's interesting." She handed him the CD. "The password's grassyknoll, lower case, one word."

"Grassy knoll?" Dillon said, but he didn't say more and took the CD from her and slid it into the drive of his computer.

Alpha, do you have Carrier?
Negative. Monument blocking.

When he had finished listening to the recording, he said, "Now that *is* interesting. What do we know?"

"What do we know?" Claire repeated. "We *know* nothing. But would you like me to speculate?"

"Oh, please do, Claire. Speculate away."

"First," she said, "I think these guys were military."

"Logic?"

"These people were on radios, not cell phones, and the radios were something special. They weren't using walkie-talkies from RadioShack. They were using encrypted AN/PRC-150s."

"Really?"

"Yes," Claire said. "They had hard-to-get, encrypted, military com gear. Then you have the lingo: roger this, roger that, return to jump-off. And the discipline. When Transport didn't respond, the guy-in-charge never lost his cool, and when the two males showed up, *instant* damage assessment. Told his guys to beat feet and they did, no backtalk, no nothing. We're talking serious discipline here, the kind that gets pounded into soldiers."

Dillon waggled a hand, exposing a monogrammed cuff link. "Maybe," he said, "but not definitive. What else?"

"Well, just the obvious. This was a hit. They knew Carrier was meeting Messenger. They may have been following Carrier. They went high-tech on the radios because they were afraid someone might intercept their chatter, maybe somebody like us, which further indicates they could be military or part of the G."

Dillon nodded. No disagreement so far.

"This conversation took place at approximately one A.M., and I think this means that the meeting between Carrier and Messenger was intended to be secret. It was two people, for whatever reason, sneaking around in the dark. And now I'm winging it here, going totally from my gut, but I think Alpha and Bravo took long shots. I'm seeing snipers with night-vision scopes, sound suppressors, the whole enchilada."

"Could be," Dillon said.

Dillon, as Claire knew quite well, didn't place much stock in gut feelings, even hers. He may have acted perpetually flippant but he preferred data.

"After they made the hit," Claire said, "they were planning to take the bodies but Transport didn't show. They got Messenger's body but not Carrier's, so for some reason getting Messenger was sufficient. If it hadn't been, I think they would have popped the two males." Claire stopped and took a breath. "And that's it. End of speculation."

"Do you have a location for this event?"

"Just the greater D.C. area. We couldn't get anything better."

"Why not?"

"We're looking into that. We could have a software problem."

"I don't see how the software—"

Before Dillon could say more, Claire interrupted him. She didn't have time to get embroiled in some nerdy technical discussion, and sometimes Dillon could be as much of a geek as her technicians. "Look, I'll deal with the location issue, but do you want me to follow up on the intercept or not?"

Dillon hesitated and she knew why. Two people may have been

killed, but solving homicides wasn't his job—or hers. They could have solved a lot of homicides had they wanted to, but simple murder, at least from Dillon Crane's perspective, wasn't really all that important. On the other hand, the fact that these particular killers had been using encrypted radios and might be U.S. military personnel put a whole different spin on things. It could mean some other agency was keeping something from *his* agency.

And that was a no-no.

"Yes, let's follow up on it," Dillon said.

4

DeMarco got a bucket of balls and carried his clubs over to a slot on the driving range between two women in their fifties. His plan was to spend the next two hours whacking golf balls, concentrating particularly on his pitching, because he couldn't pitch for shit. He was gonna play a lot of golf in the next seven days, and as he hadn't played since last fall, he wanted to get the kinks out of his swing before he played an actual round.

Normally, he wouldn't have a week to devote solely to golf, but he did at the moment because the two most important people in his life—and, therefore, the two people who most often prevented him from doing what he wanted to do—were both out of town. The first of those people was his boss.

His boss was inconsiderate and selfish and never gave a moment's thought as to how his decisions adversely impacted DeMarco's life. He was also cunning, conniving, corrupt, and unscrupulous—and, if all that wasn't bad enough, he was an alcoholic and a womanizer. Now had his boss been a used car salesman, all those negative character traits might not have been so surprising—or maybe even expected. But his boss wasn't a used car salesman. His boss was John Fitzpatrick Mahoney, Speaker of the United States House of Representatives.

DeMarco was, for lack of a better term, Mahoney's fixer. He was the guy the Speaker assigned when he had some shady job he didn't want to give to a legitimate member of his staff, jobs that were often morally questionable if not downright illegal. Jobs such as collecting undocumented contributions from Mahoney's constituents or finding things out about other politicians that Mahoney could use to control their vote. There was very little DeMarco liked about his job, but when Mahoney was not in D.C. DeMarco was often left to his own devices, and right now his employer was lying in a hospital having his gallbladder removed—and no doubt complaining mightily to anyone forced to care for him.

DeMarco had no idea what function the gallbladder performed, but he presumed it wasn't anything too important if they were simply plucking it out of Mahoney's corpulent corpus. He wouldn't have been surprised, however, if the surgeon removed several other organs as well. Mahoney not only drank too much, he also smoked half a dozen cigars a day, and DeMarco figured a heart-liver-lung transplant was overdue.

The second person currently absent from his life was Angela DeCapria, his lover—who also happened to be an employee of the Central Intelligence Agency. They met last year when DeMarco was trying to figure out which member of Congress had leaked a story to a reporter that resulted in a CIA agent being killed. When they met, Angela had been married; she was now divorced and living part-time with him.

Unfortunately—and unlike DeMarco—Angela was serious about her career, and when her boss told her she had to go to Afghanistan for a while, she packed her bags without hesitation and flew away. And because she worked for the CIA, she couldn't tell DeMarco exactly what she would be doing, how long she'd be gone, or how to reach her—all of which annoyed him. He was sure his annoyance would be replaced by loneliness—and horniness—within a few days.

So for at least a week he was on his own, and he intended to take advantage of the situation by doing only things he liked to do—one of those things being golf. He took his place on a square of green Astroturf, placed a ball on the rubber tee inserted into the carpet, pulled his driver from his bag, and made a couple of practice swings to loosen up. *Wham!* The heavy-set grandma on his right hit a ball—smacked it about a hundred and fifty yards. Using a three iron. Jesus! He wished he'd found someplace else to stand. He stepped up to take his first shot of the year—and his cell phone rang. *Shit!*

"Is this Joseph DeMarco?" the caller asked.

"Yeah," DeMarco said, relieved it wasn't Mahoney calling from his hospital bed to make his life miserable.

"This is Detective Jack Glazer, Arlington County Police. I'd like to talk to you."

"Police? Why?" DeMarco said.

"Hasn't the FBI called you or been to see you?" Glazer asked.

"No, why would they?" DeMarco said.

"Huh," Glazer said. To DeMarco it sounded as if Glazer was surprised the FBI hadn't already contacted him.

"What's this about?" DeMarco asked.

Glazer hesitated. "Mr. DeMarco, I'm sorry to have to tell you this over the phone, but Paul Russo was killed last night. You were listed as an emergency contact on a card he had in his wallet."

"Paul Russo?" DeMarco said—and then he remembered who that was. Geez, he hadn't talked to the guy in three, maybe four years.

"Are you saying you don't know him?' Glazer said.

"No. I know him. He's like a second cousin or something. His mother was my mother's cousin. How was he killed?"

"I think it would be better if we talked about this face-to-face. Would you mind coming to my office?"

Glazer's office turned out to be a desk in a room filled with half a dozen other desks—and the room was bedlam. Guys in shirtsleeves that DeMarco assumed were detectives were sitting at some of the desks, shouting into phones, and four uniformed cops were also in the room. Two of the uniformed cops were holding on to a guy who had a shaved head and tats all over his arms. The guy's hands were cuffed behind his back and he was screaming obscenities at the top of his lungs.

DeMarco told one of the detectives that he was there to see Glazer, and the detective pointed to a man sitting at a cluttered desk at the back of the room. When DeMarco introduced himself, Glazer stood up, said, "Let's go someplace where we can hear each other talk," and led DeMarco to a small, windowless space equipped with a table and four metal chairs. DeMarco noticed a surveillance camera mounted high on one wall, pointed down at the table, and assumed he was in an interrogation room, which, for some reason, made him feel uncomfortable.

Glazer was a stocky, serious-looking guy in his fifties. He was wearing a wrinkled white shirt, his tie was undone, and he appeared harried and tired. After he thanked DeMarco for coming and asked if he wanted a cup of coffee, which DeMarco declined, Glazer told him that Paul Russo had been found dead last night at the Iwo Jima Memorial, killed by a single gunshot wound to the head.

"He was shot?" DeMarco said, unable to believe what he was hearing.

"Yeah. What can you tell me about him?" Glazer asked.

Still stunned by what he'd been told, DeMarco said, "I barely knew him. He moved to Washington about five years ago. He said he wanted to get out of New York and try someplace else, that he needed a change of scenery. When he got here, he looked me up, probably because my mother told him to, but, like I said, I hardly knew him. When we were kids, I didn't have much to do with him because he was younger than me, and the only times I ever saw him were at family things—weddings, funerals, things like that."

"So why would he have your name in his wallet as an emergency contact?"

"I don't know, but I'm the only relative he had that lives around here. He wasn't married, both his parents are dead, and he didn't have any brothers or sisters, so maybe he couldn't think of anyone else to write down. When he first moved here, we had lunch one day and I showed him a few areas where he might want to rent an apartment, but that was about it. I spoke to him a couple times on the phone afterward, but I never saw him again."

"Huh," Glazer said.

DeMarco wasn't sure what that meant. "Huh" seemed to be something Glazer said whenever he heard something that didn't match what he was thinking.

"Was your cousin wealthy or famous or connected to someone important?"

"Famous? No, he wasn't famous. He was just a nurse, as far as I know. Look, I appreciate you calling me, but if you're thinking I can help you figure out who killed him, I'm afraid I'm not going to be much help."

"And you said the FBI didn't contact you?"

"Yeah, I already told you that. Why would they? Are they involved in this?"

"Yeah," Glazer said. "Actually, it's their case."

"Then why are you—"

"Like I said, Russo was shot at the memorial, which is in Arlington County, and when the body was discovered the Arlington P.D. responded. But the thing is, the park's federal property and it was sort of a toss-up as to who had jurisdiction, us or the feds. Well, I had just gotten to the scene—this was about two A.M.—when an FBI agent shows up and takes the case away from me. And that's what I don't get, Mr. DeMarco. I mean, if your cousin had been some kinda big shot I could understand it, but based on what you're telling me, he wasn't. So why's the FBI so interested in him?"

"I have no idea," DeMarco said, but what he was really thinking was: since there wasn't anyone else to do it, he was going to have to get Paul's body and arrange for a funeral. Shit.

"One thing I didn't tell you," Glazer said. "When we found your cousin he had cash in his wallet and his credit cards hadn't been taken, so he wasn't killed in a robbery. So there's a possibility—no offense intended—that he might have been pedaling meds. I mean, since he was a nurse he probably had access to all kinds of medications and maybe he was dealing painkillers, tranks, things like that. But—"

"Narcotics? Paul? I kinda doubt that. Like I said, I didn't know him too well, but he always struck me as being pretty straitlaced."

"Yeah, you're probably right, and that's what I was going to say. He didn't have a criminal record, and guys who get killed over narcotics usually do. Which made me wonder if he was a witness involved in some sort of federal case."

"Well, if he was, I wouldn't know," DeMarco said. Glazer started to say something else, but DeMarco interrupted him. "Detective, if this isn't your case, why do you care why Paul was killed or why the FBI's involved?"

Glazer rubbed a hand over his face as if trying to scrub away the fatigue. Finally he said, "Because he was killed on my turf, DeMarco. And because there's something strange going on here. If your cousin was just some ordinary schmuck who had the bad luck to get shot, the feds wouldn't have wanted anything to do with him and would have insisted I take the case. But that's not what happened and it bugs me. I was hoping you could help me figure out what the hell's going on."

It sounded to DeMarco like this was some sort of pissing contest between the local cops and the Bureau, and he had absolutely no interest in it. "Well, I'm sorry, but I can't help you," he said. "Unless there's something else, I need to get his body and make arrangements for a funeral."

"You'll have to talk to the FBI about that," Glazer said. "And they won't release the body until an autopsy is done. The agent in charge is a guy named Hopper."

5

Charles Bradford didn't like the expression *shit happens* because too often fate was blamed for poor preparation and execution. But sometimes, shit did happen. Sometimes, the best-planned operations went awry for reasons the planners could have never imagined. The attempt to rescue the hostages in Iran in 1980 was one of the best examples he could think of.

In 1979, the American Embassy in Tehran was taken over by an Iranian mob, fifty-three Americans were held hostage and, after almost a year of attempting to negotiate their release, the president finally authorized a military mission to free them. The mission was planned for months, all possible intelligence was collected, the best personnel were selected—and then everything went to hell. One helicopter had an avionics system failure, another had a hydraulic system failure, and an unexpected sandstorm occurred. The mission finally ended in total disaster when a refueling plane crashed into a third helicopter, killing eight U.S. servicemen.

Shit happens.

Bradford knew something similar had happened with Levy's operation. John Levy was a careful man, a man who thought things through. He had worked for Bradford for a long time and had always performed admirably under the most difficult conditions. So even before Levy gave him the details, Bradford was sure that whatever had gone wrong had been totally out of Levy's control—an act of God, if you will. As it turned out, he was right.

"A drunk hit the ambulance I had staged for moving the bodies," Levy said. "It was a . . . a total fluke."

"Why didn't you have the ambulance right at the scene?" Bradford said.

"I thought it might stand out and somebody might remember it. And it was only two blocks away, less than a minute away. But this drunk? He takes a corner going about sixty and hits the ambulance head on. The drunk was killed, a woman with him is in critical condition, and my man was injured."

"What sort of injuries?"

"Internal injuries and major head trauma. He's in a coma. I have someone inside the hospital, and if he comes out of the coma I'll be called immediately. I'll make sure he doesn't talk to anyone, but it may take a few days to get him out of the hospital because—"

Bradford interrupted him. "John, you know what's at stake here. This man poses a significant risk. He may talk and not even realize he's talking. I know he's a good man, but—"

Bradford stopped speaking and just stared at Levy. Finally, Levy said, "Yes, sir. I—I understand."

Bradford could see the fate of the driver bothered Levy—and this was understandable. Levy wasn't a demonstrative man, but neither was he without compassion. Nor was Charles Bradford. Nonetheless, and as Bradford had said, Levy knew that the life of a single man couldn't be allowed to compromise everything they were doing.

John Levy was tall and broad-shouldered and had a marathon runner's physique: no excess fat, long ropy muscles. His hands were huge and his wrists were the size of two by fours. Levy had the most powerful-looking wrists Bradford had ever seen. He wore his dark hair short and his face was long and somber with sunken cheeks and dark circles under deep-set, morose brown eyes. He looked like a man who rarely slept and never smiled; Bradford sometimes visualized him in a Franciscan monk's brown cowl, the hood covering his head, shadowing his face. But Levy wasn't religious, at least not in the conventional sense. What he was, above all else, was a patriot.

"Does the driver have a family?" Bradford asked.

Levy shook his head. "No wife or children. His mother and father are in Kansas. Farm people."

Salt of the earth, Bradford thought.

"Have him die somewhere overseas, in combat," Bradford said. "I don't want his parents to think their son was wasted in a senseless traffic accident."

"Yes, sir."

"And the rest of your team?" Bradford asked.

"They're already on their way out of the country."

"Good. And the two men who stumbled upon the scene?"

A second act of God, those two men showing up near the Iwo Jima Memorial at that time of night.

"I had Hopper interview them," Levy said. "They didn't see anything. They don't know anything. They're not a problem."

"Good," Bradford said. He said nothing more for a moment as he analyzed everything Levy had told him. "I think the only thing I'm concerned about was bringing in Hopper too fast. Taking the case away from Arlington and giving it to Hopper was the right thing to do, but it might have been better if you had delayed that a bit."

"I didn't know what those two men had seen at the time," Levy said. "And since I had to leave Russo's body, I didn't want to give the Arlington cops time to study the wound or do an autopsy and figure out what type of ordinance was used."

"I understand," Bradford said. "It was a judgment call. And you certainly made the right choice regarding which body to leave."

"I think so," Levy said. "Russo didn't have a lover, and his parents are dead. Nobody will really push for a solution. I've told Hopper to say he was most likely dealing drugs and, with Russo being a nurse, the people who matter will buy the story."

Bradford nodded. It appeared as if Levy had thought of everything. There were some risks—in any military operation there were always risks—but not large ones.

"All right, John," Bradford said. "Keep me posted."

"Yes, sir," Levy said.

Bradford noticed Levy started to raise his right hand to salute but then stopped himself. Old habits die hard—and it was good they did. John Levy would always be a soldier, with or without a uniform.

Bradford stood, hands clasped behind his back, looking out a window. In the distance he could see a portion of Arlington National Cemetery: a rolling green hill and row after row of white headstones. He loved the view from his office and took pride in the fact that one day his body would be interred at Arlington, his grave marked only by a simple white stone marker. That was all he wanted—no grand tomb, just the same stone that marked the graves of his fallen comrades.

He could also see Levy standing on the sidewalk talking to someone on his cell phone. He was most likely checking on the young man in the coma. He was probably wishing the driver would simply die, and then he wouldn't have to execute the order he'd been given. But Bradford had no doubt that Levy would follow the order.

He was so lucky to have a man like John. The people of this country, blissful in their ignorance, had no idea how much their survival depended on men like him.

And Martin.

Ah, Martin, I miss you so.

There was a rap on his office door. Bradford turned and saw one of his secretaries standing timidly in the doorway.

"I'm sorry to disturb you, General, but your meeting with the Secretary of Defense begins in two minutes."

6

"Dillon, I'll see your five and raise you five," Harry Cramer said.

"Harry," Dillon said, "are you sure you want to do that? The odds of you making your straight are less than sixteen percent."

"Maybe you've lost track of the cards," Harry said. "We all know you hired that young lady to distract us, but you've been paying more attention to her than anyone else at the table."

The bartender Dillon had hired to serve the poker players was indeed a distraction. She was a six-foot-tall, twenty-seven-year-old brunette with lavender eyes and exquisite proportions.

"Harry, I'm shocked you'd suggest such a thing," Dillon said. "I hired her because she makes a perfect martini and can pour with either hand. Ambidextrous bartenders are hard to find."

Marge Fielder boomed out a laugh. Marge was the only woman player present. The other attendees of the monthly game held at Dillon's home on the Maryland shore were: Harold Cramer, a federal judge who served on the D.C. Court of Appeals; Paul Winfield, special assistant counsel to the Chairman of the Federal Reserve; Stephen Demming, deputy to the Under Secretary of Defense for Policy at the Pentagon; Clyde Simmer, assistant to the Solicitor General at the Department of Justice; and Dillon Crane, deputy to the deputy director of the National Security Agency. Marge Fielder worked at the State Department and her title was Undersecretary for Political Affairs—making her the third highest ranking official in the department.

The six poker players had four things in common. They were all in their late fifties or early sixties and incredibly bright; no one player had any particular advantage over the others. Second, they were absurdly wealthy. Five of the six were heirs to obscene amounts of money willed to them by their ancestors. The exception was Stephen Demming, who had married money and then his wife had been kind enough to die and leave it all to him.

Each player occupied a powerful position in the federal government, yet none of them were known to the general public. Dillon, had he desired the job and had he been willing to contribute to whomever was running for president, could have been the Secretary of Defense; Harry Cramer had once been short-listed for a seat on the Supreme Court but had made it clear he wouldn't serve. Marge had twice declined the job of Secretary of State, having seen all too often how the press—and Congress—devoured the person in that position. Which was the third thing they all had in common: they all loved power but were astute enough to realize that the real power in Washington lay in the hands of the long-serving bureaucrats who occupied positions below the radar—the special assistants, the undersecretaries, the deputies to the deputies. The people in these positions were less likely to be changed out when a new administration occupied the West Wing and, because of their experience and longevity, they all knew exactly which levers to pull to make the gears of Washington spin. The reason Dillon had organized the game was that his friends not only had the wealth to play for staggering amounts but the game was also a forum for exchanging information—although all the players were extremely tight-lipped about giving away secrets. They came to acquire knowledge, not to dispense it.

The last thing they had in common, maudlin as it might sound, was they all believed in public service. Like Dillon. He was a Rhode Island Crane and before the terms *conservationist* and *environmentalist* became common to the English language, in an era where worker safety was the employee's problem and not the employer's, at a time when the word *union* was most often associated with the word *communism,* Dillon's great-grandfather ripped from the earth as much timber, coal, copper, and oil as he possibly could—and then emerged as a respectable fellow because he would occasionally build an orphanage or add a wing to a hospital. Dillon could have squandered his life sailing yachts or owning baseball teams, yet both he and his father, similar to the Kennedys, whom they knew quite well, had elected to devote their considerable abilities to government service. Dillon's father had been a congressman for thirty-five years, but Dillon had opted for his nearly invisible position at the NSA.

Of all the poker players, Marge found Dillon to be the most interesting—and the best-looking. He dated stunning women but—as far as she knew—he had never come close to marriage. He was quite vain about his appearance, spending a fortune each year on clothes, but wasn't the least bit vain about his accomplishments. His drab title of deputy to the deputy director disguised the fact that he was one of the most powerful players in the intelligence community, and although his attitude toward his job was typically flippant, as if he were completely above the fray, there was no one more adept—or more ruthless—in dealing with the Machiavellian maneuvers that occur within all bureaucracies. But the oddest thing about him was his education: he had a doctorate in physics, a field of study quite out of the norm for people from his class and background. One of the reasons he'd gone to work for the NSA was that he could actually understand what the wizards did at Fort Meade.

Dillon casually tossed five one-thousand-dollar chips into the center of the table, and Marge calculated that the pot was now at thirty-two thousand. "Okay, Judge," Dillon said, "you've been called. What do you have?"

Cramer fanned his cards out on the table.

"A straight, jack high. Did I mention, Dillon, that today's my birthday? I'm feeling very lucky tonight."

Marge watched a look of irritation flit across Dillon's face. He hated to lose—they all did—but the look passed quickly. He was too gracious—and too rich—to pout over the twelve thousand he'd lost on the hand. He turned to the bartender and said, "Katherine, would you mind looking below the bar? There's a bottle of Dom Perignon Oenotheque there. Please pour us each a glass so we can toast Judge Cramer's continued good health."

It was Marge's turn to deal. "Seven-card stud, threes and nines are wild."

The men all groaned. Marge liked wild card games because even geniuses like Dillon had a harder time calculating the odds.

As she was dealing, she asked Dillon, "Who do you think will replace Martin Breed?"

Paul Winfield, who worked at the Federal Reserve, said, "Who's Martin Breed?"

"My God, Paul," Stephen Demming said, "don't you read anything but the financial section of the papers?"

"Why would I?" Winfield said.

Marge knew that Winfield actually read every word in four papers daily—including the entertainment sections and gossip columns. He did this because he firmly believed that *everything* affected the markets. Marge assumed he was pretending to be ignorant of General Breed because he thought he might learn something he didn't already know. She loved these devious bastards.

"Martin Breed," Demming said, "was a two-star army general who would have gotten his third star this year. The word is that Charles Bradford was grooming him to be his replacement as the army's chief of staff. Breed died a few days ago from cancer. He was only fifty-two." Turning to Dillon, he said, "I've heard that Stan Parche will most likely end up in Breed's spot."

"I don't think so," Dillon said. "My guess is Jillian Chalmers. But, of course, the final decision will be made by Bradford."

"And you think Bradford would select a woman for that position?" Marge said.

Dillon winked at her. "Who said Jillian is female? No one has bigger balls than her."

7

Claire approached Dillon's office but didn't enter because he was talking with his boss, the deputy director.

The building was buzzing with an operation in progress. One of Dillon's other divisions—Claire's organization was just a small part of his domain—had intercepted several cell phone calls from Yemen indicating there was something onboard a ship that would soon dock in Long Beach. But whether the cargo was a bomb or a biological weapon, or something mundane like drugs or illegal aliens, wasn't clear. The NSA was trying to get more information so the Coast Guard would have a better idea of what they were dealing with before they stopped the ship. However, and because of the deputy director's body language, Claire suspected they weren't talking about the California-bound vessel.

The deputy director was simultaneously nodding and frowning. The nods implied that he agreed with everything Dillon was saying, but the frowns indicated that he didn't like anything he was hearing. This meant, Claire was fairly sure, that they were discussing Dillon's budget. Dillon's attitude toward his authorized annual budget—a budget that totaled several hundred million dollars and which he agreed not to exceed each year—was that what he was doing was so important that if more money was needed, Congress could either raise taxes or take the money from some other federal agency that was less important. In other words, not an attitude the deputy director appreciated, since he was the one who would have to crawl up to Capitol Hill and beg for the money. And judging by the deputy director's simultaneous nods and frowns, Dillon was telling the man the significance of everything he was doing and providing a reasonable explanation as to why it all cost so much—but he was also saying there was no way he could reduce his spending.

But Claire knew the real reason why Dillon could never meet his budget—and it had nothing to do with any mismanagement on Dillon's part. The real reason was that Claire's organization was not included in the budget and was being secretly funded out of Dillon's other operations. This, however, was not a fact Dillon could share with his boss.

The deputy director left five minutes later, still frowning, while Dillon appeared completely unperturbed. "That poor fellow," Dillon said, "is going to give himself an ulcer."

Claire didn't care. "The grassyknoll hit," she said. "I have data now."

Dillon's smile widened. "I love data," he said.

"That night three men in the D.C. area were shot at approximately one A.M."

"Only three?"

"It was a quiet night in Dodge. One guy had his face blown off by a convenience store clerk who was staunchly defending the fifty-six dollars in his till. The second man, poor bastard, was shot by his wife when he lost his house keys and broke into his own home."

"And the third person?"

"A man named Paul Russo was found shot in the head near the Iwo Jima Memorial."

"Could that be the monument we heard mentioned in the intercept?" Dillon asked.

"Probably. And it gets better. Russo's body was discovered at approximately one fifteen and, as you might expect, the Arlington cops were called to the scene. I had a tech take a peek into Arlington's computers this morning, and, lo and behold, before the body was even loaded into the coroner's wagon, an FBI agent by the name of David Hopper shows up and takes over the case."

"At one in the morning?" Dillon said.

"Closer to two, actually. But that's not all. As you heard on the intercept, Transport failed to show. Now, assuming Transport's function was to remove the bodies, how might one go about that? Well, I discovered that at almost exactly the same time as whatever occurred, an ambulance was in a traffic accident two blocks from where Mr. Russo's body was found."

"Why would they use an ambulance?"

"An ambulance is an ideal vehicle for picking up and transporting dead bodies. And if traffic is jammed up or you're in a hurry, you can use lights and sirens."

"I agree, but what makes you think, other than the time, that this ambulance accident is related to Russo?"

"I don't know for sure that it is. The accident was just an interesting coincidence which became even more interesting after I learned the ambulance had been stolen from a company in Fairfax and the driver, though dressed like a medic, did not work for the company and had no ID on him. The driver is currently a John Doe car thief in a coma at Arlington Hospital."

"Now that is a fascinating . . . anomaly," Dillon said, his choice of the word a reminder to Claire that she shouldn't confuse anomalies with relevant facts until she had supporting data—a reminder Claire didn't need or appreciate.

"But we missed an opportunity," Claire said. "Messenger, we assume, was removed from the scene. But how did Messenger get to the scene?"

"Damn it," Dillon muttered. "His car."

"Right. His car. Based on what we heard, Messenger must have parked fairly close to where Russo's body was found, so I sent agents to the memorial and had them get license plates on every car within two blocks of the kill site. All cars currently in the area belong to people who are alive, which means the shooters must have removed Messenger's car last night, maybe even while the cops were still at the scene."

"Nervy," Dillon said.

"Not just nervy but connected. Very connected. Who could get the FBI to show up at two in the morning to take a case away from the Arlington cops?"

"Is that a rhetorical question?"

"At this point, no."

"So what are your next steps?" Dillon asked.

"I'll see if I can figure out who Messenger is. I'm checking missing persons reports and watching to see who shows up dead in the next few days."

"Good. What else?"

"I'll get a copy of Russo's autopsy and learn more about the FBI agent who was dispatched to the scene. And I'll find out everything there is to know about Mr. Russo himself. All I know at this point is that he was a nurse."

"A nurse? Why would someone want to kill a nurse?"

"Wrong question, Dillon. The question is: Why would someone who has access to encrypted radios and possibly military personnel, and who is able to make the FBI take away a case from the local fuzz in the middle of the night, want to kill a nurse?"

"I stand corrected, my dear. Keep me apprised."

DeMarco called his mother in Queens and told her Paul had been killed. She spent a few minutes saying things like "Oh, my God. Oh, my God. He was so young. He was so sweet." She cried a bit and talked about how Paul had looked when he was a child. "Like an angel he was, with all that curly hair, those big blue eyes."

Then, being a practical person, she got down to business.

"Well, Joe, you're going to have to take care of the funeral. And you better find out where he lived and take care of his things, too."

Aw, for Christ's sake. He was sorry Paul was dead but he hardly knew the guy, and he could already see that dealing with his death was going to eat up a lot of time—time he had allotted for playing golf.

"What am I supposed to do with his things?" he whined to his mother.

"I don't know. Give them to the Goodwill or something. And maybe he had a will. You need to see what his wishes were."

Yeah, a will. A will was good. If Paul had appointed an executor, the executor could deal with all this shit.

"But didn't he have any other relatives?" DeMarco said. "I thought Aunt Vivian had a sister—Tina, Lena, something like that."

Aunt Vivian was Paul's mother, and although she wasn't literally DeMarco's aunt, that's what he'd always called her.

"Joe, what's *wrong* with you!" his mother snapped. "Lena's eighty-seven years old. You can't burden her with this. It's your responsibility. It's the right thing to do."

Sheesh.

"Agent Hopper, my name's Joe DeMarco. I'm calling about Paul Russo."

Hopper didn't say anything.

"Agent, are you still there?"

"Yeah, I'm here. How did you hear about Russo, Mr. DeMarco?"

"The Arlington cops told me about him. They said they found a card in his wallet identifying me as the person to contact in case of an emergency. In fact, I'm kinda surprised you didn't call and tell me he'd been murdered."

"Well, we must have overlooked the card. Or maybe the Arlington cops removed it from his wallet when they found the body."

Overlooked the card? This was the fucking FBI. They were supposed to be able to find gnat DNA on the head of a pin. How could they have overlooked the card? But DeMarco didn't say any of this. All he said was, "I just want to know when I can claim the body."

"Why would you want to claim the body?"

"Because I'm Paul's cousin and his only living relative." That was a lie but he didn't want to go into a long complex explanation of his relationship to Paul and the fact that Paul's real closest living relative had one foot in the grave herself.

"I'm sorry to have to tell you this," Hopper said, "but his body was cremated."

"What?"

"Yeah, I apologize, but we don't have a lot of room in the morgue we use, and when we found out Russo's parents were dead and he didn't have any siblings, after the autopsy, we—"

"You completed the autopsy already? He was only shot yesterday."

"We're pretty efficient," Hopper said. "But like I was saying, after the autopsy when we couldn't locate a next of kin, we cremated the body. I guess we really screwed up and I'm embarrassed. I hope cremation wasn't against Mr. Russo's religious beliefs."

Actually, this wasn't bad news, DeMarco thought. Now he wouldn't have to deal with the hassle of a funeral. It seemed odd that they would have cremated the body so quickly, but he could understand how they might not have been able to locate Paul's next of kin. Paul's Aunt Lena's married name was Hennessy, not Russo, and he wasn't sure how the FBI would know that people named DeMarco were related to Paul—other than the damn card in Paul's wallet.

"Where are his ashes?" DeMarco asked.

"Give me your address and I'll send them to you."

DeMarco gave Hopper his home address. "Can you tell me what you've learned about who killed him?"

"We're still investigating and we don't have any suspects yet, but . . . well, I have to be honest with you, Mr. DeMarco. We think your cousin may have been dealing prescription drugs—illegally, that is. He was a nurse and he had access to things like OxyContin, and he may have been shot because of that. There are some pretty violent people in the world of drug trafficking."

DeMarco felt like telling Hopper the same thing he'd told Detective Glazer, that the Paul Russo he had known hadn't seemed like the drug-dealing type. But the fact was, he didn't really know anything about Paul's circumstances in the last three or four years. So all he said was, "Do you have any proof Paul was doing anything illegal?"

"No, it's just a hunch based on the time he was killed and where he was killed. But like I said, we're still investigating. I gotta go now, Mr. DeMarco, but I apologize again for not contacting you before we cremated the body."

"Look, I'm not going to make a big stink about the fact you cremated him without talking to me, but I'd appreciate it if you could keep me in the loop on the investigation," DeMarco said. And then he did something he didn't normally do: he flexed what little political muscle he had. "By the way, I'm a lawyer who works for Congress."

Lawyers, in general, can be a pain but a congressional lawyer could be a significantly larger pain to Hopper because there's nothing employees in the Legislative Branch of government enjoy more than twisting the nuts of those employed by the Executive Branch. If Hopper was impressed, however, by the fact that DeMarco worked on Capitol Hill—along with several thousand other lawyers—he kept his awe hidden quite well. "I'll keep that in mind," he said, and hung up.

Claire Whiting in motion: long-legged strides, staring straight ahead, intense, unsmiling, her heels striking hard on the linoleum floor. She was always in a hurry—a woman forever at war against the clock.

She entered a room containing thirty cubicles, and in each cubicle sat two technicians, most wearing headsets, all pecking away at keyboards and studying the monitors on their desks. Large plasma screens were mounted on the walls of the room and fiber-optic cables snaked in thick bundles, invisible beneath the floor. The cables were connected to large Cray computers and rack upon rack of servers in nearby buildings. The room was always somewhat chilly because the temperature was set to meet the rigid needs of the machines and not for the comfort of human beings.

The room was part of the Net.

The word *Net* was not shorthand for *Network,* as one might assume. It was instead exactly what the name implied: a device for capturing things, in this case the whispers of a planet. The mesh of the Net consisted of acres of computers, thousands of miles of fiber-optic cable, fleets of satellites orbiting the globe, vast arrays of dish antennae on desert plains—and much, *much* more.

The Net never slept. It was always awake—and always listening.

It recorded, analyzed, and transmitted.

It translated and interpreted.

There were some who believed it might even be able to think.

The Net was the heart, if not the soul, of the NSA.

Claire strode over to Gilbert, the technician who had brought her the intercept of—she was sure—Paul Russo being killed. Gilbert had tubular arms, straw-in-the-manger dirty-blond hair spiking up from his head, and nails chewed to the bloody quick. He was addicted to caffeine and sugar and, even sitting, was in constant motion—fingers tapping, right knee bouncing, nose twitching. Because his eyes were now closed and he was absorbed completely in whatever he was listening to, Claire used a polished fingernail to tap on one of the headset earpieces, causing a burst of noise to explode in the technician's ear. She preferred to touch the headset rather than him.

"Fuck!" Gilbert said, ripping his headset off and spinning around to confront his tormentor. Then seeing it was Claire and not the man he shared the cubicle with, he sat up a bit straighter and said, "Oh, it's you. Look, I'm still working on that software problem, but I haven't found—"

"I want you to get into the Bureau's system and get me the autopsy report on Paul Russo. I also want you to get me every record you can find on Russo himself: tax returns, employment records, scholastic history, credit reports, et cetera, et cetera. I want you to do the same thing for an FBI agent named David Hopper."

"Okay," Gilbert said.

Okay. That's all.

That Claire had just asked him to invade several federal, state, and private record-keeping systems, including the Federal Bureau of Investigation's heavily protected computer network—to obtain information on two American citizens—didn't faze Gilbert at all.

He'd done it before.

Claire summoned an agent to her office.

Claire's technicians manned the machines and, in general, matched all the nerdy stereotypes: fingers grafted to keyboards and the social skills of bright, obnoxious twelve-years-olds, more comfortable in online chat rooms than at office parties.

Claire's agents—many of whom were women—did the fieldwork Claire and Dillon needed done and, like her technicians, they shared certain common characteristics: they had the intelligence to understand the high-tech gear used by the NSA but they were also cocky and aggressive and physical. And they carried weapons. They rarely got to fire their weapons—but they all wanted to.

This particular agent was dark-haired, slim, and wiry and was dressed in jeans and a black T-shirt that hugged his body. One advantage to being an agent was that the dress code was flexible. That is, what the agents wore to the office was irrelevant, but there were certain standards regarding appearance. The first of those was that the ideal agent was blessed with a face that no one would remember: no albinos, Jimmy Durante hooters, or tattoos of writhing snakes encircling their necks. The other requirements were short hair—bald was acceptable—no facial hair, and no glasses, contacts only. The reason for these requirements was Claire's agents had to be able to change their appearance often and rapidly and it was best—when required to don wigs or mustaches or any other type of disguise—to start with a relatively blank canvas.

The other thing about agents—and she often had to remind Dillon of this when he wanted to fire one—was that they were expensive. Not their salaries but their training. They had to know how to break into buildings with sophisticated alarm systems; how to follow a subject and not be seen; how to plant listening devices that would not be detected. The agents didn't have to know how the listening devices worked—that was knowledge only the technicians were given—but they did have to know enough to install the gizmos.

Yes, agents were expensive and therefore not casually discarded, so when one of them misbehaved or acted rashly, he or she wasn't usually fired. Instead, the agent was disciplined and Claire was the one who decided upon the appropriate punishment—and Claire could be quite cruel and quite inventive.

Even the agents feared Claire Whiting.

"I want an FBI employee named David Hopper smothered," she said to the agent. "Twenty-four/seven surveillance. Landlines tapped. Cell phone monitored. Bugs in his house and his car."

"Yes, ma'am," the agent said.

Paul Russo had lived in a duplex near the Court House metro station and his landlady had been his next-door neighbor, a sweet old woman in her eighties with snow-white hair and Dresden-china blue eyes. The landlady's name was Betty.

DeMarco explained to Betty that he was Paul's cousin—it was easier to say cousin than second cousin—and he was dealing with Paul's estate. That is, he was dealing with it until he could find someone else to stick with the job.

"I need to get into his place," DeMarco said. "I need to see if he had a will and try to figure out what to do with his things."

He was surprised Betty didn't ask to see proof that he was related to Paul but she didn't. Maybe she was trusting and naïve—or maybe she was just happy to have someone take care of Paul's furniture so she could lease out his side of the duplex.

"I just can't believe he's dead," Betty said. "He was such a wonderful young man. If I ever needed anything, he was always there for me. When that FBI agent told me he'd been killed, my heart almost stopped."

"The FBI called you?" DeMarco asked, wondering why they'd called his landlord and not him.

"No, an agent came here and told me."

"Do you remember the name of the agent?"

"Oh, what was his name? Whoever he was, he was a very handsome man but very serious."

"Was his name Hopper?"

"Yes, that was it. He said he had to look inside Paul's apartment. For clues, I guess."

"When did he come here?"

"Yesterday morning, about six. Fortunately, I'm an early riser. I don't know what he did, but he spent a couple hours inside Paul's apartment."

It sounded to DeMarco like the FBI was really moving on Paul's case. They perform an autopsy on him faster than you can dice an onion and then Hopper rushes right from the murder site to Paul's apartment to search it. DeMarco didn't know how the FBI normally did things, but he couldn't help but think of what Glazer had said. If Paul had been somebody famous he could understand the FBI making his case a high priority, but he couldn't imagine what made Paul so important.

DeMarco concluded his cousin wasn't into material possessions in a major way. There was no big-screen TV or fancy audio system inside his apartment, and his furniture was inexpensive and mismatched, like stuff you'd buy at yard sales or from secondhand stores. He noticed a crucifix over the bed and one of those Sacred Heart pictures of Jesus in the living room.

The second bedroom in the apartment had served as an office, so DeMarco took a seat behind Paul's small desk and spent some time looking through the file folders in the desk. He didn't find what he was hoping to find: a will. He did find a bunch of pay slips from a hospice organization. A hospice? He'd always assumed that Paul worked at a regular hospital, and again he felt guilty that he hadn't made a better effort to get to know the guy. He also found statements from a bank where Paul had his savings and checking accounts. As of two weeks ago, Paul had almost four hundred in checking and thirty-eight hundred in savings. If he'd been a drug dealer, it didn't appear that he was a very successful one.

He sat back, trying to decide what to do next, when he noticed there was a printer and a monitor for a computer on the desk, but no computer. He wondered if Hopper had taken Paul's computer or if the computer was being repaired.

His next thought was that the money in Paul's bank account should go to somebody—probably his Aunt Lena—but how in the hell was he supposed to get access to the money if he couldn't find a will? And if Paul did have a will, it might be in a safety deposit box at his bank, but how was he supposed to get into that? This whole thing was becoming a gigantic pain in the ass.

He decided he was probably going to have to talk to an estate lawyer to figure out what the procedure was if he couldn't find a will—and it was gonna really piss him off if he had to spend his own money on the lawyer. As for Paul's possessions, he'd do like his mother said and call Goodwill and see if they could pick up the clothes and furniture. He'd take Paul's files over to his place and shred the paper, but he wasn't going to do that right now.

What he wanted to do next was go to the place where Paul had worked. Maybe his boss or one of his coworkers would know if he had a lawyer and where his will might be. Or maybe he kept his will at work. Yeah, right, like he would ever get *that* lucky.

He knocked on Betty's door again and told her he was leaving and it was going to take him a few days to figure out what to do with Paul's things. She said that was all right, and started to go on again about what a fine young man Paul had been and how much she was going to miss him. Then she said, "Even if he was gay, if I had a son, I would have wanted him to be just like Paul, to be as decent as he was, I mean."

"He was gay?" DeMarco said.

"Yes. Didn't you know?"

"Uh, no. We weren't close. Was he dating someone?" DeMarco was thinking that a lover might know about Paul's will.

"No, not at the moment," Betty said. "At least I don't think so."

"How 'bout close friends?"

"As far as I know, all his close friends were people at his church. He spent most of his free time there."

"Which church is that?" DeMarco asked.

8

"Good morning, gentlemen," the president said, as he took his seat at the head of the conference table.

Charles Bradford didn't like the president—but then, he couldn't remember the last president he *had* liked. He didn't agree with the man's social programs, disagreed completely with his handling of the recent financial crisis, and thought he was overly ambitious, as if he were trying to create a legacy in the first year of his first term. He was a bright guy, though—that much he had to admit—and no president since Kennedy could give a speech like he could. But overall, Bradford had the same disdain for him that he had for every other so-called commander in chief who had never worn a uniform.

There was one good thing about the president, however: on any matter even remotely related to national defense, he relied heavily on the opinion of the chairman of the Joint Chiefs of Staff. Bradford suspected the president trusted him on military matters not only because of his experience and reputation but also because of his appearance: Charles Bradford looked the way army generals were supposed to look. He was six foot four and his stomach was washboard-flat because he exercised religiously. His skin was tanned and leathery; he wore his gray hair cut close to his skull; and he had a large bony nose that gave him the profile of a bird of prey. The left half of his chest was covered with campaign ribbons and medals, and he had two Purple Hearts and a Silver Star. The Silver Star had been awarded when he was a second lieutenant in Vietnam; he'd always believed he should have received the Medal of Honor but never said so publicly.

Also present in the White House Situation Room were Gregory Hamilton, the Secretary of Defense; Martin Cohen, the president's national security advisor; Cohen's deputy, an idiot named Clark Palmer; CIA Director Samuel Mentor; NSA Director Admiral Fenton Wilcox; and one of Wilcox's top men, a man named Dillon Crane. Bradford had met Crane before. He was a rich smart-ass. Bradford suspected that if times ever got tough, Crane would run back to the silver-spoon mansion where he'd been raised.

Not present in the room, but appearing on a video screen, was the American general who had overall command in Afghanistan, and the purpose of the meeting was to discuss the status of the war, which wasn't going well at all. Bradford believed the reason the war was taking so long and costing so many American lives was because the president was too concerned about public opinion polls and placating our so-called ally, the Pakistanis. If Bradford had been given a free hand, he would have sent in thirty thousand more troops, pushed directly into Pakistan, dropped bunker busters on every cave in the region, and disarmed the entire population.

Forty minutes later—and after no decisions of any magnitude had been made—the president was ready to adjourn the meeting. But at that point, Clark Palmer, the deputy national security advisor, said, "Mr. President, there's one other issue."

The president looked at his watch. "What is it?"

"It's something the NSA brought to my attention a couple of days ago. Admiral Wilcox, if you wouldn't mind," Clark said, nodding to the NSA director.

Admiral Wilcox was a short, slim, perpetually frowning man with iron-gray hair. He quickly explained that the NSA had intercepted a phone call between an opium warlord in Afghanistan named Sayed Wafa and one of his underlings discussing the elimination of a provincial governor whose province bordered Pakistan.

As Bradford listened to Wilcox, his knuckles turned white gripping the edge of the conference table. He couldn't believe Wilcox had spoken to the White House about the situation before he had consulted with Bradford.

"Admiral, are you positive he was talking about assassinating Governor Falah?" the president asked.

Wilcox turned to his man Dillon Crane, and Crane said, "We're as positive as we can be, Mr. President. It was a very short conversation and there's always a risk in translation, but three of our best translators have listened to the intercept. And our conclusion is consistent with other intelligence acquired by Director Mentor's people."

The president now looked over at the CIA director. The man was reported to be brilliant, but Bradford found him physically disgusting. He was grossly overweight, his face was always shiny with perspiration, and his clothes looked as if he'd slept in them. Bradford had liked Mentor's predecessor a lot better, a man named Jake LaFountaine, but LaFountaine had resigned unexpectedly earlier in the year.

"Admiral Wilcox is correct, sir," Mentor said. "One of our assets has confirmed that Wafa wants the governor out of power." When the president didn't say anything, Mentor continued. "Our problem with Governor Falah is that he's afraid to take on the Taliban and has become an actual hindrance to military operations in his province. If Wafa replaces him, which is quite likely, he'll be much more inclined to support our objectives in the region. All he cares about is money."

"But he grows opium," the president said.

"Yes, sir," Mentor said.

The issue now hanging over the conference table like a noxious cloud was should the U.S. government warn Governor Falah that Wafa was trying to assassinate him or should they allow the assassination to take place, giving them a chance to put a more malleable person in power. Bradford could tell that the president was furious to be put in the position of having to decide this matter, and Bradford didn't blame him. It wasn't as if Falah was the president of the country; he was a relatively minor politician and a bad one, at that. After this meeting was over, Bradford was going to chew out Wilcox like he was a boot camp seaman instead of a three-star admiral.

Wilcox knew that the right thing to do was to let Wafa kill the governor, and he should never have brought this issue to the president's staff. The problem with Wilcox, though, was that he was a damn three-star Boy Scout. If he was given a lawful order to nuke Australia, he'd execute it without hesitation, but if he had to do something that was morally ambiguous—on the difficult-to-interpret fringe of the law—he was unwilling to shoulder the burden unilaterally even when he knew the outcome was in the country's best interest.

It was because of men like Fenton Wilcox that Charles Bradford employed John Levy.

Before the president could commit himself, Bradford said, "Admiral, could you please repeat what Wafa said on that intercept?" After Wilcox had done so, Bradford said, "Mr. President, I don't think you should decide anything at this time. One interpretation of that phone call is that Wafa is planning to kill Falah. But another interpretation could be—well, let me put it this way. The other day I was talking to a friend about something my wife did, and I said, 'I could just strangle that woman.' I suppose that could be interpreted as a legitimate threat on her life, but in reality I was just venting my frustration."

Bradford noticed Dillon Crane smiling slightly, and he figured this was because Crane was bright enough to know what Bradford was doing: giving the president a way out. Wilcox opened his mouth to object to Bradford's last statement, but before he could, the president said, "What do you recommend, General?"

"I recommend that we continue to monitor Mr. Wafa's actions and communications for just a bit longer."

Long enough, in other words, to give Wafa a chance to blow Falah to kingdom come with a roadside bomb.

Bradford could see that the president liked this answer because the burden of responsibility had now shifted to Bradford. If Falah was killed, and if the subject of this meeting ever became public knowledge—which was extremely unlikely—the president would be able to say he had been relying on the judgment of his military advisors, and they had advised him badly. Before the president even had a chance to say anything else, Bradford said, "Well, okay," in an I'm-glad-that's-settled tone, and then, to change the subject, he turned to the CIA director. "Sam, I saw something in yesterday's briefing package about the Chinese upgrading their submarine sonar equipment. After the president leaves, maybe you could tell us all a little more about that."

Bradford returned to the Pentagon still annoyed by the meeting at the White House. He was so damn tired of it: inexperienced, gutless civilians meddling in military matters; a Congress that delighted in making him beg for money and men; a Secretary of Defense who cared more about awarding contracts to his cronies than he did about the quality of the equipment they were buying. The only people he had any respect for were those like himself: men who had given their blood—and too often their lives—to defend this country. Men like Martin Breed.

He spent the next half hour in his office editing the eulogy he would deliver at Martin's funeral. It was a good speech. It gave Martin the tribute he deserved and paid homage to the man he had been. It praised him without exaggerating in any way his dedication, his love of country, his boundless patriotism.

His only regret was that he could only speak to Martin's public record.

He couldn't talk about the truly great things Martin had done.

9

A man and a woman, both dressed in blue scrubs, approached the main doors of the hospital. They were chatting with each other, the woman laughing at something the man had said, then punching him lightly on the arm as if he was teasing her. The man was white and slender, about five foot eight. He had curly dark hair, a thin mustache, and a small goatee. He thought he looked like Johnny Depp. He didn't. The woman was black, a bit shorter than the man, stocky, her dark hair streaked with blond highlights. She wore large framed glasses, what she called her Elton Johns.

Entering the hospital, the man went toward the elevators and the woman toward the admissions desk. She made sure the hospital ID badge she wore was visible.

"Hey, sorry to bother you, sweetie," the black woman said to the gray-haired white woman—a hospital volunteer—sitting behind the information desk. "This doctor, you know, he calls the lab, talkin' all fast. He sounded like he was *Indian* or something. Anyway, he tells me to go get blood from some John Doe head trauma in ICU, but he didn't tell me the room number and he hung up before I could ask. Can you look it up for me, honey? Some of these doctors, they're so *rude*."

A moment later the black woman stepped away from the admissions desk and held her left wrist up to her mouth. "Confirmed. It's Room 5116," she said.

The goateed male who had accompanied the black woman into the hospital was already on the fifth floor where the intensive care unit was located. He approached the door to room 5116 holding test tubes and disposable syringes in his hand. He turned into the room, then immediately stopped when he saw four people standing over a bed. He heard a man, a doctor he presumed, say, "I'm pronouncing at 9:17 A.M."

The man backed out of the room and waited in the hall until a nurse came out. "Hey, I'm Gerry," he said to the nurse. "From the lab. What's going on? I'm supposed to get blood from that guy."

"Sorry. He's gone. They're getting him ready to take down to the morgue. They'll get all the blood they need during the autopsy."

"What happened to him?"

"Don't know," the nurse said. "He was in a coma but doing fine, when all of a sudden his blood pressure dropped like a rock and we lost him. Pathology will have to tell us why."

The man thanked the nurse and walked back toward the elevators. He checked to make sure no one was nearby and then muttered into his wrist. He concluded by saying, "There're too many people up here. We're gonna have to go to Plan B. I'll let you know when they take him down to the morgue."

He walked over to the nurses' station. From there he could see the entrance to room 5116. He looked for the nurse he'd been talking to—she was kinda cute—but she wasn't there. He started to chat up one of the other nurses, a little blond who looked like Renee Zellweger from the waist up—and like a Budweiser Clydesdale from the waist down.

The black woman quickly left the hospital and returned to a van parked in a loading zone. She stepped into the back of the van and stripped off the scrubs, tossing the hospital ID badge into a gym bag. Beneath the scrubs she had on a white blouse and dark blue pants. She put on a jacket that matched her pants, ripped the blonde-streaked wig off her head, and put on one that was henna colored. She replaced her Elton John jumbo frames with serious black-framed glasses. She needed to look the part. From the gym bag she pulled out another ID, this one in a badge case.

She was waiting by the elevator when the doors opened to let off a man pushing a gurney. On the gurney, covered by a sheet, was a body.

"Hold it," the woman said. She snapped open the badge case. "Arlington P.D."

"What?" the man said.

"I said, Arlington P.D. Is this the John Doe from ICU?"

"Uh, yeah. I'm takin' him to—"

"I need to get his fingerprints. We're still trying to ID him."

"Well, can't you wait until I get him to the morgue?"

"No."

She didn't want to take the fingerprints in the morgue; there were likely to be more people in there and she wanted to minimize the number who saw her. Before the gurney pusher could say anything else, she pulled the corpse's right hand from beneath the sheet and pressed the hand down on an inkless fingerprint pad. She flipped the pad over, repeated the procedure with the other hand, put the fingerprint pad into a plastic bag and into her purse, then pulled down the sheet, exposing the man's head. She used her cell phone to snap a picture of his face, although it was horribly bruised and swaddled in bandages.

"Thanks," she said to the gurney pusher, and walked away.

When the black woman arrived back at the van the white man was already sitting behind the wheel waiting for her. He no longer had a mustache or a goatee. She climbed into the van, told her partner to get going, and opened her cell phone.

"Claire, it's Alberta," she said. "I got his fingerprints and a photo that probably won't do us much good, and I'll transmit everything in two minutes to that freak, Lorene. But the guy was dead when we got to the hospital."

"Dead?" Claire said.

"Yeah. A nurse told Darryl he was doing fine when all of sudden he flat-lined on 'em."

"Claire, I got an ID on that guy."

Lorene was one of Claire's few female technicians. Her hair was dyed jet black, chopped off at the ends as if it had been trimmed with gardening shears, and she used a white makeup base that gave her the pallor of a day-old corpse. Her fingernails and lipstick matched the color of her hair.

Claire couldn't even imagine what people would think if they knew that this woman—though not in person—routinely provided information to the secretary of Homeland Security.

Claire took the printout from Lorene and looked at it. "Jesus," she muttered. She didn't know what she'd expected, but this sure as hell hadn't been it.

Lorene said, "Uh, if you don't need me . . ."

"Be quiet," Claire said. "And quit snapping that gum."

Claire's eyes fixed on an unseen horizon as she tried to comprehend the information she'd just been given. Refocusing her gaze on Lorene, she said, "I want you to get into the Pentagon's personnel records for the Third Infantry Regiment stationed at Fort Myer and . . ."

"We may have a serious problem," Levy said.

Bradford looked up from the report he'd been reading on the new Chinese mid-range missile, a missile with a guidance system almost identical to a similar American missile. He was convinced that every defense contractor in the country was infested with Chinese spies. He was also convinced—he was absolutely positive—that someday the United States would go to war with China. He was sure whatever problem Levy thought he had wasn't as serious as his problems with the Chinese, but Levy wasn't a man given to hyperbole.

"What problem?" he said.

Levy sat there flexing his big hands, the expression on his face solemn as it always was. Bradford knew Levy's family history, but did the man always have to look so grim? Charles Bradford rarely smiled, but even he smiled more than Levy.

"Gilmore called me," Levy said.

Gilmore was a colonel stationed at Fort Myer in Arlington, Virginia, and he commanded the Third Infantry Regiment. Charles Bradford had personally selected him for the position. Other army personnel were not surprised at the interest Bradford had taken in selecting the regimental commander of the Old Guard because Bradford had once held that position for a short time. People would be very surprised, however, if they knew how Bradford had changed the Old Guard's mission.

"He said he received a call from a woman," Levy said, "a Staff Sergeant Marian Kane over at the Pentagon. She was calling about the two men I used on the Russo problem."

"You mean the men you shipped out?"

"Yes, sir. Sergeants Pierce and Gannon. Anyway, Kane knew that Gannon and Pierce had been reassigned and she said her boss wanted to know who had authorized the transfer. According to Sergeant Kane, her boss was upset because these men were not supposed to be rotated out of Fort Myer for at least a year. Gilmore naturally said he couldn't help her, that he didn't get involved every time some low-ranking soldier was reassigned, and then he called over to the Pentagon to see if a Sergeant Kane really works there. He discovered that there is a Sergeant Marion Kane in personnel—but that's Marion spelled M-a-r-i-o-n, and Sergeant Kane is a male. Whoever called Gilmore screwed up."

"I don't understand," Bradford said. "Why would anyone be asking about those two soldiers?"

"I did some backtracking after Gilmore called me. I discovered that after Sergeant Witherspoon—uh, died, that—"

"Witherspoon?" Bradford asked.

Levy didn't speak for a moment and Bradford could sense Levy's disapproval. "Sergeant Witherspoon," Levy said, "was the soldier driving the ambulance, the man who was—"

"Oh, yes," Bradford said. "I'm sorry, John," he added, and he truly was. He was embarrassed he'd forgotten Witherspoon's name, a man who died in the service of his country.

"I found out that someone claiming to be from the Arlington Police Department took Witherspoon's fingerprints before his body was taken from the hospital," Levy said.

"So what?" Bradford said. "He was a John Doe and the police wanted to identify him."

"That's possible. But if the cops had taken his fingerprints, they would have drawn a blank. Witherspoon's fingerprints are not in any criminal database, and if Arlington tried to access military fingerprint files, they still would have come up empty. As you know, Witherspoon's prints are flagged, I would have been contacted, and his name wouldn't have been released to the police without my approval."

"John, I'm confused," Bradford said. "What are you saying?"

"I'm saying the only way the Arlington cops could have identified Witherspoon through his fingerprints was if they had contacts at the Pentagon or the ability to hack into a military data base and override the don't-release tag on Witherspoon's name. The detective who was assigned to the case before Hopper took it away from him is ex-military, but he was just a grunt in the marines more than twenty years ago. I think it's highly unlikely, sir, that this detective or anyone associated with him could have identified Witherspoon. So the big question is this: How did they make the leap?"

"The leap?"

"Yes, sir. What caused them to take the next step? What made them start asking questions about the cadre at Fort Myer after they identified Witherspoon?"

"Maybe they were just checking to see if Witherspoon had accomplices. Looking at other men in his unit would be a logical step."

"I don't think so," Levy said. "The ambulance he stole was recovered when it was wrecked, it wasn't involved in any crime the police know of, and I doubt there's some big auto-theft ring in the area dealing in stolen ambulances. No, sir. The cops just wouldn't have dug this hard for one stolen ambulance.

"General, I don't know what's going on here. All I know is that Witherspoon and the two men I used for the operation have been identified and someone is asking questions."

Bradford could feel a bubble of panic began to form in his chest, which he quickly suppressed—he had never panicked in his life—but there was reason for concern. In the past, there had never been a direct connection between him and Levy's operations—other than Levy himself, of course, and Levy would never talk. But this thing with Russo was different. He couldn't separate himself from Russo's death if the reason for his death were to become known. He started to rise from his chair to . . . to what? To tell Levy what was at stake? He didn't need to tell John Levy that.

But before he could say anything, Levy said, "I'm pursuing a lead, sir. I think I can find out who took Witherspoon's fingerprints."

"Pursue it fast, John," Bradford said. "Find out what the hell's going on."

10

The lady in charge of the hospice where Paul Russo had worked was a plain-faced middle-aged woman with short gray hair, no makeup, and a prim set to her mouth. She wore a blue skirt with a hem that fell a good two inches below her chunky knees, a short-sleeved white blouse, and she had a small cross on a thin gold chain around her neck. She made DeMarco think of a nun in civilian clothes. Her name was Jane Sealy.

DeMarco explained to Jane that he was trying to find his cousin's will so he could deal with his estate. At the mention of Paul's name, Jane crossed herself and then basically told him that Paul had been the saint who walked among us: extremely religious, gave his time and money to charities, loved his fellow man, wouldn't hurt a fly, and his patients and their families loved him. There was no one better suited, more compassionate, more caring, Jane said, when it came to helping people die.

DeMarco was sure all this was true, but he'd always thought that Paul had been a rather boring, mousy guy. Even as a kid, he hung back, awkward and shy, barely saying a word. DeMarco recalled the one time he had lunch with Paul when Paul first arrived in Washington. His cousin didn't like sports, nor did he play any. He rarely watched television and didn't go to many movies. He had no interest in politics whatsoever. So after they had discussed the few relatives they had in common, they had very little to talk about. At one point, Paul told him he was looking for a good congregation to join and asked where DeMarco attended church—and DeMarco lied. He said he didn't attend any particular church, that on Sunday he just went wherever the mood struck him. The truth was, he only went to church for weddings and funerals. The consequence of all this was that it had been an uncomfortable lunch filled with long periods of silence, and DeMarco was relieved when it was over. But based on everything Paul's landlord and his boss had said, it sounded as if his cousin had been a good man and DeMarco regretted that he'd never made the effort to know him better.

He asked Jane if he could look through Paul's desk and his computer to locate a will or the name of Paul's lawyer, but when he said this Jane told him, quite firmly, that she wouldn't allow him to do that unless he had some authority, like documentation confirming he was the executor of Paul's estate. DeMarco pointed out the catch-22: he wouldn't know if he was the executor of Paul's estate unless he could find Paul's will, but he couldn't find Paul's will because he couldn't prove he was the executor of the estate.

"Well, I'm sorry about that," Jane said, "but you're a complete stranger to me and I can't let you go pawing through his desk. And anyway," she added, "the FBI took his computer."

"They took his computer?"

"Yes."

"When was the FBI here?" DeMarco asked.

"A couple of hours ago."

"An agent named Hopper?"

"Yes. He had a warrant and he looked through Paul's desk. And he took his computer."

It looked like all this had happened while DeMarco was at Paul's place.

"Okay," DeMarco said, "but would you mind looking through Paul's desk for me? All I'm trying to do is settle his estate."

"Yes. I have to clean out his desk and if I come across a will or a reference to one, I'll let you know. But I can tell you that Paul wasn't the sort of person who did personal business at work, and I doubt if he kept any of his private correspondence here."

DeMarco was about to leave but said, "Let me ask you something. Did Paul have access to drugs?"

"Of course," Jane said, and then she explained.

People under a hospice's care were not given medications to stop them from dying or to even slow down the pace of whatever was killing them. Nonetheless, they had mini-pharmacies in their homes: drugs to help them sleep, to help move their bowels, to help reduce their pain.

"Things like Valium?" DeMarco asked.

"Why are you asking about this?" Jane said.

"Because the FBI thinks Paul may have been stealing meds from his patients and selling them. Didn't Hopper tell you that?"

"No, and that's absurd. Paul would never do something like that. He was the most honest person I've ever known."

"So no one—family members, drugstores, doctors—ever complained of drugs being missing or having to refill prescriptions too often?"

"I just told you, no. It's offensive that you'd even suggest such a thing."

"I'm not suggesting anything; the FBI's the one who's saying that. But what I can't figure out is why he was at the Iwo Jima Memorial at one in the morning and got shot. And, as much as I hate to say it, dealing drugs is a possibility."

"No. It's. Not."

"Then why do you think he was there at that time of night? I heard once that the park near the memorial was a gay pickup place. Do you think he could have been—I don't know—sneaking around, trying to meet a lover there?"

"Paul wasn't in the closet; he didn't need to sneak around. He *wouldn't* have snuck around."

"Well, maybe he hooked up with some married gay guy and then decided to tell the guy's wife, and the married guy whacked him to keep him from telling."

"I think you should leave."

"Hey, I was just thinking out loud," DeMarco said defensively. "And I believe you when you say he was a good guy. So who would want to kill him?"

"I don't know," Jane said, "but something was bothering him last week. He was spending a lot of time with one particular patient and when I stopped by to see how things were going, he was . . . I don't know. Different. Subdued. Nervous, like he was worried about something. He was always so upbeat I was surprised."

"Did he tell you what was bothering him?"

"No."

"Who was this patient he was taking care of?" DeMarco asked.

11

Claire stood in front of the mirror in the ladies' room—and shook her head in dismay.

Her mother had an expression, some nonsensical thing she'd probably read in Ann Landers or heard on *Oprah: You make the face you get.* Silly, irrational saying—but maybe it was true.

Claire had been a pretty young woman: a nice slim body, long blonde hair, a perfect nose, light blue eyes. She once had that healthy All-American girl look you see in leggy models who advertise sportswear for upscale clothing stores. At thirty-eight, she still had the long blonde hair and the slim build—but in the last ten years she'd become downright *gaunt.* Her face had become narrow, almost predatory, her arms muscular yet stringy. She had the look of a person who burned calories standing still.

She was still undeniably feminine—it wasn't as if she'd become mannish looking—but there wasn't anything soft about her anymore. That day, the day it happened, the softness just began to fade away—and, along with it, any sense of playfulness she once had. She now looked like . . . well, like the person she was: driven, relentless, perpetually restless. Her eyes had become cold and lifeless; her lips thin and bloodless; and those lines etched into her cheeks, bracketing her mouth. . . . Where the hell had those come from?

She couldn't help but wonder: Would she have this face if he had lived?

Enough, she said. You don't have time to feel sorry for yourself. Get back to work.

Gilbert was not in his cubicle, so Claire had to walk all around the damn room until she spotted him, talking to Irwin, another one of her techs. As she walked up behind him, she heard Gilbert say, "Jessica Biel, man, she's way fuckin' finer than Jessica Simpson."

That was *just* what she needed to hear.

She cleared her throat and both techs looked at her, deer-in-the-headlights expressions on their faces, embarrassed to have been caught bullshitting instead of working.

"Bring me what you have on Russo and Hopper," she said to Gilbert, and walked away without waiting for an answer.

As Gilbert stood anxiously in front of her desk, eating his fingernails, she ignored him and read the printouts. Regarding Russo, the guy sounded like some sort of gay angel: hospice worker, didn't cheat on his taxes, gave to charity like he was Bill Gates. He'd never had a traffic ticket, much less committed a real crime.

"Autopsy report," she said.

Gilbert handed it to her.

The first thing she noticed was that the autopsy had begun at five A.M. the day Russo died and had been completed at six A.M. No way. Speedy-friggin'-Gonzales couldn't have chopped the guy up that fast. But the bell ringer was the cause of death: death by gunshot wound to the head at close range and, based on entry and exit wounds, the weapon had most likely used 9mm ammunition. No bullet had been recovered.

Bullshit. Double bullshit.

The report in the Arlington cop's computer said there had been *no* exit wound, which there would have been if Russo had been shot at close range with a nine mickey-mike. And she was convinced from the transmission they'd intercepted that Russo had not been shot at close range. He'd been popped from some distance away by a sniper, and if there was no exit wound, the ordnance involved was probably the type the SWAT boys used, the kind of ammo that penetrates the skull and then explodes into a jillion little fragments, instantly shutting off all voluntary motor functions. But a 9mm would fit the story that the nurse had been killed in some drug deal gone bad, such a weapon being gangbanger, drug-dealer, street scum preference.

Claire sat there looking at Gilbert, but she wasn't really looking at him. She was staring at his chest, his shirt a narrow blue wall for her to focus on.

"Uh, you need me for anything else?" he said.

"Hush," Claire said.

Hospice worker. Nurse. Drugs. No. Hospice worker. Dying people. Death-bed secrets.

"Get me the names of Russo's last ten patients," she said. "Leave the file on Hopper with me. Oh, and do a data dump on this doctor who did the autopsy, this Dr. Lee."

David Hopper.

Claire reviewed the file Gilbert had compiled on the FBI agent, noticing that he had served in the army before joining the Bureau. She also noticed he was on the take.

Hopper was a GS-14 and thus made a decent salary, but he had two ex-wives and four children and had never been in arrears on either alimony or child support. Not only was he father-of-the year, but based on his credit card statements, he dined at some of the best restaurants in town, purchased his clothes from high-end stores, and owned a pricey and relatively new Mercedes. The supposed source of Hopper's additional income was a trust fund established by a dead uncle, but a little research—the sort of research Claire's people could do in their sleep—showed that the uncle had been an alcoholic insurance salesman who had three DUIs in an eight-year period. No way had Uncle Boozer left Nephew David any money.

Turning last to his phone records, she noted no calls to anyone who struck her as unusual. However, at about the same time as Paul Russo's body was discovered, Hopper had received a call on his cell phone from another cell phone whose owner Gilbert had not identified.

She marched back out to the technician's desk.

"Who made this call to Hopper?" she said, jabbing her finger at the phone record.

"I don't know," he said.

"Well, find out."

"I've tried," Gilbert whined.

"Try harder. Don't leave until you get me an answer."

"Geez, Claire, I was hoping to get out of here on time for once. Can't someone else—"

"Look at me," she said.

Gilbert looked at her with the eyes of a martyr. None of her employees knew the demons that drove Claire Whiting. All they knew was that she was fanatical about her job and she would work until she dropped—and she would work you until *you* dropped. Gilbert also knew of another technician, a man with three kids all younger than eight, who had been transferred to a listening post on the North Korean border because he'd failed to meet Claire Whiting's expectations.

12

General Martin Breed's flag-draped casket sat in the main aisle of the National Cathedral, bathed softly in the light coming through the cathedral's magnificent stained-glass windows. The cathedral, even as big as it was, was half full, the pews occupied by men and women in uniform, high-ranking civil servants, and media-conscious politicians. Charles Bradford had just delivered Martin's eulogy; after he stepped away from the lectern, he saluted the casket—his last tribute to Martin—and sat down with Martin's family.

Replacing Bradford at the lectern was Martin's brother, Jerry, a soft-looking dentist who bore little resemblance to his soldier sibling. Jerry began to speak about an incident that had occurred when he and Martin were boys, the point of the story being that even as a child Martin Breed had been fearless. Charles Bradford knew that Jerry Breed had no idea how truly courageous his brother had been.

Martin's wife, Linda, begin to cry again as Jerry was speaking. She'd been incredibly brave during Martin's illness and had held up well throughout the service. Her daughters, two pretty teenage girls, were pale and still as statues, stunned seemingly motionless by their father's passing. Bradford put a fatherly arm around Linda Breed's shoulder and pulled her close for a moment, letting her know he would always be there for the wife of a warrior.

Bradford had met Martin at the Pentagon. He had just received his second star and Martin, only a major at the time, had been assigned to his staff. One evening, after a particularly frustrating day, he discussed with Martin his dissatisfaction with a member of the National Security Council who was preventing the army from dealing directly with an obvious threat. He wasn't surprised Martin agreed with him—Bradford was, after all, his boss—but he knew Martin wasn't simply telling him what he wanted to hear. He sensed immediately that Martin Breed was one of the special ones, one of those men like himself and John Levy, men who were willing to do whatever was necessary to protect their country.

It took many long philosophical discussions before he was totally satisfied that Martin was a man he could take into his confidence. These discussions primarily focused on three critical questions. Is it ethical for men in power, men entrusted by their countrymen with that power, to go outside the law if the situation demands it? Second, is it reasonable to expect the average citizen to understand what needs to be done? And last, is it logical to expect self-serving politicians to act on what needs to be done?

It was the politicians who frustrated Bradford the most. It seemed to him that their primary agenda was not losing the *next* election rather than accomplishing something meaningful once they were elected. They never agreed on anything, and by the time a decision was made it was often too late and the damage was already done. So as dangerous as it was for him personally, Bradford finally decided that it was cowardly and irresponsible for a man in his position to ignore obvious threats to national security and blame his failure to act on others. There was no one in a better position than he was to do what needed to be done. He had superbly trained personnel and virtually unlimited funding, and he was privy to almost as much intelligence the true mission of the soldiers who protect the Unknowns' tomb. He also told him about John Levy, but he didn't tell him Levy's name. He trusted Martin, but security procedures had to be followed.

Bradford knew that many Americans—not all, but many—would condemn what he and Martin had done in Turkey. Yet if those same Americans were asked, Do you wish Osama bin Laden had been eliminated when we first knew he posed a threat? what do you think their answer would be? Bin Laden and his al-Qaeda organization were known to be behind the first World Trade Center attack in 1993, the bombings of two U.S. embassies in Africa in 1998, and bombing of the U.S.S. *Cole* in Yemen in 2000. So why didn't we kill him before 2001? The answer was because the politicians vacillated until it was too late. They were concerned about violating international law and what our Muslim allies might think if we killed bin Laden on their soil and without their approval. They were concerned the intelligence wasn't one hundred percent accurate (it never was) and worried about the international reaction if innocent civilians were killed. They debated if we should capture him rather than kill him, and if there was some way to get the Saudis or some other Islamic government to do the capturing for us. They vacillated over *everything,* and because of this bin Laden was allowed to live, and three thousand American civilians died, and nothing has been the same since. Had Bradford taken the initiative before 2001—and he blamed himself to this day for not having done so—9/11 might not have happened. But now—thanks to men like Martin Breed and John Levy—he was taking the initiative.

Yes, Martin Breed had done much for his country, and the most important things he had done would never be known. Bradford always believed that if he had ever asked Martin to die for him, he would have done so without hesitation—and then it turned out, when it was time for Martin to die, that Martin turned against him. But he didn't feel bitter toward his friend. Who knows what effect the cancer had on his mind at the end? And who knows what any man might do when faced with the prospect of meeting his Maker? He liked to think that impending death would never change his principles, but he had no right to judge Martin harshly. He had not yet walked in Martin's shoes.

Linda Breed let out a heart-wrenching moan, and Bradford took her small hand into his. But as he held her hand, his thoughts turned to John Levy. Bradford prided himself on his ability to compartmentalize issues and problems, and his focus this morning had been on Martin's funeral and his eulogy. Now that his part in the service was over, however, he couldn't help but wonder how Levy was faring.

Levy *had* to find out who had identified that young soldier through his fingerprints.

"That's her," Perkins said, pointing at the monitor on his desk.

Perkins—a lanky, balding, bookish man in his forties—was an agent who worked for the PFPA, the Pentagon Force Protection Agency. The PFPA is the Pentagon's police force and is composed of guards, criminal investigators, and highly trained technicians responsible for protecting the Pentagon and other DOD assets in the D.C. area. John Levy was nominally the deputy director of the agency. The reality, as Perkins and every other member of the force knew—including Levy's boss—was that Levy reported to no one. And people in the Pentagon quickly learned to do whatever Levy asked of them. If they didn't, someone very, very high up the chain of command would make a phone call and instruct them in the error of their ways. Levy was a shadowy presence who, for reasons no one could understand, was incredibly powerful and totally autonomous.

Levy looked at the monitor and saw a stocky black woman with henna-colored hair and black framed glasses wearing a dark pantsuit.

"We got that picture from a surveillance camera located near the hospital pharmacy," Perkins said. "We started with a general description of the woman from a nurse's aide, who said that a black woman identified herself as an Arlington police officer and took the fingerprints of the John Doe corpse. We showed the aide this surveillance photo, and he confirmed this was the woman."

"So who is she?" Levy said.

"Her name is Alberta Merker. I used Homeland Security's facial recognition software." A second photo flashed up on the screen, showing a round-faced black woman, her hair cut in a short Afro. "That's her Maryland driver's license photo, minus the wig and glasses."

"Put both photos on the screen at the same time," Levy said. Perkins did and Levy studied the two pictures. Yes, it was the same woman, but the simple disguise she'd worn made it tough to tell.

"She's not an Arlington cop, is she?" Levy said.

"No, sir. All I could find out about her is that she's ex-army enlisted and works for the Department of Defense. DOD personnel records identify her as a GS-Eleven procurement specialist, but her file has nothing in it that identifies exactly what she does or which division she works for. And a title like *procurement specialist* is not much help; she could be procuring anything from combat boots to tanks.

"I mean, this is really strange," Perkins added. "I'm certain this woman is connected in some way to the Pentagon, but it's like her personnel records have been sanitized."

Levy just stood there, looking at the two pictures of Alberta Merker still visible on the monitor. He didn't say anything, but he was thinking that the Department of Defense employed over two million military personnel and almost a million civilians. It was spread over the entire planet and had more departments, divisions, and bureaucratic niches than anyone could possibly imagine or keep track of. The fact that Merker's personnel records were incomplete didn't necessarily mean that someone was trying to hide the identity of her employer—but he suspected that in this case someone was.

"Where does she live?" Levy asked.

"College Park, Maryland, according to her tax returns. Also, per her tax returns, she's single. But I don't know if she lives alone or not."

When Levy didn't say anything, Perkins added, "Sir, if you told me why you're interested in this woman, maybe I'd be able to get more data."

"You don't need to know anything else," Levy said. "All you need to know is that she's a security risk and I don't want you talking about her to anyone."

"Yes, sir."

Levy turned to leave, then, realizing he'd been too harsh with the man, he said, "You did a good job on this, Perkins, and I appreciate it. And I'd tell you more if I could. It's just that the situation with this woman is very sensitive."

"Yes, sir. I understand."

For your sake, I hope not, Levy thought.

13

DeMarco ate a can of chili for dinner and, while he ate, he felt sorry for himself. Mahoney's absence was a gift—a gift that was now being squandered because he was wasting his time dealing with his cousin's death. He also wondered what the hell the FBI was doing. He agreed with Glazer, the Arlington cop, that something very odd was going on.

He grabbed a beer from his refrigerator and went into his den to watch the evening news, but just as he was about to turn on the television his phone rang. He looked at the caller ID but the number was blocked.

"Hello?" he said.

"Hi, it's me."

It was Angela. Thank God. He could picture her: the long dark hair, the laughing eyes, the trim body he loved.

"Are you back?" he asked, hoping like hell that she was. She'd only been gone a few days, and he couldn't believe how much he missed her.

"No. And I probably shouldn't even be calling you, but I just wanted to let you know I was all right and that I was thinking about you."

"I know you can't tell me exactly where you are, but are you someplace safe? Tell me you're not running around in the mountains looking for al-Qaeda guys in caves."

She didn't answer for a moment, as if she was trying to choose her words carefully. "I'm in a safe place, so don't worry about me. I can't tell you any more than that, because if the NSA intercepted this phone call I could get in trouble."

"The NSA!" he said. "You think they're listening to this?"

"No, not really, but you can never tell with those guys."

"Well, in case they are, let's give them something interesting to hear. Tell me what you're not wearing."

"Don't be silly. Anyway, I miss you and I love you."

"I miss you too. When are you coming back?"

"I don't know." To change the subject, she asked him what he'd been doing. He told her Mahoney was in the hospital, nothing serious, and he'd been planning to play golf until his boss returned to work. He was just about to tell her about his cousin getting killed when he heard a thud in the background and she said, "Joe, I'm sorry, but I have to go. I'll call you again as soon as I can."

The thud could have been anything—something falling off a shelf, a door slamming—so why did he think it was an explosion? God, he hated her job.

He turned on the television, listened to the local news as he sipped his beer—and tried not to think about Angela in Afghanistan. The anchorman was yapping about a *Washington Post* reporter being missing, saying how the reporter had been an investigative journalist and had broken a number of big political stories. DeMarco had never heard of the guy. Except for the sports page, he rarely paid attention to the bylines in the paper.

The newscaster went on to say that management at the *Post* was concerned that the reporter's disappearance could be related to whatever he was working on, although his editor didn't know what that could be. Which made DeMarco think that maybe they oughta supervise their damn people a little bit closer. It sounded to him like a reporter could goof around all day and his bosses wouldn't have a clue what he was doing.

Kind of like DeMarco.

The last thing the news guy said was the reporter drove a yellow Volkswagen bug, last year's model, and if anyone saw one abandoned someplace, they should call the DC cops.

Volkswagen bug. What man would drive one of those? DeMarco wondered. They were *cute* cars. Cute was, in fact, their defining quality. They were the cars rich daddies bought their college-age daughters when they sent them off to school.

The news gal who was paired up with the news guy—for some reason they always worked in pairs, like it takes two people to read a teleprompter—was now talking about some brand of pet food that was making cats sick. This had happened before and the public was going nuts and it sounded to DeMarco as if the FDA was spending more money on the problem than they would have spent if people were dying.

His mind switched lanes again, back to his cousin. If Paul wasn't mugged and if he wasn't selling drugs, why was he killed at one in the morning? He could have been meeting someone—maybe a lover like he'd told Jane, the hospice boss—and they had some kind of lethal spat. But that didn't sound right either, not from everything he'd heard about Paul. And why meet your lover at a public park at one in the morning? No, it was something else.

Paul was a nurse who helped people die. What if one of his patients had told him something? What if some guy on his deathbed had gasped out *I did this terrible thing* or *I know this horrible secret about so-and-so*. Then what? Paul tries to blackmail somebody? Nah, he wouldn't do that. But what if he'd decided to tell a reporter about something he'd learned from a patient? That was a stretch, but possible. The problem with that bright idea was the time. Why the hell would he be telling a reporter something at one in the morning? And why even meet with a reporter? Why not just call the reporter?

Whatever the case, there was something he really wanted to know: the name of Paul's last patient. Good ol' Jane had refused to tell him.

He picked up the remote to change the channel, to watch something less depressing than the news, when the female newscaster said, "This just came in. Speaker of the House John Mahoney is reported to be in a coma at Walter Reed Army Medical Center. Speaker Mahoney was admitted to the hospital two days ago for a routine gallbladder operation, but—"

DeMarco turned off the television and immediately called Mahoney's chief of staff, a man named Perry Wallace. Wallace was bound to know more than the press. Wallace said that after they removed Mahoney's gallbladder everything looked fine, but then he got some kind of infection, something called gram-negative septic shock, and went into a coma.

"They think they might have nicked his appendix when they took out his gallbladder," Perry said. He paused before he added, "He could die, Joe."

DeMarco couldn't imagine Mahoney sick, much less dead. The man was just too robust, too full of life, too ornery and mean to die. He thought about calling Mahoney's wife, Mary Pat, but decided not to. She was probably at the hospital at her husband's bedside or in the hospital chapel praying. He'd give her a call tomorrow and see how things were going.

Then another thought occurred to him, one which made him feel small for even thinking it: *What would happen to his job if Mahoney died?*

14

Dillon was speaking to someone on the phone and laughing when Claire entered his office. He hung up, still chuckling, and said to her, "There's a Nigerian cabdriver in Pittsburgh. He wasn't considered high risk, but we've been monitoring him periodically. Last night he called his mother and asked her to take care of his dog if something should happen to him. Mama, naturally, asks, Why would anything happen? Our cabbie's evasive, but mama persists, and he eventually blurts out that he's decided to become a martyr." Dillon paused for a beat. "The man had turned his cab into a rather sizable bomb. The federal courthouse was his target. My God, these people! Why didn't he just take the damn dog with him? They could have both been martyrs."

"You think this is *funny*?" Claire said. "It sounds like it was only dumb luck that we caught this guy."

Dillon shrugged. "Luck's an ingredient in any game, Claire, including ours. Maybe more so in our game."

They had had this discussion before. Dillon maintained that you had to approach the spy business as a game because if you didn't—if you allowed yourself to dwell constantly on the enormity of the task and the consequences of failure—it would drive you mad.

Dillon had been playing the game for over thirty years. He began his career at the tail end of the Cold War, at a time when the world had been continually on the brink of Armageddon. And he was still playing, but now he watched religious fanatics more than communists; now it was trying to keep the Chinese rather than the Russians contained; now he worried more about the Russians selling their nuclear warheads to terrorists than launching them.

The game just went on.

Dillon, cynic that he was, believed the human race was incapable of any sort of lasting peace, that there would always be some tribe determined to destroy some other tribe because of greed or ideology or religion or bigotry. And when it came to solving conflicts with words rather than weapons, he maintained that we hadn't advanced since the days when we killed each other with clubs and stones. Today's stones were just radioactive.

There was no way all of America's spies and warriors could keep the country totally safe. There just wasn't enough time in the day. There weren't enough people, money, and machines to keep the enemy constantly at bay. All you could do, he said, was come to work each day and take your seat at the table of the most fascinating game on the planet—a game that never ended and where just being alive to play was prize enough.

Well, it wasn't a damn game to Claire Whiting.

"I've got something new on Russo," she said. "Something potentially very big."

"Yes?" Dillon said, the mirth still in his eyes.

"Russo was a hospice nurse. His last patient was Martin Breed."

"*General* Martin Breed?"

"Yes, *that* Martin Breed."

"I'll be damned," Dillon muttered, recalling how he and his poker buddies had been discussing Breed the other night. "So what's the significance of this?" he asked.

"I don't know."

"Okay. Continue."

"The FBI falsified Russo's autopsy report—I don't think they even did an autopsy—and then they immediately had the body cremated."

"How could they falsify the autopsy report?"

"The doc who supposedly performed the autopsy is a man named Lee. Dr. Lee visits the casinos in Atlantic City quite often and the day after Russo died, his checking account increased by three thousand dollars. That could be a coincidence, but I doubt it. Anyway, the autopsy report said Russo was killed at close range, most likely with a 9mm handgun, and we know he wasn't."

"This isn't really new information," Dillon said. "I mean, we already suspected the FBI was involved in some sort of cover-up when they took over the case."

"That's true, but claiming that Russo was killed with a handgun supports the story they're dishing out that Nurse Russo was dealing meds and his death was drug-related, further obfuscating what really happened."

Dillon's mouth twitched, a gesture that Claire knew meant *I am not yet impressed.*

"The third item is that Hopper, the FBI agent, is on the take. Someone is feeding money to him from a phony trust fund."

"But I take it you don't know who's behind the trust fund."

"No. Next is the person who called Hopper the night Russo was killed. This person used a cell phone that was one of three hundred bought for personnel stationed at Fort Myer, but the owner of the phone is only identified as being the Fort Myer public works department and not a specific individual. When we contacted the public works department, they had no idea who the phone had been given to. They just pay the bill."

"Certainly you can locate him via his cell phone, Claire."

It irritated her that he would say something so obvious, but she didn't bother to tell him that the cell phone in question was an older model without a GPS chip, and it appeared that its owner not only shut it off when he wasn't using it, he also removed the battery. But all she said was, "We'll locate him the next time he uses the phone." Then, before Dillon could interrupt again, she said, "And now the big item. The ambulance driver, the one with no ID who was injured in a wreck two blocks from the memorial? The guy I thought might be Transport? I sent people to the hospital to get his fingerprints so we could identify him but when my guys arrived they discovered the driver had died suddenly and unexpectedly from his injuries."

"How convenient."

"Yes, too convenient. And no autopsy was performed on the driver. One was supposed to be but it wasn't because before the autopsy was performed, the body disappeared, and whoever took it was smart enough to disable the surveillance cameras first. *But* we got fingerprints before they got rid of the body. My guys did good on that."

"So who was the driver?" Dillon said, his tone implying that he'd appreciate it if she got to the point sooner rather than later. Claire didn't know it, but he had an appointment with his Milanese tailor in an hour.

"Sergeant Mark Witherspoon, U.S. Army. And guess what? He was stationed at Fort Myer. The Third Infantry Regiment."

"The Old Guard? The Tomb of the Unknowns?"

"Right."

The soldiers who guarded the Tomb of the Unknown Soldier were, in Claire's opinion, just plain weird. Claire understood the value of pageantry and patriotic symbolism but had to wonder what normal young man would volunteer for an assignment where he had to march like a robot in front of a grave. And becoming a tomb guard was no easy matter. They didn't take just anybody. The men selected were rigorously screened and tested, and the wash-out rate was fairly high. But what really concerned her about the sentinels was their fanaticism. Fanatics could be valuable or dangerous—depending on which organization they worked for—and these particular fanatics didn't work for the NSA.

"Is that all?" Dillon said.

"No. Since Witherspoon was one of the tomb guards, I decided to check out the rest of the cadre over there. Two men, both infantry, both expert marksmen, were transferred to Afghanistan four hours after Russo was killed. They reassigned them to a unit that sneaks across the Pakistan border and hunts Taliban. We made some calls trying to find out who authorized the transfer, hoping that might lead us back to whoever's running this thing, but we didn't have any luck."

"So what's the significance of all this?" Dillon asked.

"I think the significance is fairly obvious," Claire said. Was Dillon playing devil's advocate and being deliberately obtuse? "Those men in the Third Infantry are the kind of zealots you'd recruit if you wanted to pull off some kind of wet black op in the United States. They'd tell those soldiers that Russo was a terrorist and for the sake of God and Country he had to go, and those boys would do it. Then, after the hit, they moved them so far from civilization that they wouldn't have to worry about them talking to anyone. They've basically put 'em on ice until they need them again."

"But who's *they,* Claire?"

"Well, obviously I don't know yet, Dillon," she said, making no attempt to hide her irritation. "But whoever *they* is, they have major clout. We're talking about people with heavy pull at the Pentagon to be able to get those soldiers transferred the way they did."

"But you don't know for sure that the soldiers who were transferred were involved with Russo's death."

"No, I don't. But it feels right."

Dillon said, "Hmm," which Claire knew meant: *Maybe, but data would be nice.*

"So, is that all?" Dillon asked.

"Is that all! I'd say that's quite a bit."

"I apologize if I implied otherwise. I'm just asking if you have any more facts."

"No."

"Then could you summarize, please."

Claire just stared at him for a moment—she didn't have time to repeat herself—but she took a breath and complied. "We have a man who was one of the last people to see General Martin Breed alive. He was killed by some person or organization using encrypted military com gear, and the killers may have come from the Third Infantry Regiment stationed at Fort Myer. We also have an FBI agent who is on the take and appears to be trying to cover up how Russo was killed. And, last, the person who controls Hopper, based on the cell phone he's using, may have some connection to Fort Myer."

"But who was Messenger, Claire? You haven't discussed him—or her—at all."

"I don't know. I'm still looking at accidental deaths and homicides that occurred around the time Russo died. So far, nobody who's died looks right."

"Did you read the funnies this morning?" Dillon said.

The funnies was Dillon's term for *The Washington Post* because they got the facts wrong so often.

"Yes," she said. And then Dillon watched her blue eyes focus on the wall behind him as she tried to recall what she'd read.

"Oh, shit," she said. "I'm so used to looking at data we've pinched that it didn't even occur to me to consider the *Post* as a legitimate source. God, I'm sorry, Dillon. I'm . . . I'm embarrassed."

He could tell she was. "That's all right. You have a lot on your plate. And the fact that Robert Hansen is missing doesn't mean he's Messenger, but the possibility is . . . interesting."

Dillon smiled as Claire left his office, thinking it was extremely rare when she overlooked something. She was incredibly bright, very good at her job, and she just hated to lose. And she was, without a doubt, the most driven person he knew. In fact, it worried him that she had nothing else in her life: no lover, no pets, no hobbies—no joy. She had her job and nothing else, and that wasn't healthy. She had never learned, as Dillon had a long time ago, that some days you had to forget the work and simply enjoy being alive.

Dillon also knew that Claire wanted his job, but not for the usual reasons. She didn't want it because she desired advancement or status or higher pay. She wanted it because she thought Dillon was blasé about the work and she could do it better. But Dillon never considered her ambition a threat; it was merely a characteristic he exploited.

Nor was he worried that Claire might one day turn against him and tell his bosses what he was *really* doing—tell them about the shadow net that he'd created. He wasn't worried because *he* knew the demons that drove Claire Whiting.

The headquarters of the National Security Agency at Fort Meade, Maryland, is located in an immense cubic structure that appears to be constructed of black reflective glass. It looms like an obsidian monolith—mysterious and ominous—over parking lots large enough to accommodate eighteen thousand vehicles.

Dillon's office was on the ninth floor, and after Claire left he walked over to a window—a window designed to prevent anyone from seeing into his office or record what was being said there—put his hands in his pockets, and looked eastward. As he stood there, he didn't think about Paul Russo. He thought, instead, about how it was that he and Claire came to be involved with Russo at all. He had been standing at the same window on September 11, 2001, and had just witnessed, on television, Tower Two of the World Trade Center collapsing into a mound of rubble.

That was the image burned most vividly into Dillon's brain. Not the image of the jets flying into the towers but the image of the towers collapsing. It was *America* collapsing. He had never before experienced such a sense of failure, and he vowed, on that day, that he would do anything to keep such a thing from happening again.

The day the towers collapsed, Dillon knew—he knew with absolute certainty—that politicians would never have the courage to do what needed to be done. And the recommendations of the blue-ribbon bipartisan commission that had investigated the causes of 9/11 had proven him correct. The commission's most significant recommendation was that a National Security Director—an intelligence czar—be appointed: a single individual who would ensure that sixteen divergent and competing federal intelligence agencies would act in a coordinated fashion in the future.

What a joke. What a horrible joke. There was no way sixteen agencies—agencies staffed by bureaucrats who protected their rice bowls more fiercely than any tigress ever protected a cub—would give up their authority, their autonomy, or their budgets for the sake of cooperation.

More importantly, what the 9/11 Commission didn't seem to understand was that the War on Terror was a war for *information*. The U.S.

government was no longer fighting other governments—governments that declared their policies and advertised their intentions, governments that could be penetrated and spied upon. Now they were dealing with thousands of isolated terrorist cells spread about the globe, under no centralized control, independently plotting America's destruction—and an unknown number of those cells were operating in America, just as the 9/11 hijackers had done. The men who flew the planes into the towers on September 11 were on American soil almost two years before the event, chattering to each other on cell phones about the best places to take flying lessons and how easy it was to sneak box cutters on to airplanes. The 9/11 Commission concluded the government's failure to stop the hijackers was an interagency *coordination* problem, whereas Dillon knew the failure occurred because the right people weren't listening—and the reason they weren't listening was because the law prevented them from doing so.

What the 9/11 Commission should have concluded was that the NSA needed to start monitoring all communications occurring inside our borders as well as outside—that the agency needed to spy upon citizen and foreigner alike, to identify any future mischief being planned. But even before the commission issued its spineless report, Dillon had known that would never happen. So on that morning, as the dust was still choking the inhabitants of Manhattan, he began to think about what needed to be done.

Although most Americans have no idea what the National Security Agency does, it is America's largest intelligence service both in terms of personnel and funding. It employs more than thirty thousand people, and their primary mission is eavesdropping on foreigners, friend and foe alike. And as practiced by the agency, eavesdropping is not a man with his ear pressed to the wall. Eavesdropping means capturing any communication in any medium. Buried fiber-optic cables are tapped; microwave, radio, and telephone transmissions are intercepted; satellites listen; codes are broken. No communication is safe from the Net. To do what Dillon wanted to do wasn't, therefore, a technical problem; it was instead a legal one—a pesky law called FISA, the Foreign Intelligence Surveillance Act.

The father of FISA was the late Edward M. Kennedy, and he introduced his legislation following years of Senate investigations into Richard Nixon's use of domestic intelligence agencies to spy on political activists. Surprisingly—or maybe not—Democrats *and* Republicans supported Ted's bill, including folks like Republican Strom Thurmond, a man not known for leaning far to the left. It appeared that neither conservative nor liberal liked the idea of presidents ignoring the privacy protections guaranteed Americans by the Fourth Amendment.

FISA strictly prohibits randomly monitoring the communications of U.S. citizens. That is, it does not allow an intelligence agency to listen to as many phone calls as it possibly can just hoping to hear two guys talking who might be terrorists. FISA basically says that if you want to eavesdrop on the communications of Americans and foreign residents on American soil, you need a warrant, and to get said warrant, the government has to be able to show that these folks are suspected of being engaged in terrorism or espionage. Now getting these warrants isn't particularly difficult, because the warrants are approved by the Foreign Intelligence Surveillance Court, a group of federal judges who act in total secrecy and whose decisions are not really monitored by anyone. Furthermore, *suspected* isn't a particularly challenging legal standard to meet. Nonetheless, obtaining these warrants takes time—and in a war, minutes count—but more importantly, there was an obvious catch-22. You might suspect that an American named Muhammad who attends a mosque led by a radical, fire-breathing, anti-American imam is plotting nefarious things, but you couldn't really be sure until you listened to a few of Muhammad's calls. In other words, just being named Muhammad wasn't sufficient justification for a warrant.

Then, to Dillon's immense surprise and delight, he found that there was, in fact, one politician who had the courage to do what needed to be done: the president of these United States. Following 9/11, the president concluded that FISA was a major roadblock to his forces engaged in the War on Terror, and he issued an Executive Order—which no one ever saw—which said that in the future the NSA didn't need a warrant to eavesdrop on folks suspected of terrorism. The president's intention was never to spy on Americans communicating with other Americans, however. His intention was that if an American or a foreigner on American soil was a suspected terrorist and was calling *overseas,* no warrant was required anymore. And to calm the nerves of those people at the NSA who were worried about going to jail for breaking the FISA laws, he sent them to his top lawyer, the Attorney General. The AG told the spies not to worry, that the president's directive trumped FISA—and the NSA was off to the races, with Dillon leading the pack.

Dillon did have one other small problem, though. It was relatively easy for the NSA to capture wireless signals—signals that swam through the atmosphere like blind fish, bouncing from satellite to satellite. The Net just vacuumed these babies up. The problem was that in the twenty-first century the majority of all communications—voice and e-mail—were being routed through fiber-optic cables, and to tap into a fiber-optic cable wasn't a matter of simply attaching a couple of alligator clips to a wire. To tap into fiber-optic cables, it was necessary to go into communications company switching stations and connect complex equipment and sophisticated computers to the cables. Fortunately, thanks in large part to the Justice Department's interpretation of the law, companies like Verizon and AT&T agreed to cooperate. And once this equipment was installed it became possible to monitor *everyone's* communications—and Dillon began doing so. Again, this was not what the president had in mind, but once he opened the door, Dillon jumped right through it.

It was impossible to listen to everything, of course. Every twelve-year-old in America—and maybe in the world—has a cell phone, and *billions* of calls, e-mails, and text messages pass through fiber-optic cables every day. So the NSA's marvelous computers listened for key words and phrases, or calls going to certain locations, or calls spoken in certain languages. To use a simple example—the actual process was much more complicated—if a man in Washington speaking in Arabic said the words *white house* and *ka-boom* in the same sentence . . . well, the spies at Fort Meade perked right up.

But Dillon knew it wouldn't last. The NSA's warrantless eavesdropping program was a secret being kept by politicians, several thousand spies, telecommunications company employees, and big-mouthed lawyers at the Department of Justice. It was, in fact, amazing the secret was kept for as long as it was—for nearly four years—but in 2005 one of the big-mouthed lawyers squealed. He squealed to a reporter named James Risen who dwelled in that bastion of anarchy known as *The New York Times,* after which *The Times* told everybody what the NSA was doing and things came to a screeching halt—for everyone but Dillon, that is.

Since Dillon had expected this development, he had set up Claire's division well in advance of Mr. Risen's party-spoiling revelation. The division consisted of a few hundred handpicked folk out of the thirty thousand employed by the NSA, and they were moved into an isolated annex on the sprawling grounds of Fort Meade. And when the rest of the agency went back to playing Mother-May-I with the FISA Court, Claire's technicians just continued to monitor communications as they pleased—and warrants be dammed.

The majority of the work that Claire's techs did was accomplished inside large computers, and it's rather difficult to tell what a person is doing when all that's evident to the naked eye is a man sitting in front of a machine. It becomes even harder to tell when that same person controls the reports generated by the machine. And the functions accomplished by Claire's eavesdroppers were not in any way unique to the agency, and almost everything they did was electronically piggybacked on top of legitimate FISA-sanctioned operations. That is, when the NSA obtained a FISA warrant to tap into certain cables to monitor certain folk, the work would be assigned to Claire's division and they significantly expanded the scope of the warrant.

It was also amazingly easy for Dillon to hide the activities of Claire's secret division from his superiors. It was, in fact, depressingly easy. The current Director of the NSA was a three-star navy admiral; the deputy director, Dillon's immediate superior, was a civilian whose primary function was defending the agency's massive budget. The reason it was so easy for Dillon to keep these folks in the dark was not, however, because they were stupid. Earlier in his career, Admiral Fenton Wilcox had commanded a nuclear submarine, one of the most complex machines ever designed by man. No, the problem with the admiral and his deputy was not their intelligence. The problem was a prevailing American management practice: in America, these days, managers were not expected to *technically* understand the things they managed. Not long ago the CEO of Boeing became the CEO of Ford—it apparently didn't matter that one company made airplanes and the other automobiles. Management was management, or so some thought, and the principles that applied to running one company efficiently should certainly apply to any other—and the government subscribed to this faulty thinking. Dillon's bosses, bright as they were, did not really understand the complex technologies associated with NSA eavesdropping. Very few people did, Dillon being one of the few.

The end result of all this was that if Admiral Wilcox were ever to ask Dillon what Claire's small division was doing, Dillon could spout pure gibberish and the admiral wouldn't know any better. But the fact was, the admiral never asked, nor did the general before him. These men assumed that the people who worked for them would never do something illegal, that a bunch of civil servants—the word *servant* almost always said with a sneer—would never have the audacity to go beyond the agency's authorized and lawful mission. This was the single biggest problem with managers who didn't understand the technology: they had to trust the nerds who worked for them because they couldn't tell when they were lying.

And so Dillon had created the *other* Net—the Shadow Net—and no one, to date, was any the wiser.

15

When DeMarco visited the hospice, he had asked Paul's boss who Paul's last patient had been—and good ol' Jane had turned mulish on him. "Our patients and their families have a right to privacy," she said.

"Yeah, but you said Paul had been acting strange around this guy," DeMarco countered. "So maybe he knows something related to Paul's death. Don't you want to find out why Paul was killed?"

"I'm not going to tell you his name," Jane said, and before DeMarco could say anything else, she added, "And anyway, he's dead."

"Oh," DeMarco had said, momentarily taken aback. "Well, maybe his family knows something."

"I'm not giving you a name." Jane was a rock.

"Fine. But did you tell the FBI about this patient and that Paul looked upset the last time you saw him?"

"No. Agent Hopper never asked about Paul's patients."

"What did he ask?"

"Nothing. He just said he wanted to look through Paul's desk and then took his computer."

So DeMarco had been rather perturbed at Jane, but after thinking about the situation a bit more, he reminded himself that it wasn't his job to find out who murdered his cousin. Paul's death was a tragedy, and he hoped the killer would be found, but the FBI was much better equipped than he was to figure out who did it. No, his job wasn't to play detective. His job was to find Paul's will and dispose of all his secondhand crap, and since Paul's landlady had told him that all of Paul's close friends were associated with his church, DeMarco decided to stop by there.

"Father, my name's Joe DeMarco. I'm Paul Russo's cousin."

Father Richard Porter was in his thirties, a good-looking guy with rimless glasses and brown hair touching his collar. He'd been on the church's grounds pruning bushes with an electric hedge trimmer when DeMarco had driven up, and DeMarco had been surprised that the young guy dressed in jeans and an old Duke sweatshirt was not only a priest but pastor of the church.

"I was so shocked to hear about Paul," the priest said. "He was a wonderful man."

"Yes, he was," DeMarco said. Why tell the priest that he barely knew his cousin? "The reason I'm here is I'm trying to settle Paul's estate and I can't find his will or the name of his lawyer. I was told he was close to people at your church and I was hoping one of them could help me."

"Well, let's see," the priest said. "Your best bet would be Mary Albertson. She and Paul worked together a lot. And Mary's the motherly type. If Paul confided in anyone, it would have been her." The priest placed his hedge trimmer on the ground. "Come up to the rectory and I'll give you her phone number."

As they were walking away, DeMarco looked down at the extension cord attached to the hedge trimmer to see if the cord was wrapped with black electrical tape in a couple spots like his was. About every other time DeMarco used his hedge trimmer, he cut the cord; it looked like the padre was a more careful trimmer than he was.

The priest gave DeMarco Mary Albertson's phone number and asked if there was anything else he needed. After a moment's hesitation, DeMarco said, "Were you Paul's confessor, father?"

"Yes."

"I know you can't tell me anything Paul told you in confession. I'm Catholic too"—an extremely lapsed Catholic, but there was no point bringing that up—"so I understand that. But can you think of anything Paul might have told you, uh, indirectly, that could give me—and the FBI—some reason as to why he was murdered."

"I'm afraid not," Father Porter said. He smiled sadly, remembering Paul. "I shouldn't be telling you this, but Paul's idea of a major transgression was losing his temper if a clerk in a store was rude to him or cursing—mildly, I might add—when someone cut him off in traffic."

Once again, the FBI's theory that Paul had been dealing drugs sounded more far-fetched than ever.

Mary Albertson ran a church program that served breakfast to the poor and homeless on weekends, and Paul Russo was always there with her, dishing out bacon and eggs to the needy.

Mary was a big lady in her sixties: six foot, easily two hundred and fifty pounds, cheerful brown face, warm, caring brown eyes. She teared up when DeMarco said he wanted to talk about Paul, but smiled when she talked about him. She'd known him ever since he joined the congregation four years ago and had worked with him on many a church committee. He was one of the few people, she said, who seemed to actually enjoy feeding the poor.

"Most folks, they serve these people and they act all happy and hardy, but they're really not. They don't like being near them, the way they look, the way they smell. But not Paul. He realized they were human beings and, but for the grace of God, he could have been the one getting served instead of doing the serving. I appreciated that because there was a time when *I* was on the other side of that serving line."

DeMarco's attitude toward street people was that the majority of them were pain-in-the-ass drunks, but Mary Albertson's comment made him squirm a bit and she noticed, wise woman that she was.

When DeMarco asked her if she knew if Paul had a lawyer, Mary said she didn't. She'd never heard him speak of one.

"Shit," DeMarco muttered and then mumbled, "Sorry," when he noticed the look Mary gave him. He thanked her for her time and started to leave, but then something occurred to him. "There's one other thing I'm curious about," he said. "Do you have any idea who Paul's last patient was? The lady at the hospice where Paul worked couldn't give me his name because of medical confidentiality rules, but she did say that something was bothering Paul the last time she saw him at this patient's house. I really want to talk to the man to see if he knows anything related to my cousin's murder."

Unlike Paul, the occasional small white lie—in this case, that DeMarco already knew that Paul's last patient was dead—didn't bother DeMarco all that much. For that matter, telling whoppers didn't bother him all that much either.

"Yes, he was really down about something the last time I saw him too," Mary said.

"Do you have any idea why?"

She shook her head. "No. When Paul talked about the people he was caring for, he'd usually say there was something beautiful in watching how they accepted that the end was near, how it was inspiring—that's the word he used—the way they readied their souls to meet their God. This last one, though? All Paul said was that the poor man was tormented, as if he was already burning in Hell, and Paul was trying to help him make peace with himself."

"You mean he was trying to convert him to Catholicism?"

"Oh, no. Paul wasn't the type to ram his religion down someone's throat. But if a person asked for help, spiritual or otherwise, he would have given it."

"Huh," DeMarco said. "So do you know who this man is? Like I said, I'd really like to talk to him."

"Well, I'm afraid you're too late for that, Mr. DeMarco," Mary said. "They held the funeral for him yesterday, paid him the honor he was due. Paul's last patient was General Martin Breed."

As DeMarco was walking back to his car, he thought maybe that explained why the FBI had taken Paul's case away from the Arlington County cops. Maybe there was some connection between Paul's death and a two-star army general, a man who would have access to a lot of classified information. And maybe that's why Hopper had searched Paul's apartment and taken his computer. Yeah. Maybe.

The next thought he had was that if Paul's death was connected in any way to a Pentagon heavyweight like Martin Breed, he'd be smart to keep his big nose out of it. He should just do what he was supposed to do: find a lawyer to deal with Paul's four-thousand-buck estate and then go play golf like he'd originally planned.

Yep, that definitely sounded like the smart thing to do.

16

Claire returned to her office, still embarrassed that she had overlooked the *Post* reporter, Robert Hansen, as the man Paul Russo might have met with. She didn't know for sure that Russo had met with Hansen, but it sounded right. It felt right. It sang to her.

Russo, this gay altar boy, just didn't strike her as the type who would have been involved in anything illegal or even underhanded. But what if General Breed—a man privy to the Pentagon's dirty little secrets—had told Russo something before he died? He might have even told Russo something while under the influence of whatever drugs he was being given, maybe delirious, not even knowing what he was saying.

But what about Martin Breed? The man had been an absolute poster boy for the United States Army. Handsome, charming, articulate, a born leader of men. He'd risen up through the ranks at a meteoric pace and had been involved in all the recent wars. In Afghanistan, he'd even managed to get himself wounded, which is quite hard for a general to do, so he got a Purple Heart to go along with all his other medals.

But there had been nothing in Breed's career to indicate he was anything other than a good soldier. There'd been no financial scandals—no awards of huge army contracts to pals in big business—and his marriage had been rock solid, as far as anyone knew. Nor had he shown any desire for public office, so it didn't seem likely that he would have compromised his principles to get himself elected after he retired. Breed's only known ambition was to reach the pinnacle of his profession: to replace General Charles Bradford as the army's chief of staff.

Assuming Russo had learned something significant from Breed—which was a hell of a big assumption—what could it have been? What could have been so important that someone would want to kill Russo because of what he'd heard or seen? And then there was the question of *how* Russo's killers would have known that Breed told Russo anything?

Too many questions—not enough answers. Insufficient data, as Dillon would say.

Claire called Gilbert and two other technicians into her office and proceeded to issue orders, giving them four hours to do what she knew would take them twice as long.

The first thing she had them bring her was Martin Breed's medical records, which had been easy to obtain. Breed had been a high-ranking army officer so Claire assumed, correctly, that he'd been treated by someone over at Walter Reed. His oncologist was a Dr. Stanley Fallon and Dr. Fallon's notes, entered into his computer, stated that Breed had died from brain cancer, a particularly aggressive, fast-moving form of the disease. The last entry regarding Breed recommended that the general call in a hospice, as he was not expected to last more than a month, six weeks at the outside.

This gave Claire pause. Martin Breed died only three weeks after the doctor made his final entry on his patient. Did this mean anything? Maybe, maybe not. She doubted a physician could predict exactly how long a patient would last, and three weeks was pretty close to a month. Still, it made her wonder.

What she really wanted to know was who, besides Paul Russo, had talked to the general as he lay dying. That is, could General Breed have told one of his last visitors that Russo posed some kind of threat? General Breed's phone records didn't point to any logical person—his last calls had primarily been to family members—and the only other way Claire could think of to get the answer to her question was to ask General Breed's grieving widow, an idea she instantly rejected. Talking to people always posed a risk because it left a human trail, and Claire was not ready to go down that path just yet. She much preferred to gather information through purloined records—and eavesdropping, if necessary.

Claire was frustrated, and not just because she wasn't making progress on the Russo intercept. What was really frustrating her was that she might be wasting her time investigating Russo at all. Claire's organization had been established by Dillon to spy within the country's borders for the purpose of preventing attacks which could make 9/11 seem insignificant by comparison. The detonation of a nuclear bomb in Manhattan or Washington, D.C. wouldn't just kill thousands of people; such an event could destroy the economy and cripple the very infrastructure needed to safeguard the nation. If Claire's technicians had just heard Russo being murdered in some mundane way for some mundane reason, she wouldn't have spent any time on him at all. But because his death might be linked to rogue elements of the U.S. military and a dead two-star general, she needed to know what the hell was going on—and she was getting nowhere.

Claire had a four-hundred-calorie lunch and then went to the gym to kick and hit the heavy bag for half an hour. She liked hitting the heavy bag. She had so much aggression in her that it sometimes seemed like hitting the bag was her only outlet. It was either hit the bag or hit Dillon.

As she was walking to the locker room, a guy waved to her—a good-looking guy maybe a year or two younger than her. She pretended she didn't see him. She knew he was working up the nerve to ask her for a date, and she dreaded the prospect of turning him down, as she knew she would.

She'd been on a total of six first dates in the last ten years and she never saw any of the men again. They had all been decent guys—men that most single women her age would kill for. She even had sex with one of them—or tried to—because she thought having sex might jump-start her emotions. God, what a disaster that had been. Now, instead of sex, she worked and she exercised—and cleaned. She had to have the cleanest condo in Laurel, Maryland.

Following her workout, Claire had a brief unproductive conference with her technicians. They were striking out everywhere. They still couldn't identify the cell phone owner who had called Hopper, and they could find no link via phone records or e-mails connecting Russo, Martin Breed, and the *Washington Post* reporter, Hansen.

The whereabouts of the reporter was another dead end. Neither his body nor his car had been found. And his damn bosses at the *Post*—based on statements they had given to the D.C. Metro police, and which the police had helpfully entered into their computers—were clueless as to what Hansen had been working on before he disappeared. All Claire could tell was that Hansen had been a political firefly, constantly flitting from story to story, investigating anything involving Congress or the administration that smacked of scandal or corruption. But he didn't normally work the military side of things.

She also had a tech hack into the *Post*'s computers to look for anything Hansen might have filed that seemed relevant. Zip again. The last story he submitted had been written two weeks before he disappeared and was about a sixty-two-year-old congressman using a corporate jet for a trip to the Bahamas with a thirty-four-year-old ex-Redskins cheerleader. A story, in other words, as old and tired and tawdry as Washington itself.

The tech did find one interesting thing while poking through the *Post*'s electronic files. A GS-11 analyst at Langley had leaked a story about the CIA giving money to a psychopath in Hamas, the analyst apparently having some pro-Israeli bias. Claire couldn't tell from the *Post*'s files why the CIA was funding a Hamas murderer and she finally decided she didn't care. It just made her furious when low-level government employees leaked things to the media; leaking information was a management prerogative. She anonymously e-mailed the name of the CIA tattletale to a heartless prick at Langley she knew, confident that the leaker would soon be stationed in Greenland.

She looked up at the clock. It was seven P.M. and she could feel the onset of a migraine, so she turned off the lights in her office to see if that might make her headache go away. As she sat there in the dark, she reflected on the fact that the day had been a total waste. Goddammit, she needed to go *proactive* on this thing. She needed to stop looking at records and make something happen. She needed . . .

Two of her male technicians were slinking toward the door. They had their coats on.

"Hey, where do you think you're going?" she said quietly.

The techs practically jumped out of their skins. With the lights out in her office, they thought she had left for the day. Fat chance.

"Uh, home," one of the men said.

Claire didn't say anything.

"Geez, Claire, we've been here like *twelve* hours. We're tired."

Twelve hours. Big deal. She thought about their current assignments. They weren't involved in the Russo op, but what they were working on was important. Hell, it was all important—but she couldn't afford to burn them out.

"Good night," she said.

The two men looked at each other, surprised, and moved quickly toward the door.

Claire closed her eyes again.

She could see him: her fiancé, Navy Commander Mark Daniels. He had called her on her cell phone to tell her he'd just been summoned to a meeting over at the Pentagon and he didn't know when he'd be home that day. At the time they were sharing an apartment in Annapolis, not sure when they'd get married, just knowing marriage was inevitable and that life was perfect the way it was.

She remembered being annoyed by the call. Of course he'd be late, she'd thought at the time. She'd be late, too. Half the people who worked in Washington, D.C., would be late that night because thirty-seven minutes earlier the second plane had struck the World Trade Center. So when Mark called, she'd been practically sprinting down a hallway toward a conference room because things were going crazy at Fort Meade. Half the bosses at the NSA were trying to figure out what had happened, and it seemed like the other half were already working on a story to exonerate the agency.

He'd been wearing his dress blues that day because he'd had some sort of ceremony to attend that morning. She could see him: tall, dark-haired, beautiful physique; two gorgeous dimples formed in his cheeks when he smiled. He wouldn't have been smiling when he called, though; he would have looked serious, his eyes flashing, worried and angry, yet still courteous enough to call and let her know that he'd be late. And she could see herself, all impatient, no time to chat, striding down the hallway, irritated that he had called when he did. And then she heard him scream. She'd never forget that sound.

She could see him—and hear him—as he was incinerated by thousands of gallons of exploding aviation fuel as American Airlines Flight 77 crashed into the Pentagon.

She'd never see him again—and she'd always see him.

17

Levy watched Alberta Merker enter her house. It was nine P.M. Merker put in a long day, doing whatever it was that she did.

Merker's house was in a quiet middle-class neighborhood and her next-door neighbors appeared to be at home. He could see people moving about in one of the houses and lights were on in the other. The houses across the street from Merker's, all except one, appeared to be occupied as well.

He would have to wait until her neighbors were asleep.

He wondered if he was doing the right thing. He could have followed Merker tomorrow when she went to work to see where she would lead him, but he didn't have time for that. He needed to know immediately what she was doing and who employed her.

He closed his eyes and thought, as he often did at quiet moments, about the last time he'd seen his brother. When his father had left he'd been too young and he didn't really have a clear memory of the man. But his brother he remembered vividly: standing there in his uniform, his pant cuffs tucked into the top of his combat boots, the green beret on his head, the broad smile on his face—and then his brother vanished. Forever.

He also thought back to the day he met Charles Bradford for the first time. Bradford had been a colonel then and his commanding officer. It was midnight and Levy was sitting alone in the sentinels' changing room, only nineteen years old, feeling totally alone and more depressed than ever. Bradford sat down next to him and asked how he was doing, and he was shocked to find Bradford knew about his father and brother. And when Bradford spent an hour with him, talking to him about the army, about the country, about patriotism, Levy was moved to tears. He never forgot that night. He didn't speak to Bradford again for ten years, and when he did, he was astonished Bradford remembered him.

He was even more astonished by the job Charles Bradford asked him to do.

By one A.M., Merker and her neighbors appeared to be sleeping. Levy put on a ski mask, took a small gym bag from the trunk of his car, and picked the lock on Merker's back door. He wasn't particularly good with lock picks, and it took him almost five minutes. As he entered the house, he noticed a pleasant odor. Merker might have been burning incense or candles before she went to bed.

Merker slept on her back, her mouth slightly open, and there was a lamp on a small table next to her bed. Levy placed the gym bag on the floor, found the lamp's switch, then pulled the Colt from his shoulder holster. He placed the barrel of the gun against the center of Merker's forehead and turned on the light.

Merker came awake instantly and saw Levy looming over her, the gun in his hand, the ski mask covering his face. She opened her mouth to scream but Levy prodded her head with the gun and said, "Don't." She clamped her mouth shut; her brown eyes were huge with fear.

"If you scream," Levy said, "I'll pistol-whip you. If you fight me, I'll pistol-whip you. I'll make your face look like a Halloween mask. Do you understand?"

Merker nodded. He noticed that although the woman was clearly frightened, she wasn't panicking, she wasn't on the verge of hysteria. She was thinking about how to escape. She was a professional, of some sort.

"What do you want?" Merker said.

Levy didn't answer. He threw back the sheets covering Merker. She was wearing what looked like men's boxer shorts and a Garfield-the-cat T-shirt.

"Roll over on your stomach," Levy said.

"I have money in the freezer," Merker said. "There's five hundred dollars in a little Tupperware thing. My credit cards are in my purse."

"If you don't turn over onto your stomach immediately," Levy said, "I'm going to hurt you."

Merker turned over and Levy reached down into the gym bag for a roll of duct tape. He used the tape to bind her hands, then took her by the shoulders and turned her so she was lying once again on her back.

"What do you want?" Merker asked again.

"I want to know who you work for," Levy said. "I want to know who sent you to Arlington Hospital to get that man's fingerprints."

"What?" she said, feigning confusion, but Levy could tell she wasn't confused.

"Alberta, tell me who you work for and I'll leave. If you don't tell me, then . . . well, I'm going to make you tell me."

"I work in the commissary at Fort Meade. I buy stuff: you know, the produce and meat and shit. You got me mixed up with somebody. I don't know what the hell you're talking about, about fingerprints."

Levy shook his head. "Stand up."

"Look in my purse if you don't believe me," Merker said. "You'll see my badge for the commissary."

He was sure she did have such an ID badge. That meant nothing.

"Stand up," Levy said again.

Merker rose from her bed and for an instant she seemed relieved, probably thinking that if Levy wanted her out of the bed he wasn't planning to rape her.

"Go to the kitchen," he said, and gave her a small push in the back.

In the kitchen, Levy turned on the lights. "Sit down in one of those chairs near the table."

"Look, you got me confused with—"

He backhanded her. He didn't slap her that hard but she stumbled against the kitchen table.

"Sit in the chair," he said.

He took the roll of duct tape and wrapped the tape around her chest and legs, binding her to the chair. Her hands were still taped behind her back.

"What do you *want*?" Merker said.

"I told you. I want to know who you work for."

"I work for the goddamn army! I work in the commissary at Fort Meade. How many fuckin' times do I have to tell you? You're making a mistake."

Levy took a cloth sack from the gym bag and placed the sack over Merker's head.

"What are you doing?" she said.

Levy didn't answer. He tipped back the chair she was sitting in so that she was now lying on her back, her head on the floor, bound to the chair. He then searched the cabinets in the kitchen until he found what he was looking for: cooking pots. One was a five gallon aluminum pot that she probably used for making spaghetti or stews. Two other pots were cast iron and about half that size. He filled all three pots with water.

Waterboarding is a very effective form of persuasion. The prisoner is immobilized, usually on a board or table, a cloth sack is placed over his head, his head is placed in a position lower than his feet—and then water is poured onto the sack. It sounds harmless, and the prisoner isn't marked in any way—except psychologically. Prisoners subjected to this procedure can have nightmares for life and often develop a number of phobias, some of them completely debilitating, such as an inability to take showers or having panic attacks whenever it rains.

During waterboarding, as the water cascades over the prisoner's face and into his nose and mouth, his gag reflex kicks in. He begins to choke and cough uncontrollably, and the sensation is identical to drowning, a drowning that never stops. Interrogators have found the technique so effective that hardened men, fanatical terrorists, will sometimes confess in less than five minutes.

"Who do you work for?" Levy said.

"I told you. I . . ."

Levy began to pour the water onto Merker's face and she whipped her head from side to side, coughing and choking and gagging, straining against the tape binding her to the chair, the chair bucking off the floor. He poured for almost two minutes—two minutes that would have seemed like an eternity to the woman. When he stopped pouring, Merker sucked in air in huge, ragged gasps, her chest heaving.

"Who do you work for?" Levy said.

She didn't answer. It sounded as if she might be hyperventilating because of the panic she was certainly feeling, but she didn't seem to make any attempt to speak.

He began to pour the water again.

Then something strange happened: Merker stopped moving. She just lay there, not choking or trying to evade the water. It appeared as if she'd passed out, but that didn't make sense. That was one of the nice things about waterboarding: prisoners normally remain conscious, or at least semiconscious, throughout the process.

Levy reached down and felt for a pulse in Merker's throat.

There was no pulse!

Levy ripped the sack off Merker's head and performed CPR on her for five minutes. It did no good. Merker was dead.

Levy knelt next to the woman, breathing heavily, completely shocked. There was no way she should have died, not from what he had done to her. She must have had a heart attack or a stroke. She was a chunky woman, but she wasn't obese. In fact, she looked like she was in pretty good shape. She must have had some sort of preexisting medical condition. That was the only thing that made sense.

What the hell had he done? He hadn't wanted to kill her—and he wouldn't have killed her if she'd told him what he wanted to know. She hadn't seen his face. But now she was dead—and, worst of all, she was the only lead he had. He had just killed the one person who could tell him who their opponent was.

He cut the tape binding Merker to the chair, examined her body, and was relieved to see that he hadn't taped her so tightly that he'd bruised or marked her. He took a washcloth and soap, gently scrubbed the tape residue from her legs, and pulled the wet Garfield T-shirt off her. He carried her back to her bedroom, placed her back in her bed, put a dry T-shirt on her, then found a hair dryer and blow-dried her short hair. He noticed that her lower lip was somewhat puffy from where he'd struck her, so he took her out of the bed and laid her face down on the floor. That was better: it would look as if she'd risen from her bed and collapsed when she had the first symptoms of whatever killed her, and falling to the floor would account for the bruise he'd caused when he slapped her.

Levy returned to the kitchen, placed the cooking pots back in the cupboard, and, using rags he found in a closet, mopped up the kitchen floor. After he placed all the wet rags in a clothes hamper, he spent the next hour looking for anything that might identify Merker's employer. All he found was the Fort Meade commissary ID in her purse. He walked back to the bedroom for one final look around and noticed a photo of Merker and another black woman who might have been

Merker's sister. She and the other woman were wearing sombreros and grinning and drinking drinks that looked like margaritas.

First Witherspoon and now this young woman. Witherspoon had been a brother in arms and Merker . . . well, she had been a soldier in her way as well. She had been his adversary—but not his enemy.

This was not the way John Levy wanted to serve his country.

18

DeMarco was a lawyer who had never practiced law. And what he had learned about estates and wills back in law school wasn't even a distant memory; he had no memory of those subjects at all. So he looked in the phone book, found the name of an Arlington lawyer who specialized in wills and estates, and made an appointment.

He told the lawyer his problem, that his cousin had been killed and he was the only relative young enough and close enough to deal with Paul's estate. But he couldn't find Paul's will and he needed to clean out Paul's apartment and do something with the four grand Paul had in the bank.

The lawyer—a crusty, ill-tempered old fart named Crenshaw—said if Paul had died intestate, DeMarco or some other relative would have to deal with the state of Virginia to probate Paul's will.

"So can you give me the form I have to submit?" DeMarco asked.

"It's not quite that simple," Crenshaw said, after which he went through a mind-numbing discourse about how DeMarco would have to qualify as the administer of the estate, get something called a surety bond, provide lists of all of Paul's known assets and heirs, and submit reports on a periodic basis to some bureaucratic entity known as the Commissioner of Accounts Office. Then, after what sounded to

DeMarco like a decade of paper shuffling, the state would divvy up Paul's possessions to his relatives in accordance with formulas they used.

"But his only relatives are me, my mother, and an aunt who's eighty-seven years old," DeMarco whined. "And none of us want his furniture, and me and my mom both agree Paul's aunt can have the money. Can I at least clean out his apartment and get rid of his sh—his stuff?"

"No. Mr. Russo's possessions don't belong to you," the lawyer said.

"But what's Paul's landlady supposed to do with his furniture? Store it someplace until his estate is settled?"

The lawyer shrugged. "She could get rid of the furniture, I suppose. But if she did, and if one of Paul's relatives wanted the furniture or the money that could have been obtained if the furniture had been sold, well, then she might have a problem. Someone might sue her."

"We're not gonna sue her! I already told you: none of his relatives want the furniture. It's a bunch of secondhand crap. And his landlady would have to pay about a hundred bucks a month to put it in storage."

"She could be reimbursed from Paul's estate," the lawyer said. "The other thing is that if Paul made a will, he might not have left his possessions to his family. He could have left his estate to a charity or a close friend."

This was hopeless.

Before he left Crenshaw's office, the lawyer gave him a stack of paper that contained all the rules and forms—and charged him a hundred and twenty bucks.

DeMarco's curses trailed behind him as he walked back to his car.

DeMarco stopped at a restaurant in Georgetown to get lunch—and a martini. It could be said that dealing with all the bullshit associated with Paul's death was driving him to drink, but DeMarco didn't need to be driven to drink. Like his boss, he drank too much as it was.

Which reminded him to check on Mahoney. This time, he called Mary Pat and asked how her husband was doing. Not good, she said, and started to cry. Mahoney was still in a coma, his vital signs were getting weaker, and the doctors were noncommittal. To all this, DeMarco responded with the usual useless platitudes people are reduced to in these situations: *Don't worry. He'll be fine. He's strong. He's getting the best medical care in the country. I'll pray for him.*

And he would.

He sat there a few minutes, sipping his martini, thinking about the walking contradiction that was John Mahoney: corrupt yet intensely patriotic, self-serving and self-centered but incredibly loyal and generous to those he considered friends, a serial adulterer who was deeply in love with his wife. He hoped Mahoney had made a confession before he went into surgery; he wasn't sure God knew about Mahoney's good side. He finished his drink and his lunch and then called Hopper at the FBI. Agent Hopper did not sound delighted to hear from him.

"Did you happen to come across Paul's will?" DeMarco asked.

"No, why would I?" Hopper said.

"Because you searched his house and you took the computers from his home and his office."

Hopper didn't say anything for a moment. "How do you know that? Are you bird-dogging my investigation, DeMarco?"

"I'm not bird-dogging anything. I went to Paul's place because I gotta deal with the crap in his apartment, and his landlady told me you'd been there. And when I went to the place where he worked, his boss told me the same thing: that you searched his desk and took his computer. Anyway, I looked through the desk in his apartment and—"

"You were in his apartment?"

"Yeah. Like I was saying, I looked through his desk hoping to find his will, but I didn't. I was thinking maybe it was on his computer, that maybe he made one of those online do-it-yourself wills. Or maybe his lawyer's identified in the address book in his e-mail."

"I didn't find anything related to a will in his computer," Hopper said. "Nor did I see anything about a lawyer."

"Why did you take the computer?"

"Because we're investigating his death and we're looking for a drug connection."

"From what I've been told about him, it's pretty unlikely he was dealing drugs."

"Is that right?" Hopper said. "Well, it may interest you to know that I found a bottle of Librium capsules in his apartment, and your cousin's name wasn't on the prescription label. It was only twenty pills, but—well, you know."

"Yeah, I see what you mean," DeMarco said, but he was thinking: *Horseshit, you found any pills.*

"And DeMarco, one other thing," Hopper said. "Stay out of Russo's house. It's part of a crime scene."

"A crime scene? I thought he was killed at the Iwo Jima Memorial."

"Just stay out of his house," Hopper repeated, and hung up.

DeMarco sat for a moment, spinning his empty martini glass in his hand, and reflected on his discussion with Hopper. The guy was lying to him; no doubt about that. There was no way he had found a stolen bottle of pills in Paul's apartment. But *why* was he lying? Once again, he thought about the fact that General Breed had been Paul's last patient and that maybe Hopper was lying because there were national security issues involved.

Then another thought occurred to him. When he searched Paul's desk he'd been looking for file containing a will or a bill Paul had received from a lawyer. He hadn't come across an address book in Paul's desk, but then he hadn't really been looking for one. DeMarco didn't have a paper address book; he kept addresses on his computer at home and all the important phone numbers were in his cell phone. But maybe Paul was like his mother. His mom kept the addresses and phone numbers of her friends in a little black notebook, and she kept the notebook in a drawer in the kitchen near the phone.

He should take one last look in Paul's place, try to find an address book stashed in away in a drawer, and see if the book contained the name of a lawyer. No way in hell was he going to go through the hassle of dealing with the state to settle Paul's estate if he didn't have to. Then he thought about Hopper's warning—or maybe it had been a legal directive—for him to stay out of Paul's place. And then he thought, Fuck Hopper. He wanted to get this bullshit with Paul's estate settled and go play golf.

19

Charles Bradford watched through his office window as an Asian man wearing a stained gray fedora slowly pruned a rhododendron. He wondered what it would be like to have a job like that, a simple job, a job with no real responsibility, a job where *other* people worried about protecting the country.

"So all you know is that she worked for the Department of Defense," Bradford said.

"Yes, sir, " Levy said. He paused and added, "I'm sorry I let you down, but she was a young woman. There was no reason to think—"

"Do you think she might have really worked at Fort Meade, John?"

"It's possible. She had a badge to get on base, for the commissary like she said."

Bradford didn't say anything for a moment, as he mulled over what Levy had told him. "Fort Meade. Could someone have heard you that night, John?"

"Heard us? Do you mean could someone have intercepted our radio transmissions during the operation?"

"Yes."

"That's possible, of course, but it doesn't matter. We were using encrypted com gear and we never mentioned any names."

"Encrypted com gear," Bradford repeated. "John, what's the one organization in this country that might be able to listen in on an encrypted transmission?"

Levy was silent for a moment. "The NSA," he said.

"Yes, the National Security Agency. And where are they headquartered, John?"

"Fort Meade."

"The NSA helps design encrypted communications systems used by the military. And if they develop an encrypted system, you know damn good and well they know a way to break the encryption. They have to be able to do that in case the enemy gets their hands on our gear."

Levy shook his head. "No, sir, I don't buy it. The radios we used have a Type I encryption system with a 256-bit encryption key. It would take the NSA a million of hours of computer time to break the code, assuming they could ever break it."

"Do you know that for a fact, John? Even I don't know the latest advancements in NSA encryption technology. What I do know is that they're always light-years ahead of the people using the radios."

Levy nodded his head. He knew Bradford could be right.

Neither man said anything for a moment, then Bradford said, "I think I'm going to have someone poke around a bit over at the NSA."

"Sir, that could be a mistake. Right now the only thing anyone knows is Witherspoon was driving a stolen ambulance and two soldiers from Fort Myer were reassigned to Afghanistan. And if the NSA had heard something, wouldn't they have told somebody? Wouldn't they have alerted someone here at the Pentagon, or maybe even the White House?"

Bradford laughed. "That's the last thing they'd do, because then they'd have to admit they were conducting an illegal eavesdropping operation. But they might initiate their own investigation."

Bradford looked out at the Asian pruning the rhody again. Now the gardener was just standing, head cocked, studying the bush, like a painter assessing a work in progress. Bradford supposed that bush-trimming *was* an art in its way, and again he envied the man his task.

He turned back to Levy. "John, let's consider the worst case scenario. Let's assume someone—the NSA, whoever—knows Witherspoon and those two other soldiers were involved in Russo's death. Let's even take it a step further. Let's assume they know Russo was meeting with Hansen. Is there anything you said that night that would have told them *why* Russo and Hansen were meeting?"

"No, sir. Absolutely not."

"And Russo didn't leave anything behind that says why he and Hansen were meeting?"

"No, sir. Hopper searched Russo's house after the operation and I had searched it before, as soon as we knew that . . . that General Breed had talked to Russo."

Bradford could tell Levy was still very much bothered by Martin's death.

"And as for the reporter," Levy said, "the *Post* has repeatedly stated that they have no idea what Hansen was working on prior to his disappearance."

"I agree," Bradford said.

"And there's no way to prove the two soldiers we shipped out were involved in the operation. There's no evidence that they were at the memorial and, with Hopper handling the case, no evidence will ever be found."

Bradford was silent for a moment. "John, our biggest liability at this point is those two soldiers talking."

"They won't, sir. I know those men. They won't ever discuss what happened that night."

"I'm not sure we can afford to take the risk."

Levy didn't say anything for a moment, then he looked directly into Bradford's eyes. "Sir, I am not going to do anything to harm those soldiers."

There was no doubt Levy meant what he said. Killing Martin Breed on his deathbed was one thing, and even eliminating Witherspoon, a man who would most likely have spent the rest of his days as a vegetable, was different from killing two loyal soldiers who had only followed orders. At least that's the way Levy would see it. When things settled down a bit, he needed to talk with Levy some more about the sacrifices that men in their positions were sometimes required to make. But not now.

"I'm not asking you to harm them," Bradford said. "All I'm saying is that you need to make sure those men understand the importance of not talking to anyone, and if anyone tries to talk to them, they need to let you know immediately. Can you get word to them where they're stationed now?"

"Yes, sir."

"Good. For now, just keep tabs on everything. Keep in touch with Hopper at the Bureau and tell Colonel Gilmore to call you if he gets any more inquiries about the sentinels. And I'll do a little quiet probing over at the NSA."

"And if we find out the NSA did hear us that night?" Levy asked.

"Then I'll deal with it," Bradford said.

Bradford had to participate in a teleconference with his NATO commanders in two minutes, but he continued to sit at his desk. He didn't tolerate people being late to his meetings and, consequently, he didn't like it when he was late. But he needed to do something about the NSA, and right away.

As he'd told Levy, he needed to know if the agency had any knowledge of the Russo op. He didn't, however, want it known that anyone at the Pentagon was interested—and he really didn't want it known that *he* was interested. He thought about this problem for a moment before he came up with the perfect answer: Aziz. Yes, the Aziz fiasco would provide the cover he needed.

He picked up the phone, punched in a number, and said, "This is General Bradford. Tell him it's not urgent, but I need to speak to him." Forty minutes later, his NATO teleconference was interrupted when the president returned his call.

"Is there a problem, General?" the president asked, and Bradford could hear the stress in his voice. The man was struggling with two wars, an intractable Congress, and a domestic agenda that appeared to be mired in the mud. He didn't need another problem—which was exactly what Bradford was counting on.

"No, Mr. President, there isn't a problem," Bradford said. "In fact, I'm calling to suggest doing something to avoid one, and it would be best if the issue was handled by someone outside of the Department of Defense."

20

"We got something on that guy Hopper."

Claire looked up. It was the agent she'd assigned to watch the FBI man. He was wearing a short-sleeved shirt that said POTOMAC ELECTRIC POWER COMPANY over the pocket, and she assumed the shirt was part of whatever ploy his team was using to stay close to the subject, maybe a power company truck outside the Hoover Building or near Hopper's home. What Claire didn't like was that he looked hung over, his eyes two bloodshot holes in his unshaven face. She made a mental note to have him checked out. Drunks were a liability.

"What did you get?" Claire said.

"Maybe you should just play this," he said, and offered her a CD.

"Password," she said.

"Feebwatch," he said. "One word, lowercase."

She started to berate him for using a password so closely related to the contents of the CD, but didn't. She would talk to him about that when she spoke to him about the booze. She inserted the disc into one of her computers and listened to a phone call from a man named DeMarco to Hopper. When the call was over, she said, "So what? So this guy DeMarco is trying to find Russo's will. What's the big deal?"

"Listen to the next phone call," the agent said.

I got your message. What's going on?

The man speaking was the one who had directed Paul Russo's execution. Hopper responded by saying:

It's about the nurse.

What happened?

I got a call from a lawyer named DeMarco who works for Congress. He's related to the nurse, and he's trying to find out if the nurse had a will. The thing is, he's searched the nurse's apartment at least once and he seems to be following my investigation.

Do you think he's conducting his own investigation?

I don't think so. But I get the impression he isn't buying the story that Russo was killed because of drugs.

There was a moment of silence.

Look, it's probably nothing.

It was Hopper speaking again.

I'm just letting you know because you told me to keep you informed. You might want to put somebody on this guy, but that's up to you.

It bothers me that he works for Congress.

Yeah, it bothers me too, but I don't think his job is related to this. He's just the nurse's cousin trying to settle the estate. If you want, I could make up a will for the nurse. You know, fill out one of those online forms and give it to DeMarco. That would probably get him off my back.

No, don't do that. If the real will shows up, that could just complicate things. Anyway, thanks for calling.

"Were you able to identify the man who called Hopper back?" Claire asked the agent.

"No," he said. "We got a fix on his position when he was talking to Hopper and he was in a car on the beltway, but after he completed the call he powered down the phone."

Claire made sure the agent had all the assets he needed to stay on Hopper, then dismissed him.

Her next thought was: DeMarco. Yeah, he might do.

"We need to spook Hopper."

Claire said this as she paced Dillon's office and she made him think of a walking pipe bomb, some completely unstable device that could detonate at any moment.

Claire Whiting just *sucked* the tranquillity out of any room she entered.

"I think we should use this guy DeMarco," she said.

"Use him how?"

"We'll give him something that'll make him suspicious of Hopper. I mean, he's already suspicious; you can tell by the sound of his voice that he doesn't believe Russo was dealing drugs. So we'll give him something else. We'll tell him no autopsy was performed on his cousin and Hopper lied about Russo being killed with a handgun. Or maybe we tell DeMarco the night Russo died he was meeting with a reporter from the *Post,* and the reporter's disappeared."

"How would you leak all this to DeMarco?"

"I don't know yet. I'll figure something out. But the idea is we give him something that'll make him call Hopper again and make Hopper meet with whoever's controlling him."

"That could be rather dangerous for Mr. DeMarco, don't you think?" Dillon said.

Claire stopped pacing and looked at Dillon. The expression on her face said *and your point is?*

"We actually don't have to use DeMarco directly," she said. "We've recorded his voice and I can have a guy imitate him. Then Hopper will run to his boss. Or maybe Hopper's boss will send people to watch DeMarco . . ."

"And maybe kill him," Dillon tossed in.

". . . but we'll be there covering DeMarco, and we'll follow these people right down the rabbit hole."

"No, Claire. I don't want this DeMarco person involved, and I definitely don't want him killed. Let's leave him out of this, for the time being."

Claire opened her mouth to debate this directive but, before she could, Dillon asked, "Tell me what else you've learned."

Claire stared at Dillon for a moment, making no attempt to hide her annoyance. She was probably thinking how things would be different if she had his job. "We checked traffic cameras," she said. "There wasn't one right near the Iwo Jima Memorial but there was one half a mile away. The camera caught Hansen's car going through the intersection half an hour after Russo's body was discovered."

"What about before Russo was killed? Did any of the cameras show Hansen going toward the memorial?"

"No. We looked at cameras on the most likely routes from Hansen's apartment to the memorial, but none of them picked him up. He's a local boy, so maybe he knew some back-road way to get there. Or maybe he didn't drive from his apartment."

"And I take it you couldn't see who was driving the car."

"No. Just the license plate. I don't know why they don't set up those fucking cameras so you can *really* see what's going on."

"They're designed to catch people running stoplights, Claire, not to spy on the citizenry."

"Well, that's pretty damn shortsighted, if you ask me."

"So you don't really know who was in the car, Hansen or the people who might have killed him."

"No, but you have one hell of a coincidence. Hansen goes missing the same day as the hit, and half an hour after the hit his car is spotted near the memorial. That's good enough for me. They popped Russo and Hansen, and whoever was in charge took Hansen's body. Then, while all the cops were looking at Russo's corpse, one of the guys on the hit team comes back and picks up Hansen's car."

"And did what with it?"

"I don't know," she said, exasperated with Dillon's mania for detail. "They took it to a wrecking yard and squeezed it into a little metal cube. Or they took it to a chop shop and had it cut up into a hundred pieces. It's gone, just like Hansen, and neither will be found again. Hansen'll be like that old-time reporter you like so much."

"Do you mean Ambrose Bierce?"

"Yeah, the guy who walked into Mexico and disappeared. And that's what they'll say about Hansen twenty years from now: he was on to something big and he vanished."

Dillon liked to quote Ambrose Bierce, one his favorites being: *An idiot: a member of a large and powerful tribe whose influence on human affairs has always been dominant and controlling.*

"I also had an agent search Hansen's apartment," Claire said, "but she didn't find anything helpful. She said the place might have been searched before she got there, but Hansen was such a slob it was hard to be sure."

"I know Hansen's laptop went missing with him," Dillon said, "but could he have e-mailed something from it?"

"No. Hansen used his laptop like a typewriter and when it was time to file a story he'd copy it to a disc and take the disc to work. He never e-mailed anything related to his stories. Maybe he was afraid to."

"So another dead end," Dillon said.

"Yes. Which is why I need DeMarco for a Judas goat. Please, Dillon. Let me tether his ass to a stake and see who comes to eat him."

"No, Claire," Dillon said. "Find another way."

21

DeMarco knocked again on Betty's door, and she frowned when she saw who was standing on her porch. He wondered if she'd forgotten who he was.

"Hi, Betty. Joe DeMarco, Paul's cousin? Remember?"

"Of course I remember. Why do people your age always assume someone my age can't remember anything?"

Sheesh. "I'm sorry, I wasn't implying—"

"Oh, never mind. What do you want?"

"Well, I was wondering if you'd mind letting me into Paul's apartment again. I still can't find his will."

And then he told Betty what the lawyer had said, how she might be forced to store all of Paul's things until Paul's estate was settled by the state, which could take until the next ice age. He could tell Betty wasn't too happy to hear that—and she gave him the key.

There was no Rolodex or address book in Paul's apartment.

This whole thing was really beginning to piss him off. He'd just blown a hundred and twenty bucks on a lawyer who'd been no help at all, and now he was wasting more time on a guy he barely knew. And the worst thing was, it was a gorgeous day outside, a perfect day for golf, and he was inside a stuffy apartment.

The money he'd paid the lawyer made him think he should go through Paul's bills again. If a lawyer had prepared a will for him, there would definitely be a bill, and since he couldn't find a file labeled LAWYER, he spent forty minutes looking at old Visa bills and canceled checks. No joy.

Then another thought occurred to him: he kept his really important papers in a safe deposit box at his bank, things like his own will and the deed for his house. But he also had a little fireproof box down in his basement where he put semi-important stuff like his passport, his insurance policies, and his disaster cash. Maybe Paul had a box like that, too.

He rooted around in Paul's closets—one in his bedroom, one in his office, and one by the front door. It was a small house and there was no basement. All he found was the usual crap people dump on the top shelves of their closets, things they never use but are too lazy to throw out. He didn't find a strongbox, but he did find a cardboard box filled with photographs.

He flipped through the box and saw a picture of his mom, Paul's mom, and Paul's Aunt Lena—the person who, if she wasn't eighty-seven years old, should be dealing with this. Then there were the usual snapshots people take and never look at again: pictures of people sitting at barbecue tables, in front of Christmas trees, posed like they were guests at a wedding or some other celebration. There was one guy who was with Paul in a lot of the pictures, and there were several pictures of the guy standing alone. Hmm, he thought.

He knocked on Betty's door again—he could tell Betty was becoming a wee bit tired of him—and showed her the picture of the man he'd found so frequently in Paul's photo collection. "Do you know who this is?" he asked.

"Oh, that's Anthony," she said. "He and Paul dated for about two years, but they broke up over a year ago. Paul took it very hard. I felt so sorry for him."

"Huh," DeMarco said. "Do you know Anthony's last name?"

"McGuire. He lives in Fairfax."

An ex-lover. Maybe he'd know if Paul had a will.

But then he looked up at the sky—that beautiful, cloudless blue sky—and he thought, Life is too short. Look at Mahoney. One day he's running around, on top of the world, and the next day, with no warning at all, he's on his back, in a coma, half a step from death's door. Yeah, life is too short and to hell with Paul, his furniture, and his will. He was gonna spend the afternoon playing golf. He'd go see this McGuire guy tomorrow.

The small conference table in Claire's office was piled with paper, stacks of paper, all the records she'd asked her people to pull on Russo and Hopper. And because she didn't know what she was looking for, she couldn't tell her techs to go through the papers and find whatever it was she needed to find; she had to do it herself, and the task was taking forever. She was just *burning* time and it was really pissing her off.

That damn Dillon. If he would just let her use DeMarco like she wanted.

The records provided a fairly complete picture of Russo: he was heavily involved in his church, donated much of his salary to charities, had no expensive hobbies, ate lunch at Subway almost every day. One thing she couldn't find from the records, however, was a person Russo was particularly close to—somebody he might have confided in, somebody who might have been able to explain what he was doing at the Iwo Jima Memorial. Based on his phone bills for the last six months, this person didn't exist. There wasn't anyone he called every day or every other day, the way a husband might call his wife or a guy might call his girlfriend.

"I want Russo's house searched," Claire said. "*Really* searched."

Claire was speaking to her favorite agent, a young lady in her thirties named Alice. Unlike most of the people who worked for her, Alice wasn't afraid of her. Alice sat there impassively, saying nothing.

Alice was very good at her job, but she had the emotional range of cork.

The reason Claire was talking to Alice was because she knew one thing to be absolutely true: *Men can't find anything.* This was an axiom as certain and valid as any law of physics.

One night—she remembered it like it was yesterday—Mark had decided he wanted peanut butter after they finished making love. God knows why he wanted peanut butter at one in the morning, but he did. She was still lying in bed, feeling kinda sore between her legs but sore in that *good* way, and he yelled out to her, *Hey, where's the peanut butter? Top shelf of the cupboard,* she yelled back, *right next to the stove.* A minute later, he yelled again: *I can't find it.* So she had to get up, put on a robe, go into the kitchen, and there he was, buck-naked, staring helplessly into the cupboard. Claire remembered thinking at the time how absolutely perfect he looked and what a lucky girl she was. *I thought you said it was on this shelf,* he said. *It is,* she said, and she moved one box out of the way—*one box*—and there was the peanut butter.

Mark may have been perfect but he was still a man—and men can't find anything.

So when Claire wanted a place searched she assigned a woman, in this case Alice. She would have assigned Alberta because Alberta had more patience than Alice, but Alberta was dead.

Claire still couldn't believe it. Alberta had only been thirty-seven. One of the agents who knew her well said her mom had died of a coronary at forty-two, and it looked as if the same thing had happened to Alberta. They were holding a wake for her tomorrow night but Claire didn't plan to attend. She wanted to go but she knew her presence at the event would make Alberta's co-workers uncomfortable.

"An FBI agent has already been in there," Claire said. "He took Russo's computer and I'm guessing he searched the place as well. So if Russo hid something and it's still in his apartment, it's not going to be in any of the usual places."

"What am I looking for?" Alice asked.

"I don't know," Claire said. "Anything he thought was important enough to hide really well, and in particular anything associated with an army general named Martin Breed."

"Breed?" Alice said.

"Yeah," Claire said, but she didn't tell Alice anything more and Alice didn't ask.

"How many guys can I take with me?" Alice said.

"One. Russo's place can't be that big."

"Okay," Alice said.

"And one other thing," Claire said. "Russo lived in a duplex and his landlord is the old lady who lives next door. I don't want the old woman hurt. I don't want her to have a stroke or something. So you need to figure out a way to deal with her if she wakes up and hears you while you're searching."

"Sure," Alice said, with an indifferent shrug.

22

"Admiral," the Attorney General said, "this is Aaron Drexler. Aaron works for me now, but before coming to Justice he was on the legal staff at the Pentagon. He has a top secret security clearance."

Robert Scranton was a large, hearty, gregarious fellow. Add a fake white beard and he'd make a good Santa. He hailed from the president's home state and, before being made the country's top lawyer, had been a mediocre district attorney in a fair-sized city. The fact that it had taken him three tries to pass the bar exam apparently bothered no one—or at least it didn't bother the fifty-eight senators who had voted to confirm him. Scranton had more important qualifications than intelligence and experience; he was rich, had contributed hugely to the president's campaign, and was arguably more loyal than a golden retriever.

Admiral Fenton Wilcox brusquely shook Drexler's hand. He had no idea why he'd been summoned to the Attorney General's Office—but he had been summoned. Nor did he know why he was being introduced to Drexler, a whip-thin six-footer dressed in a dark suit. Drexler had short black hair and hooded eyes and he just sat there staring at Wilcox, seeming not at all impressed by a man who wore three stars and directed the largest, most secretive intelligence organization in the country.

There was a palpable arrogance about Drexler that instantly annoyed Wilcox.

"Aaron," the Attorney General was saying, "graduated from MIT with a degree in computer science and then obtained his doctorate of law from Harvard."

Maybe that explained Drexler's arrogance: his education. MIT and Harvard weren't the easiest schools in the country to get into. But just to put the guy in his place, Wilcox said, "I know a lot of bright guys, Mr. Scranton. They work for me. Why are you introducing me to Mr. Drexler?"

"Admiral, Aaron specializes in Internet fraud here at Justice because he knows his way around a computer. In other words, with his Pentagon background, his work experience, and his education, he's capable of understanding a lot of what you folks do in the dark over there at Fort Meade."

Scranton smiled after he said that. His "do in the dark" comment was intended to be humorous, but Fenton Wilcox, a man with a small sense of humor to begin with, didn't smile back. He looked at his watch. "Mr. Scranton," he said, "what does this—"

"The president has asked me to audit your operation for compliance to FISA and I've assigned Aaron."

"Audit! What the hell is this all about?"

"Aziz," Scranton said.

"Goddammit," Wilcox muttered. Then, more loudly: "Aren't we *ever* going to get beyond that? The damn guy was guilty, and my people didn't do anything illegal."

"Well, the president wants to make sure of that, sir. There were rumors that you knew more about Dr. Aziz than you could have learned from the authorized wire taps."

"Rumors! What rumors?" the admiral said.

Ignoring the question, Scranton said, "Because of these rumors, the president is concerned you folks might be illegally spying on our citizens again, and he won't stand for a repeat of what happened in 2005. So he's asked for a small, independent look to make sure you're doing things by the book."

The admiral's eyes bulged and his complexion turned an unhealthy shade of crimson. "My agency is doing no such thing! I've testified to Congress about that. Under oath." Testifying under oath may not have meant much to crooks and politicians but it meant something to the admiral. "The kind of crap that happened back in 2005 is not happening on my watch."

The Attorney General nodded his large head, as if concurring, but then said, "I'm sure you believe that, Admiral, but there's always the possibility that some of your people are not as honest as you."

"I run a tight ship," Wilcox responded, through clenched teeth. "My people are not monitoring American citizens unless we have a FISA warrant."

Wilcox personally believed that FISA was making him work with one hand tied behind his back, but the law was the law and he followed it—and he was damn certain his people did too.

"Admiral," Scranton said, "I don't doubt your integrity. Nor does the president. The fact remains, however, that he's authorized this audit. I imagine he just wants some peace of mind. I'm sure you understand. And even though we don't expect Aaron's review to uncover anything improper, Congress will also be pleased we're doing this little—ah—spot check, if you will."

"The only thing that's going to come out of this so-called audit is that this guy—" the admiral jerked a thumb toward Drexler—"will be given access to programs where he has no need to know. And that could jeopardize—"

Need to know in this context was not an idle phrase but a fundamental principle applicable to the protection of classified information. One of the best ways to keep from spilling the beans—loose lips, sinking ships, et cetera—was to limit the number of people allowed access to classified data, and only those with a valid job-related *need* were permitted access.

"The president's giving him the need to know, Admiral," the attorney general said, flexing some of Santa's muscle. "And, by the way, I've already discussed this with your boss."

Meaning the Secretary of Defense, Wilcox assumed.

"Now I know you're not happy about this, but . . ."

"You're goddamn right I'm not," the admiral muttered, but he knew he'd already lost this battle.

The goddamn Aziz case. Would it never end?

Dillon entered the director's office and noticed immediately that Admiral Wilcox's perpetual frown was even more pronounced than normal. His face looked like a fist with eyes. He assumed the cause of the admiral's displeasure was the other man already in the room.

"Dillon, this is Aaron Drexler," Wilcox said. "He's from the Justice Department. The president has asked Justice to review our operation to ensure that . . . that we're doing everything by the book. More fallout from Aziz."

Dillon nodded pleasantly at Drexler, noting the man's shoes as he did. Penny loafers—hardly appropriate with a suit.

"Drexler, this is Dillon Crane, one of my senior people. He reports to the deputy director. He'll give you everything you need. Now you'll have to excuse me. I'm late for a briefing."

Dillon smiled at Drexler.

Drexler didn't smile back.

Aziz. What a debacle that had been. That is, it had been a debacle as far as Admiral Wilcox and the administration were concerned. For Dillon Crane it had been a roaring success, justifying everything he did.

It began with the NSA's machines intercepting a phone call, and what the machines captured were certain words spoken in Farsi. Had the words been spoken in English it's quite likely nothing would have happened, as the words were innocuous words, boring words, words like *alloy, heat treatment,* and *thermal expansion.* But when the machines heard those particular words in Farsi, it was like a marble falling in a Rube Goldberg device: the marble rolled down a chute, dropped onto a cog, turned a gear, and a little mechanical man spun around, arm outstretched—and one of Claire's technicians was electronically smacked on the back of the head.

Claire's techs rapidly discovered that one of the people talking was an Iranian but now a U.S. citizen. This was Dr. Ahmed Aziz, a metallurgist who worked for Owens Corning. Aziz was talking to another Iranian, also a metallurgist, and these two smart fellows were trying to reverse-engineer a particular component—a cast alloy able to withstand high temperatures in a radiation-rich environment. After consulting with various experts, Claire's techs concluded the casting under discussion was part of a gizmo used to speed up the enrichment of uranium—enriching uranium being one of the crucial steps in building a nuclear weapon.

Normally, if the U.S. government even *suspected* that Dr. Aziz was talking to a nuclear scientist in Iran, this would have been sufficient information to obtain a FISA warrant. And that's what Dillon needed—a warrant—so he could legally record more of Dr. Aziz's conversations. If he had such a warrant, the next time Dr. Aziz phoned his bomb-making pal, the FBI would have just cause to detain Aziz and question him and do all those things civil libertarians objected to but which made perfect sense to Dillon if you were trying to keep

Iran from becoming a nuclear power. But since Dillon had recorded Aziz's initial conversation illegally, this wasn't possible.

So Dillon fudged. Just a bit.

There's a mosque in Houston known to nine of the sixteen U.S. intelligence agencies. The mosque funnels money to al-Qaeda and the U.S. government allows this to occur because it can learn more by following the money trail than it can by arresting the money movers. This being the case, one of Claire's people hacked into the computer of the bank where Dr. Aziz kept his money and made it appear as if money had been sent from the man's checking account to the mosque. The FBI saw where the money came from, obtained a warrant to eavesdrop on Dr. Aziz's communications, and asked for the NSA's help—and Dillon pretended to be surprised when they did. And when Dr. Aziz made his next phone call, Dillon's people—now operating in a completely legal fashion—recorded him and the FBI whisked Dr. Aziz off to a cell. After three days, Aziz admitted that he had indeed been trying to help the Iranians build a bomb. "Why shouldn't a good Muslim country have the right to protect itself?" the scientist said.

Unfortunately, Dr. Aziz's family obtained a very loud lawyer who pointed out to the media that the metallurgist was a virtual pillar of his community and he had been *disappeared* by his own government. Where are we living, the lawyer screamed, Nazi Germany? And because the media listened to the lawyer, the lawyer was able to get Dr. Aziz's congressman to listen to him as well. And the congressman—delighted to have all the free publicity—called over various people from the NSA, the FBI, and the departments of Justice and Defense, and asked them to explain why they had incarcerated his constituent without the benefit of a trial.

So the FBI explained. They said they had detained Dr. Aziz as a suspected terrorist under the provisions allowed by the Patriot Act, and they did this because he was helping Iran build a nuclear weapon.

And, they pointed out, Dr. Aziz confessed. He confessed because you tortured him! the congressman shouted. We didn't torture him, the FBI said, we just didn't let him sleep too well for a couple of days.

Then there were problems with the legally obtained intercepts. There were some questions regarding the accuracy of the translation, but the biggest problem was Owens Corning, Dr. Aziz's employer. Owens Corning, unfortunately—at least it was unfortunate from the FBI's perspective—utilizes high-temperature castings to make fiberglass, which is in turn used for insulating houses. Dr. Aziz was now claiming that's what he'd *really* been talking about with his Iranian buddy—how to make fiberglass—and it was only because he was tortured that he'd said otherwise. Bullshit, the FBI said, and complex technical arguments were given to show Aziz was lying, but because the arguments could only be understood by egghead scientists, and because Dillon couldn't let the FBI have the recording the NSA had illegally made, Dr. Aziz and his congressman eventually won the day.

But Dillon Crane was satisfied, even though Dr. Aziz would most likely win a very large judgment in his upcoming lawsuit related to all the mental and physical anguish that he'd suffered. He was satisfied because he'd identified a traitor and because the U.S. government now knew the Iranians needed a bomb-making component that they couldn't currently buy or build. Dillon knew that this wouldn't stop Iran from eventually building a nuclear weapon but it would slow them down, and that was the best he could do.

Dillon escorted Aaron Drexler back to his office and pointed the lawyer-scientist to a chair in front of his desk. "Coffee?" he offered. "A soft drink, perhaps?"

Drexler just shook his head, his hooded eyes taking in Dillon's office.

"I'm curious, Mr. Drexler. What's the relationship between Aziz and this review you're conducting? We did everything by the book on Aziz."

Drexler smirked and repeated the statement made in the attorney general's office. "There are rumors the NSA knew more about Dr. Aziz's activities than you could have possibly discovered via the legally obtained recordings submitted into evidence. The president is concerned about those rumors."

"I see," Dillon said, although he'd heard no such rumors, and if there had been any he certainly would have. "So exactly where would you like to start? *Mi casa, su casa,* as they say."

That would be the day.

Drexler ignored the question. He was staring at a painting on one wall of Dillon's office.

"Is that a Picasso?" he asked.

"Yes. From his blue period."

"That's an odd size for a print."

"A print?" Dillon said. "Oh, no. That's the original. My mother gave it to me when I graduated from high school."

"Your mother gave you a Picasso? When you were eighteen?"

"Sixteen, actually. But, yes, she was quite fond of me. My brother only received a Grant Wood when he graduated, but then his grades weren't quite as good as mine."

Drexler frowned, not sure if Dillon was pulling his leg. He looked away from the Picasso, and said, "What I want is a random sample of a few intercepts, and all warrants and reports associated with those intercepts. To narrow things down, I'd like to see transmissions originating in the D.C. metro area on . . . oh, let's say, April nineteenth. That day's as good as any."

Dillon Crane played poker at the professional level. Had he not done so, he was quite sure the shock of what he'd just heard would have registered on his face.

Dillon called in a few mid-level managers and had them start compiling the records Drexler asked for, and then he phoned Clyde Simmer, one of his poker-playing friends. Clyde worked at the Department of Justice.

"Do you know a man named Aaron Drexler?" Dillon asked, when Clyde came on the line. He wouldn't have been surprised if Clyde didn't know Drexler; Justice was a big place.

But Clyde did. "He slinks," Clyde said.

"Pardon me?" Dillon said.

"He slinks. He's a slinker. I mean, I really don't know him all that well but that's the impression I get, that he's an arrogant bastard who slinks about looking for an opportunity to stab someone in the back. There's something ferret-like about him, but I've been told he's quite bright and not afraid to work."

"Is that it?" Dillon said.

"Well, let's see. I know he came to us from some other agency, some odd place for a lawyer to have come from, but I can't remember which one."

"The Pentagon," Dillon said.

"Yes, that's it. The rumor was that he came to us under a cloud of some sort and we wouldn't have normally hired him, but his wife's family was cozy with the fool who was attorney general at the time. Not Scranton, but the fool before him. I can find out more if you'd like, Dillon."

"No, don't bother. If I need to know anything else I'm fairly certain I can obtain the information."

Dillon wondered if Clyde appreciated the understatement.

Claire didn't understand why Dillon was wasting her time telling her about this man Drexler. So what if he was doing a review to see if they were complying with FISA? The head of the NSA didn't know what Dillon was doing; there was no way some outsider from Justice was going to find anything. And right now she was up to her ass with a million other things and she didn't have time to deal with nonsense like this.

"Dillon," she said, "what does this have to do with me?"

"Claire, Mr. Drexler has asked to see the transmissions we intercepted in the D.C. area on the day Paul Russo was killed. He pretended he was selecting a random date and place for this so-called spot check he's doing, but I would assume his selection wasn't the least bit random."

Claire sat for a moment, stunned—just as stunned as Dillon had been when Drexler had told him what he wanted. Then she said, "Aw, shit!" Then she said it again, "Aw, shit, Dillon, what did I do? I must have screwed up. I must have tripped an alarm somewhere."

"Yes," Dillon said quietly, "I think you did."

Dillon, in spite of his life-is-but-a-game attitude, took mistakes made by his subordinates quite seriously.

"But what?" Claire said. "What could I have done that would have told anyone we were looking into Russo? Mostly all I've done is record searches, background checks on Hopper, the tomb guards, that sort of thing. I wonder if Hopper could have spotted the surveillance we have on him." She was thinking about the agent she suspected might have a drinking problem—and kicking herself for not pulling him immediately off the detail.

"Possibly," Dillon said. He paused before he added, "Claire, what was the name of that agent who died recently? That young woman?"

"What?" Claire said, confused for an instant by the question. "Her name was Alberta Merker. She had a heart attack." Then Claire realized what Dillon was getting at. "The fingerprints? You think they caught on to us when I had that soldier fingerprinted?"

"Either that or when you accessed the fingerprint files. I believe you said the files were flagged."

"Are you saying you think Alberta was killed by these guys?" Before Dillon could answer, Claire said, "I *know* she had a heart attack, Dillon. She was autopsied by one of the docs we use. And because she was an agent, I had them do a complete tox screen on her. She had a heart attack. She had a family history of heart problems."

"I don't know if she was murdered or not, Claire, but the fact that she took the man's fingerprints and died soon afterward is probably not something we should assume to be a coincidence."

"What does this have to do with Drexler?"

Normally Claire would have been able to answer that question without any help from Dillon, but he could tell she was having a hard time concentrating. She had just been told it was possible that one of her agents had been killed in the line of duty—and Claire had never lost an agent before. Dillon knew how devastating that could be, even for someone so seemingly cold-blooded.

"Well, this is what I think is going on," Dillon said. "Whoever killed Russo knows somebody is investigating his death and they suspect it might be us, the NSA. Why they suspect this I don't know, but they do. And so they sent in Drexler, and his job is most likely threefold: to confirm the NSA is aware of Russo; to determine exactly what we know; and, most important, to determine who at the NSA knows about Russo."

"But what does this have to do with Alberta?"

"It may have nothing to do with Alberta. She may have simply had a heart attack. But what if they identified Alberta, questioned her, and *then* she had a heart attack?"

"Are you saying they tortured her, Dillon? If you are, I don't buy it. Her autopsy didn't show anything like that. And if they did torture her, she must not have told them anything."

"I agree with your last conclusion," Dillon said. "If she had told them anything, Mr. Drexler probably wouldn't be here."

What Dillon meant, but didn't say, was that if Alberta had told anyone about the Russo intercept, Claire Whiting might have found herself strapped to a chair watching someone extract her long, polished fingernails.

"So what are you doing about Drexler?" Claire asked.

"I'm complying with his request, of course."

"You're what?"

"I've given him all the transmissions we intercepted in the D.C. area on the night in question—verbal, e-mail, and text. The legal intercepts, that is." Dillon laughed. "Drexler had no idea how much information he was asking for. I've buried the poor fellow in electronic files and paper. Then, to make his job even harder, I've told him we're behind schedule transcribing some of the conversations we've recorded—I didn't tell him the computers do most of the transcribing—so he's going to have to listen to hours of garbled, barely audible transmissions. It'll take Mr. Drexler *weeks* to review everything I've given him."

"I don't get it, Dillon. Why would Drexler even think you'd give him an illegal intercept, whether it was related to Russo or any other case?"

"He may think he swooped down on us so fast that we wouldn't have time to separate the legal from the illegal. But I suspect Mr. Drexler knows it's unlikely that the Russo intercept is lying in the stacks of files I've given him. I think this is just his opening salvo, and what he's doing is getting the lay of the land. He's trying to figure out how we operate and who does what, and what he's really looking for is the people who might have listened to a transmission of Russo being killed."

"Then he's wasting his time. He'll never identify the techs who work for me by reviewing authorized wire taps and, if by some fluke he did, none of them would talk."

"If Mr. Drexler asked them politely, I'm sure they wouldn't, Claire. But how long do you think the redoubtable Gilbert would resist if somebody connected a car battery to his—uh—manly appendage?"

Claire reluctantly nodded her head in agreement. A couple of bitch slaps to the head, and Gilbert would give up his own mother.

"So what are we going to do?"

"I'll keep an eye on Mr. Drexler," Dillon said. "What you need to do, and quickly, is figure out why Russo was killed and who ordered the killing."

"I know that!" Claire snapped. "What do you think I've been trying to do?"

"I also think you need to do a little research on Mr. Drexler. A friend of mine has given me reason to believe that there might be a skeleton or two lurking in his closet."

"Okay," Claire said, rising from her chair, anxious to be on her way.

"Oh, and one other thing," Dillon said. "Your idea to use Mr. DeMarco? I think you should proceed with that."

Claire Whiting wasn't the type to pump her fist into the air and shout, "Yes!" She simply nodded her head but Dillon saw the gleam in her eyes. She made him think of a cat creeping up on an inattentive canary.

23

"*This is Joseph DeMarco, Agent Hopper, and I wanted you to know that—*"

"No, no!" Claire said. "You have the voice down, the New York accent and all, but the . . . the *tone* is wrong. He's not so formal. He's sort of laid back. And if he was pissed, it'd be more like: *Hey, Hopper, this is DeMarco, and I just found out*—Do you understand?"

"I guess," the impersonator said. He could imitate almost anyone, including most females. At Christmas parties, after a couple of drinks, he'd do an impression of the president and his wife talking after sex that was so funny that even Claire laughed. At this point she didn't know what she wanted him to tell Hopper but, when she did know, she wanted the impersonator to be ready.

"Go practice some more," she said.

Claire needed to spook Hopper.

She needed to make him run, literally, to whoever was controlling him and the best way she could think to do that and keep the agency's involvement secret was to use DeMarco. If she could get Hopper to meet his boss, that would be ideal. The other possibility was that Hopper would call his boss and his boss would decide to do something about DeMarco. They—whomever Hopper was working with—had already killed Russo and most likely the reporter, Hansen. They'd kill DeMarco, too, if they had to. So she would put people on DeMarco and when they tried to kill him or snatch him, she'd follow whoever was assigned—and try to protect DeMarco as best she could.

DeMarco. Again, records could only tell you so much, but the impression she had was: average guy, maybe *below*-average guy. He was a lawyer and had passed the Virginia bar, but had never practiced law. He was a GS-13—a rank that wasn't all that impressive in D.C.—and had been one for a long time, meaning that his career had most likely stalled. He had an office in the subbasement of the Capitol—the location of his office another indicator that he wasn't a power player—but he wasn't on the staff of any member of the House or Senate. So she couldn't figure out exactly what he did but finally decided it didn't really matter. He was just some sort of low-level legal weenie stuck in a dead-end job.

As for his personal life, nothing leaped out at her. He'd been married once, divorced about six years ago, and the divorce had cost him a bundle. He lived in a townhouse on P Street in Georgetown; the house wasn't all that big but the mortgage was enormous. He drove a mid-sized Japanese car, didn't appear to cheat on his taxes, and didn't gamble online or spend hours looking at porn sites on the Internet.

The only thing unusual about him was his father. Gino DeMarco had been a button man for Carmine Taliaferro, an old-time Mafia guy in Queens. Taliaferro died from cancer a few years ago, and Gino DeMarco died from lead poisoning—three bullets in the chest. She supposed it was possible that Joe DeMarco, like his father, could have connections to organized crime, but based on his bank statements and his lifestyle, she didn't think so.

She looked at his photo again. He was a good-looking guy: a full head of dark hair, a prominent nose, blue eyes, and a big square chin with a dimple in it. Good-looking, yet at the same time hard-looking. It was most likely her imagination, and probably because of what she knew about his father, but she could picture him in a Scorsese movie playing a knee-breaker working for a loan shark. And there was something in his eyes: toughness, stubbornness, *something* that made her think, If you pushed him, he'd push back.

Then she laughed, thinking that if the NSA was doing the pushing, it wouldn't matter how hard he pushed back.

Another of Claire's agents—a guy, skinny, droopy-eyed like he was always on the verge of falling asleep—was slumped in a chair in front of Claire's desk, sitting more on the base of his spine than on his butt. Claire thought about telling him to sit up straight, but she wasn't his mother—or anyone else's mother—and never would be.

"I want this guy's house and car bugged and I want a GPS tracking device installed on his car," she said, handing the agent the slim file on DeMarco. "But I also want *him* bugged, and I want it done tonight. He's got a cell phone, and he probably has it on him all the time. So bug the phone and put a GPS chip in it, too, so we always know where he is. And his belts. Bug them." She paused for a beat, then said, "Use the gas."

A few years ago, Chechen terrorists invaded a theater in Moscow and took a few hundred people hostage. The Russian government responded by shooting nerve gas into the theater, the idea being that the gas would knock everybody out—the Chechens and their hostages—and then the Russians could just walk in and scoop up the bad guys. The only problem was that the gas killed more than a hundred people, mostly hostages.

The United States, not to be outdone in any sort of weaponry, had a similar gas. There were, however, a couple of problems. The first was that the gas wasn't particularly fast-acting, taking about ten minutes before it incapacitated the gasee, which wasn't really a problem when it came to DeMarco. Claire's droopy-eyed agent would wait until DeMarco was in bed, slip into his house wearing a gas mask, release the gas, then wait ten minutes and do what he needed to do. The next morning, DeMarco would wake up with the mother of all hangovers but would be otherwise healthy. Unless, of course, he was allergic to one of the ingredients in the gas, which about one person in ten thousand was, and if this was the case he wouldn't ever wake up. That was the second problem with the gas.

But when directed to gas an American citizen with a chemical that might turn that citizen into either a brain-dead vegetable or a corpse, all Claire's agent said was, "Okay, boss."

When Dillon decided to spy illegally on American citizens, he and Claire had discussed the likelihood of their employees becoming a problem—that is, telling the media or Dillon's bosses what they were doing. But Dillon had told Claire not to worry, their employees wouldn't betray them, and the reason for this had to do primarily with the *culture* of the NSA.

The NSA, though staffed with many civilians, is primarily a military organization, and in military organizations people tend to follow orders. NSA employees assume, if they've been directed to spy on someone, that their mission is lawful and their bosses have the proper warrants and authority. The employees, in other words, typically act without questioning their orders because they know it's the bosses who'll get in trouble if they've been directed to commit an illegal act.

Then there's the fear factor. From the minute an employee is hired, it's beaten into his or her head that you do *not* talk about your job—not with anyone, for any reason. One safeguard taken to ensure that NSA employees understand this golden rule is that they are annually briefed—the word *briefed* being a thinly disguised euphemism for *threatened*—by a man who works in counterintelligence. The man who does these so-called security briefings has white hair, Nordic features, and unblinking, pale-blue eyes, and everyone who meets him instantly envisions a reincarnated Gestapo officer. The briefer, in a voice devoid of emotion, warns the employees during these annual chats that if they ever divulge classified information to anyone without a need to know—and everything they work on is classified—they will be incarcerated in a federal prison and gang-banged to death by huge tattooed sadists. That is, if they are lucky they'll go to prison. Another possibility, implied but never directly stated, is that they might simply disappear.

However, as effective as these yearly pep talks were, Claire felt she could not rely solely upon a sinister warning. She took things one step further.

NSA employees, depending on the nature of their work and the classification level of their jobs, are randomly and periodically polygraphed. Random and periodic was not good enough for Claire, however. All her people were polygraphed monthly—and they all knew they'd be polygraphed. Only one question was asked during these electronic truth-seeking sessions: *Have you discussed anything you're working on with anybody outside of the division?* So far no one had answered this question in the affirmative; if anyone ever did . . . well, the white-haired counterintelligence officer would be brought in to finish the questioning.

Claire's agents wouldn't talk—and they did what they were told.

24

DeMarco took two more Tylenol, which made a total of six that he'd taken since he had gotten out of bed. His head ached so badly his hair actually hurt. It felt like every little follicle was a wood auger boring a hole in the top of his skull.

He couldn't understand it. After he played eighteen holes yesterday afternoon, he sat around the clubhouse and had a couple of beers with the guys he played with, but he only had a couple. And last night, he had dinner at a steakhouse and a glass of wine with his meal, but that was it. No martini before dinner, no brandy after dinner, and no booze when he got home. So why did his head hurt so damn much? He wondered if he was coming down with the flu.

Anthony McGuire, Paul's old boyfriend, lived on a block in Fairfax where all the homes were one-story brick boxes that had obviously been built from the same set of boring architectural plans. The only thing that distinguished one house from another was the color the owner selected to paint the trim and shutters. McGuire had chosen hunter green.

DeMarco rang the bell and a man he assumed was McGuire opened the little peephole installed in the front door and asked DeMarco what he wanted. A cautious guy, had been DeMarco's first impression. DeMarco introduced himself, said he was Paul's cousin, and wanted to ask a few questions about Paul's will. To this McGuire had responded by saying, "How do I know you're related to Paul?"

Speaking to the brown eye in the peephole, DeMarco said, "Well, let's see. I knew his mother when she was alive. Her name was Vivian. I know his Aunt Lena, and Paul was pretty close to my mom. He called her Aunt Maureen, although she's not really his aunt. And when Paul first came to Washington, I took him around and showed him some apartments."

"Oh, you're *that* guy. The one who works for Congress."

"That's right," DeMarco said.

"Paul didn't like you very much."

That embarrassed DeMarco. "Well—uh, we didn't really get a chance to know each other. And from everything I've heard about him, I regret that. Now could I please come in and talk to you?"

McGuire finally opened the door but didn't immediately allow DeMarco to enter. He looked up and down the block, as if he was looking to see if anybody was with DeMarco or maybe watching his house. The guy was really paranoid, which made DeMarco wonder if he'd been robbed before, maybe the victim of a home invasion.

As DeMarco entered the house, he noticed two matching suitcases and a laptop case sitting in the foyer. "Taking a trip?" he asked.

"Uh, yes. I'm visiting a friend in . . . who lives out west. The airport shuttle will be here in a couple of hours, so I don't have much time to talk to you."

They took seats in McGuire's living room which, unlike DeMarco's living room, was as neat as a pin and smelled of furniture polish.

DeMarco couldn't recall ever using furniture polish. McGuire was also as neat as a pin: pressed jeans, pressed long-sleeve shirt, and tennis shoes so white they looked as if they'd just come out of the box. He had curly dark hair, was short and slim, and had eyelashes long enough for a Maybelline commercial. He sat on the edge of his chair, bouncing a knee, giving DeMarco the impression he was nervous, although he couldn't imagine why.

"How did you know Paul and I were friends?" McGuire asked.

DeMarco said Paul's landlady had told him, and then explained—for what seemed like the ten-thousandth time—that he was trying to find out if Paul had a will and where it might be. To his relief, McGuire said that Paul did indeed have a will. When your career was watching people die as Paul's had been, and when the people dying were sometimes quite young, you learned very quickly you weren't immortal. And since his financial life had been pretty simple, Paul had used an online form and had named St. James Church in Falls Church as the beneficiary of all his worldly possessions. He had kept his will in a safe deposit box at his bank.

DeMarco felt like leaping to his feet and cheering. "Who was the executor of his will?" he asked.

"I was. Or at least I was when we broke up a year ago. I don't know if he changed his will after that, but I would assume he did."

DeMarco was willing to bet that Paul hadn't changed his will—people tended to put off things like that—but decided it didn't really matter. He was going to tell the pastor at St. James that Paul had left him four grand and, if he wanted the money, *he* could go through all the hassle of getting the state to give it to him. He was through screwing around with this whole mess.

It occurred to DeMarco later that he should have left right then—but he didn't. Instead he said, "I'm curious about something, Mr. McGuire. The FBI thinks Paul was shot because he might have been involved in a drug deal. What do you think?"

"I don't know," McGuire mumbled. "I have no idea why he was killed. Look, if there's nothing else, I have to—"

Now that was *wrong*. No one who knew Paul believed he was dealing drugs. Everyone, in fact, was adamant he wouldn't do something like that. So why wasn't McGuire, the person who had possibly known him best, not equally adamant? And McGuire's body language was off. He didn't look DeMarco in the eye when he made the statement. He did what DeMarco called rabbit eyes: eyes darting away as if looking for a place to run to, a hole to crawl into. In DeMarco's experience, rabbit eyes indicated a lie—a lie told by an incompetent liar—which made him wonder why McGuire was lying.

"Well, what do you think he could have been doing at the Iwo Jima Memorial at one in the morning?"

"I really don't know," McGuire said, but there it was again: the mumble, the rabbit eyes.

"Do you know something about Paul's death, Mr. McGuire?"

"No. Why would I?"

McGuire didn't say this calmly, however. He practically shrieked, *Why would I?* as if he was desperate for DeMarco to believe him, but then he added in a calmer voice, "We hadn't seen each other in over a year."

But DeMarco wasn't buying it. "Mr. McGuire, Paul was my cousin," he said. "He was your friend, your ex-lover. And he was murdered. Right now the FBI—"

"Oh, God, the FBI's involved?"

Why in the hell would he say that?

"Yes," DeMarco said, "and right now the Bureau thinks his death was drug related. But if you know it's not—if you know what really happened—you need to tell the Bureau."

McGuire held his hands palm outward at chest level, as if he was fending DeMarco off. If he hadn't been sitting down, he would have backed away. "I'm *not* going to get involved in this," he said. "And I want you to leave. Right now."

"Are you leaving town because of what happened to Paul?"

"No, I've had this trip planned for months."

Liar, liar, pants on fire.

DeMarco stared at McGuire for a long moment, then said, "Mr. McGuire, I'm a lawyer and an officer of the court." DeMarco actually had no idea if he was an officer of any court; that was just an expression he'd heard on TV. "And I think you know something about Paul's death and if you won't tell me what you know, then I have a legal obligation to contact the FBI and tell them that I think you're withholding information in a homicide investigation."

"You can't do that!" McGuire shouted. "You could get me killed."

"Get you killed?" DeMarco said. "What in the hell are you talking about?"

"Please, just stay out of this. You could get killed too."

"McGuire, I wanna know what you know. Now tell me."

"Oh, God," McGuire said.

"Come on. Spit it out. You can either talk to me or you can talk to the feds."

McGuire didn't respond immediately. He just sat there, looking down into his lap, shaking his head—but he wasn't shaking his head as a sign he was refusing to talk. Instead, it was as if he couldn't believe this was happening to him.

In a softer, less threatening tone, DeMarco said, "Anthony, please, tell me what you know. You owe it to Paul."

McGuire finally raised his head and said, "Paul called me the day he was killed. He made a big deal about how he was calling from a pay phone, which I thought was strange, and he told me that a patient of his had told him something important." McGuire then took a deep breath and said, "Paul said he thought this patient may have been killed. By the government."

"By the government?"

"Yes. And he said he might be killed too because of what he knew."

"Who was this patient?"

"He didn't tell me."

It had to be General Breed, DeMarco thought. "Did he tell you what this patient told him?"

"No. He said if he told me then I'd be in danger, too."

"Then why'd he call you?"

"He said that if anything happened to him, I was to call a reporter at *The Washington Post* named Robert Hansen."

"And tell Hansen what?" DeMarco asked.

"That Paul had hidden something at the church."

"What church?"

"His church. St. James."

"Did he tell you what he hid?"

"No."

"Well, did he tell you where he hid it?"

"No. He just said to tell Hansen it was hidden at the church. And then I saw on the news that a reporter named Hansen had disappeared."

"So then what did you do?"

"Nothing. I was afraid. I didn't know who to call."

"You didn't do anything? You knew Paul might have been killed because of whatever this patient told him—and you just sat here?"

"He said the *government* killed his patient. The government, for Christ's sake! Who the hell was I supposed to call?"

Gilbert made a copy of the DeMarco-McGuire recording. He stood up, poked his head over the top of his cubicle like a timid gopher peering out of its hole, and saw that Claire wasn't in her office. He left a message on her answering machine and went to lunch.

25

Aaron Drexler had Dillon worried.

Clyde Simmer, his friend at the Justice Department, had told him that Drexler wasn't a fool and Dillon confirmed this when he looked at the man's academic record. And, as Clyde had also stated, Drexler worked quite hard; he spent fourteen hours his first day at Fort Meade. Bright and hardworking were good attributes in an employee. They were very bad attributes in an adversary.

Drexler spent the first day going through the intercepts Dillon had given him and then focused in on one particular operation. The NSA, in conjunction with the FBI and Homeland Security, had been watching three young Palestinian students for over a month. The men were registered as students at George Mason University but spent very little time at the school they were supposedly attending. The reason why they were being watched was because they had made an abnormally high number of tours of the U.S. Capitol and had taken extensive notes and photographs while touring. Some of their e-mails, written in an extremely crude code, discussed security procedures they had observed. The entire surveillance operation was being conducted in a completely legal fashion and with all required warrants.

Drexler called Dillon at one point and said he wanted to see all the paperwork associated with the Palestinian student operation—requests for warrants, interagency memoranda, surveillance observations, that sort of thing. Then he added, almost as if it were an afterthought, that he also wanted a list of NSA personnel who were monitoring the Palestinians' communications—and Dillon immediately understood what Drexler was doing. Drexler was thinking that since the Palestinians lived in Arlington and not too far from the Iwo Jima Memorial, that maybe the NSA technicians who were monitoring the Palestinians had intercepted the Russo transmission inadvertently. When Drexler made his request, Dillon said. "Oh, I thought you understood, Mr. Drexler. We don't have *people* monitoring those men. Our computers do all that for us. And as for the those intercepts I gave you, no one's even listened to them yet."

"You gotta be shittin' me!" Drexler said. "What the hell's the purpose of recording all this crap if you don't listen to it?"

"Well, we will. Eventually," Dillon said, doing his best impression of a flustered, fumbling bureaucrat. "It's just that we're so understaffed. It's the budget cuts, you know."

The next request Drexler made was for a list of all personnel on duty between the hours of midnight and six A.M. on the night Russo was killed—and Dillon happily gave him the information he wanted.

Whenever a person entered and exited an NSA facility, they swiped their ID badge through bar-code readers so that security personnel—including those in counterintelligence—would have a record documenting where people went and what time they arrived and departed. What Drexler still hadn't grasped, however, was the size of the NSA. There were almost three thousand people working the night Russo was killed, and Dillon gave him all three thousand names, including the names of security guards, cleaning and maintenance personnel, and folks who came in early to prepare breakfasts in the cafeterias. When Drexler asked that the list be sorted by people's occupations, Dillon said, "Oh, I'm sorry, we can't sort the information that way, not automatically. All we want to know is who's on base and where they've been in case something happens."

The reality was that Dillon could have sorted the information by shoe size and eye color if he'd wanted to, but Drexler had no way to know that.

But now Drexler was no longer looking at the files Dillon had given him. In fact, he'd called Dillon and rudely demanded that the files be removed from his office, saying he couldn't work surrounded by such clutter. For the last six hours, Drexler had been talking to people in the NSA's Human Resources department—the folks who handled hiring and promotions and personnel records. And that's why Dillon was worried. He couldn't understand how talking to the folks in HR could possibly help Drexler, and therefore he was concerned that he was missing something.

Dillon placed his feet up on his desk and looked at the Picasso on the wall. The painting, as he'd told Drexler, was a self-portrait of the artist from his blue period and actually had been given to Dillon by his mother. In the painting, Picasso wasn't bald as he became later in life. In this portrait he had a full head of dark hair, a thin, scraggly beard, and wore a heavy cloak buttoned to the collar as if he'd painted himself in an unheated room during the winter.

"What's he up to, Pablo?" Dillon said to the painting. "Why's he talking to the drones in HR? Those people can barely find their offices; they don't have the slightest idea what we really do here.

"Come on, don't sit there looking cold and confused. Help me out. Why's he looking at personnel files? What will that gain him?"

As there were more than thirty thousand people who worked for the NSA, reviewing personnel files to find whatever he was looking for would take Drexler forever. And as for the files themselves, they didn't give details related to classified assignments or specific operations. Drexler had to know that and, if he didn't at first, he must know it by now. So what was he up to?

He sat glaring at Picasso another full minute, and when the Spaniard remained mute, he said, "Oh, all right, I'll call him."

Dillon hated talking to the people in HR. They had shelves of manuals filled with confusing and contradictory regulations, and none of these manuals ever told them how they could do something, only how they *couldn't.* If you wanted to hire, fire, demote, or promote an employee—it really didn't matter which action you had in mind—the HR people could always find a regulation that stopped you but never one that aided you. Dillon had always suspected that somewhere in the warren where the HR folks lurked like troglodytes was a hidden Mission Statement that read: *We will help no one—and be proud we didn't.*

The other reason he didn't want to call the people in HR was Dillon figured that he should be able to figure out what Drexler was doing without having to talk to anyone. He was a good poker player, and a good player knows the hand his opponent is holding even though he can't see the cards. Such should be the case with Drexler: Dillon should have been able to deduce his intentions from the actions he'd taken without having to ask the people in HR a thing.

But, dammit, it didn't seem as if he could.

He picked up the phone, called the head of HR, and said, "You imbecile! Do you have any idea what you've done?"

Dillon, of course, had no idea what the man had done either, but he'd learned over the years that when dealing with HR it was best to put them immediately on the defensive.

"I want you in my office. Now!"

When the HR man was standing on his carpet—large, lumpish, and sullen—Dillon asked him what Drexler was doing.

"He's asking about m-m-m-managers," the HR man stammered.

"Managers?" Dillon said.

The HR man started to say something else, but Dillon raised a hand to silence him. He sat there for a moment, thinking, then said, "Ah!" Turning to the Picasso, he said, "Now I understand."

He asked the HR man a few more questions, to confirm that he was right, and then dismissed him.

"How are you doing on researching our friend Mr. Drexler?" Dillon asked.

Claire shrugged. "I'm making progress."

"Well, my dear, you need to speed things up. Drexler has seen through my little ploy, the one where I buried him under a mountain of useless intercepts, and now he's taking a different approach."

"For Christ's sake, Dillon, can't you just make that sour-faced shit disappear? What the hell's he doing now?"

This was why Dillon sometimes preferred to talk to Pablo rather than Claire: Pablo didn't swear at him.

"Mr. Drexler is now looking at *people,* Claire. Not intercepts."

"I don't understand," Claire said.

"You will. Drexler's been talking to folks in HR and, based on the questions he's been asking, I've determined that he's made a very nimble intellectual leap. He's concluded that somewhere within the NSA there is very likely a group of people doing exactly what your division does and that this division is hidden among other legitimate divisions."

Claire smiled. She smiled so rarely that when she did it made Dillon think of those cactus plants that bloom only once a year.

"Well, good luck with that," she said. "My division's not on any org chart and my people aren't even assigned to me."

Dillon knew what she was thinking. Everyone who worked for Claire—as far as personnel records showed—was assigned to a legitimate staff position in Dillon's other divisions. In the terminology the HR folk used, Claire's people had been *temporarily detailed* to her division, but no paperwork existed to show these temporary assignments. And then there were people like the late Alberta Merker, people who had cleverly crafted background covers that made it appear as if they didn't work for the NSA at all. Compounding Drexler's task was the fact that the NSA's HR division was notoriously slow and a lot of personnel paperwork was out of date.

Claire consequently thought it would be impossible for Drexler to find the people in her organization—and she was right. And this meant that she still didn't understand what Drexler was doing.

"Claire, it's not your people he's looking for. It's you he's trying to find."

"What?"

"How many GS-Fifteens are there in this agency like yourself, people who hold a senior supervisory rank yet don't manage people? In other words, people who don't appear to have a function that matches their pay grade?"

"Well, there're a lot," Claire said.

And she was correct about this too. There were a fair number of high-ranking folk at the NSA, GS-14s and 15s, who didn't manage people. Many were overeducated technical types—mathematicians, linguists, code-breakers, computer wizards—brainiacs, in other words, stuck off in cubicles by themselves. And there were a few other high-paid folk walking aimlessly about who had been removed from upper management positions due to their incompetence and then given semi-useless staff assignments because that alternative was less painful than firing them. But there were relatively few people like Claire Whiting: seemingly talented senior people who were not scientific specialists and yet didn't appear to have any clearly defined role in the agency.

People, in other words, who would make Mr. Drexler say, Hmm. I wonder what *this* person does?

"What Drexler is doing in HR is eliminating managers in large batches," Dillon said. "For example, all managers overseas and all managers engaged in noneavesdropping functions, like research or security or encryption, he crosses off his list."

"Yeah, but—"

"He will eventually cull the pile down to a couple hundred people who don't seem to fit into some normal and clearly defined bureaucratic niche, and then he'll start pulling the string. He'll find out where these people are located and ask them what they do, and there's a possibility, although it may be remote, that he might eventually find you: the beautiful lady tucked away in an annex with a division that doesn't exist."

Claire waited impatiently for one of her agents to pick the lock on the door to Aaron Drexler's temporary office. Drexler was currently in the cafeteria eating lunch, and one of Claire's people was watching him, but Claire knew he wouldn't be there for long.

When Drexler arrived at Fort Meade, Dillon had helpfully provided him an office. And Dillon, having the foresight to know something like this might be necessary, gave Drexler an office that had a simple key lock on the door. Dillon claimed office space was tight—which was true—and he apologized that he didn't have a room available with a more sophisticated lock—which was not true. Had he wanted to, Dillon could have put Drexler in an office like he and Claire had, one with both a cipher lock and a thumbprint reader.

But, Dillon said to Drexler the day he showed him his temporary office, he understood that Drexler needed to have a secure place in which to store information. So inside Drexler's office was a very impressive-looking safe. It was six feet high, three feet wide, and three feet deep, and its walls were four inches thick. It had a massive combination lock, eight inches in diameter, and one that required *five* numbers—not the usual three or four to open it—and it was made from an alloy that Dillon claimed was impervious to diamond-coated drill bits. It was so heavy, Dillon said, that if they ever had to move it from the office they'd have to knock out a wall and use a construction crane. And this was all true. Dillon then provided Drexler with instructions on how to change the combination for the safe to one of his own choosing.

What Dillon didn't tell Drexler was that any decent safecracker—and Claire had three at her beck and call—would be able to open the safe in about the same amount of time as it would take to smash a kid's piggy bank. The safe belonged in some sort of bank robbers' museum, and the only reason it was still at the NSA was because they really would have to knock out a wall to get the monster out of the building.

Claire was surprised to find that the safe was practically empty. The only things inside it were a classified personnel directory, an outdated (and also classified) NSA organizational manual, and a stack of file folders. There were maybe a hundred folders, certainly no more than a hundred and fifty. Claire looked at the tabs on the file folders and saw people's names. She flipped open the first folder and saw it was the personnel file of a GS-15 lawyer who was attempting to find a legitimate legal defense for secretly monitoring the ever-increasing volume of seemingly innocuous conversations occurring on Facebook and Twitter.

The folders were in alphabetical order. Claire Whiting, GS-15 Supervisory Intelligence Analyst, was six folders from the bottom of the stack.

26

"Goddammit!" Claire said, and slammed a small fist down on her desk. She had just listened to the recording of Anthony McGuire telling DeMarco that Paul Russo might have hidden something at a church. The recording had been obtained via the listening devices planted in DeMarco's belt and cell phone.

"When did this conversation take place?" Claire asked.

"About an hour ago," Gilbert said. "Hey," he added defensively, "you were gone. I left you a message."

Jesus Christ! She had that bastard Drexler breathing down her neck and now this happens.

"Where's DeMarco now?" she said.

"At the church. We have an agent watching him and—"

"Shit! Is he—"

"Calm down. He's just—"

"Don't you dare tell me to calm down!"

"He's just sitting in his car outside the church. There's a funeral service going on, and it was just getting started when DeMarco got there."

Thank God for that. Claire did *not* want DeMarco searching that church before she did. She sat for a moment, thinking and then called the agent who had planted the bugs in DeMarco's house.

"Start a fire at his house," she said.

"What?" the agent said. Arson wasn't one of his normal duties.

"Start a fire at his house. I don't want the place burned down, just start a fire. Lots of smoke. Then call the fire department right away. Then call DeMarco, pretend you're from the fire department, and tell him his house is burning."

"Won't he wonder how the fire department got his cell phone number?"

"If your house was burning down," Claire said, "do you think you'd be thinking about something like that?"

DeMarco stood at the back of the church, thinking he shouldn't be there at all.

What he should have done after speaking to Paul's ex-boyfriend was call the Bureau and tell them what McGuire had said. The problem was that McGuire's story was pretty farfetched—the part about the government having killed Paul's patient, who DeMarco was sure was General Martin Breed. He didn't think McGuire had lied to him; he believed Paul really had told McGuire that the G had killed Breed—but just because Paul had said this didn't make it true.

DeMarco had always found government conspiracy theories hard to swallow, and the reason for this was because he worked for the government. Most government employees he knew—the exception being Mahoney—were not only incapable of organizing an effective conspiracy, they were, more importantly, incapable of keeping anything secret. And a conspiracy isn't a conspiracy if everyone knows about it. The other problem he had with calling the Bureau was he didn't trust them—or at least he didn't trust that guy Hopper.

So if Paul really had hidden something in the church, it would be nice to know what it was before he started making outrageous claims about the government killing a two-star general. But that presented another problem: St. James wasn't St. Peter's in Rome, but it was still a good-sized structure. There were over a hundred rows of pews, and whatever Paul had hidden—most likely some sort of document—could be taped to the bottom of any one of them. There was also a big altar with lots of nooks and crannies, a choir loft, a pipe organ, confessionals, restrooms, and the place where the priests dressed before saying mass, whatever that space was called. It would take him a week to search the church by himself—and there was no way he was going to spend a week doing that.

But he figured there had to be *some* kind of clue. Certainly Paul hadn't intended for the reporter to have to search the entire church. Maybe one of the statues was St. Paul. That is, he assumed Paul was still a saint; his knowledge of saints currently approved by the Vatican was rather spotty. He started to walk around the church, not sure exactly what he was looking for, when his cell phone rang.

His cry of "Son of a bitch!" echoed loudly throughout God's house.

"You got any idea who might want to burn your house down, Mr. DeMarco?" the fireman asked.

"No," DeMarco said, but what he was really thinking about was the mess the damn firemen had made—they'd caused more damage than the fire. He was also thinking about the upcoming battle he was sure to have with his fucking insurance company.

"Whoever did this," the fireman said, "took a bunch of old magazines, put them against your back door, and doused them with gasoline."

DeMarco wondered if he should tell the fireman that the old magazines were his. He'd put them outside by his garbage can intending to take them to one of those newspaper recycling bins they had in some shopping malls, but he'd never gotten around to it. But if he told the fireman the magazines were his, then his insurance company could probably come up with some reason for saying the fire was his fault, and then the bastards would try to deny his claim. Hell, they'd try to deny his claim no matter what the facts were.

"The good news," the fireman said, "is somebody called us as soon as they saw the smoke and we got here in three minutes and it only took us a couple of minutes to put the fire out."

Because his house was made of white-painted brick, there didn't appear to be any structural damage. The bricks near his back door were all blackened, but they could be repainted. The only thing that had been destroyed by the fire was his back door, which was made of wood, but his door wasn't the big problem. The big problem was the damn firemen had sprayed down the door with a hose that pumped about eighteen thousand gallons a minute and the water pressure had blown out the door's window, turning his kitchen floor into a small lake with soot floating on top. His stove, which was directly in line with his door, looked as if it had been hit by a tsunami, and everything on the kitchen counter near his stove—his coffeepot, his toaster, and a never-been-used Cuisinart given to him by his mother—had been blown off the counter. He wondered if there was water in the electrical outlets and if the linoleum floor was going to curl up and have to be replaced.

But what good would it do to bitch to the fireman about all this?

After the firemen left, DeMarco stood on his back porch looking morosely into his kitchen. He was going to have to spend the day mopping up the room and figuring out what else had been damaged.

He'd also have to get a piece of plywood to nail over the opening where his back door had once been until he could get a new door. And then he'd have to call up his insurance company and have a giant fight with them to force them to honor all the false promises they made when they sold him his homeowners policy.

The last thing on his mind was whatever Paul Russo had hidden at St. James.

Claire was going to have someone search the church before DeMarco had a chance to do so, but she doubted—now that she'd calmed down somewhat—that anything was hidden there. Since Russo had met with the reporter, it seemed logical that if he had some sort of document to show him, he would have brought it with him the night he met Hansen at the Iwo Jima Memorial—and whoever had killed Russo now had the document. But maybe not. Maybe Russo was afraid of being killed before he met with Hansen so he left the document—or whatever it was—in the church for the reporter to retrieve. Or maybe he took the original of whatever he had hidden and left a copy in the church as a backup. She didn't know. All she knew was that there was a remote possibility something was hidden in the church and she had to search it before DeMarco did and before DeMarco called up somebody—like the FBI—and told the FBI what McGuire had said.

The good news was she'd know if DeMarco made a call. Right now her technicians were laughing as they listened to him curse as he cleaned up his kitchen.

She picked up her phone. "Where's Alice?" she said, to the agent who answered.

"Don't you remember?" the guy said. "She's runnin' all around Northern Virginia."

Claire had forgotten. She'd told a technician to hack into Virginia law enforcement computers to identify shady garages and wrecking yards where the reporter's Volkswagen might have been taken after he was killed, and Alice was now checking out those places. Claire figured Alice would be wasting her time but if they could get some physical evidence regarding Hansen's disappearance it could prove useful.

But since Alice wasn't available, who could she use? She wished Alberta was still with them; she still couldn't believe Alberta was dead. "How 'bout Sylvia?" she asked.

"She's in New York. Her mother—"

"Oh, that's right," Claire said. Christ, she was losing her mind.

"Hey, I can search the church if you want," the guy said.

Claire's lips drooped with scorn. Yeah, right. Men can't find anything. She was going to have to search the church herself.

"No. Your job," she said, "is to make sure DeMarco doesn't go to the church anytime today or tonight. If he heads in that direction, stop him."

"How am I supposed to do that?"

"Hell, I don't care. Use your damn head. Ram him with your car if you have to. Hit him hard enough they have to tow his car away."

"With *my* car?" the agent said, realizing Claire was serious. "How 'bout I get a car from the pool?"

"And what? Hit him with a government vehicle that can be traced back to this agency?"

"But what about my insurance rates?" the agent said.

Claire was thinking about who she'd take with her to search the church when Henry, the technician who shared the cubicle with Gilbert, walked into her office.

"What is it?" she snapped. Henry was a whiner, constantly bitching about something, and she wasn't in the mood to deal with him right now.

He handed her a manila folder. She opened it and began to flip through the documents. As she flipped, a small smile appeared, and the more she flipped, the wider the smile became. She closed the folder and looked up at Henry who was still standing before her desk, shuffling his feet, hoping Claire was not displeased. She was not.

"You did *good,* Henry," Claire said.

Henry exhaled in relief.

On the cover of the folder were the words AARON TYLER DREXLER.

It was time to remove a thorn from Dillon's paw.

Claire removed her ID badge and walked into Drexler's temporary office without knocking.

"Who are you?" Drexler asked, frowning at her.

Claire noticed his eyes were bloodshot and he needed a shave, and she wondered if he'd worked through the night.

"Oh," Drexler then said, answering his own question, "you must be the gal that putz Dillon was supposed to send over to give me a hand with some of this crap. I'm telling you, honey, this is the most fucked-up, disorganized operation I've ever seen. It's no wonder you people couldn't stop nine/eleven."

Claire sat down, unasked, in the only other chair in the room.

"To answer your question, Aaron, I'm not the gal sent to help you. I'm the gal who's been sent to straighten your ass out."

"What the hell are you talking about? Who are you?"

"I'm a messenger, Aaron. And the message is: Go home. Go back to whoever sent you and tell them you couldn't find whatever they sent you here to find."

"Who the hell do you think . . ." Pointing a finger at Claire's face, he said, "Now you listen to me, lady. I was sent here by the attorney general and I'm not leaving until I—"

Claire slapped a file folder on Drexler's desk, the sound like a bomb exploding.

"What's that?" Drexler said.

"That's the end of life as you know it, Aaron."

"What are you—"

"When the bottom fell out of the market in 2008, you lost almost a half a million dollars."

"So what? Everybody lost money during that time."

"That's true, but everybody didn't do what you did to recover their losses. At the time your portfolio turned to dust, you were a member of the Pentagon's legal staff assisting the Justice Department in their case against Ames Incorporated, and—"

"Again, so what?"

Ames Inc. was a company that had received a multimillion-dollar contract to design and install improved body armor on army personnel carriers, and a whistleblower informed the Pentagon that Ames was screwing its Uncle Sammy. Ames was charging for work that had not been performed, for overtime that had not been worked, for materials that had not been used, and anything else they could think of to increase their profit margin. The Justice Department had a strong case against a colonel at the Pentagon and a couple of executives at Ames, but Justice also wanted to nail Burton Ames, the company's founder and CEO—a man reportedly worth three billion dollars who owned multiple mansions, a private jet, and a yacht the size of a light cruiser.

Burton, naturally, claimed he had no idea what his executives were doing with regard to the Pentagon contract; he just wasn't a hands-on manager. Bullshit, the federal prosecutor said. Unfortunately, the case against Burton Ames was complex and hardly a slam-dunk but the prosecutor felt, if he presented his evidence clearly and cleverly, he could convince a jury to put greedy Burton in a cell for a few years. However, when the prosecutor got to court it became apparent that Burton's lawyers knew his strategy and every weakness in his case. Burton Ames walked out of the courtroom smiling, and the prosecutor ended up with egg all over his face.

The prosecutor knew someone on the legal staff at the Pentagon had helped Ames's lawyers. He knew, in fact, that the person who had done this was Aaron Drexler. He knew it—but he couldn't prove it. Drexler was placed on administrative leave while the prosecutor attempted to get enough evidence against him to convict him for abetting Ames but gave up after four months when he couldn't find any. And then, in the ultimate irony, Drexler sued the government, saying the prosecutor's investigation had destroyed his reputation and ruined his career at the Pentagon, and Drexler was awarded three hundred thousand dollars in damages. Then, to add insult to injury, Drexler obtained a job at the Justice Department—the same organization that had been trying to convict him. The daughter of the last attorney general—the one who preceded Robert Scranton—had been in the same sorority with Drexler's wife, and Drexler's wife was able to convince the AG that her brilliant husband was the innocent victim of a Pentagon witch hunt.

"I'll tell you *so what,*" Claire said, answering Drexler's question. "The only reason you're a free man today is because one very pissed-off prosecutor couldn't prove you tanked his case against Burton Ames. Well, Aaron, I can prove it."

"Bullshit," Drexler said. He was obviously thinking that if Justice couldn't find any evidence against him after four months of digging, it was highly unlikely the NSA had been able to find anything in the few days he'd been at Fort Meade.

Aaron Drexler did not yet fully appreciate the NSA's capabilities.

"When the government was preparing its case against Burton

Ames," Claire said, "they got warrants for his computers, and in those computers they found several encrypted e-mails. They asked the NSA to decode the e-mails but we said we couldn't. The truth is, Aaron, we could decode them but we didn't want to because doing so would give away the fact that we had that ability. In other words, putting you in jail just wasn't worth it to us, as that would have meant revealing some of our secrets. Well, Aaron, now it's worth it."

Claire didn't tell Drexler that she had been unaware at the time it was happening that the NSA had been asked to assist Justice in the Burton Ames case. That work had been assigned to another division and it wasn't something she would normally see. But when her tech, Henry, started rooting around in Aaron Drexler's past, he found the correspondence between Justice and the NSA and decoded the e-mails.

Claire opened the file folder and passed four sheets of paper to Drexler. "That's selected bits of text we took from the encrypted e-mails you sent to Burton Ames, including one in which you said you would help him for half a million dollars. On the next page is an electronic banking transaction depositing half a million dollars in a numbered account at a bank in Nassau. On the following page is a proof that you're the owner of that account."

Drexler smirked and shook his head. "This is a bad bluff. There's no way you can prove who owns this account. Nassau banking laws don't allow them to give you that information."

"You're correct. That is, if we were to ask the bankers they wouldn't tell us. But we didn't ask them. We just looked inside their machines."

"That's not legal."

"Legal is for wimps, Aaron. Finally, we can also prove that money from that same account in Nassau was used to purchase your vacation home in Tampa. I guess you figured that, since three years had passed, no one would notice that you suddenly had the money to purchase a second home."

"You can't prove—"

Claire raised a hand, stopping him. "Aaron, please stop telling me what I can't do. That file contains all the information the federal prosecutor wished he'd had three years ago, and when I give him this information you'll lose your current job at Justice and be prosecuted to the fullest extent of the law by a guy who has a major hard-on for you. You will go to jail, Aaron."

Drexler looked at her for a long time, saying nothing; then the arrogance drained out of his face like air escaping from a pin-pricked balloon. "What do you want?" he asked.

"What do I want?" Claire repeated. "I want you out of here, Aaron. I also want to know who sent you and what you were asked to do."

"I don't know who sent me. I was called and told I was going to be assigned by the attorney general to do a review here at the NSA. My job was to find out if the NSA had intercepted a radio transmission on April 19th that contained the words *messenger* and *carrier* and to identify who had knowledge of the intercept."

"Why did you agree to help them?"

"Because they knew some of the same things you know. They didn't know what was in the encrypted e-mails, but they knew about the Nassau account and my place in Tampa. I don't know how they found out, but they did. So I agreed to do what they wanted because they weren't asking me to do anything illegal."

"But you must have some idea who called you."

"No, I don't. I swear. But it has to be someone at the Pentagon because they knew all about the Ames case."

"How were you supposed to contact them?"

"I was given a phone number."

It turned out to be the untraceable Fort Myer cell phone number, the same number that had been calling Hopper.

Claire rose and looked down at Drexler. He was no longer the supercilious jackass he'd been when she first walked into his office.

Drexler was finished. Her tone softened somewhat when she said, "You know something, Aaron? It just might be a good thing for you that we had this conversation. If you had heard the intercept they wanted you to find, there's a very good possibility you would have been killed."

"Killed?" he said.

"Oh, not by us, Aaron. By the man who sent you here."

Eleven P.M. Claire was parked in a van in front of St. James Church with four of her agents, all men, and the van had magnetic signs attached to the side panels advertising a cleaning company. Everyone, including Claire, was dressed in blue coveralls. Claire sat in the passenger seat of the van, feeling tired but at the same time relieved that Drexler was out of her hair.

Her cell phone finally rang. "It's safe," the caller said, and hung up. This meant the priests were asleep—and wouldn't wake up for at least six hours.

Claire had assigned one agent to watch the two priests who lived in the rectory and told him that after the priests had gone to bed, to gas them with the same magic gas they'd used on DeMarco. She wanted to be able to turn on all the lights in the church when she searched it and she didn't want the priests interfering.

Claire's men grabbed vacuum cleaners, mops, and brooms and marched up to the double doors of the church. The lock barring entry delayed them for all of twenty seconds and as soon as they were inside, Claire dispersed her team: two to start looking under pews, one to check out the choir loft and altar area, and one to poke around in the confessionals and restrooms. She had no faith, however, that they would find anything.

She stood in the center aisle of the church and did a slow three-hundred-and-sixty-degree spin. She was thinking, although she didn't realize it, exactly what DeMarco had thought: No way would Russo have hidden something in the church, just hoping the reporter would find it. There had to be some clue as to its location.

She made a complete circuit of the church, touching nothing. She looked at the Stations of the Cross, the stands of votive candles, the high altar, and the baptismal font. She examined the statues of the saints. She noted that the most distinctive feature about the church was its stained glass windows. There must have been thirty windows, each about six feet tall and three feet wide, and each window depicted a Catholic saint. She saw St. Anthony of Padua—the saint Catholics prayed to when something has been lost, possibly the one she should be praying to now.

Claire Whiting wasn't a Catholic, however—she was a lapsed Presbyterian—and she knew very little about the Catholic Church. But there was one thing she did know: she knew how to Google.

She sat down in a pew, took out her BlackBerry and typed into the search field various combinations of words: Paul, St. Paul, nurse, hospice, Catholic saints. It took less than five minutes before Claire smiled, put away the BlackBerry, and toured the church again, looking at the name of the saint on each stained-glass window.

And there he was: St. John of God.

St. John of God founded the order of the Hospitallers. He was the patron saint of nurses—and of those who were dying.

There was a downward-sloping ledge below each stained-glass window, creating a shallow depression, the bottom of which couldn't be reached by a person of average height. She called her tallest agent and had him reach up to see if he could feel anything in the depression.

He pulled out a sealed white business envelope.

Inside the envelope were a handwritten letter and a small digital recorder.

27

My name is Paul Russo. I'm a hospice nurse, and I was taking care of General Martin Breed at his home before he died. One day he told his wife he needed to see General Bradford. Up until then, he had refused all visitors because he was embarrassed by the way he looked and wanted people to remember him the way he was before the cancer. After Bradford's visit, he told his wife he needed to see Justice Antonelli, but Antonelli couldn't come because he'd just been admitted to the hospital for a hip replacement.

General Breed became really agitated when Antonelli couldn't come and started acting strange. He wrote me a note saying there might be listening devices in his room and that the phones were tapped, but I thought it was just the cancer and the meds making him paranoid. Then he got a small tape recorder and had me take him into the bathroom and turn on all the faucets. When he finished in the bathroom, he wrote another note telling me to hide the recorder and said if he died before he could talk to Antonelli, I needed to get the recorder to him. He died that night, after I went home.

I've been a hospice nurse for ten years and I have a pretty good idea when someone's time has come, and I thought General Breed would last at least another week, maybe even two. But then he died and I wondered if he might have been killed but then I laughed that idea off, thinking I was getting paranoid, too. The next day, the day after he died, I listened to the recording he'd made. I couldn't believe what I heard and I have no idea if the general's telling the truth but why would a dying man lie?

Now I'm really scared. And if General Breed's house was bugged, I can't remember what I said in there, if maybe I said something that would tell someone I have the recorder. I'm going to hide it, but I'm not going to give it to Antonelli. I have a friend who's involved with a big-time reporter and I'll get the recorder to him and let him deal with it. If what the general said is true, the public needs to know.

I don't know who might be reading this letter but I hope you'll do the right thing.

Paul Russo

"Is this Russo's handwriting?" Dillon asked.

"Yes," Claire said.

"I wonder why he didn't just tell Hansen over the phone where he'd hidden the recorder. Why meet with him?"

"Maybe Hansen insisted on a meeting. Or maybe Russo was afraid to take the recorder with him when he met with Hansen. We'll never know," Claire said. "What I wonder is why Breed wanted the tape delivered to Antonelli?" Thomas Antonelli was the Chief Justice of the Supreme Court.

"I would assume because of his position," Dillon said, "but I think I read somewhere that he's related to Breed through his wife's side of the family. What I don't understand is why Russo didn't want to give the recording to him."

"I think after Russo heard the recording he wasn't willing to trust anyone in the government. You'll understand when you hear it," Claire said.

Dillon started to say something else, but stopped.

He hit the PLAY button on the recorder.

Thomas, this is about things I did for Charles Bradford during my career. I know when you hear this you're going to be disappointed in me, but at this point that's the least of my concerns. You're the only one I can trust with this information, and the only one I know who has the courage and the influence to do what needs to be done.

Martin Breed's voice was weak, raspy, often barely audible. It was the voice of someone in a lot of pain; it was the voice of a dying man. Water could be heard running in the background.

The first thing I did for Charles involved the Incirlik Air Base in Turkey. A member of the Turkish Parliament, a man named . . .

Dillon knew there was nothing unusual about the American government attempting to influence policy in other countries. We did it all the time by giving money and weapons to foreign politicians we believed were sympathetic to American interests, men like the Shah of Iran for example. And then we turned around and supported Saddam Hussein when Iraq attacked Iran. Our decisions regarding which foreign regime to support sometimes backfired on us; nonetheless, that was global politics as practiced by the United States and other wealthy nations.

But what Martin Breed was describing was different in several respects.

Dillon wasn't so naïve as to think the U.S. government had never authorized the assassination of a high-ranking foreigner for national security reasons. Although he didn't know of any cases personally, he could certainly imagine past directors of the CIA—and a couple past presidents—authorizing such executions, particularly during the bad old days of the Cold War. But those instances would have been extremely rare, acts of last resort and only undertaken after a great deal of hand-wringing.

Charles Bradford didn't wring his hands.

In 2003, or maybe it was '04, we took out a Saudi banker while he was visiting London. I can't remember his name now, my head's just not working right, but he was funneling millions to al-Qaeda and, because he was related to the royal family, the Arabian government refused to do anything about him. We could have made his death look like an accident but Charles decided he wanted to send a message to the Saudis, so I had a man pose as a room service waiter and simply shoot him.

The second thing that was unusual was that when the United States government did deem it necessary to eliminate a foreign politician, we tried our best to get foreigners to do the killing. Castro was the best example Dillon could think of: three U.S. presidents were obsessed with the idea of removing Fidel from the planet: Eisenhower, Kennedy, and Johnson. And while these presidents approved the expenditure of millions of dollars and countless schemes to do away with Fidel, they never sent in a U.S. Army sharpshooter to bump the man off. And the reason these presidents never authorized an official military operation to execute Castro had little to do with morality or legislation. It was instead that most presidents thought it might set a poor example to achieve regime change in this manner; other countries might be inclined to imitate the practice.

In 2006, Charles decided he had to do something to slow the pace at which the Iranians were developing nuclear weapons. He knew they'd eventually become a nuclear power, but he wanted to delay that as long as possible and he could see the U.N. sanctions and all the other diplomatic nonsense weren't working. At the time, the Iranian weapons program was being steered by a brilliant Iranian physicist who'd been trained in the United States. We used a roadside bomb to take him out, and the killing was eventually traced back to a dissident in Iran. The dissident was later executed by the Iranian government.

That same year, we killed the deputy director of the ISI, the Pakistani intelligence service, because he was selling information to the Taliban. . . .

Breed went on to describe the assassinations of several other men, all foreigners, most with links to terrorist organizations, but some who were senior politicians or businessmen who were aggressively, dangerously, anti-American. The men who assisted Breed on these missions were selected from the sentinels who guard the Tomb of the Unknowns.

But Breed wasn't finished with his revelations.

There's another man like me. I've never met him and I don't know his name, but I know he exists. For security reasons, Charles kept us apart. He used him for some foreign missions when I wasn't available and to deal with American citizens that he considered to be traitors.

There was a long interruption when Breed started coughing, then choking. He sounded extremely weak when he resumed, as if he might not have the strength to finish the recording.

The U.S. operations were different from the ones overseas. Deaths were always made to appear to be accidents: car accidents, fires, illnesses actually caused by poison. Sometimes people simply disappeared. The only one I know about for sure involved a journalist named Moore who had obtained information about a covert operation in China. Charles considered Moore a traitor, and I agreed, because if Moore had published his story it would have endangered Chinese operatives the DIA had recruited.

As Dillon listened to Martin Breed talk about the things he had done for Charles Bradford, he wondered why Breed had turned against Bradford in the end. It sounded as if Breed always concurred with his superior's decisions. As in the case of the American journalist: Breed clearly agreed the journalist was a traitor. Then Breed's own voice gave Dillon the answer, or at least a partial one.

Six months ago, right before I was diagnosed with cancer, we killed a man named Piccard. Piccard worked for a French defense contractor and Charles learned he was meeting secretly with buyers from North Korea, Iran, and a couple of South American countries. The French government said they were aware of Piccard and would stop any sales he tried to make, but Charles didn't believe the French. He never believed the French. I tried to convince Charles that killing Piccard was unnecessary and we should let either the

U.S. State Department or the French deal with him, but Charles insisted that I proceed. But I screwed up, Thomas. I screwed up terribly. We killed Piccard with a car bomb—but we also killed his twelve-year-old daughter. She wasn't supposed to have been with him that day. When I heard about the girl, I was absolutely sick. But that wasn't the worst of it. After Piccard was dead, we found out that he had been acting in concert with French intelligence. He was only pretending to negotiate with these buyers because by doing so he was giving the intelligence guys a better idea of the enemy's capabilities and the players involved. If Charles hadn't acted on his own, we might have discovered this, and we never would have killed Piccard or his daughter.

That was the last thing I did for Charles Bradford. Thomas, I don't have the strength to tell you about all the soul-searching I've been through. I don't have the strength or the time. I don't regret most of the things I did for Charles, but he's becoming more aggressive, more impatient. He's not giving the government sufficient time to deal with problems before he takes action, and I'm afraid he's going to make more mistakes like he did with Piccard.

I met with Charles two days ago and told him he had to resign before I died. I felt I had to give him the opportunity. I still admire him and I don't want to see him disgraced, but I told him if he didn't resign he'd be exposed. The truth is, I don't want to expose him, because I sincerely believe that doing so would be bad for the country. I also don't want him exposed for frankly selfish reasons. I don't want my wife and girls to know what I've done. Thomas, I know you have the courage to stop him and if you must go public with this information, so be it, but I'm hoping you won't. And God forgive me for what I've done.

When the recording finished, Dillon just sat there, rubbing his chin, looking at the Picasso on the wall as if waiting for Pablo to comment.

"So what do we do with this?" Claire said.

Dillon looked away from the painting. "I don't know, but I agree with General Breed. It's not in the nation's best interest to go public with this information. Even though Bradford may have acted on his own, the fact that the chairman of the Joint Chiefs of Staff, in collusion with another American general, took it upon himself to kill a number of prestigious foreigners is not something we want the world to know."

"So what do we do?" Claire asked again.

"I've been in meetings with Charles Bradford a number of times. He's arrogant, caustic, impatient, ruthless—and brilliant. After Saddam Hussein was overthrown, he wanted to do what MacArthur did in Japan after World War II and run Iraq as its de facto president until he was able to place the right Iraqi politicians in power and restructure their government. I think if the White House had listened to him, we wouldn't be mired down in the country the way we are today."

"Well, MacArthur may have been his role model, but even MacArthur didn't do the kind of things Bradford's done," Claire said.

"I don't know what General MacArthur did," Dillon said. "All I know is that Charles Bradford is one of those soldiers—and I'm sure he's not alone—who believes that civilians, including Congress and the president, should have no say in matters of national defense. He thinks the Pakistanis got it right, when Musharraf was both the president and the chief of the army over there."

"We need to make a decision, Dillon."

"And the way he uses the tomb guards. As I'm sure you know, before Bradford got his first star, he briefly commanded the Third Infantry Regiment. He must have realized at the time what an asset those soldiers could be. It was like you said, Claire, they're the sort of zealots—or patriots—Bradford could use as assassins, and those young men would have no idea that what they were doing was illegal."

Before Claire could ask him again what they should do, Dillon said, "How many incidents were mentioned on that recording?"

"Thirteen. It sounded like the first one happened in February 2002."

"So nine/eleven was probably the catalyst, the same as it was for us, but Bradford took a more direct approach than we did. If an individual appeared to be a significant national security threat, and if he could penetrate that person's security, he eliminated him. He wasn't going to stand by and let the politicians fail to deal with the next Osama."

"One of those people he killed was a Chinese politician!" Claire said. "He could have started a damn war. Is he insane?"

"The Chinese politician was a financial terrorist," Dillon said. "He was bent on destroying our economy. But to answer your question, I believe Charles Bradford is completely sane. He did nothing for personal gain, and he doesn't appear to have some mad delusion like overthrowing the president and becoming absolute ruler of the country. He obviously doesn't want credit for what he's doing, so he's not doing this for glory or to go down in the history books as the country's savior. As misguided as he may be, Bradford considers himself a patriot. Throughout his career, he's seen soldiers' lives wasted because politicians didn't have the courage or the foresight to deal directly and quickly with obvious threats to the country, and he finally decided he *had* to act—just as we did."

"Yeah, but still—" Claire started to say.

"And, unfortunately, that recording is not enough to remove Charles Bradford from his position, much less send him to jail."

"You've gotta be—"

"There's no *proof* that Bradford ever ordered Breed to do anything." Pointing at the recorder on his desk, Dillon added, "What you have there are the ramblings of a dying man, a man with cancer eating away his brain, his blood full of morphine and God knows what else. Not exactly an iron-clad case."

"So, for the third damn time, Dillon, what do you want to do?" Claire said.

Dillon walked over to the window and stared down at the street below. There was some sort of security drill in progress, or at least he thought it was a drill. A group of men in SWAT gear had surrounded a delivery van and were aiming their weapons at it. But maybe it wasn't a drill. These were dangerous times.

"About Charles Bradford, I don't know," Dillon said. "I need some time to think about that. What I want to do right now is figure out who directed the hit against Russo. If we can identify that man we may be able to use him against Bradford."

"That's what I was planning to do with DeMarco," Claire said.

"Yes. Mr. DeMarco," Dillon said. He paused a moment, then added, "Here's what I want you to do, Claire. Make a copy of that recording but then modify it, just a bit. I want . . ."

When he finished speaking, Claire said, "I'm not too sure how smart this is, Dillon."

"Nor am I, my dear, nor am I."

28

"Mr. DeMarco, this is Anthony McGuire. Uh, Paul's friend."

"Yeah?" DeMarco said. "What can I do for you?" The last thing he was in the mood for was dealing with McGuire.

"Well, I remembered something," McGuire said. "Something that may—uh, tell you where Paul hid whatever he hid."

Claire patted the impersonator on the shoulder. "Good job," she said. "You got that perfect. I particularly liked the little catch in your voice when you said *Paul.*"

"Uh, thanks," the impersonator said. Claire Whiting scared the hell out of him.

"Now go work on the DeMarco voice some more. I don't think we're gonna need it now, but I want you to be ready, which you're not quite yet."

DeMarco was seated in a pew near the stained-glass window depicting St. John of God. McGuire had called him while a guy from Home Depot was installing his new back door, but after the guy finished he decided to go to the church, because the contractor he'd called to give him an estimate on the cost to repair his kitchen couldn't come until tomorrow. The reason he'd asked the contractor to give him an estimate was because the insurance company claims adjuster was offering to settle for about one half of what DeMarco figured it would take to make things right.

McGuire had said that Paul always made a big deal out of the St. John of God window because St. John was the patron saint of nurses and Paul, being a nurse, always mentioned it whenever he and McGuire attended mass together. McGuire wasn't sure Paul had hidden anything near the window, but he said that might be a good place for DeMarco to look.

DeMarco had yet to approach the window, however, because there was an old woman at the front of the church, in a pew by herself, fingering rosary beads. She seemed absorbed in her prayers and probably wouldn't notice if he searched near the window, but he thought he'd wait awhile, hoping she'd leave pretty soon.

While he waited, he closed his eyes, clasped his hands together, and prayed to God to bring down a plague upon his insurance company, like the plagues He'd brought down upon the pharaoh when the pharaoh refused to let Moses and his people go. DeMarco wanted locusts to eat his insurance agent. He wanted the agent's office to be set upon by lice, frogs, and flies. Slaying the firstborn son of every executive in the company might be going too far, but maybe their dogs and cats could all get fleas.

In his opinion, insurance companies were like guys who welch on bets. In fact, that's exactly what insurance was: a bet between a homeowner and the company. The homeowner was betting that one day his house might burn down, and the insurance company was betting it wouldn't. The homeowner then put his money into the kitty by paying premiums for twenty years, and the insurance company used the money to invest in things that made them rich. Or richer. Then, if the house *does* burn down, the insurance company, in spite of all the money it's made, refuses to honor the bet. And that's what his insurance company was now doing by trying to get him to settle for half the money it was going to take to repair his kitchen. And when they finally did pay, they'd raise his rates.

Thank, God. *Finally,* the old woman was finished praying. He watched as she genuflected and crossed herself about a dozen times, then walked up the main aisle of the church. She gave DeMarco a little smile as she walked by him, which he returned, then he looked down at his lap, trying to look like a pious man saying his prayers, which, in a way, he had been doing.

As soon as he heard the church door close, he hustled over to the window. He could see a ledge below the window but was too short to reach it. Shit. He opened the door to one of the confessionals and got the chair the priest used. He took the chair over to the window, climbed up on it, and there it was: an envelope.

The only thing in the envelope was a dinky digital recorder.

Sitting in the operations room, Claire watched on a large plasma screen as DeMarco pulled his car off the Memorial Parkway and into a parking lot where people could look across the Potomac at the District. From this particular vista, DeMarco had a good view of the Lincoln Memorial, the Kennedy Center, and the dome of the Capitol shimmering in the distance—although Claire doubted DeMarco was thinking about the view.

Through three different bugs—one in DeMarco's car, one in his cell phone, and one in his belt—Claire listened as DeMarco played Martin Breed's recording. The sound quality was excellent and when DeMarco muttered, "You gotta be shittin' me," Claire felt like she was sitting right next to him.

Claire had sent her technicians out of the room while DeMarco played the recording. Dillon had told her that he didn't want anyone but him and her—and DeMarco—to know about the things Martin Breed had done for Charles Bradford. Claire still didn't think it was smart giving the recording to DeMarco, even one that had been doctored, but Dillon had overruled her objections. Once DeMarco listened to the recording, he would know almost as much as they did—and that was dangerous.

But the oddest thing about Dillon's plan—if you could call it a plan—was that he didn't appear to have an endgame. He said he hadn't decided what to do with the information on the recording, whether to use it to destroy Bradford or simply force him to resign, as Breed had planned. It was very unlike Dillon not to have thought things completely through.

Then another thought occurred to her: maybe Dillon did have an endgame and he just wasn't telling her what it was.

What in the hell was he supposed to do with this thing? DeMarco wondered, looking down at the small recorder resting in the palm of his hand. He knew it was his imagination, but the damn recorder actually felt *hot,* like it was going to burn right through his flesh.

He was only sure of two things—neither of which he could prove. First, he was sure Paul had been killed because of what he'd just heard, and second, Paul had wanted to get the recording to that reporter, Hansen. But other than those two things, he was completely confused.

He assumed the man who had made the recording was General Breed. That made sense, considering the things he claimed to have done for this guy Charles, but Breed never identified himself on the recording nor did he ever state Charles's last name or the last name of this guy Thomas, who he'd obviously made the recording for. He found it odd that their last names weren't mentioned, but even worse, it made the recording almost useless in terms of evidence. The other thing he didn't understand was why Paul decided to give the recording to a reporter instead of Thomas, whoever the hell Thomas was. He didn't know. He didn't know shit.

Well, he did know one thing: the damn recording was a political A-bomb and way, way too big for him to handle. He needed to give it to somebody who had the clout to deal with it. But who? Normally, he would have given it to the FBI, but he was afraid to do that because he didn't trust Hopper. He did know someone personally at the Bureau, a woman he'd once dated, and he knew he could trust her but he didn't feel comfortable taking this to her. He hadn't seen her in three years.

Another thing bothering him was that *somebody* had assigned Hopper to take the case away from the Arlington PD. Maybe it was this guy Charles—and Charles, based on the recording, was a guy big enough to boss around a two-star army general, which made Charles pretty damn scary.

So if he couldn't go to the Bureau, who could he go to? He supposed he could go directly to the Justice Department. The only problem with that bright idea was that the FBI, at least theoretically, worked for Justice and, for all he knew, Charles worked for Justice.

The guy he needed was Mahoney. Mahoney was Speaker of the House. Mahoney had *major* clout and could definitely force Justice to investigate and make sure they didn't try to cover anything up. But Mahoney was still flat on his back in a coma from which he might never wake up.

The only other person he could think of was his friend Emma. Emma had retired from the DIA—the Defense Intelligence Agency—but she'd been a power player when she worked there. She had helped him on cases in the past and she knew powerful people all over Washington, people who could be trusted. But, right now, like everyone else in his life, she wasn't available. She was cruising the Mediterranean with her lover, and DeMarco didn't even know what cruise line she was on.

The more he thought about it, he concluded that Paul had the right idea: turn this whole mess over to the press. They'd print a front-page headline in eighty-five-point font and all hell would break loose. Congress would call a bunch of hearings, special prosecutors would get assigned, and, if the FBI was told to investigate, every politician on the Hill would be watching them. Yeah, that sounded like the best idea. Just do what his cousin had been trying to do: set up a meeting with some reporter—which one, he didn't have a clue—and hand over the recording.

Or he could just mail the recorder to the press. No, that wouldn't work. Without an explanation as to where it came from and its connection to Paul and General Breed, people might just ignore it or take it for a hoax. No, he had to talk to a reporter and convince the reporter that the recording was the real thing.

And he had to do one other thing: he had to make sure he didn't get killed like Paul.

Dillon walked into the operations room Claire was using. Three of her technicians were now back in the room, sitting in front of computer monitors, earphones on their heads. DeMarco was still visible on the plasma screen, still sitting in his car on the banks of the Potomac, pondering what he'd just heard. Alice, Claire's favorite field agent, was the one filming DeMarco and transmitting the picture.

"How many people do you have on him?" Dillon asked Claire.

"Four," she said. "More than enough to follow a guy like him. And I've got a tracking device on his car and we can use his cell phone to track him, too. If I need to, I can cover him with a satellite."

"I certainly hope it doesn't come to that, Claire."

"Me too."

"So what do you think he's going to do next?" Dillon said.

"How would I know?" Claire said. "We can record his voice, not his thoughts."

"Well, not yet," Dillon said, smiling slightly.

DeMarco had no idea whom to call at *The Washington Post*. At one time, he'd known a *Post* reporter, an old alcoholic named Reggie Harmon. But Reggie got married for the fourth time last year—to another reporter, also an alcoholic—and moved to Houston where his new bride worked. The only other reporters at the *Post* whose names he knew wrote for the sports page. Yeah, he knew all the sports guys, especially that one pessimistic son of a bitch who started off every football season by saying how bad the Redskins were gonna be that year. Unfortunately, most of the time, he was right.

Then he thought: Woodward and Bernstein—although he wasn't sure Bernstein even worked there anymore. But this thing he was holding, this recording, it was right up Woodward's alley: an army general admitting he'd killed a bunch of people because some guy named Charles told him to. Oh, yeah. Woodward would drool like a rabid dog when he heard the recording.

The problem with Woodward, DeMarco figured, was he probably had a thousand conspiracy nuts calling him every day of the week. There was no way he'd take a call from DeMarco even if he worked for Congress. No, wait a minute. The *Post* had lost a reporter. Woodward might take a call from somebody who said he had information related to the disappearance of a brother scribbler. Yeah, that would work.

Dillon and Claire watched as DeMarco opened his cell phone.

"Are you ready, Claire?" Dillon asked.

"Gilbert?" Claire said.

"Yeah, I'm ready," Gilbert said.

Claire listened as DeMarco punched a number into his cell phone.

"Who's he calling?" Claire asked.

Gilbert and Dillon both said at the same time, "*The Washington Post.*"

Gilbert could tell DeMarco was calling the *Post* because as soon as DeMarco dialed the *Post*'s number, the number showed up on his screen and the software he used automatically gave him the identity of the party being called. That's how Gilbert knew who DeMarco was calling. But how had Dillon known? Answer: because he was Dillon.

Dillon put on a headset, one which had earpieces covering his ears and a microphone on a wand in front of his lips. Then Dillon, Claire, and Gilbert all listened as DeMarco navigated the *Post*'s voice mail system until he finally reached an operator.

DeMarco said, "I need to speak to Bob Woodward. I have information relating to the disappearance of—"

At that moment, Dillon made a slashing motion across his throat and Gilbert cut off the call to the *Post*.

DeMarco heard his cell phone make a funny click and cursed, figuring the operator at the *Post* had accidentally disconnected him. But then he heard: "You don't really want to talk to Bob Woodward, Mr. DeMarco."

"What?" DeMarco said, and then looked at his cell phone like it had turned into a snake. "Who the hell's this? How the . . . how the fuck did you get on my phone?"

"Magic, sir. The same magic I used to determine that you're in possession of a recording made by the late General Breed."

"You got me *bugged*?" DeMarco said.

"Three ways from Sunday, my friend," Dillon said.

"Who the hell is this? FBI? Is this you, Hopper?"

It didn't sound like Hopper, though.

"No, Mr. DeMarco. As I think you know, Special Agent Hopper is not your friend. I, on the other hand, am the man who can keep you alive."

"Keep me alive? Who the hell is this?"

"Mr. DeMarco, you are now in possession of the same information that got your cousin killed. And since I know this, and if I was the person who killed Paul Russo, you'd be dead right now, right there where you're parked on the banks of the Potomac."

"What? How the hell do you—"

"Turn around and look behind you. No, turn the other way. Do you see the SUV, the black one with the tinted windows? The driver's a nice young lady named Alice. I want you to join Alice. She's going to drive around for a while to make sure she's not being followed, and then she's going to bring you to me."

"Hey, screw you, whoever you are. I'm not going anywhere with your people."

DeMarco heard the guy laugh. "DeMarco, I can see you. I can hear you. I can cut in on your cell phone conversations. Think about that. So, please, just calm down and do what I say. I want to help you. There are some other people out there, however—the kind of people General Breed speaks about on that recording—who want to kill you. And maybe they'll kill your girlfriend as well. Killing someone in Afghanistan isn't all that hard to do."

Jesus, they knew about Angela and where she was. Who the hell *was* this guy?

"Please join Alice in her car, Mr. DeMarco."

29

Alice was an athletic-looking young woman in her early thirties, wearing a black blazer over a white blouse, jeans, and running shoes. She had a cell phone gizmo in her ear. She was kind of cute, DeMarco thought: long black hair, brown eyes, a long straight nose, and a red-bronze complexion. Because of the nose and her coloring, DeMarco thought she might have some Native American in her, but the main impression he had of Alice was: *serious.*

Alice was as serious as a heart attack.

"Kneel on the seat," Alice said. "I need to frisk you to see if you're carrying a weapon."

"I'm not carrying one," DeMarco said.

"I still need to pat you down."

"Bite me," DeMarco said.

Before Alice could respond to DeMarco's childish comment, the man who had spoken to him previously, said, "It's okay, Alice. I doubt Mr. DeMarco is armed. I'm sure I'll be safe from him." The man's voice came from a speaker in Alice's vehicle which was directly behind DeMarco's head and he jumped in his seat when he heard the voice.

Alice stared at DeMarco for a few seconds—letting him know she wasn't pleased that he'd interfered with her job—then said, "Buckle your seat belt." She didn't speak to him again for thirty minutes.

Alice drove onto the Memorial Parkway, crossed the Fourteenth Street Bridge into the District of Columbia, and then got on 395. She stayed on 395 until she came to the Capitol South exit, took the exit, and then made a tour of Capitol Hill, turning frequently, backtracking occasionally. A couple of times she spoke to someone, saying, "Am I clear?" Apparently whoever she was talking to said she was. From Capitol Hill she took surface streets to reach the D.C. Beltway and then took the beltway exit to Silver Spring, Maryland, where she once again began driving through residential areas, this time dodging down the occasional alley, blowing through stop signs as if they didn't exist, scaring the shit out of DeMarco. Finally, she stopped in front of a small house whose lawn was badly in need of cutting. There was a kid's big-wheeled tricycle sitting on the grass near the front door.

DeMarco followed Alice into the house. The front door opened into a living room filled with inexpensive, mismatched furniture and smelled musty, as if the house had been locked up for some time. DeMarco stood in the living room for a moment, not sure what to do next, until a voice called out, "Mr. DeMarco, I'm in the kitchen."

DeMarco entered the kitchen and saw a white-haired man in his sixties pouring coffee into two cups, and the guy was dressed like he'd just posed for the cover of *GQ*. DeMarco couldn't afford to spend a lot of money on his clothes. He bought the suits he wore for work at a Men's Wearhouse in Alexandria and his casual clothes at outlet malls. He figured the guy pouring coffee had spent more on his tie than he had spent on his suit.

"I believe you take your coffee black," the man said, as he handed DeMarco a cup.

DeMarco nodded. He wasn't about to give him the satisfaction of asking how he knew that.

The man sat down at the small kitchen table and gestured for DeMarco to take a seat. As soon as he did, DeMarco said, "Who are you?"

"Before we start," the man said, "would you mind giving Alice the recorder you took from St. James?"

DeMarco looked over his shoulder. Alice was standing behind him, about four feet away, her face expressionless. He turned back to the white haired man and said, "I don't think so."

"Alice," the man said, and because of the tone of voice he used, DeMarco glanced back at Alice again. This time she was holding an odd-looking plastic gun with a yellow hand grip.

"That's a Taser, Mr. DeMarco," the man said. "It won't kill you but I understand being shot with one is rather uncomfortable. So, please, may I have the recorder?"

DeMarco thought for a moment about shoving his chair back into Alice and hopefully knocking her off balance long enough for him to wrestle the Taser away from her. Not a chance. If he tried he was just going to end up on the floor twitching like a guy with St. Vitus dance. He pulled the recorder from his pocket and slid it across the table to the white-haired man, and he tossed it to Alice.

"Thank you," the man said to DeMarco. To Alice he said, "Alice, would you please wait in the living room until I'm finished talking to Mr. DeMarco."

What the guy meant was, *Stick around, Alice, in case I need you to shoot DeMarco.*

After Alice departed, DeMarco asked for a second time, "Who are you?"

The man smiled slightly, this annoying Cheshire Cat smile. "Do you know what the NSA is, Mr. De—May I call you Joe, please? Mr. DeMarco is just too cumbersome, too formal."

"Yeah, you can call me Joe. And what do I call you?"

"As I was saying, Joe. Do you know what the NSA is?"

"The National Security Administration."

The man shook his head. "The National Security *Agency,* Joe. Not Administration. The NSA is the largest intelligence service in this country, both in terms of money and manpower, and yet you, like most people, don't even know its proper name."

DeMarco started to say that he didn't give a rat's ass about the proper name, but the man asked, "And do you know what the NSA does, Joe?"

"I know you guys got caught bugging a bunch of telephones without warrants a few years ago."

"That's not *quite* accurate, but close enough. At any rate, the NSA has two primary functions. The first of those is cryptography. To keep it simple, we devise codes and encrypted systems to protect America's secrets, and we break the codes of nations who may be unfriendly toward us. Our second mission is, in a word, eavesdropping. We eavesdrop in every way imaginable, Joe, on America's enemies and our allies. We eavesdrop on cell phones and faxes and e-mails. We eavesdrop on satellite and microwave transmissions and undersea cables. There is virtually no form of communication that we can't intercept and record.

"When you think of spies, Joe, you probably imagine Richard Burton in *The Spy Who Came In from the Cold,* a cynical man in a rumpled trench coat paying greedy communists for their secrets. Well, that's not the way it works most of the time. Not in the twenty-first century. The NSA *is* the spies, Joe. Spying today, the largest part of it, the most effective part of it, is done by eavesdropping on our enemies.

"So you asked who I am. Well, I'm a spy. Think of me as Richard Burton, minus the bad trench coat."

"What does this have to do with—"

"Unfortunately, when we're listening to all these transmissions—these radio and telephone communications—sometimes, although not intentionally, we intercept transmissions here in this country. We don't mean to but . . ."

"Bullshit," DeMarco said.

". . . but sometimes we do. And therein lies the problem, Joe. *Our* problem. Yours and mine. We overheard, quite by accident, a very disturbing conversation. And now I'm going to play that conversation for you."

He took a small digital recorder from the inside pocket of his suit coat, a recorder similar to the one DeMarco had found in the church. He hit the PLAY button and DeMarco heard:

Alpha, do you have Carrier?
Negative. Monument blocking.
Bravo, do you have Carrier?
Roger that. I have him clear.
Very well. Stand by.

DeMarco sat, mesmerized, listening to the recording until the NSA man tapped the STOP button.

"Well, Joe, what do you think of that?"

"I think somebody popped Carrier and Messenger. And I think Carrier was my cousin and Messenger was a *Washington Post* reporter named Hansen."

"Very good. And they were killed because of what General Breed said on that recorder you found in the church."

"But what the hell does this have to do with me?" DeMarco said. "I mean, if you know all this stuff—"

"Joe, your country needs you."

"My country! What is this horse—"

"The NSA can't admit that we overheard Paul being killed. I'm afraid that would cause us a major political problem."

"Well you know something, Richard Burton? I don't give a shit about your political problems."

As if DeMarco hadn't spoken, the man said, "It would erode the public's trust in us, which in turn would make us less able to do our mission—which is to protect the country. So you see, we need you. We need you to pursue what you heard on that recording."

"Pursue it how? What the hell am I supposed to do? You guys need to go to the FBI with what you have. Or somebody in Congress, somebody who has the clout to deal with this, not somebody like me."

"Joe, clout is the least of our problems. We have *clout.* What we can't do is involve more people in this issue, because the more people we talk to, the greater the likelihood becomes that what we've done will become public knowledge. But since you already know what we've done, and since you're already involved in Paul's murder, you're the perfect person to help us."

"Help you do what, for Christ's sake!"

"We want you to help us find the man you heard directing your cousin's execution. And then we need to bring that man and his boss to justice, not only for killing Paul but for doing the things that General Breed accuses Charles of doing on that recording."

"And who the hell is Charles?" DeMarco asked. "And who's Thomas?"

Dillon had directed Claire not to give DeMarco Paul Russo's letter and to delete last names from the recording. So what DeMarco had ended up with was a recording that described all the things that Breed had done for Charles Bradford, but Charles Bradford and Justice Thomas Antonelli were identified only by their first names.

Answering DeMarco's question, Dillon said, "Thomas is retired Senator Thomas Whitman. He was a former chairman of the Armed

Services Committee and he worked closely with General Breed. He was incorruptible."

"Was?"

"Yes. Unfortunately, Senator Whitman had a stroke four days ago and died last night. He was eighty-three."

It had taken some effort for Claire to come up with a plausible and unavailable man whose first name was Thomas. She'd looked at army officers that Breed had worked with, senior civilians at the Pentagon, and finally settled on Senator Whitman when the man fortuitously kicked the bucket. Dillon did not want DeMarco to know the recording had been intended for the Chief Justice of the Supreme Court, at least not yet.

"Okay," DeMarco said, not sure he believed this. "But who's Charles?"

Dillon paused. "Charles is Charles Bradford, Joe. Chairman of the Joint Chiefs of Staff."

30

"Is something bothering you, honey?" the bartender asked.

"What?" DeMarco said.

He was at the bar in Sam & Harry's on 19th Street, having a Stoli martini. The bartender was a good-looking gal a little younger than him, and he flirted with her whenever she was behind the bar. He had thought about asking her out before he met Angela; he had no intention of doing that now, but he still flirted with her. But tonight he didn't feel like flirting. Tonight he was stewing over the trap he was caught in—and the bartender had noticed.

He told her everything was fine, that he'd just had a bad day at work. What he wanted to tell her was: *Yeah, something* is *bothering me. I'm being manipulated and lied to and threatened by an evil old prick who works for the NSA.*

When he'd asked the NSA guy what he wanted him to do, he said he just wanted DeMarco to meet with Hopper. And to make sure Hopper met with him, he would give DeMarco some additional information about Paul's death.

"But what's the purpose of the meeting?" DeMarco had asked.

"We believe, after you meet with Hopper, that Hopper will contact the man he's working for and we'll be able to identify that man."

"But why do you need to identify him? You already know Bradford's responsible."

"We know it but we can't prove it. General Breed's recording doesn't include Bradford's last name and the recording alone isn't proof that Bradford ordered Breed to do anything. And although we've recorded the voice of your cousin's executioner, we don't know his name. Furthermore, the radio intercept of your cousin being killed is inadmissible as evidence."

"It's not *inadmissible,*" DeMarco had said. "You just don't want to admit you've been intercepting communications in the U.S. without a warrant."

"Be that as it may," Richard Burton had said, "we need proof. We need evidence. We need to know who's working for Bradford and maybe, using the intercept, whether it's legal or not, we can convince him to testify against Bradford." Before DeMarco could pose another argument, the man said, "Come on, Joe. I'm not asking for all that much. I just want you to meet with Hopper and then we'll take it from there, and you can go back to doing whatever it is you do."

DeMarco had mulled over the request—he mulled it over for about a nanosecond. "I don't think so," he had said. "I don't know you, I don't trust you, and I'm not going to become part of whatever game you're playing. You need to turn over everything you have to some law enforcement agency. If you don't, I'm gonna talk to the press. Even without the recording, somebody will listen to me."

And that's when the threat came.

"Joe, do you know what you are right now?" the NSA man said, his eyes twinkling.

"Yeah. I'm a guy who doesn't work for you."

"No, Joe. You're a suspected terrorist."

"A suspected . . . Are you out of your fucking mind?"

"Not at all. You received a call from Afghanistan the other night, a call we intercepted, quite legally by the way, since it originated from

Afghanistan. The transmission was somewhat garbled, however. We had some sort of problem with our equipment, but we recorded you saying something about al-Qaeda and caves. Yes, that part of the transmission was quite distinct."

"I was talking to my girlfriend," DeMarco had said. "That was a joke."

"We don't know who you were talking to, Joe. Like I said, we had some equipment problems. But when an American citizen gets a call from Afghanistan discussing al-Qaeda. . . . Well, it's not a joke to us. We take that sort of thing rather seriously, and I'm afraid that when we pass this information on to Homeland Security, you're going to be detained for questioning. And you may be detained for quite some time."

"Oh, bullshit," DeMarco had said, instantly dismissing the threat. "Homeland doesn't have any basis for detaining me, and no judge would ever allow it."

"Who says a judge will ever know you've been detained? The world's changed since nine/eleven. And once you're detained for possibly being in allegiance with terrorists. . . . Well, Joe, if you think you have a hard time getting on an airplane now, wait until you've been added to the TSA's watch list. And then there's the fact that you have a security clearance and access to the Capitol. I don't think the Secret Service and the Capitol Police will look kindly on a man on the no-fly list working in such a sensitive place."

Before DeMarco had been able to say anything else, Richard Burton had smiled and added, "All we want you to do is *meet* a man. What's so horrible about that? And you'll be helping us catch the people who killed your cousin. Don't you want to catch those people?"

In the end, DeMarco agreed to do what the NSA man wanted—but he'd only agreed to give himself time to figure a way out of the mess he'd gotten himself into. He'd been an idiot to go to St. James after McGuire had told him that Paul might have hidden something there.

There was no doubt about it: curiosity did kill cats—or, if not cats, morons who didn't have the good sense to mind their own business.

Another thing bothering him, as he sat there sipping his martini and feeling sorry for himself, was that he couldn't even be sure the recording he'd heard of Paul being killed was legitimate. For all he knew the NSA had fabricated the recording, which in turn meant he could be involved in some devious NSA plot against Bradford, some sort of internal Pentagon feud.

Christ, he didn't know who he could trust. He couldn't trust the FBI and he sure as hell couldn't trust the NSA. And he didn't know what was really going on because he was sure the NSA man wasn't telling him everything he knew. But there was one thing he knew for sure: *He was the mouse in the elephant cage.* These elephants—the FBI, the NSA, the chairman of the Joint Chiefs—they were all stomping around the cage, dancing with each other, and if DeMarco's little mouse ass tried something, one of the elephants was going to squash him.

He figured he still had the option of going to the press. Get in his car tomorrow, make a beeline for *The Washington Post,* and run inside like a guy seeking sanctuary in a cathedral. The problem with that bright idea was, since he knew he was being watched—hell, they had cameras on him today, for Christ's sake—he suspected he'd never get inside the building. And after Alice had dropped him off back at his car, he went home, looked up the NSA on the Internet, and learned that some three-star admiral ran the organization. Just what he needed: another guy with stars on his shoulders involved in this thing.

Yeah, he could just see it: him getting out of his car and running for the front door of the *Post* and some navy SEAL sniper putting a bullet through his head from a mile away.

Which also made him think: how did he know that the *NSA* hadn't killed Paul and Hansen? How did he know it wasn't really *their* op he'd heard on that recording?

Yep, he was the mouse in the elephant cage. He'd read somewhere that elephants were actually afraid of mice—and maybe they were—but he was pretty sure these particular elephants weren't afraid of him.

Hey, Hopper, this is DeMarco.

DeMarco had been told to call Hopper at ten fifteen the day after meeting with Dillon at the safe house. Claire was sitting in the operations room with Gilbert, listening to his conversation with Hopper. She nodded her head when she heard DeMarco speak. The way he spoke was just the way she had predicted, the way the damn impersonator had never been able to get quite right.

What is it, DeMarco? I haven't got time to talk right now, and I don't have anything new to tell you about your cousin's murder.

Well, you better make time to talk to me, or the next call I'm making is to the press.

Why would you talk to the press?

Because the FBI—or maybe it's just you—is involved in a cover-up.

That's an asinine thing to say. What are we covering up?

For starters, your autopsy report says that Paul was shot at close range with a 9mm. But I talked to the Arlington detective who saw Paul's body, and he said there was no exit wound. He said if Paul had been shot with a nine at close range there would have been an exit wound the size of my fist.

That's not necessarily true, DeMarco. I'm sure our ballistic experts know more about gunshot wounds than some county cop. But how do you know what the autopsy report said?

I work for Congress, Hopper. I told you that. Getting information out of bureaucrats is what I do for a living.

Good. DeMarco was following the script, Claire thought.

Who told you about—

And I've talked to Paul's friends, and there's no way he was dealing drugs. You lied about finding that bottle of pills in his apartment. I also found out that Paul's last patient was General Martin Breed. I think that puts a whole new spin on things, Paul maybe being the last guy to see a Pentagon big shot like Breed alive. Maybe that's why you're not being straight with me about the investigation.

Hopper didn't say anything for a long time, which made Claire think that Hopper had no idea that Russo was connected to Breed.

What do you want, DeMarco?

I want a meeting. And when we meet, you're going to tell me what's really going on.

Forty seconds later, Claire heard: *Why did you page me?*

"Yes!" Claire said. The man speaking was the man with the Fort Myer cell phone. Hopper had apparently paged him and then the guy had turned on his cell phone and called Hopper back. She looked over at Gilbert, making sure he was paying attention. She wanted the damn guy's location.

We need to meet. It's about . . . about the case I took over from the Arlington PD. That lawyer I told you about. You know, the cousin. Well, he just told me some things I think you need to know.

What did he say?

Not over an open line.

Claire laughed and said, "It's a little late for that, Bozo."

I'll meet you where we met last time, at three thirty.

Hopper's boss hung up.

"Well, where's the guy Hopper was talking to?" Claire asked Gilbert.

"He's on Route One, just outside Alexandria, heading north. And he just powered down his phone."

"Shit," Claire said. Was this guy always on the move?

Claire had told Alice that she wanted Hopper smothered—and Alice was smothering him. She was leading an eight-man team in four separate vehicles, two agents per vehicle. One of the vehicles was a pickup truck, and in the bed of the truck was a dirt bike with big knobby tires. She could follow Hopper anywhere. Her team also had parabolic mikes so if Hopper met his contact outside or sitting near a window, they would be able to record whatever was said. But Claire had made it clear that recording the conversation was a secondary objective. Her primary objective was to identify the man Hopper was meeting.

Hopper was scheduled to meet his contact at three thirty. By three o'clock, when Hopper's car had still not exited the Hoover Building garage, Alice assumed the meeting was going to be someplace close by, unless the meeting had been canceled. Then, at three twenty, one of Alice's team radioed her. "He's leaving the building. The Pennsylvania Avenue exit."

Alice was parked in her vehicle with another agent on the corner of 9th Avenue and Pennsylvania, and she looked down Pennsylvania and saw Hopper walking directly toward her. What was he doing? She'd expected him to drive somewhere, but it appeared as if was walking to meet his contact. This was good. Maybe the meeting would take place outdoors and she could easily record what was said. The National Mall was just one long block away from the Hoover Building, and that was a likely place for a meeting. Or maybe Hopper would meet his contact in one of the public buildings on the Mall, like the Museum of Natural History, which was close, and where she could easily follow him.

Alice watched from her SUV as Hopper stopped on the corner of 9th and Pennsylvania and waited for the light to change. She was positive by now that he wasn't looking for a cab and was planning to walk to the rendezvous site, and she ordered three members of her team to leave their vehicles and proceed in the direction of Pennsylvania Ave to follow Hopper on foot. If a car stopped and picked Hopper up, all she had to do was radio the agents who were still in their vehicles and they would take up the pursuit.

When the light changed and Hopper started to cross the street, Alice put on sunglasses and a baseball cap, exited her SUV, and fell into step behind him. At some point, she would walk past him and one of her team members would assume the tailing position, and by then her other agents would be in positions where they would effectively have Hopper boxed in between them. From that point forward, they would be constantly switching positions to keep Hopper in sight so he wouldn't become used to seeing the same person behind him. They would also frequently change their appearance, donning and removing hats and jackets and glasses.

Hopper crossed Pennsylvania but didn't proceed down 9th Ave toward the National Mall as Alice had expected. Instead he turned to his right, walked half a block west, and entered the Department of Justice—and Alice knew she was screwed.

The Robert F. Kennedy Department of Justice Building has a beautiful Indiana limestone façade, a red-tile hip roof, and decorative colonnades. It is a five-story one-point-two-*million*-square-foot behemoth, and occupies one enormous city block. And, as is the case with almost all federal buildings since nine/eleven, people don't simply walk into the building. You either had to have identification showing you were an employee of the department—and, as an FBI agent, Hopper had such identification—or you had stop at a security checkpoint where guards would examine your ID, verify you were an approved visitor with an appointment, and then provide you with a temporary badge and most likely someone to escort you to wherever you wanted to go. Whomever Hopper was meeting was most likely already inside the building. He could be an employee of the Justice Department or some other federal agency that was permitted access. Even if Alice were to show the security guards her NSA credentials—which she had no intention of doing—it would still take time to convince the guards to let her enter the building, and by then Hopper would have disappeared into one of the hundreds of rooms inside the place.

She was screwed.

Alice stood outside the building for half an hour and at four o'clock, people began to stream out of the building, going home for the day. One of the people who exited was Hopper, and his contact could be any one of the hundreds of other people exiting at approximately the same time. She watched without any indication of the frustration she was feeling as Hopper crossed Pennsylvania Avenue again and walked back into the Hoover Building, then she pulled out her cell phone, called Claire, and told her what Hopper had done.

Claire went ballistic.

31

"John," Bradford said, "I feel like things are spinning out of control. It should have ended with Russo and the reporter. But now this lawyer . . . what's his name again?"

"DeMarco," Levy said. "Joseph DeMarco."

Bradford was attending a barbecue later that day at Camp David. It was the president's wife's birthday but hardly an occasion, in Bradford's opinion, worth taking him away from his duties. Had the chairman of the House Appropriations Committee not been attending as well, he would have come up with some last-minute emergency that required him to stay at the Pentagon. Unfortunately, part of his job, whether he liked it or not, was cozying up to the people who funded the military.

Not only did he not want to attend the function, he didn't want to attend in the attire he was wearing. The invitation had emphasized casual dress, indicating they might be sitting around a bonfire, and he was consequently dressed in stiff new blue jeans, a red and blue striped shirt, and loafers. The president was a man who looked comfortable in jeans—hell, he *was* comfortable in jeans—but the only casual clothes Bradford liked were combat fatigues. And the damn jeans, for some illogical reason, made him feel less powerful, less able to handle the situation with this DeMarco character. He knew he was being irrational and mentally shrugged off the feeling.

"So now this lawyer knows that Hopper's involved in some sort of cover-up and he knows Martin was Russo's last patient."

"Yes, sir," Levy said.

"How did DeMarco connect the nurse to Martin?"

"He could have simply talked to Russo's employer," Levy said. "I didn't have him under surveillance—maybe I should have, but I didn't—and I had no idea he was investigating Russo's death."

"But *why's* he investigating?"

"I don't know. All he was trying to do was find his cousin's will, but he keeps digging things up. I guess I should have watched him closer."

"Yes, maybe you should have." Bradford was quiet for a moment. "You know, we've been very lucky up until now, John, but we can't rely on luck any longer. We can't afford any more mistakes. We need to wrap this up, once and for all."

They had been incredibly lucky. When Martin had told him he was going to expose him if he didn't resign, he'd taken the precaution of having Levy place a listening device in Martin's bedroom. To install the device, Levy waited until nightfall and simply drilled a small hole through the siding of Martin's house. The bug was about a quarter inch in diameter and connected to a small recorder that Levy hid in the shrubs outside of the bedroom, and the recorder could be accessed remotely by phone like a telephone answering machine. Bradford knew Martin was so ill he rarely left his sickbed, and he figured a single device in the Martin's bedroom would be sufficient. If anyone was seriously looking for a listening device they'd find the bug, but it was so small he doubted Martin's visitors or his family would notice it, and he knew Martin was too weak to conduct a search himself.

Thanks to the listening device, they heard Martin tell the nurse he had to talk to Thomas Antonelli before he died. Bradford had no doubt he was going to tell Antonelli about their relationship, and that's when he ordered Levy to kill Martin, as much as he hated to do so. Levy picked the lock on Martin's backdoor when Martin's family was asleep and after the nurse had left for the day, and killed him painlessly with an overdose of morphine.

But where they really got lucky was with the nurse.

Bradford wasn't sure if Martin had told the nurse anything specific but he thought he might have, so he took the precaution of having Levy watch Russo after Martin died, and one day, as Levy was tailing him, Russo suddenly stopped his car to use a pay phone. This took Levy by surprise and by the time he parked, the nurse was already on the phone, but Levy heard enough to know that Russo was planning to meet a reporter at the Iwo Jima Memorial.

So much luck—and the problem with Martin should have ended when Martin, the nurse, and the reporter died. But then this congressional flunky comes along. How much did DeMarco know? And what did he want? And the big question: was anyone helping him?

Levy had apparently been thinking the same thing. "Sir," he said, "that man Drexler you sent over to the NSA. He called me yesterday. He said he didn't find anything that tied the agency to Russo, but he sounded strange. There was something off about his . . . his tone of voice. I'm thinking I should talk to him in person."

"We don't have time for that," Bradford said. "And I'm not surprised that Drexler didn't find anything. They're not fools over there at Fort Meade and, for that matter, we really don't know the NSA is involved."

"Well, somebody's involved," Levy said. "The woman who took Witherspoon's fingerprints worked for some organization."

"I know," Bradford said. "Has anyone made any attempt to contact the two soldiers you used?"

"No, sir."

Bradford rose from his desk, too agitated to sit, and began to pace his office. He wasn't the type to feel sorry for himself, but there were times when it felt as if the responsibilities he bore were overwhelming.

The Chinese were growing stronger, both financially and militarily, and the Indians weren't far behind. Good-paying jobs for middle-class Americans were disappearing, the country's manufacturing base was collapsing, and we were at war with religious fanatics, a war that would never end. He wondered, some days, if he was going to live long enough to witness the end of an empire.

He had no doubt that the course he had embarked on ten years ago with the help of John Levy and Martin Breed was the right course. It was simply unconscionable to sit back, doing nothing, while the politicians wrung their hands and Americans died and suffered. But sometimes . . . sometimes it was just too much. Yet what choice did he have? He could retire, of course. Simply walk away and leave all this for the man who replaced him. But what was the likelihood that his replacement would do what needed to be done? Not much. He squared his shoulders. Wallowing in self-pity was unacceptable. His only choice was to keep moving forward, to keep on fighting, no matter how terrible the cost might sometimes be.

He took a breath. "John, here's what I want you to do. Have Hopper meet with DeMarco and, when he does, he needs to find out what DeMarco knows. Do you understand me, John? Hopper needs to do whatever's necessary to make DeMarco talk. Do you think he has the stomach for that?"

"Yes, sir. He won't have any qualms about that. But why don't I do it?"

"No," Bradford said. "Right now it doesn't appear that anyone knows about you, and I want to keep it that way. But afterward, Hopper needs to go. I've never trusted him; he only helps us because we pay him. And at this point he's a liability, particularly considering the magnitude of what's involved."

"Sir," Levy said, "if something happens to a guy who works for Congress *and* an FBI agent, their deaths are going to be vigorously investigated."

"I'm sure they will be, John, so the trail can't lead back to us. See if you can find someone who might have a motive for wanting to kill DeMarco."

"Somebody tried to burn down his house the other day."

"Well, there you go," Bradford said. "That's perfect. The man obviously has enemies."

"And Hopper?"

"Hopper should simply disappear. Arrange for a deposit to his bank account, a large deposit—use the emergency fund—and a couple of hours later withdraw the money and route it to Geneva, the Caymans, somewhere like that. Hopper's not popular at the Bureau. His bosses will think he sold information to somebody they're investigating, and then took his thirty pieces of silver and fled the country. But, John—and this is really important—are you positive Russo didn't leave any sort of written record?"

"Sir," Levy said, "I searched Russo's body. He had nothing on him. Hopper and I both searched Russo's house. I looked at the reporter's laptop and there was nothing on it. Nor did the reporter have any notes on him or in his house. I monitored Russo's cell phone—he didn't have a landline in his house—and the only time he left his house before he met with the reporter was when he stopped at his church."

"How long was he in the church?"

"Less than ten minutes, closer to five. And when I looked inside he was just kneeling there, praying."

"Is there a pay phone in the church?"

"No." Then Levy hesitated. "Or I should say, I don't think there is. There isn't one outside the place or on the main floor, but I suppose there could be one in the basement or a landline in an office. But it doesn't matter; I'm sure Russo wasn't in the church long enough to tell anyone what he knew."

Bradford was silent as he thought all this over. "Okay, John, but you have to find out what DeMarco knows and if anyone's helping him."

"Yes, sir."

32

Claire and Alice were already in the briefing room when the three men entered. The men were all in their late twenties, with short hair and flat bellies, and were harder than slabs of granite—and Claire noticed the look Alice gave them as they took seats facing the projection screens at the front of the room. Claire rarely thought about the sex lives of her personnel, but she'd always suspected that Alice was a lesbian. Apparently not.

As soon as the men were seated, Claire tapped a keyboard and two photographs of DeMarco appeared on the screen. One photo was his driver's license photo. The other was the one on his Congressional ID badge.

"Your job tonight," Claire said, "will be to protect this man. For this op, his code name is White, as in white knight. White is meeting a man tonight and we believe this man will have a team with him and they may try to kill White or snatch him during the meeting. We don't know for sure, but that's a possibility we have to be prepared for."

A photo of Special Agent David Hopper appeared on the screen. "This is the man White is meeting. His code name is Black."

Most of Claire's agents specialized in surveillance and intelligence acquisition. The three agents she was speaking to performed those functions, too, but they had been picked for this mission because they were all ex-military and all had recent combat experience—meaning killing experience. Because Claire suspected that Russo and Hansen had been killed by soldiers from Fort Myer, she had to be prepared for something similar tonight and therefore she needed comparable talent—talent just as lethal as the tomb guards.

"Gentlemen," Claire said, "this meeting tonight is tied to an operation that is classified so far over your heads that I can't give you even an inkling as to what's involved. All you need to know is that this op is so sensitive and so vital to national security that we can't involve the FBI or any other law enforcement agency. We can't afford *any* leaks, so this op is being handled totally in house. Do you understand?"

"Yes, ma'am," the agents said in unison.

"Alice," Claire said, "will have tactical control of the op in the field. I'll be here at Fort Meade providing technical support." Claire paused then and looked each man in the eyes. "Now listen closely. Even though Alice will be in charge, you'll be allowed to use your discretion regarding actions necessary to protect White. The problem, obviously, is if the opposition plans to kill White there may not be time for you to get permission from Alice to take them out. What this means is that you are authorized to remove any deadly threat to White without obtaining Alice's prior approval. Are we clear?"

"Yes, ma'am," the agents said, realizing they'd just been told that they had license to kill, just like James-effing-Bond.

"Okay," Claire said. "Alice, it's all yours."

As Alice walked to the front of the briefing room, a map appeared on one screen and a satellite surveillance photo of the rendezvous site appeared on another screen.

"The meeting between Black and White," Alice said, "will take place at midnight on a baseball field at Tuckahoe Park in Falls Church, Virginia."

When DeMarco spoke to Hopper, Hopper had tried to delay giving DeMarco a time and a place for their meeting. Hopper's excuse was that he couldn't be sure when he'd be available and would call DeMarco later—at the last moment—to identify the meeting place. But DeMarco, following instructions he'd been given by Dillon, refused to go along with that and insisted that Hopper identify the rendezvous spot in advance.

Alice shined a laser point at the map. "Tuckahoe Park is enclosed by the Lee Highway on the south, Sycamore Street on the east, 26th Street on the north, and Tuckahoe Elementary School on the west. The baseball field is here, adjacent to the park, and the location was most likely chosen by Black because a hit team can hide in these woods, on top of these buildings at the elementary school, or across 26th Street at the Bishop Connelly School behind this long hedge. The ball field cannot be seen by vehicles traveling on the Lee Highway because of the woods, and the field is in a slight depression and therefore cannot be easily seen from Sycamore Street. You can, however, see the field from 26th Street, but this street is not heavily traveled at night because its primary purpose is to provide access to the elementary school. Any questions on the geography?"

The agents shook their heads.

"We expect," Alice said, "that opposition will most likely be using weapons with sound suppressors and night-vision scopes. You will be similarly equipped."

Pointing at the three agents in turn, Alice said, "You're Alpha. You're Bravo. You're Charlie. Alpha, you'll be going to the rendezvous site as soon as this briefing is concluded. Your primary job is to protect White from Black and you'll take up a position near these bleachers. There's a mound of sod there—they're resodding the outfield—and the mound will make it more difficult for someone to see you from the woods, which is the most likely position for a sniper.

"Bravo and Charlie, at the start of the operation you'll be with me. I already have people watching the park. I assigned them as soon as Black identified the rendezvous site. We expect that the opposition will move in some time before the meeting, most likely two or three hours before. My spotters are located here, here, here, and here," Alice said, using the laser pointer again. "I will be stationed here. My spotters and I will have night-vision binoculars and thermal imaging equipment and we'll see the opposition when they arrive. As soon as they take up their positions, you will move in behind them, close enough to take them out if necessary. Do you understand?"

Bravo and Charlie nodded.

"Gentlemen," Claire said, "there's something you need to understand. The opposition will have men just as capable as you are. Do not underestimate them in any way."

Claire couldn't tell the agents that they were going up against the sentinels from the Third Infantry Regiment. That was information that Dillon didn't want anyone else to know. But it was important for these agents to understand how lethal their opponents were. This was going to be like pitting two boxers against each other that were perfectly matched in every way: size, reach, conditioning, and experience. The advantage Claire had was that the other side didn't know the NSA was involved.

At least she hoped they didn't.

"This vest," Alice said, "will stop anything smaller than a fifty-caliber round."

DeMarco didn't know what to say to that. *Gee, thanks* didn't seem right. He just tugged on the straps to tighten the vest.

"And you'll be wired and you'll have an ear bud," Alice said.

"A what?"

"You'll be wired so we'll be able to hear whatever you and Hopper say to each other, and you'll have a nearly invisible communication device in your ear so you'll be able to take orders."

"Who'll be giving the orders?" DeMarco said.

"It doesn't matter. You just need to know that whoever's talking to you is a person you better obey. If you want to live."

Alice was a bundle of joy.

She turned to leave the room, but before she did she said, "Wait here. Someone will be here in a minute to hook up the com gear. And then Dillon wants to talk to you."

Dillon?

Alice, DeMarco thought, you just fucked up. Dillon had to be Richard Burton, the white-haired man with the expensive clothes. Yeah, the slick son of a bitch looked like a *Dillon*.

A young guy who could have worked for the Geek Squad at Best Buy came into the room next. He told DeMarco to remove his belt and gave him another belt; then he stuck an American flag lapel pin onto DeMarco's jacket. Lastly, he jammed a little clear plastic thingamajig into DeMarco's left ear and made sure all the stuff worked.

Two minutes after the geek finished, the old man walked into the room. Once again he was dressed immaculately and, just as he'd been the first time DeMarco had seen him, he seemed completely relaxed and appeared to be enjoying himself tremendously.

"Are you all set, Joe?" Dillon asked.

"Yeah."

"Good." Dillon handed a piece of paper to DeMarco. "Here's what you'll say when you meet Hopper. You don't have to say all that verbatim, just use it for guidance."

DeMarco looked at what was written on the paper. "I'm not saying this," he said.

"You're not saying what?"

"I'm not going to say I want money from these guys to stay quiet."

"Why not? You need to give Hopper some reason why you're pursuing the case and why you haven't talked to the authorities about what you know. A payoff is a plausible reason."

"Yeah, well, you think of another plausible reason," DeMarco said, "because I'm not gonna let you assholes record me asking for a bribe. All the rest of this stuff, I'll say, but not that."

Dillon nodded his head as if DeMarco's demand was reasonable but then he said, "The phone call you received from Afghanistan the other night. We analyzed the transmission again, and it appears the person who called you was a CIA agent named Angela DeCapria—your girlfriend, like you said."

"So what?" DeMarco said, not liking where this conversation was going.

"Well, Joe, I don't know if you know this but Ms. DeCapria's in an extremely vulnerable position right now. She's on the Afghanistan-Pakistan border near Kandahar posing as an aide worker for an NGO."

"How the hell do you know where she is and what she's doing?" DeMarco said.

"I think you'll agree that's a rather silly question, Joe, when you think about what the NSA does."

"Then what's your point? Are you threatening to reveal what she's doing over there if I don't do what you say?"

"Of course not, Joe. I'd never do that. But as I told you, Charles Bradford is chairman of the Joint Chiefs, and he could find her just as easily as I did. And then, if Bradford so desired, a mistake could be made; someone might tell the wrong person that Ms. DeCapria isn't who she claims to be."

Bullshit. He was threatening Angela.

"Listen to me, Dillon," DeMarco said, and Dillon's right eyebrow elevated in surprise.

"How do you know my name?" Dillon said.

DeMarco saw no reason to tell him that Alice had let it slip. Instead he said, "You're not the only guy who can find things out. I know your name and I know where you live. And if anything happens to Angela DeCapria, I'll kill you, *Dillon,* and that's a promise."

"I'll keep that in mind," Dillon said, but there was a smile tugging at the corner of his lips. DeMarco could tell Dillon considered it more likely he'd be struck by a meteorite than killed by DeMarco.

"Now back to the script," Dillon said. "Are you clear on what you need to say?"

"Yeah," DeMarco said. "I'm clear."

33

Dillon was worried.

He was sitting with Claire in the operations room at Fort Meade. Four of Claire's technicians were in the room as well, poised in front of monitors, wearing headsets. There was a satellite image of the rendezvous site on one large plasma screen. On another screen was a computer-generated map of the rendezvous site, and data from the satellite and information provided by Alice's spotters were being continuously added to the map so that Dillon would have real-time information regarding the locations of all the players. Blinking green lights on the map showed the location of Alice and her spotters; red lights showed the location of the three agents assigned to protect DeMarco; yellow lights were being reserved for the opposition. A solitary blinking blue light was DeMarco.

Although he was thirty-five miles from Tuckahoe Park in Falls Church, Dillon was the wizard behind the curtain. He could control the satellite overhead; he could direct the actions of all his people. He could hear everything Alice said to her team and everything they said to her, and he would be able to hear everything Hopper said to DeMarco. Yet in spite of all the marvelous technology at his fingertips and all the clever people helping him, Dillon was worried.

Dillon dealt in worst-case scenarios. One such scenario was that the man who had directed the operation that killed Paul Russo would bring in a team—probably more sentinels from Fort Myer—and his team would either kill or kidnap DeMarco during his meeting with Hopper. But no team had shown up and the meeting was scheduled to begin in fifteen minutes. Which brought Dillon to the most worrisome worst-case scenario: maybe the opposition team *had* shown up. Maybe they had infiltrated the rendezvous site and Alice's people hadn't seen them. That seemed impossible, but . . .

"Alice," Dillon said into his mike, "tell DeMarco to go stand on the pitcher's mound."

Roger that.

Dillon was hoping that when DeMarco took up his position on the pitcher's mound that the opposition team would give themselves away—assuming there was an opposition team. Alice immediately transmitted his order.

DeMarco, go to the pitcher's mound. Alpha, White is moving into position.

Alpha was the agent hidden near the bleachers at the ball field, the man assigned to protect DeMarco from Hopper if necessary. He and the other two agents could only hear Alice; they were not able to hear Dillon nor would they be able to hear DeMarco talking to Hopper. The original plan had been to wait until the opposition team was in place, and then send Bravo and Charlie into the woods, placing them in positions where they could neutralize the opposition if needed—but again, there appeared to be no opposition.

"Alice," Dillon said, "send Bravo and Charlie into the woods now. Have them search for intruders."

Roger that.

"There are no intruders," Claire said.

Dillon ignored Claire's comment. "Alice, if they find no intruders, position Bravo and Charlie where they have the widest field of vision."

Roger that.

Dillon watched as two red lights and a single blue light changed position on the electronic map. Via the satellite, he could also see DeMarco walking slowly across the ball field but, because it was night and the ball field was only dimly lit from nearby streetlights, DeMarco was just a dark moving form.

Thirty minutes passed. Hopper was now fifteen minutes late. Bravo and Charlie had found no intruders in the woods. Dillon was beginning to think that Hopper had decided not to make the meeting.

A Mercedes sedan has just parked on Sycamore Street.

That had been one of Alice's spotters speaking.

A man is exiting the Mercedes. It's Black.

Hopper had arrived.

Black is approaching White.

Dillon glanced at the satellite image and watched a dark image of Hopper striding across the baseball field toward DeMarco.

Thirty seconds later: *A Cadillac SUV has pulled into the parking lot of the Bishop Connelly School.*

Dillon looked at the map. DeMarco wouldn't be able to see the SUV. It was hidden by the long hedge running along the perimeter of the Bishop Connelly School.

The man in the Cadillac SUV just put on a headset.

The man in the Cadillac *had* to be with Hopper but Dillon wouldn't know if he was the one who had directed Russo's execution until he heard the man's voice.

All personnel, listen up.

It was Alice speaking.

The man in the SUV is opposition. His code name is Cadillac. Bravo, Charlie? Can you see Cadillac's vehicle? It's behind the hedge on 26th Street.

This is Bravo. Negative.

This is Charlie. Negative.

Even though the agents had night vision equipment, the hedge was apparently blocking their view of the Cadillac SUV. This wasn't good. Alice had expected the opposition to use the woods on the south side of the ball field for cover and not the hedge across the street from the field, and she'd positioned Bravo and Charlie in the woods. Alice had guessed wrong.

One of Alice's spotters said: *Cadillac is exiting his vehicle. He's removing something from the rear seat of his vehicle.*

Alice immediately asked, *What did he take from the vehicle?*

Cannot identify. Cadillac is on the ground. Cadillac is belly-crawling toward the hedge. Cadillac is taking up a position at the east end of the hedge.

The satellite image of Cadillac crawling was barely visible. It looked like a shadow slithering across the ground. Then suddenly the plasma screen showing the satellite image went completely black.

"What the hell's going on?" Claire said.

"We've lost the satellite," one of the techs said.

"Why? What happened?"

"I think it's because . . ."

Claire didn't need to hear geek babble. "Get it back! Now! We're blind!"

Bravo, Charlie. Can you see Cadillac? He's in a prone position at the east end of the hedge.

It was Alice speaking.

This is Bravo. I can see his head.

This is Charlie. I have him too.

Thank God for night-vision goggles, Dillon thought.

"The satellite's down hard," Claire's tech said.

DeMarco watched as Hopper approached. He was a good-looking guy, a couple inches taller than DeMarco. He was dressed casually in a lightweight jacket over a T-shirt, jeans, and running shoes—he was dressed like a man ready for action. The way he was dressed also matched the story he'd given DeMarco, which DeMarco suspected was pure bullshit.

"You're late," DeMarco said, when Hopper reached the pitcher's mound.

"Kiss my ass," Hopper said.

"And I still don't understand why we had to meet out here in the middle of the damn night."

DeMarco said that because he figured the complaint would be expected, but Hopper had already told him why they were meeting at this time of night. Hopper's lie was that he was part of an FBI surveillance team watching some bad guy around the clock, and this was the only time he could break away. The park had been chosen for the rendezvous because it was close to the location of Hopper's fictitious surveillance team. DeMarco suspected the real reason Hopper wanted to meet at midnight was that there would be less chance of anyone seeing Hopper kill him, particularly if Hopper took him into the woods near the ball field.

"I already told you why we're meeting now," Hopper said. "So just get to it, DeMarco. What do you want?"

"I told you what I want. I want to know what the hell's going on with my cousin. I know you falsified his autopsy report and I think you're covering up why Paul was really killed."

"He was killed because he was peddling meds."

"You gotta quit lying to me, Hopper. It won't work. I know this isn't about drugs."

"Oh, yeah," Hopper said. "What do you know?"

"I know a *Washington Post* reporter is missing, and right before Paul was killed the reporter was headed toward the Iwo Jima Memorial."

Ask him how he knows that.

"That's him!" Dillon said.

The man who had just spoken was the man who had directed the operation at the Iwo Jima Memorial. Tonight, however, he wasn't using encrypted radio equipment—most likely because the equipment was too bulky—and Claire's technicians were easily able to lock in on his radio frequency and listen to him talking to Hopper. It appeared that just as DeMarco was wired so Dillon could hear him and give him orders, Hopper was wired so Cadillac could hear Hopper and give him orders. Dillon smiled. It was like DeMarco and Hopper were two radio-controlled robots, their speech and movement controlled remotely by their masters.

As soon as Dillon said, "That's him," Alice said, *Delta, Echo, Foxtrot. Cadillac is your target. We've lost satellite coverage so you will not—I repeat—you will not lose Cadillac when he departs.*

Delta, Echo, and Foxtrot were Alice's spotters—and the agents Claire had assigned to follow and identify Hopper's boss. Their job was the most critical part of the operation. Their job, in fact, *was* the operation since the only reason Dillon had wanted DeMarco to meet with Hopper was so Hopper could lead them to the man they now called Cadillac.

The only thing that remained to be done at this point was to keep DeMarco alive and, frankly, keeping DeMarco alive was secondary to identifying Cadillac.

"How do you know about the reporter?" Hopper said.

"Traffic cameras," DeMarco said. "I asked that cop, Glazer, to look at them."

He's lying. That was Cadillac speaking.

"You're lying," Hopper said.

"I also know General Breed was Paul's last patient," DeMarco said.

"Yeah, you already told me that. How'd you find out about Breed?"

"I found out because I know how to get information out of people. I also know one of the last people to see Breed before he died was Charles Bradford."

"What?" Hopper said.

When Dillon heard Hopper say *what*? it sounded to him as if Hopper was genuinely surprised to hear Bradford's name, which made Dillon wonder if Hopper even know about Bradford's role in this whole thing. He couldn't help but wonder if he'd just signed Hopper's death warrant. Knowing the connection between Breed and Bradford was what had gotten Paul Russo killed.

Ask him what he wants.

That was Cadillac speaking to Hopper again.

"What do you want, DeMarco?" Hopper said. "Money to stay out of this thing?"

"No, I don't want money. I just want to know what's going on."

Dillon smiled when he heard this; DeMarco was a stubborn bastard.

Tell him that Russo is a classified op and you need to know where he's getting his information from.

"Okay, I'm gonna level with you," Hopper said. "Russo's death is connected to a classified operation, and that's why I had to take the case away from Arlington and why I haven't been straight with you. You've stumbled into something *way* over your head, pal, something related to national security, but that's all I can tell you. So now you listen to me. I need to know who's feeding you information, and don't tell me fuckin' traffic cameras."

"No, no," DeMarco said. "I'm not buying that classified national-security crap. You feds chuck that out whenever you want to hide the truth."

"DeMarco, goddammit, I'm telling you the truth. And if you don't tell me what I need to know, I'm gonna call your boss and get your dumb ass fired for sticking your nose into an FBI case after you were told to back off."

DeMarco doubted Hopper knew who his boss was, but he didn't say that. Instead he said, "You're not gonna talk to my boss, because if you do, I'll have to tell him what you're up to—and then you'll have Congress all over your ass."

Hopper, make him talk. Take out your gun and threaten to kill him. Shoot him in the knee if he doesn't talk.

Thirty-five miles away, in the operations room at Fort Meade, Dillon screamed, "No!"

He knew what was going to happen the instant Hopper pulled his weapon.

"Alice!" Dillon yelled. "Tell Alpha not to kill Hopper!"

Dillon was too late.

DeMarco watched Hopper's right hand go up, toward his chest—and he immediately realized that Hopper was going for a gun in a shoulder holster. DeMarco was too stunned at first to move, then he started to back up, holding his hands in front of his chest, saying, "Wait a minute. Wait a minute."

But Hopper didn't wait. His drew his gun and started to bring the weapon to bear on DeMarco—and then he dropped to the ground like his legs had evaporated and there was a small red-black hole in the exact center of his forehead.

DeMarco had no idea who had killed Hopper.

No one had told DeMarco about Alpha, Bravo, and Charlie.

Levy saw Hopper fall, and his mind registered that, a millisecond before Hopper fell, he'd seen a muzzle flash from a weapon that he thought came from *behind* DeMarco, from the bleachers, but everything happened so fast he wasn't sure.

Now DeMarco was running. Why was he running if he had protection? And why was he running toward the woods and not up to the street where he'd most likely parked his car?

All Levy knew for sure was that he couldn't let DeMarco leave the ball park. The damn guy knew too much.

Levy picked up the object he'd taken from the backseat of his SUV: a short barreled rifle with a sound suppressor and night-vision scope.

Cadillac has a weapon. I repeat. Cadillac has a weapon.

It was one of Alice's spotters speaking.

Dillon cried out, "Alice! Tell your men they can't kill Cadillac."

Dillon wanted to use Cadillac to squeeze Charles Bradford if he could. Cadillac dead was of no use to him.

Alice immediately relayed the order, speaking rapidly, sounding like an auctioneer.

Bravo, Charlie. Do not shoot Cadillac. I repeat, do not shoot Cadillac.

When Hopper had been shot, DeMarco didn't know who had shot him. He'd stood there for about a second, stunned by what had happened, and then sprinted toward the bleachers. He wasn't going to stand in the middle of a baseball diamond, a perfect target for whoever was shooting, and the bleachers were the closest cover he could see.

The bleachers suddenly seemed a mile away.

Levy raised the rifle to his shoulder, sighted in on DeMarco's running form—and fired. He watched without emotion as DeMarco fell headlong into the dirt, right near third base, like a ballplayer sliding into the bag.

DeMarco was hit in the back, just to the left of his spine, with something that felt like a sledgehammer. His hands, then his chin, scraped the dirt. His right hand was touching third base. Thank God for the vest Alice had given him. He got up and started running again. He had to get under cover. The next shot might hit someplace where he wasn't protected—like his head.

DeMarco's been hit.

It was Alice speaking.

Bravo, Charlie! Put rounds near Cadillac. Drive off Cadillac but do not hit him. Fire, fire!

Without the satellite, Dillon couldn't see what was happening at the ball field, but he understood what was going on. Cadillac had shot DeMarco. He wondered if DeMarco was dead.

Levy didn't understand what had happened. DeMarco had gone down but now he was back up and running again. He must be wearing a vest. Levy aimed again. This time he aimed for DeMarco's head.

John Levy was an excellent shot.

He started to pull the trigger, but before he could, bullets began to strike the ground near him. Tree bark and dirt blew back into his face. He scooted backward where there was a slight depression in the ground but the bullets continued to hit near his head, missing him by inches. He got up and started running. The hedge would provide some cover until he reached his vehicle.

Dying wouldn't help the general.

As Levy drove away from the park, tires squealing, he was thinking that he had failed miserably. DeMarco was still alive, Levy still didn't know who was helping him, and still didn't know the extent of DeMarco's knowledge regarding General Breed.

He had failed Charles Bradford completely. He had failed him for the first time in his career.

With a small smile on his face, Dillon watched as three green blinking lights moved on the electronic map—Alice's spotters were following Cadillac.

DeMarco crouched beneath the bleachers, his heart hammering. His back hurt from where the bullet had struck the vest, he'd skinned a hand when he fell, and he was panting like he'd just run a marathon instead of maybe a hundred feet from the pitcher's mound to the bleachers.

Who the hell was out there? Who killed Hopper?

"Sir."

DeMarco whipped his head to his right. Whoever had just spoken was close—it sounded like the guy was under the bleachers with him—but he couldn't see anyone! He started to scoot backward on his hands and knees, to get out from under the bleachers as fast as he could, but the voice said. "Sir, it's okay. Calm down. You're safe."

Safe my ass! And where the fuck was *the guy?*

"Sir, it's all over. I'm going to show myself now."

And then DeMarco saw a man literally rise up out of the earth. One minute there was what looked like a mound of dirt near the bleachers and the next thing he saw was the mound turn into a man dressed in mottled black and green combat fatigues with dark green camouflage paint smeared on his face. He was holding a short barreled rifle in his hands, and there was a sound suppressor attached to the rifle along with a high-tech scope that probably allowed the man to see in the dark. The man had been less than ten feet from DeMarco. If this guy had wanted to kill him, DeMarco knew he'd be dead already.

"Sir," the man said, "you're directed to return to your vehicle and wait for further instructions."

DeMarco didn't move; he just put his head down on the dirt. "Holy shit," he said—and he didn't care how many spies heard him.

Dillon had allowed DeMarco to drive his own car to the ball field. DeMarco figured Dillon did that because it would have looked funny if Hopper had arrived at the rendezvous before him and saw someone dropping him off. DeMarco also knew Dillon wasn't worried about losing him because his car undoubtedly had some little tracking gizmo attached to it and, for all he knew, he had tracking gizmos attached to *him,* sewn into his damn clothes or something.

DeMarco.

It was Alice talking to him through the earbud.

I'll be with you in a couple of minutes. Just stay where you are. Don't move.

DeMarco looked out at the ball field. Alice was standing there with a couple of men who had rifles slung over their shoulders and, just like the man under the bleachers, and they were wearing camouflaged military-style fatigues. Alice and her pals were looking down at Hopper's body, probably trying to figure out what to do with it.

As he sat there, DeMarco decided there was no way he was going to let these NSA assholes keep jerking his strings like he was some kind of puppet. And now, on top of everything else, he was involved in the death of an FBI agent. Dillon had undoubtedly recorded him talking to Hopper, maybe even filmed him, and, for all he knew, Dillon might try to pin Hopper's murder on him.

This whole thing just kept getting worse and worse: Paul getting killed by a government SWAT team; Breed's recording implicating a four-star general in a string of international assassinations; the damn NSA virtually holding Angela hostage to make him cooperate; and then, the last straw, using him as bait to kill an FBI agent. He had to find a way out.

He needed a plan.

But he didn't have a plan.

He looked back at the ball field and noticed nobody was paying any attention to him; they were all focused on Hopper's body. Dillon's people obviously thought DeMarco would just sit there like the good puppet he was until somebody came over and told him what to do.

Then he came up with a plan. Well, actually, *half* a plan. But half a plan was better than no plan at all.

He pulled the earbud out of his ear and chucked it out the car window. When he did, he felt like he'd just pulled a tick out from under his skin. Then he started his car, stomped on the gas pedal, and drove away—wondering how long it would be before they noticed he was gone.

All he needed was a five-minute head start.

Perry Wallace, Mahoney's chief of staff, was an unattractive, disagreeable genius whose only reason for living was to keep Mahoney in office. He also lived in Falls Church, a little more than a mile from Tuckahoe Park. DeMarco had been to Wallace's home twice before and he knew he could drive there in two minutes—but he also knew he was infested with listening devices and suspected his car had a tracking device installed on it as well. So he needed to dump the car and get rid of all the bugs before he went to Perry's place.

He drove as fast as he could and less than a minute later pulled into an alley that was halfway between Tuckahoe Park and Wallace's house. He jumped out of the car, leaving the door open, and started throwing things into the car. He tossed his cell phone and watch in first and started to throw in his wallet, then realized he would need money. He took all the cash from his wallet and when he saw he didn't have much, he pulled out his ATM card. He spent a few seconds—he couldn't afford to spend more than a few seconds—running his fingers over the card looking for some kind of bug or tracking device, then gave up. He had no idea how the NSA could bug a plastic card. He'd just have to hope for the best. He put the ATM card and his cash on the hood of his car and started stripping off his clothes. He figured the last time he'd taken off his clothes that fast was when he was seventeen and lost his virginity to a girl named Patty Donatelli.

Less than ninety seconds after he'd arrived in the alley, he was standing next to his car wearing nothing but boxer shorts and socks. Holding his cash and his ATM card in his hand, he started running.

He had no idea what he'd say to a cop if one saw him.

Alice and the two agents designated as Bravo and Charlie stood there looking down at Hopper's body. Alice spoke into her mic. "Claire, what do you want me to do with—" She almost said Hopper's name, then realized Bravo and Charlie didn't know his name and didn't need to know it. "With Black," she concluded.

Claire was alone in the ops room at Fort Meade, waiting to hear back from the agents who were tailing Cadillac. Dillon had gone home and her techs were taking a break, having a cup of coffee. In answer to Alice's question, Claire said, "Take the body back to Fort Meade. I'll decide later what I want to do with it."

Hopper was a problem. Killing him may have been justified but he was still an FBI agent, and the last thing she and Dillon needed was a major FBI investigation into the death of one of their own people. So Claire didn't want the body found immediately, but she hadn't made a decision yet on whether she wanted Hopper to disappear forever or if she wanted to create some scenario to explain his death. Whatever the case, she'd figure it out tomorrow, after she had a chance to talk to Dillon and after they had identified Cadillac. To Alice, she said, "Have your men transport the body. What I want you to do is drive back to the safe house with DeMarco. I want him someplace where we can keep an eye on him." Claire hadn't figured out what they were going to do with DeMarco, either.

"Roger that," Alice said, looked over to her shoulder toward DeMarco's car—and saw the car wasn't there.

"Goddammit!" she said. Thumbing her radio to change the frequency, she screamed, "DeMarco! Where are you?" When DeMarco didn't respond, she changed frequencies again. "Claire, DeMarco's gone. He took off."

"Oh, shit," Claire said. She ran to the door of the operations room and yelled to her techs, "Get back in here!" It had never occurred to her that DeMarco would run. As soon as her technicians were back in the room, she said, "Find DeMarco." The techs returned to their monitors and Claire said to one of them, "Is the satellite still down?"

"Yeah," the tech said, "and it's gonna be for quite a while."

Claire muttered a curse and turned to another tech, "Well? Where the hell is he?"

The tech said, "He's approximately half a mile from the park, in an alley near the corner of Washington Boulevard and Quantico Street. He's not moving."

Alice heard what the tech said and began sprinting toward her car. As she ran, she was thinking: *That goddamn Demarco. She knew he was going to be trouble the first time she met him.*

Three minutes later, Alice called Claire. "I'm standing right next to his car, and he's not here. Where is he?"

Claire turned to one of the techs. "Well?"

"The GPS in his cell phone says he's right there, right where his car is."

Alice said, "Well, he's not here." Then Alice looked into DeMarco's car and said, "Claire, he dumped everything. His clothes, his cell phone, his wallet, everything he had on him is in his car. He's gotta be on foot, he's not wearing any clothes, and he can't be too far from here. I'll start driving around and see if I can spot him." Alice paused before she said, "It would sure be nice if we had a satellite that worked."

It took DeMarco five minutes to run to Wallace's house and when he got there he was breathing like he was two seconds away from a heart attack and his feet hurt from running without shoes on the hard sidewalk. He pressed down on Wallace's doorbell and then started hammering on the door with his fist. Wallace had no social life and DeMarco was positive he was home sleeping.

Finally, Wallace answered the door. He was dressed in purple pajamas constructed from enough cotton to build a circus tent and he was naturally surprised to see DeMarco standing there on his porch, semi-naked. "What the hell?" he said.

DeMarco pushed his way into the house and closed the door. "Perry, I need clothes, shoes, and your car—and I can't tell you why," he said.

"What?" Wallace said.

"Perry, wake the fuck up! I'm being chased by some of the scariest guys you've ever seen in your life, and I need—"

"What guys? And where are your clothes?"

"It involves Mahoney, Perry, and I need you to do what I'm telling you. And I need you to move fast."

DeMarco had invoked Mahoney's name because he knew by doing

so Wallace would be more inclined to help him. Wallace also knew that Mahoney often asked DeMarco to do things that Wallace knew were in his own best interest not to know about, and the fact that Mahoney was lying in a hospital bed did not mean DeMarco had stopped working for him.

While Wallace was getting the clothes, DeMarco peeked out the front window and saw a black SUV driving slowly down the street—the kind of SUV that Alice drove. It was dark outside and the windows in the SUV were tinted, so he couldn't tell who was driving, but his gut told him it was Alice or one of her gun-toting friends.

Wallace came back with a pair of sweat pants and a sweat shirt. The sweat shirt had an XXXL label and the tennis shoes were a size smaller than DeMarco wore. DeMarco had no idea why Perry Wallace owned sweat clothes as he had never—judging by his waistline—exercised in his life. Wallace refused to give him the keys to his good car, but he also owned a beat-up Mazda pickup that had about two hundred thousand miles on it.

As he was leaving, DeMarco said, "If anybody asks you about me, you haven't seen me."

"You got that right," Perry said.

34

Dillon was shoeless, standing on the carpet in his office, tapping golf balls at a drinking glass using a long-handled putter, a belly putter. When Claire entered his office, he glanced over at her and said, "Have you ever used one of these before? I know Vijay Singh used one for a while. I rather like it."

"The name of the man who was driving the Cadillac last night is John Levy," Claire said.

Dillon sighed, leaned the putter against a wall, slipped his feet back into his Gucci loafers, and took a seat behind his desk. "And what do we know about Mr. Levy?" he asked.

"He enlisted in the army at age eighteen and twenty months later showed up at Fort Myer."

"The Tomb of the Unknowns?"

"Correct. He was there at the same time that Charles Bradford was base commander. After Fort Myer, Levy spent time at Fort Benning, Fort Lewis, Bosnia, and Iraq One. Typical noncom's career. He was assigned to Washington about the same time as Bradford got his second star and just before Martin Breed did his first job for Bradford, the one in Turkey."

"Hmmm," Dillon said.

"A couple months after being posted to Washington, Levy resigned from the army, which is odd because by then he had more than ten years in the service and appeared to be having a stellar career in uniform based on his fit reps. And then he started job hopping. He did a stint with the DIA, a few years as civilian with CID, and currently he's the deputy director of the Pentagon Force Protection Agency. When Bradford was posted overseas, whatever agency Levy worked for would transfer him to the same location."

When Dillon didn't respond, Claire continued, "So it appears that the same year Bradford recruited Martin Breed, he also recruited John Levy. Two like-minded men who were incredibly dedicated to Bradford and believed completely in what he was doing. He allowed Breed to stay in the army and advanced his career and used him for certain assignments. For other assignments, particularly the stateside ones, it appears that he used Levy. Apparently he didn't want Levy attached to a military unit, because he'd have less freedom to do whatever Bradford wanted."

"*Apparently,*" Dillon said. "It *appears,*" he added, the words dripping off his tongue like bitter fruit. Before Claire could object, he said, "I don't disagree with your analysis, Claire, but it would certainly be nice to have some facts to support all this."

"How many damn facts do you want?" Claire said. "We know Levy tried to kill DeMarco last night. We know he killed Russo and we know the tomb guards helped him. And we know what Breed said on that recording. I don't care how doped up and sick he was, some of what Breed said had to be true."

Dillon nodded as if conceding the point.

"So now what, Dillon? What do we do now that we know John Levy is Bradford's man?"

Dillon didn't answer her question.

Instead he said, "Where's DeMarco, Claire?"

"What the hell happened, John?" Bradford spoke calmly, suppressing the anger—and the panic—he was feeling. Generals don't panic.

"It was an ambush," Levy said, and proceeded to tell Bradford what had happened at the baseball field in Falls Church.

"My God," Bradford said. "This is—"

He opened a drawer in his desk and began to reach for a bottle of Chivas Regal he kept there for special occasions—then slammed the drawer shut. He never drank during the day, and he wasn't about to start now. "Do you have any idea how many people were with DeMarco last night?" he asked.

What he really meant was: *How many more people now know our secret?*

"No, sir. But there was more than one shooter. Maybe two or three."

"Why in hell didn't you take a team with you, for Christ's sake?"

"I was afraid to use the sentinels again since someone was already curious about them. I figured I could handle it myself. I didn't expect DeMarco to have so much support. Or any support, for that matter."

"Who do you think was helping DeMarco?"

"I don't know. I keep coming back to whoever identified Witherspoon through his fingerprints. It's somebody in the government, but I have no idea who."

"Goddammit, John, I need answers!" Bradford shouted.

"I know that, sir, and I'm doing the best I—"

"Where's DeMarco now?" Bradford said.

"I don't know. That's what I've been doing, trying to find him."

"John, you *must* find him. You need to find out what he knows and who's working with him. This . . . this is a damn disaster!"

"Maybe not, sir. Keep in mind that the only thing DeMarco seems to know is that Russo was meeting with a reporter and that you visited

General Breed before he died. I think, if he knew more, he would have said so when he talked to Hopper."

"I can't take that chance. Find him, John. Find him and find out what he knows and kill him."

DeMarco was in a room at a motel called the Day's Inn, and the motel was located in Crystal City, a shopping and office complex near Reagan National Airport. He was lying on the bed in the baggy sweat clothes he'd borrowed from Perry Wallace and watching the morning news to see if the newscasters would mention that the body of an FBI agent had been found in the woods near Tuckahoe Park. Of course, they didn't mention any such thing.

When DeMarco had left Perry Wallace's place, he knew he couldn't go home. He needed to find a place where he could hunker down for a while and figure things out. He picked the Day's Inn because it wasn't too expensive and because it was near the Crystal City shopping mall, where he could buy some clothes. The other thing was, the motel had an underground garage where he could park Perry's truck. He was worried about the truck because he was guessing that by now the NSA knew he was driving it.

Last night, when he abandoned his car and his clothes, Dillon and his friends would have quickly concluded that DeMarco couldn't stay on the streets and would most likely go to the home of someone nearby to hide. They'd look at his phone bills to see if he knew anyone in the area and, if that didn't work, they'd start looking at people who worked for Congress. They might even know that he worked for Mahoney, although, and because of the things he did for Mahoney, he wasn't an official member of Mahoney's staff. If they knew he worked for Mahoney, they'd immediately zero in on Wallace. Whatever the case, they'd figure out pretty quickly that Perry Wallace worked for Congress and lived half a mile from where DeMarco had dumped his car and then they'd send someone to question him. They'd probably tell Wallace that DeMarco was a fugitive and that he'd broken some law, and if Wallace didn't cooperate he would go to jail with DeMarco—at which point, Perry would sing like a canary and Dillon's spies would then have the license plate number and make of Perry's old pickup and start searching for it.

He turned off the morning news but continued to lie on the bed looking up at the ceiling. What the hell was he going to do? He couldn't hide in a motel room forever. What he wished, more than anything else, was that he still had the recorder he'd found in the church—but thanks to Alice and her Taser, he didn't have it. If he had the recorder, he would have some leverage over Dillon, and the press would be more likely to believe him. Without the recording, however, he strongly doubted that anyone was going to believe him when he started babbling about the NSA and the Chairman of the Joint Chiefs and a dead FBI agent whose corpse couldn't be found.

But he needed help and he needed someone who would buy his story, and the two people who could help him most—Emma and Mahoney—were unavailable. He supposed he could track Emma down. It wouldn't be impossible to find out which cruise ship she was on, but tracking her down would involve a bunch of phone calls—and the NSA had made him leery of talking to anyone on the phone. Then it occurred to him that contacting Emma could be dangerous for her, possibly even fatal. He'd already unintentionally gotten Angela embroiled in his problems and the people he was dealing with were extraordinary adversaries—people with military-trained killers at their disposal and the most sophisticated technologies the government possessed. No, he wouldn't get Emma involved.

But he needed *somebody*. He needed somebody who could deal with the Pentagon, somebody with federal muscles, huge federal muscles.

What he needed was somebody in the damn FBI. The Bureau was the right organization to deal with this.

The problem with going to the Bureau, however, was he couldn't just pick up the phone and call them. Not without any proof. So he needed to contact somebody at the FBI he could trust, somebody who would not only believe him but be able to steer him to people who had the power and the guts to deal with something as big as this.

And he knew such a person. He just didn't know if she would help him.

About three years ago, he and Emma had been sucked into an investigation at a naval shipyard on the West Coast. It started out as a little whistleblower incident—somebody complaining how the government's money was being squandered—but then the investigation mutated dangerously into a case involving espionage and a psychotic Chinese spy. During the case, DeMarco had a brief fling with an FBI agent named Diane Carlucci. The fling might have amounted to more but Diane was transferred from Washington, D.C. to LA, and out of DeMarco's life.

But she was back in Washington now. He hadn't known she was back until he ran into her on the street in Georgetown one day. She was with a rugged, good-looking, gray-haired guy a few years older than DeMarco, whom she introduced as her husband. She and DeMarco had stood there for a moment, both feeling a bit embarrassed. They couldn't talk about the good times they once had—not with her new husband standing there—so DeMarco mumbled a few words about how good she looked, which she did, and how great it was to see her again and then walked away thinking about what might have been.

But Diane was the right person to call. Unlike Hopper, DeMarco knew she was honest. And she'd been with the Bureau long enough that she'd be able to put him in touch with the right big shot to talk to about this whole NSA mess.

So that was DeMarco's new half-assed plan: meet with Diane Carlucci and convince her to introduce him to a heavy hitter at the Bureau, a big honcho near the top who would know how to proceed with a case of this magnitude, involving people at the highest levels in the Department of Defense.

"Where's DeMarco, Claire?" Dillon asked.

"I don't know," Claire said. "We never expected him to bolt, but while Alice's people were all following Levy and removing Hopper's body, that's just what the bastard did. He abandoned his car, took off all his clothes, and dumped everything that had listening and tracking devices installed in them. After we located his car, we identified people in the area he might know and found a guy named Perry Wallace, who's John Mahoney's chief of staff."

"Mahoney? Is DeMarco connected to Mahoney?"

"I don't know. He isn't a member of his staff. He probably just knows Wallace because they both work in the Capitol. Anyway, Alice paid Wallace a visit, scared the livin' shit out of him, and he admitted he loaned DeMarco a vehicle, but said he had no idea what DeMarco was doing or where he was going. And knowing how Alice can be, I believe him. But right now, we have no idea where DeMarco is."

"You need to find him, Claire, and you need to find him before John Levy does."

"I know that," she snapped. It really irritated her when he stated the obvious. "What do I do after I find him?"

"Put him in a safe house with people who can make him stay there. I haven't decided what to do about Mr. DeMarco yet."

As deputy director of the Pentagon Force Protection Agency, John Levy had the resources at his disposal to pursue DeMarco. He called four senior agents into his office and gave them a photo of DeMarco and all the information he had obtained on the man.

"But you can't use local law enforcement to help you," he told his agents. "This agency needs to track this man down independently."

"Why are we looking for him, sir?" one of the agents asked.

Levy knew the men who worked for him resented him. He'd been brought in from the outside, elevated immediately to a senior position, and had an incredible amount of power—power that was disproportionate to his position. But they'd follow his orders—they were afraid not to—and they'd accept whatever explanation he gave them.

Answering the agent's question, he said, "DeMarco has been identified as a credible threat to Pentagon security. Why he's a threat is classified. Just find him, but don't approach him until you've talked to me."

DeMarco decided not to call Diane Carlucci from his room at the Day's Inn. He thought he could trust her but he wasn't sure how she'd react to what he was about to tell her, and she might decide to trace the call. But what he was really afraid of was the NSA tracing the call. He didn't know how they'd know about the call if he called from a randomly selected phone but he'd become so paranoid about NSA capabilities that he wasn't willing to take any chances.

He walked over to the window and peered through a crack in the drapes. Across the street from the Day's Inn, just on the other side of the Jefferson Davis Highway, was a Hyatt Regency. That would work.

The snooty-looking clerk at the Hyatt's registration desk gave him a dirty look when DeMarco entered the hotel—which was not surprising considering his wrinkled, oversized sweat suit attire—but the clerk didn't stop him when he walked over to a bank of pay phones.

"This is Agent Carlucci."

"Diane, it's Joe."

"Uh, Joe, how are you doing?"

She was obviously surprised to hear from him and she also sounded somewhat guarded, maybe thinking that he was calling to try and rekindle their affair. She had no idea that sex was the last thing on his mind.

"Diane, I need to see you. Right away."

"Why?"

"I can't tell you over the phone."

She didn't say anything. He was obviously going to have to tell her more to get her to drop whatever she was doing and come to him.

"Diane, this isn't about us. All I can tell you is that I can't talk about it on the phone, it involves the Bureau, and it's serious. Really serious. And I need you to meet me. I can't come to you."

Diane still didn't say anything. One thing he knew about her was that when it came to her career, she wasn't going to take chances.

"Diane, you know me. You know I wouldn't ask you to do something like this if it wasn't important. And like I said, it involves the Bureau, and not in a good way."

"All right, Joe. Where do you want to meet?"

DeMarco thought about that for a second. He didn't want to meet her too close to where he was staying. "Rosslyn," he said. "There's a little coffee shop on Wilson Boulevard, close to the metro station, called the Java Hut. How long will it take you to get there?"

"An hour. I can't make it any sooner."

"Okay, see you in an hour," DeMarco said, and hung up before she could change her mind.

He didn't know what Diane would do after he talked to her but at least someone else would know what the hell was going on. And once he told her Hopper had been killed, she'd do something—DeMarco didn't know what—but something.

He started to leave the phone booth, but then something else occurred to him. Last night he'd been desperate to escape from Dillon's thugs and running to Perry Wallace had been the best, most expedient solution. But this morning he also remembered that he'd called Perry just a couple of days ago to ask about Mahoney's condition and that phone call, more than anything else, would have led the NSA right to Perry's doorstep. The consequence of all this was that to save his own hide DeMarco had selfishly gotten Perry involved in this whole, deadly NSA affair and he wondered if Dillon's goons had Perry's wide-bodied frame in a little room somewhere, twisting his nuts to make him talk.

Perry wasn't a good friend, but he didn't deserve that.

Since he didn't know Dillon's phone number, DeMarco called directory assistance and was surprised to find that the NSA had a listed number, just like they were some sort of normal government agency.

"You got an old spook there named Dillon," DeMarco said to the NSA operator. "I'm pretty sure that's his first name. I need to talk to him."

"Sir," the operator said, "I have no idea who you want to speak to. This is a very large agency and I—"

"Lady, listen to me before you hang up. This guy Dillon is in his sixties, tall, white hair, dresses like a million bucks. He's probably six hundred pay grades above you and he's trying to find me. He will have you fired if you don't put this call through to him. Now I know you can't possibly know everybody at the NSA, but Dillon's not a common first name and, like I said, this guy's a big shot. *Somebody* will know him. Now I'm just gonna wait five minutes, and if I'm not talking to him before five minutes are up, I'm gonna hang up and you're gonna get fired."

DeMarco meant what he said: calling Dillon was dangerous and there was no way he was going to wait longer than five minutes. He knew that as soon as Dillon came on the line and realized DeMarco was on the other end, he'd trace the call and dispatch a bunch of armed thugs to pick him up. But DeMarco figured that unless the thugs were eating breakfast at the Hyatt, they wouldn't be able to get to him in five minutes and he'd be gone before they arrived. He hoped.

Three minutes later, he heard Dillon say, "Good morning, Joe. Where are you?"

"You know damn good and well where I am," DeMarco said, "and in two minutes I'm gonna be gone."

Dillon chuckled. "You're right, of course. I do know where you are. But really, Joe, you're safe from us. You are not safe from General Bradford's people, however. Your life is in danger. So just stay there and someone will be by shortly to pick you up."

"I don't think so," DeMarco said. "Last night you almost got me killed. Anyway, the reason I called is I borrowed a car from a guy I know because I figured you had tracking devices on my car."

"Yes, we're aware Mr. Wallace assisted you."

"Well, that's why I called. I wanted to tell you that I didn't tell Wallace anything. He doesn't know about Bradford or Breed or Hopper or anything else. I just told him I was in trouble and needed a car—and that's all I told him. So if you guys are holding Wallace and interrogating him, you need to let him go."

"Joe, who do you think we are, the Gestapo? We spoke to Mr. Wallace early this morning, very politely, and he told us he had loaned you a vehicle. We have no intention of troubling him any further. But you need to let us bring you in, Joe. I wasn't being melodramatic when I said your life was in danger."

"I don't think so," DeMarco said again. "But that's the other reason I called. I want you to know I have no intention of talking to the press or anybody else about what happened last night. I did what you wanted by meeting with Hopper and now I'm just gonna lay low and wait for this thing between you and Bradford to blow over."

Lying to Dillon didn't bother him at all.

"Claire," Dillon said into his phone, "DeMarco just called me."

"Why'd he call?"

"He called to tell me that his friend Mr. Wallace has no idea where he is and to assure me he's not planning to talk to the press. At any rate, he called from the Hyatt in Crystal City. Find him, Claire. Use a satellite, assuming we have one that's functioning."

Dillon let Claire absorb that little barb before he added, "Oh, and Claire, do one other thing. Check the phone he used at the Hyatt. See if he called anyone else."

DeMarco needed to get to Rosslyn, which was about four miles from the Hyatt. Since Dillon knew he was driving Perry's ancient pickup, he imagined a flock of NSA geeks were watching traffic cameras so he couldn't drive to Rosslyn, and the nearest metro stop was at least a mile from where he was. He decided the easiest thing would be to take a cab.

There were four cabs waiting in front of the hotel, and he started to approach the first one in the taxi line—and then realized he didn't have enough money to take a cab. He'd had about a hundred and twenty bucks when he'd checked into the Day's Inn last night and now had four bucks left. And he was hungry. He needed money.

He ran back into the Hyatt and used the hotel's ATM. He knew Dillon's people would be able to see that he'd used the machine, but he figured that didn't matter because they already knew where he was because of the phone call he'd made to Dillon. Once he had the money he'd split, and unless the NSA had somehow managed to stick a GPS device up his ass when he wasn't looking, Dillon's guys shouldn't be able to track him.

Two minutes later, he was in a cab and on his way to Rosslyn.

Claire assigned Gilbert to see if DeMarco had called anyone other than Dillon from the phone booth at the Hyatt. She then dispatched Alice and three other agents toward Crystal City. She knew DeMarco wouldn't still be at the Hyatt but she figured he'd be someplace close by and she wanted Alice headed in that direction so once they located him, Alice would be there to pick him up. And Claire knew she'd locate the bastard shortly—particularly with a satellite at her disposal.

Five minutes later she acquired the satellite she needed, and after that it was a thing of beauty, the way her technicians worked. They took a satellite image of the greater D.C. area at the exact time DeMarco had called Dillon and displayed the image on a screen in the operations room. They zoomed in until the image showed the Crystal City area. They zoomed in again until they were looking at the entrance to the Hyatt. Then they ran time forward and saw, looking down from the stratosphere, DeMarco walking out of the Hyatt and getting into a taxicab. They ran time forward again and watched DeMarco exit the cab in Rosslyn near the metro station and enter a McDonald's. Two minutes later, Claire was watching DeMarco in real time, looking like a bum in his baggy gray sweat shirt, munching on a breakfast burrito, trudging up Nash Street toward Wilson Boulevard.

Claire sat back and smiled.

The smile lasted about three seconds,

"Claire," Gilbert said, "right before DeMarco called Dillon a call was made from that same phone booth to an FBI agent named Diane Carlucci."

"Aw, shit."

Two seconds later, another technician turned away from his monitor and said, "Claire, DeMarco used an ATM at the Hyatt before he left there."

"Oh, that idiot!"

"He used an ATM when he was at the Hyatt," Claire said.

"That's not good," Dillon said.

"Yeah, but that's not the worst news. Right before he called you, it looks like he called an FBI agent named Diane Carlucci."

Dillon closed his eyes briefly, then opened them and said, "How long was he on the phone with her?"

"Thirty-eight seconds."

"He couldn't have told her the whole story in that amount of time. He probably set up a meeting with her. Carlucci must be someone he trusts at the Bureau, maybe someone he's worked with before."

"Do you want me to find out?"

"No, we don't have time for that. Find out what Carlucci knows and stop her from meeting with DeMarco."

"And how do you propose I do that?" Claire asked.

"Talk to the woman, Claire. Be convincing."

Walking back into the operations room, Claire said, "Where's DeMarco now?"

Using a laser pointer, Gilbert placed a red dot on the front entrance of a building that was visible on the wall-mounted screen. The image of the building was coming from the satellite they'd used to follow DeMarco.

"He's right there," the tech said, "in that coffee shop."

"Good. Stay on the bastard," she said.

Claire went into her office, shut the door, and dialed a phone number.

"This is Agent Carlucci."

"Agent, my name is Claire Whiting. I work for the National Security Agency."

"Five minutes ago DeMarco used his ATM card at the Hyatt Regency in Crystal City," Perkins said.

"Good work, Perkins," Levy said. He sat for a moment, thinking, and then said, "Fax a photograph of DeMarco to the front desk of the Hyatt. I'll take it from there."

Levy waited three minutes and called the Hyatt. "This is Agent Douglas Kirk, United States Secret Service."

The person at the Hyatt who'd answered the phone inhaled sharply and said, "What?"—the reaction you'd expect from a person who's just been told he's talking to the Secret Service.

"This is urgent," Levy said, "and involves the protection of the president of the United States. You've just been faxed a photograph of a man. Do you have the fax?"

"Lemme see," the man said. Two minutes later he was back on the line, sounding breathless. "Yeah, I've got it. What's this about?"

"Do you recognize the man in the photo?"

"Oh, my God! He was here just a few minutes ago. He used a pay phone."

"Did he use the ATM?"

"Yeah. How did you know that?"

"Did you see where he went after he used the ATM?"

"He left the hotel."

"In which direction was he headed?"

"I don't know. I can't see outside the hotel from the front desk. But wait a minute. I'll go ask the parking valet." A moment later the clerk was back on the phone. "The valet said he caught a cab."

"Which cab company?"

"He just said it was a maroon-colored taxi."

"Thank you, sir. We appreciate your help." Levy hung up and immediately called Perkins. "Perkins, DeMarco took a maroon-colored cab from the Hyatt after he used the ATM. Figure out which company he used and find out where the cab took him."

"Yes, sir."

"Agent Carlucci," Claire said, "you received a phone call from a man named Joseph DeMarco about fifteen minutes ago."

"How do you know that?" Diane said.

"Did you hear what I said when I introduced myself? I said I work for the National Security Agency. We've been watching DeMarco."

There was a pause as Carlucci absorbed that shocking nugget. "Why?" she asked.

"I can't tell you," Claire said. "You don't have need to know."

"How do I know you're NSA?"

"You mean other than the fact that I know DeMarco called you? Well, call the agency. We're in the book. Ask for me. Or call anyone you know at the NSA and have them verify I work here."

"I don't know anyone at the NSA."

"Agent Carlucci, I need to know what DeMarco told you."

"If you know he called me, why don't you know what he said?"

"Because we didn't have a warrant to tap the phone he was using. Now will you please tell me what he told you, or do you want my director to call your director?"

Carlucci went silent again, probably thinking: *Go ahead. Call my director*. Claire had already gotten the impression that there was some steel in Carlucci and she wasn't going to be able to walk right over her.

"Okay, Carlucci," Claire said. "I probably shouldn't be telling you this but . . ."

Claire was treading on dangerous ground here. She didn't know what DeMarco might have told Carlucci, but she agreed with Dillon that he wasn't on the phone long enough to have told her the whole story.

". . . but DeMarco has been dating a woman who works for the CIA and this woman is currently in Afghanistan. The other night she called DeMarco. We know this because we monitor almost all communications coming from that part of the world. Well, what DeMarco's lady friend passed on to him is controversial. Politically controversial. And it involves the CIA, the NSA, and high-ranking members of the U.S. military. I'm sorry to be so cryptic, but that's all I can tell you."

"Joe said it involved the FBI."

"Only in a peripheral way. DeMarco's girlfriend disagrees with what her superiors are doing in Afghanistan regarding a particular operation and when her chain of command wouldn't listen to her she spoke to the FBI's legal attaché in Kabul. The attaché had the good sense to know this was not an issue in which he should get involved, he told Ms. DiCapria's superiors that she was talking out of school, and now Ms. DiCapria is in hot water, both legally and professionally."

"And if I call our legal attaché in Kabul, he'll confirm this?" Carlucci said.

"No, he won't," Claire said. "This operation is highly classified and strictly need to know. But I imagine five minutes after you talk the attaché, the FBI's Office of Professional Responsibility will be in your office asking how it is you happen to have information on this subject."

"Why would Joe call me about this?"

"I won't know that until you tell me what he said to you."

Claire held her breath until Carlucci responded.

"All he said was that he needed to see me, that he couldn't talk on the phone, and that it involved the FBI."

"That's all he said?"

"Yes."

Thank God!

"The only thing I can assume, Agent Carlucci, is that DeMarco's trying to help his girlfriend. May I ask what your relationship is with DeMarco?"

"We were involved with each other about three years ago but I'm married now."

"I see," Claire said. "Well, all I can think is that DeMarco is trying to take advantage of your former relationship. Agent, I can't order you not to meet with DeMarco, but believe me when I tell you that doing so would not be a career-enhancing move."

Carlucci didn't say anything.

"When were you supposed to meet him?"

"In half an hour."

"Where?" Claire said.

"I thought you guys were following him," Carlucci said.

Claire almost laughed. Carlucci was testing her.

"We are. Right now he's sitting in a coffee shop in Rosslyn on Wilson Boulevard."

"That's where we're supposed to meet," Carlucci said.

"Okay, Agent. Thank you for your cooperation and, again, I want to stress that it's not in your best interest to get involved in this."

Claire had no idea if Carlucci would call the FBI's legal attaché in Kabul or meet with DeMarco, but her gut told her that she wouldn't do either of those things. All that really mattered at this point was that she knew that DeMarco hadn't told Carlucci anything significant—and she needed to get him out of that coffee shop.

"Sir," Perkins said, "the cab dropped him off in Rosslyn, near the metro station."

"Did he go into the station?" Levy asked.

"No. He went into the McDonald's near the metro but he's not there now."

"All right, Perkins. I want you to get four cars over to Rosslyn and start looking for him. Tell your men when they find him that they're not to talk to him. I want DeMarco tossed into a car and I want your people to remain outside the car until I get there."

"Claire," Gilbert said, "we're picking up radio traffic from Pentagon police vehicles. They're searching Rosslyn for DeMarco."

Shit. She knew that was going to happen. Levy's men had seen DeMarco use the ATM at the Hyatt, found out from the Hyatt's people that he'd taken a cab, and it was a cakewalk from there. The good news was they didn't know exactly where DeMarco was. But if DeMarco left the coffee shop—which he would do eventually when Carlucci didn't show up—the Pentagon cops might spot him walking on the street.

"Where's Alice?" Claire said.

"She's still ten minutes from Rosslyn."

"What the hell is taking her so long?"

"Traffic."

Even the NSA couldn't do anything about the traffic.

"Connect me to that coffee shop," Claire said.

DeMarco looked at his wrist to check the time, and realized he no longer had a watch. He asked a lady sitting near him for the time and she told him—but made it clear that she wasn't interested in starting up a conversation with an unshaven guy dressed like an escapee from a poor man's gymnasium. Diane was late. Only ten minutes late, but she'd always been a punctuality freak. Maybe she'd gotten held up in traffic.

"Sir, is your name Joe DeMarco?"

DeMarco had been looking out the window. He turned to see who was speaking and saw it wasn't the lady who had reluctantly given him the time. It was the barista, a cute gal in her twenties—but she really should lose the nose ring.

"Uh, yeah," he said, but he was wondering how the girl knew his name. He'd been in the place a couple of times but had never introduced himself. The hairs on the back of his neck began to stand at attention.

"You have a phone call," the barista said.

"A phone call?"

"Yeah. Some lady. She said it's real important."

It must be Diane calling, probably to tell him that she'd been delayed—or maybe to say that she'd changed her mind about meeting him.

"Sir, do you want to take the call?"

"Yeah, I'll take it," DeMarco said. He walked over to the counter and picked up the phone. "Hey, Diane, are you on your way?" he said.

"This isn't Diane."

Oh, shit, if it wasn't Diane, it could only be the NSA. Goddammit! How in the *fuck* did they find him?

"Is this you, Alice?" DeMarco asked. "How did you find me here?"

"It's not Alice, it's Alice's boss—and how we found you is irrelevant. All you need to know is that the Pentagon Force Protection Agency is cruising Rosslyn looking for you, and the Pentagon cops work for John Levy."

"Who's Levy?"

"He's the man who tried to kill you last night at Tuckahoe Park." Before DeMarco could ask another question, the woman said, "You have a choice to make, DeMarco. You can either stay in that coffee shop—"

"Goddammit, how did you know where I was?" DeMarco asked again.

"As I was saying, you can either stay in the coffee shop and wait until we pick you up or you can take your chances with Charles Bradford's people. You have to believe me, DeMarco. We are your best option. We are your only option. And keep in mind, we're the ones who kept Levy from killing you last night. If we wanted you dead, you'd already be dead. So what's it going to be?"

DeMarco didn't answer.

"And one other thing, DeMarco. Agent Carlucci is not going to be meeting with you."

Son of a bitch! DeMarco had never believed any of that paranoid Big Brother nonsense the antigovernment crowd was always spouting—but he'd become a true believer in the last few days.

And he'd had enough. He was sick of these people controlling his life.

"I'll tell you what I'm gonna do. I'm going to call the Arlington P.D., a detective named Glazer I know over there. I'm going to tell him the FBI and the NSA are covering up why my cousin was killed, and that you guys are trying to kidnap me. And after I talk to the cop I'm gonna call the closest TV station. Then I'm going to hold a fucking press conference while I'm being protected by a bunch of SWAT guys. Oh, and one other thing. I've got a .38 in my pocket—I got it from Perry Wallace last night—and if Alice's pals come through the door, I'm gonna shoot 'em if they try to take me out of here."

How do you like them apples, you bitch?

"DeMarco, the landline you're currently using will be dead the minute you hang up. And if you or anyone else in that shop has a cell phone, you'll find that the cell phone isn't getting a signal. I repeat: we are your only option."

DeMarco didn't answer but at that moment he saw a Pentagon patrol car cruise slowly past the coffee shop, the two officers inside it swiveling their heads as they looked at pedestrians on the sidewalk. He quickly turned so his back was to the window.

"And one other thing, DeMarco. If you don't cooperate, somebody is going to whisper into the ear of the Afghanistan government that a certain CIA agent is playing around in their backyard. So I'm not screwing around here. You either do what I tell you or your girlfriend is going to become a gigantic embarrassment to the CIA and an international headline—and that's the best-case scenario."

"You goddamn—"

DeMarco stopped swearing and took a breath.

"Okay," he said. "I'll wait for your people to get here."

"Alice will be there in five minutes. She'll park in front of the shop but don't go to her until she signals you. Do you understand?"

"Yeah, I understand," DeMarco said. He was so tired of this; he had never felt more impotent in his life.

A couple minutes later he saw a black SUV double-park in front of the coffee shop, but since the vehicle's windows were tinted he couldn't see who was in it. Then the passenger-side window powered down. It was Alice. He watched as she looked around and then saw her speak into the phone mike protruding from the headset she always seemed to be wearing. He wondered if she slept with that thing on. She still hadn't looked over at the coffee shop. She just kept checking the street around her, talking to someone, and then she finally turned and faced him and made an arm motion for him to join her in the car.

DeMarco hustled out of the coffee shop and jumped into Alice's SUV. Alice immediately said, "Buckle your seat belt."

Without thinking, DeMarco looked down to find the seat-belt latch and when he did Alice pressed a Taser against his throat.

"Give me the gun, DeMarco."

"I don't have a gun. I just said that."

Holding the Taser against his throat, Alice ran her hands over his torso, behind his back, down his legs. She was close enough to him that he could smell the scent of the shampoo she used. When she finished patting him down, she said, "Okay. But if you give me any shit at all, I'm gonna run fifty thousand volts through you just for the fun of it."

DeMarco had always liked women—with the possible exception of his ex-wife—but after meeting Alice and talking to Alice's unnamed boss, his perspective was beginning to change.

35

Dillon had always been rather indifferent toward automobiles, and he didn't enjoy driving at all. It was just too frantic—the stop-and-go traffic, the maniacs constantly switching lanes, honking, maneuvering for position. He took cabs as often as possible. Today, however, he decided to drive himself.

It had always been a Crane family tradition to own Jaguars, and he owned a maroon XJ-Series sedan that sold for about ninety thousand with all the bells and whistles. Naturally, his had all the bells and whistles. He drove out the gates of Fort Meade and headed toward Washington, D.C. He had decided to go to the National Mall to ponder on Charles Bradford as it seemed the perfect place to make a decision that would indeed affect the nation.

Dillon may have come across as a jaded cynic but he was, in fact, terribly sentimental when it came to the National Mall. It symbolized all that was good and great about America: her past, her glory, her promise. The long, broad expanse between the Capitol and Lincoln's memorial, Washington's obelisk, Jefferson's temple, the memorials to those who had died in war, the magnificent buildings surrounding the mall containing art and history and the machinery of democracy . . . After all these years, the sight still took his breath away.

He parked near the Vietnam Veterans Memorial, in front of a fire hydrant. He didn't care if he got a ticket but he didn't want the car towed, and to prevent that from happening he placed a placard on the dashboard that read FEDERAL BUREAU OF INVESTIGATION. TOWING OR TAMPERING WITH THIS VEHICLE IS A CLASS B FELONY. The placard had the FBI's official seal on it.

Dillon had no idea what a class B felony was, or if there even was such a thing, but the sign had worked in the past. Traffic enforcement folks probably figured an FBI agent who drove a Jag was someone special.

He took a slim leather briefcase out of the car and began to walk.

He sincerely believed, as he had told Claire, that exposing Charles Bradford would be disastrous for the country. The United States was not well regarded in large parts of the world, and even our allies believed that to safeguard our fragile economy, much less our security, we wouldn't hesitate to subvert any regime that posed a threat. Dillon imagined citizens in other countries would not even be surprised that an American general went about assassinating high-ranking foreigners.

Dillon also had to admit he agreed with most of Bradford's decisions—not the executions themselves but the fact that the men Bradford killed had indeed been national security menaces. It could be argued that Bradford had acted without proper authority and shouldn't have acted unilaterally, but it was clearly better to eliminate a single foreigner than go to war. How many American lives could have been saved if a single well-placed bullet had been used to fell Saddam?

He didn't concur, however, with Bradford killing American citizens whom he considered traitors. Morality aside, if it ever became known that Bradford had assassinated fellow Americans, every bleeding-heart liberal in the country—as well as every right-leaning anti-government militia nut—would have all the evidence they needed to justify their paranoia.

By the time he reached the Lincoln Memorial, Dillon found himself in exactly the same position where Martin Breed had been before he died. He saw the *logic* in the things Charles Bradford had done but knew in his heart that the man had gone too far. He also knew if Bradford remained in power that the assassinations would continue and the possible unintended consequences could be disastrous. As Claire had said, Bradford could actually start the war he was trying to prevent if he killed the wrong foreign politician.

Dillon's thoughts were interrupted by a peal of laughter from a small girl, the sound of a child absolutely delighted by something. He looked over and saw a man his age holding the hand of a girl of four or five: a grandfather taking his granddaughter for a walk. The little girl was pointing a short, chubby finger at a fat, waddling pigeon.

Dillon had never even come close to getting married. He knew he'd make a terrible husband. And the thought of rearing children . . . well, that was absolutely terrifying. Yet for some reason after his sixtieth birthday, he occasionally wished that he had a grandchild to spoil, and preferably a granddaughter. It was an irrational desire.

But back to Charles Bradford.

Dillon was too objective not to recognize his own hypocrisy. What Bradford had done was in a way no different than what he and Claire were doing. Bradford had taken it upon himself to decide who America's enemies were and then he eliminated them. Dillon, although he didn't kill people—Hopper was the only exception—had taken it upon himself to invade the privacy of American citizens and trample on their constitutional rights. But Dillon knew there was a wavy gray line out there and he believed he was on the right side of that line, whereas Charles Bradford had stepped over it. Way over it. Was he deluding himself? Maybe. Nonetheless, he had made up his mind: Bradford had to go.

He stopped at a bench in front of the Lincoln Memorial, wiped off the bench with a handkerchief, and sat down, crossing his long legs. "What would you do, Abe?" he said, softly but out loud.

Abe didn't answer.

As he had told Claire, he wasn't convinced that releasing the Breed recording would be enough to force Bradford to resign, much less convict him of a crime. Unless John Levy was willing to testify against Bradford, which Dillon couldn't imagine him doing, there was no concrete evidence to support Martin Breed's claims. And Dillon could foresee congressional hearings going on for months, if not years, resulting in a national quagmire proportional to Watergate and possibly concluding with Bradford still in uniform and more popular than ever in some political circles.

Then there was the problem that exposing Bradford would most likely result in revealing the NSA's role in Bradford's downfall. That would be a calamity for the agency, and not just a public relations nightmare. If what Dillon and Claire were doing was uncovered, it could possibly result in the complete dismantlement of America's most effective intelligence organization. He couldn't allow that to happen. He *wouldn't* allow that to happen.

So how would he do it? How would he, Dillon Crane, remove General Charles Bradford, Chairman of the Joint Chiefs, without exposing either Bradford or himself?

The answer, he was convinced, was John Levy.

From his briefcase he took out the file on Levy that Claire had compiled. He'd already read it twice and knew every word in it, but he read it again, hoping something would leap out at him.

The psychic impact of Levy's tragic family history was obvious. When Levy was two, his father's helicopter was shot down on some spy mission at the beginning of the Vietnam conflict—before the United States was even officially at war—and the body was never recovered. His brother, who was several years older than Levy, enlisted in the army at age eighteen, and then he also disappeared in Vietnam during the final days of that terrible war. Like his father, Levy's brother was MIA, presumed dead, and no body was ever recovered. So it was no mystery as to why John Levy joined the army, nor was it a mystery why he became one of the sentinels at the Tomb of the Unknowns. The unnamed bodies in the tombs at Arlington *were* his father and his brother.

But Dillon believed that, for Levy, being a tomb guard was meaningful on another level. There was a religious aspect to being a sentinel but, instead of praying matins and vespers, the sentinels put on a uniform and walked at a measured pace in front of an unnamed corpse. The young men who guarded the Tomb of the Unknowns, like all those deeply committed to a particular faith, willingly dedicated themselves to ritual and sacrifice and a higher calling—and none was more dedicated than young John Levy. But Levy needed something more: he needed someone to replace his dead father, his dead brother. And when he met Charles Bradford at the time Bradford commanded the Old Guard, he found that person and later devoted himself totally to Bradford and his cause.

And that, Dillon believed, was the key to Bradford's undoing: Levy's blind, unswerving, religious devotion to a man who had become his father, his priest, his god.

36

DeMarco was going out of his mind with boredom, and at the same time he couldn't relax or sleep because he couldn't find a way to wiggle out of the box he was in.

They'd stuck him in a farmhouse west of Havre de Grace, Maryland. There were fifty barren acres surrounding the house, and he figured the land was never planted with anything that grew taller than lettuce so anyone approaching the place could be seen while they were still half a mile away.

Three men were guarding him, all guys in their thirties built like light heavyweights—and they were armed. And while one slept, the other two were always awake. DeMarco figured the only way he'd get away from them was if he had a hand grenade or if they had simultaneous heart attacks. They were rude bastards, too. They played gin most of the time but didn't include him in the game, and the only time they talked to him was to call him to dinner.

There was a TV in the farmhouse but it got only two channels. He would have thought that the NSA, being who they were, could have at least pirated a cable feed. And the only thing to read was a stack of old newspapers. He was going to hang himself if he had to stay in the place another day.

He flopped down on the couch and picked up one of the papers again, even though he'd already read every word in it. One article was about Martin Breed and showed photos of the high-ranking folk who had attended his funeral. DeMarco looked at the photos again but this time saw something he hadn't noticed before. There was an old guy in a wheelchair sitting near Charles Bradford. He studied the caption that identified the people in the picture, and then read the article again. Huh.

DeMarco heard a car coming up the driveway. He looked out the window and saw Dillon unfolding his long, lean form from the backseat of a black SUV. Dillon just stood there for a moment, looking out at the barren fields as if he were wondering why the NSA's crop was so poor. Finally, he turned and walked toward the house, and DeMarco heard his guards yes-siring the guy as he entered.

"Good morning, Joe," Dillon said. Then, after inquiring about DeMarco's health and pretending to apologize for keeping him prisoner, he got down to business. "I want you to meet with Charles Bradford," he said.

"You betcha," DeMarco said, sounding as if it would be the most natural thing in the world for him to drop in on the chairman of the Joint Chiefs. "You mind if I go home and change into my good suit for the meeting?"

DeMarco was no longer wearing the sweat clothes he'd borrowed from Perry Wallace. When Alice found his car abandoned in Falls Church, she'd been kind enough to retrieve his clothes as well as his wallet, watch, and cell phone. But the clothes were a mess since he'd been wearing them when he was shot by Levy and crawled around under the bleachers.

Dillon ignored DeMarco's sarcastic comment about changing into a suit. "I obviously can't meet with Bradford," Dillon said. "The agency's involvement in all this must be kept completely secret. I'm sure you understand."

"Oh, yeah, I understand," DeMarco said.

But he was thinking that maybe what he should do is grab Dillon and put a choke hold on him and threaten to break his neck if they didn't let him go. But then what? He'd finally figured out how they had tracked him last time: a satellite. He'd seen in movies how a satellite orbiting a zillion miles above the earth was able to take close-up pictures of a pimple on a terrorist's nose, and that's what they'd used to follow him. They knew he'd made a phone call from the Hyatt in Crystal City and then they'd parked some big-ass satellite right over his head and watched his every move. Now that he knew how they followed him, he might be able to evade them next time. Yeah, he could live in the sewers for the rest of his life.

Maybe it would be a good idea to quit being a smart-ass and listen to what Dillon had to say.

"And assuming the general will meet with me, exactly what am I supposed to say to him?" DeMarco asked.

"You won't have to say much. I simply want you to play General Breed's recording for him. Then you can tell him that you know he had your cousin and the reporter killed, and you suspect he had Martin Breed killed as well. And then tell him he needs to resign."

"And that's it? I just waltz in, play the recording, and he says: I give up, Joe. You got me. I'll pack up my desk today."

"No, the tape alone won't be enough to convince him. There are problems with the tape."

"Like the fact that Bradford's last name is never mentioned."

"Yes, like that," Dillon said. Dillon didn't tell DeMarco the recording he had found in the church had been modified.

"So what's going to make Bradford fold?" DeMarco asked.

"You're going to tell him that you know John Levy. . . ."

"The guy who tried to kill me at the ball field?"

"Yes. Levy is Bradford's creature. My people followed him when he left Tuckahoe Park and identified him. At any rate, you're going to tell General Bradford that we have Levy cold. We have voice recordings of him. We have witnesses who saw him shoot you. You'll tell Bradford if he doesn't resign, you'll inform the press and people in Congress, turn over everything you have to the FBI, and Levy will be arrested for murder and forced to admit that he was—and has been for years—operating under Bradford's control."

DeMarco shook his head. "If I know all those things, Bradford's going to wonder why I haven't already gone to the press and why I'm bothering to talk to him at all."

"No, he won't wonder that," Dillon said, "because by now he knows you're working with other people in the government. And he'll realize that those people don't *want* his activities exposed. So you need to convince him, Joe. You need to make him believe that we'll expose him if we're forced to but that we don't want to. It's not good for the country."

"Why not?" DeMarco asked.

"It's complicated, but take my word for it. Exposing Charles Bradford is bad for the country. And it's bad for the NSA."

Dillon was telling DeMarco to leave the heavy thinking to him—and DeMarco thought Dillon was full of shit.

"You think it's going to be that easy?" DeMarco said. "I just tell Bradford that Levy is going to roll over on him, and he crumbles?"

"People like Charles Bradford don't crumble. But he knows the damage this could do to the military, not to mention his own legacy. Charles Bradford wants to be remembered as a great American general—but not in this way. So if you're convincing, he'll believe Levy will be arrested and forced to testify against him, and he'll also believe that even though we don't want to expose him, we will if he doesn't resign."

DeMarco sat there, thinking about everything Dillon had told him, and shook his head again. "I don't think so," he said. "There's no reason for me to be involved in this any longer. Anybody can play those tapes for Bradford and deliver your message. Get one of your people to do it. Put Alice in a disguise. I don't care how you do it, but I want out of this."

"Sorry, Joe, but we're going to do this my way. Right now only three people know what Martin Breed said about Bradford on that recording: me, you, and an associate of mine. I don't intend for our small circle to grow any larger. And since neither my associate nor I can meet with Bradford, you've been drafted."

DeMarco opened his mouth to protest but Dillon raised a hand to stop him. "You need to keep in mind, Joe, that by now Bradford knows who you are and the only reason you're still alive is because I'm protecting you. But if you don't do as I ask then I'll have no reason to protect you, and Bradford's people—this monster Levy or somebody just like him—will hunt you down. Think about *who* your enemy is, Joe. He's the leader of the most powerful military force on the planet. How hard do you think it's going to be for him to find you and kill you?"

DeMarco didn't say anything, but if he'd ever thought that Dillon, because of his appearance, was in any way soft, he just disposed of that notion. Dillon would sacrifice him in a heartbeat if that's what he thought he needed to do.

"I'll protect you until Bradford resigns," Dillon said. "But *you're* going to deal with him. So, have we reached an accord? Are we on the same page? Before you answer, remember the problems we can cause your CIA friend in Afghanistan."

DeMarco wanted to break Dillon's aristocratic nose, but all he said was, "Yeah, we're on the same page."

"Good. Now, you were asking earlier if you should go home and get your good suit. Alice, can you come in, please?"

Alice must have driven Dillon to the safe house. She walked into the room, her face as expressionless as always, carrying a man's dark blue suit on a hanger in her right hand. Under her left arm was a black belt and a new white dress shirt still in its packaging, and in her left hand, a pair of black shoes appropriate for the suit.

"Put on the jacket, Joe," Dillon said.

Alice handed DeMaro the suit coat and he put it on. It fit perfectly. "How'd you know my size?" he asked.

Alice gave him a look that said, *You've got to be kidding.* It was the most emotion he'd ever seen the woman display.

"That coat," Dillon said, "*is* an eavesdropping device. It records and transmits and has its own power supply. When you go to Bradford's office, you'll be searched for weapons and listening devices but the devices in the coat will not be activated at that time. If they are activated, they'll be detected when you're searched. So the key to this operation is timing. You must get in to see Bradford no later than a specific time as the devices in the coat will automatically power-up at that time."

"And how am I supposed to do that?"

"Don't worry. We have that figured out. And one other thing, Joe. You'll note there are three buttons sewn on the right sleeve of the coat but only two on the left. We don't think Bradford's security people will notice the difference, but if they do you'll just tell them a button fell off. You see the little bits of thread from the missing button on the left cuff?"

DeMarco looked down at the brass buttons. They all looked the same and they all looked like ordinary buttons to him.

"Before you leave his office, Joe, you need to pull the top button off the right sleeve and drop it on the floor someplace where it won't be stepped on."

"You want me to plant a bug in the office of the chairman of the Joint Chiefs?" DeMarco said.

"Exactly," Dillon said.

"Do you really think Bradford will resign?" Claire said later, when she was alone with Dillon.

"Oh, no," Dillon said. "I'm sure he won't."

"Then why on earth are you sending DeMarco to him and giving him everything we know?"

Dillon just smiled.

God, she just *hated* it when he did that.

37

DeMarco found a parking place in the vast lot surrounding the Pentagon. Dillon had provided the car he was using, and it had all the appropriate decals to permit him to drive onto the lot. He'd been somewhat surprised that Dillon had let him drive himself to the meeting, but since Dillon had him and his car bugged, and probably had a satellite watching from above, and had Alice tailing him, Dillon probably wasn't too worried about DeMarco taking off like he had last time. He concluded again that Dillon must have been more concerned about Bradford's people seeing someone drop him off than he was about letting DeMarco drive himself.

He stepped out of the car and pulled out the cell phone that Alice had provided. Dillon had insisted that DeMarco not take his own cell phone to the Pentagon, which meant, DeMarco was pretty sure, that his own cell phone was bugged. He called the phone number he'd been given which, according to Dillon, would be answered by Bradford's secretary and not some voice mail system. And sure enough.

"Good morning. This is Mrs. Cleary."

"Hi, Mrs. Cleary. My name's Joe DeMarco, and I need to see General Bradford right away. He'll want to see me."

"Mr. DeMarco, I don't know who you are or how you got this number, but you don't simply call up and expect to get on the general's schedule."

"Mrs. Cleary, I know the general has nothing scheduled for the next hour. His calendar, the one you have in the computer on your desk, says he's dining alone today and working on some speech he's giving at Fort Hood next week."

"How do you know—"

"Mrs. Cleary, please tell General Bradford I want to talk to him about Paul Russo. Trust me, ma'am, he'll know who I'm talking about and he'll want to see me. Tell him if he doesn't see me, my next stop is *The Washington Post.*"

The phone was silent for a moment.

"Please hold, Mr. DeMarco."

The lady had wonderful manners, and less than two minutes later she was back on the line. "Mr. DeMarco, where are you?"

"Right here at the Pentagon."

"Very well. Go to the security checkpoint at the main entrance. Someone will meet you and escort you to the general's office."

Two Pentagon cops in black fatigues walked DeMarco down the wide hallways of the building. DeMarco had never been in the Pentagon before and was awed by the size of the place, not to mention all the brass walking around. He'd never seen so many generals and admirals in one spot. He was taken to a small room where he was met by two other security guys wearing suits. They ordered him to empty his pockets and to take off his suit coat, belt, and shoes. He removed his wallet, dumped all his spare change into a bowl, and handed the security guys his cell phone and a small digital recorder.

"Take off your watch, too," one of the men said.

As DeMarco removed his watch, he looked at the time. He needed to be in Bradford's office in ten minutes. In ten minutes the listening devices sewn into his suit would be activated.

While one of the men was giving him an embarrassingly thorough frisk, the other one examined his belt, shoes, and suit coat. He ran his hands all over the coat to make sure nothing was sewn inside the lining. He tried to twist the heels off DeMarco's new shoes, but they remained in place. He then took a little circular patch of cotton and rubbed it all over everything: suit, belt, and shoes. And DeMarco's hands. DeMarco assumed the cotton swab was like the type they used at the airport to see if you have explosives in your luggage. Two other electronic gizmos were then passed over him. He guessed one was looking for recording devices as Dillon had told him, but he didn't know what the other gizmo did.

Apparently satisfied, they told him he could put his shoes, belt, and coat back on, but that he wouldn't be permitted to enter Bradford's office with his watch, his cell phone—or the recorder.

"Uh," DeMarco said, "I don't care about the phone or the watch, but I have to take the recorder to the general."

"No, sir," one of the security men said.

"I'd suggest you call General Bradford," DeMarco said. "Tell him that what's on that recorder concerns General Martin Breed and you won't let me bring it to him."

The man gave DeMarco a steely-eyed stare then left the office. Two minutes later he was back and said, "The general says you may bring the recorder with you but we need to examine it first."

"Sure," DeMarco said. "By the way, what time is it?"

The security guy ignored him.

Shit. Without his watch, he couldn't know the exact time but he was pretty sure the recording equipment in the suit coat would activate in a couple more minutes. He hoped they didn't take too long looking at the recorder. They didn't. A young guy came into the room, took the recorder apart, looked at it, poked at it, and put it back together in plenty of time. These guys were good.

DeMarco, like every other TV-watching American, had seen and heard General Charles Bradford before. He was familiar with the boot-camp haircut, the eagle's beak, the rumbling voice that sounded wise and fatherly when he spoke to the public—and he was definitely intimidated.

Charles Bradford was a man who had spent most of his life in an arena that DeMarco couldn't even imagine, must less compete in. He dealt with the president, senators, and cabinet members on a daily basis and, judging by the number of stars on his shoulders and the medals on his uniform, he was exceptional at what he did. And not only that, the guy *looked* like a general; he made DeMarco—who had never been in the military—want to stand at attention and salute. Yeah, he was intimidated—and if he hadn't been, Bradford's opening salvo would have ensured that he was.

"Well, DeMarco," Bradford said, "I'm not exactly sure why I'm meeting with you. I don't know anyone named Russo, but when you said something about going to the *Post,* I decided to listen to what you had to say. But unless you're a very stupid man, I'm sure you understand that threatening me is not a wise thing to do. You're probably going straight from this office to a federal lockup."

"Sir," DeMarco said—he couldn't help but call him sir—"I'd just like you to listen to two recordings. May I play them please?"

Bradford nodded his head, his pale eyes boring into DeMarco's. Bradford's eyes had as much warmth as the point of an ice pick.

When the radio intercept of Paul Russo being killed was finished, Bradford frowned and said, "I have no idea what all that was about, all that carrier and messenger nonsense."

DeMarco didn't bother to respond to Bradford's denial. All he said was, "Now I'll play the second recording, the one made by General Breed before he died."

DeMarco saw it: Bradford's eyes widened in surprise, just for an instant, and he rocked back in his chair. The fact that DeMarco had in his possession a recording made by Breed not only surprised Bradford, it hit him hard.

DeMarco tapped the PLAY button on the recorder, and the voice of a dead general filled the room.

Thomas, this is about things I did for Charles during my career. I know when you hear this you're going to be disappointed in me.

Bradford listened to the recording without any further evidence of emotion. He just sat, his face impassive, his eyes hooded, his big hands steepled under his chin. When DeMarco hit the STOP button, Bradford didn't say anything for a moment.

"DeMarco, it seems to me that you didn't think this blackmail scheme through very well."

"General, I'm not trying to black—"

"That first recording, the one with all the messenger-carrier stuff, there's nothing on it that makes it clear what those men were talking about, much less any connection to me. Regarding the recording you *claim* is General Breed speaking—and by the way, I think you're despicable for trying to soil Martin's name—the recording doesn't mention me by name, it only refers to someone named Charles."

"You're the Charles he's referring to," DeMarco said.

"Really?" Bradford said. "Do you know there's a General Charles Paulson, the four-star at CENTCOM, and that Martin once worked for him? And I'm sure you know Congressman Charles Mallory. He sits on the House Appropriations Committee, and he and Martin attended West Point together. And do you know Charles . . . Oh, never mind. I think I've made my point."

"Sir," DeMarco said, "you can save all that for your court-martial."

Bradford's face reddened at DeMarco's impertinence and he put his hands on the edge of his desk to stand up, but before he could, DeMarco continued, "There's something else you need to know. The man speaking on the first recording, the one controlling the operation, is a man named John Levy. Levy works for you, and a couple of nights ago he tried to kill me at a park in Falls Church. Several people saw him shoot me in the back and the only reason I'm not dead is because I wore a vest. What I'm saying is that Levy is finished. He'll be arrested for Paul Russo's murder and for attempted murder, and when he's arrested, he'll admit he was working for you."

"Who are *you* working for, DeMarco?"

"It doesn't matter. All that matters is that other people know the same things I know. The recordings you heard are copies of the originals."

"Then why don't you go to the media with all this? Why haven't you told those fools in Congress? And why haven't you arrested this man Levy?"

"Because exposing you would be bad for the country, sir. We don't want the rest of the world to know an American general controls a group of assassins and runs around killing whoever he thinks represents a threat."

"You don't have any idea what you're talking about," Bradford snapped. "People like you—" But then he stopped. "What do you want?"

"We want you to resign, sir."

"Resign? Why you *pissant*. If you think I'll give into this sort of blackmail—"

"Sir, these recording are authentic. And I don't care if there are a million guys named Charles, you're the Charles on General Breed's tape." DeMarco stood up. "I'm leaving now, but if I don't read in tomorrow's paper that you're resigning, Levy will be arrested and made to confess. And then everything we have will go to the media and the fools in Congress you mentioned. We don't want to do that, but we will."

DeMarco didn't think Bradford was going to let him leave. He figured the security guys who had frisked him were going to slap handcuffs on his wrists and toss him into a cell in the basement of the Pentagon. Fortunately, they didn't.

As he was leaving Bradford's office, he looked down at the button lying under the chair where he'd been sitting.

38

DeMarco walked slowly through the Pentagon parking lot and got into his car, but he didn't start the engine. He couldn't believe what he'd just done. And he wondered, although at this point it was the least of his problems, if he'd committed a crime by planting an NSA eavesdropping device in Bradford's office. Probably.

"You did a good job, Joe."

DeMarco jerked like he'd been goosed. That damn Dillon had rigged up a speaker in the car so he could talk to DeMarco.

"So what are you going to do when Bradford doesn't resign?" DeMarco said.

Dillon didn't answer the question. Instead he said, "I'd like you to return to the safe house in Maryland, Joe. Do you know how to get there?"

"Yeah," DeMarco said, but he was wondering what would happen if he just made a run for it. But then he thought: a run to where? Where could he run to that Dillon couldn't find him? His next thought was that maybe the safe house was actually the best place for him to be. Bradford had tried to kill him once and now that he'd stuck his finger directly into the man's eye, there was a good chance he might try to kill him again.

"Good," Dillon said. "Then drive back to the safe house. I want you off the street."

DeMarco crossed the Key Bridge into the District and then wound his way to New York Avenue. It would have been faster to take the beltway back to the safe house, but he wasn't in any rush. As he drove, he wondered how many people were following him. A whole bunch, would be his guess. Alice and her NSA pals, and maybe a few of Bradford's people had joined the procession. The whole time he was driving, one question occupied his brain: What the hell was Dillon *really* doing?

There was no way Bradford was going to resign. Just five minutes with the guy, and DeMarco could tell. Bradford was going to fight back, somehow, someway.

But what the hell was Dillon up to? About the only thing Dillon had told him that he believed was that Dillon didn't want to expose Bradford, and DeMarco believed this for one simple reason: for the old spy to expose Bradford, he'd have to expose himself. But Dillon *had* to know Bradford wasn't going to resign. All Dillon had done by playing the recordings for Bradford was tip his hand. Bradford now knew everything Dillon knew.

So what was Dillon doing?

DeMarco didn't have a clue.

As DeMarco continued to drive toward Maryland, random thoughts bounced around inside his brain. He wondered how Mahoney was faring. Had it not been for Dillon, he would have called Mary Pat again to ask, but he didn't want to do that now. If he called, Dillon would know and then he might figure out DeMarco's real relationship to Mahoney and find a way to exploit the situation. And what was the point of calling? Hell, Mahoney was going to be all right. Nothing could kill the bastard. In a day or two, he'd be sitting up in his hospital bed eyeing the derriere of every passing nurse.

He thought for a moment about his kitchen; he'd missed the appointment with the contractor who was supposed to give him a repair estimate. Assuming he lived through this thing with Dillon and Bradford, he still had a fight with his insurance company to look forward to.

He also wondered how much danger Angela was in. He hadn't liked the idea of her being sent to Afghanistan in the first place, but he hadn't been too worried about her because he figured she was probably sitting in the U.S. embassy in Kabul being guarded by a battalion of marines. But now, thanks to Dillon, he knew she wasn't in Kabul; she was playing spy games on the Afghanistan-Pakistan border. He wished she'd quit her damn job and take up an occupation that was safe, sane, and normal—and one where she could be with him every night. He also wondered if Bradford knew he was dating Angela and, if he knew, whether Bradford would hold that over his head as Dillon had done.

Then, thinking about women who put their careers ahead of their personal lives, he wondered about Diane Carlucci. Had she given him up to the NSA to protect her FBI career, or did Dillon force her in some way? Whatever the case, he wondered if he'd be hearing from her in the future. It seemed unlikely.

He hit a red light—and noticed a liquor store on one corner. That's what he needed: a drink. There was no booze at the safe house and DeMarco was a man who liked a martini in the evening, and sometimes more than one. He thought of saying out loud: *I want a bottle of vodka waiting for me when I get back to the safe house,* like he was ordering from room service. He knew if he spoke inside the car a gaggle of NSA spooks would hear him, including Alice, who was following him. And then he thought: Why not? All they could do was tell him no.

But then the pinball that was his brain bounced off in another direction: Liquor store. Ray-Ray Jackson.

He stopped for the next red light and looked at the street sign. He was on the corner of New York and Florida—and the liquor store where Ray-Ray worked was about eight blocks away.

A man named Curtis Jackson supervised the janitors in the Capitol. His office was right down the hall from DeMarco's, in the subbasement of the building; as the years had passed, DeMarco and Jackson had gotten to know each other fairly well. Jackson had four children. The oldest one played catcher for the Mets Triple A team in Buffalo. His twin daughters were both in college at Howard—and the tuition was breaking Jackson's back. His other son, Raymond—Ray-Ray—had already graduated from college with a degree in computer sciences; he was the guy DeMarco called whenever his home computer went on the fritz. But now Ray-Ray was going for his MBA and, because his father couldn't afford to pay his tuition too, he was working at a liquor store in the District.

What DeMarco was about to do could put Ray-Ray in danger, but probably not too much. And he had to try. He had to do something that would give him some leverage over Dillon.

He needed paper. Then he thought: What if Dillon had put a camera in the car, too? Well, he'd find out in a minute if there was one. He slowed down so he would hit the next light on the red. Paper. He needed paper. He opened the glove box and saw the owner's manual. He flipped to the back of it where there were a bunch of blank pages and where, if you were totally anal, you could record your maintenance history. He ripped out three of the blank pages.

The light changed. While driving he searched for a pen. He needed a pen. No pen in the glove compartment. He checked the console between the front seats. No pen, but there was a Magic Marker. That would work.

He managed to hit the next three stoplights when they were red—he was probably driving Alice crazy, driving so slowly—and at every red light he wrote on the blank pages from the owner's manual, now certain there wasn't a camera in the car or somebody would have scolded him.

"DeMarco, why are you turning?" Alice asked, her irritation apparent.

DeMarco ignored her.

"DeMarco! Get back on New York and stay on it until you reach—DeMarco, goddammit, why are you stopping?"

"You see that liquor store over there, Alice? I'm gonna buy a bottle of vodka. There's no booze at the safe house, and after what I've just been through, I feel like getting drunk."

"We'll get you some booze. Just keep going."

"And I gotta use the can."

"I said keep going."

"Alice, I want some booze and I wanna take a leak, and if you don't like it, you can kiss my ass."

He heard Alice scream something as he got out of the car.

He walked into the liquor store and saw Ray-Ray was alone behind the counter, sitting on a stool, reading a college textbook. His laptop, which he practically slept with, was sitting on the counter. Ray-Ray smiled when he saw DeMarco and started to say something, but DeMarco held up his first piece of paper and waved it frantically in the kid's face. The paper said, RAY-RAY, SHUT UP! DON'T SAY A THING! NOT A WORD!"

"Hey," DeMarco said, still showing the paper to Ray-Ray. "I need a fifth of Stoli and a small bottle of vermouth."

Ray-Ray stood there, frowning now, not having a clue what DeMarco was doing—and that's when DeMarco handed him the second note.

"You got a bathroom here?" DeMarco said as Ray-Ray read the note.

DeMarco held up the third note. It said: YOU GOTTA DO THIS FOR ME, RAY-RAY. IT'S IMPORTANT, REALLY IMPORTANT.

Ray-Ray nodded and said, "The bathroom's back there, sir. I'll get your vodka."

DeMarco grabbed up the notes and walked to the bathroom. Once there, he flushed the notes down the toilet, then flushed it a bunch more times, and then made as much noise as possible pulling toilet paper off the roll. By then he figured Ray-Ray had accomplished his task—it would have only taken him a minute—so DeMarco left the restroom and walked back to the sales counter.

"Thanks," he said to Ray-Ray, as he took a bag from him containing the bottles of vodka and vermouth—and at that moment Alice stepped into the liquor store. She looked at DeMarco, then over at Ray-Ray, and then stood in the doorway, blocking the exit, until DeMarco reached her. Speaking softly, so Ray-Ray couldn't hear her, she said, "Give me the recorder, DeMarco."

"Sure," DeMarco said, and he switched the brown paper bag containing the booze from his right hand to his left, reached into the pocket of his eavesdropping suit coat with his right hand, and passed her the recorder. Alice looked down at the recorder to make sure it was the one he'd been given by Dillon, and as she was studying it he stepped around her and walked back to his car.

With Alice on his bumper, he continued on to the safe house, smiling slightly, feeling somewhat smug. He'd pulled it off.

"Hey, Alice, do I take the next left?"

"Yes," Alice said, sounding all tight-jawed.

"You know, this is kinda cool. You're like my own personal navigation system."

"Shut up, DeMarco," Alice said.

39

Charles Bradford was spit-shining his shoes when Levy entered his office. As a four-star general and the army's chief of staff, Bradford obviously could have had some soldier shine his shoes but, as he'd told Levy once, he'd started spit-shining his shoes as a cadet at West Point and had always found the task relaxing in a Zen-like way. And he sounded relaxed now as he told Levy about DeMarco's visit and the recordings DeMarco had in his possession.

"Why didn't you detain him when he came here?" Levy asked.

"I considered that," Bradford said. "And if you'd been here, I might have, but I didn't want DeMarco talking to anyone other than you. Where have you been, John?"

"Trying to find DeMarco. I got copies of his phone records and I've been checking out people he calls frequently. One's a woman, and based on how often he calls her, I'm guessing she's his girlfriend. I found out she works at Langley and is out of the country right now, but I haven't been able to get a fix on her location."

"She's with the CIA?"

"Yes, sir."

"Could she be helping DeMarco?"

"I doubt it. I don't know exactly what she does, but I do know she was overseas when all this started."

"Well, don't waste any more time on her," Bradford said. "Everything's going to be fine."

Fine? "Sir," Levy said, "you don't seem very upset by all this."

"Oh, I was very upset at first, John. And I imagine that's what these people were counting on, me panicking and giving in to their demands, resigning because I was afraid they'd go public with what they know. But then I calmed down and thought things through."

"So you're not worried about DeMarco going to the media?"

Bradford ignored Levy as he placed his gleaming shoes on the floor, slipped back into them, and tied them with a double knot. "Of course I'm worried," he said, "and if he did, it would be a three ring circus. But that's not going to happen. I think DeMarco was telling the truth, and whoever he's working with has the intelligence—or maybe the patriotism—to know that going public with those recordings would be bad for the country."

"But what if they did release the recordings?" Levy said.

"John, they have no proof of anything. I suppose the president could order me to resign, but frankly I doubt he has the balls to do that. I'm more popular than he is. And I'd deny everything, of course, but a lot of people will still admire these things I've *allegedly* done."

Levy didn't like the way Bradford was acting. The calmness he was displaying was unnatural—and disconcerting. Bradford should have been angry, worried, demanding action. He should have been developing a plan to neutralize DeMarco and whoever was controlling him. It was as if DeMarco's visit had shocked him so badly he was in a state of denial. Or was it possible, Levy wondered, that Bradford didn't believe anyone could bring him down? Had he stepped over that thin line separating confidence from egomania?

John Levy thought all these things, but he said none of them. All he said was, "Sir, what do you want me to do?"

"Nothing. Don't you understand, son? These people made a huge tactical blunder in sending DeMarco to me with those recordings. Now I know everything they know, and I know they have no evidence linking me to anything Martin did. And I'm about ninety percent certain that whoever's helping DeMarco works for the NSA and this person realizes that to expose me he would have to expose himself, and he's too much of a coward to do that." Bradford inhaled deeply, centering himself. "They took their best shot, John—and they missed."

Levy just stood there, not knowing what to say.

Bradford rose and came out from behind his desk. Putting an arm around Levy's shoulders, he walked him toward the door.

"Go home, son," Bradford said. "Get some rest. It looks like it's been awhile since you've slept."

Bradford wasn't as confident as he had pretended to be with Levy. He was in an extremely vulnerable position, and the only way to negate that vulnerability was to do something he hated to do. He stood up and walked away from his desk, looked briefly out the window, then turned and looked at the photos and plaques on the wall behind his desk—the wall that told the story of his life.

There were photos of him at various stages of his career, from cadet at West Point to chief of the army. He was shown receiving medals, posed with other army generals, and shaking hands with four U.S. presidents. But it was the battlefield photos that meant the most to him: photos with combat troops—his troops—in every arena where the army had waged war in the last thirty-five years. In the center of the wall was the photo he loved the most, the photo that had appeared on the cover of *Time* magazine—the photo that launched his career and defined his life.

It had been taken when he was a second lieutenant in Vietnam, just after the battle for which he'd been awarded the Silver Star. The photographer had captured him in a shot that made it appear as if he was just stepping out of the jungle, pushing his way through an almost impenetrable wall of green foliage. His head was bandaged, the left sleeve of his shirt was missing and his left arm was bandaged from shoulder to elbow. In his right hand he carried an M-16. He was tall and lean and muscular, and his face was smudged with camo paint. And while he looked gaunt and haggard—when the photo had been taken he hadn't slept in three days—his strength and his determination were evident in the grim set of his mouth and in his eyes. He was, in that photo, the nightmare warrior that no enemy would want to face.

His eyes moved from the *Time* cover to one of him standing next to Colin Powell when Powell occupied the chairman's office. He had always liked Powell and had publicly supported him, but he'd always known that Powell wasn't a Patton or a MacArthur—or a Bradford. The difference between those generals and Powell was that Powell didn't have the stomach to *willingly* sacrifice a battalion if it meant winning a major battle, whereas men like Patton and himself had that sort of bloody resolve. It was this same quality that caused Lincoln to ultimately chose Grant over his other generals because Grant *accepted* that thousands of his own men would have to die to reunite the country. And it was not that men like Grant or Patton had been callous or unfeeling. They cared deeply for their soldiers—just as Charles Bradford cared deeply for every man and woman who wore an American uniform—but they understood that preserving a nation was more important than preserving the life of any one person, no matter how much you might love that person.

Bradford returned to his desk and picked up the phone.

Dillon smiled as he listened to Bradford's phone call.

He was a lucky man. The button bug DeMarco had dropped on the carpet in Bradford's office was battery-powered and would stop operating in the next half hour. Fortunately, Bradford had met with Levy before the battery died, and he made the phone call as soon as Levy left his office.

Someone had once said that it was better to be lucky than good—and Dillon was both lucky *and* good.

The most interesting thing about the discussion he'd just listened to between Levy and Bradford was that Bradford never told Levy that DeMarco knew who Levy was and knew what Levy had done.

Yes, it was good to be lucky. But was he lucky enough?

"Do you understand, Alice?" Dillon said.

"Yes," Alice said.

Alice was so *wooden*. Claire could be just as ruthless as Alice, maybe more so, but at least Claire showed some emotion. Not this young lady, though. She was a machine. She was his Terminator.

"You can't lose sight of either man, not for an instant. Use as many people as you think you need."

"I won't lose them," Alice said.

"And the timing has to be perfect. Absolutely perfect."

"I understand," Alice said.

"I wouldn't normally ask you to do something like this but—well, with what's at stake. . . ."

"I said I understand, sir."

Dillon had been reluctant to tell Alice everything that he and Claire knew but finally decided he had to.

"I mean, what Charles Bradford is doing—"

"Dillon, for God's sake," Claire said. "She gets it."

40

It was after midnight when Levy pulled into the parking lot of a small four-story apartment building in Alexandria. He had a two-bedroom unit on the second floor and had lived there for three years. He could have afforded something better but had never seen the need. The apartment was just a place where he slept and occasionally ate. The only reason he had a second bedroom was that he needed space to store his books, all history books, and most of them about the Vietnam War—the war in which he'd lost his father and his brother. He had promised himself that one day he would travel to Vietnam and see the places where they had fought—the places where they'd vanished from the earth.

Alpha, do you have Sentry?
Roger that.
Bravo, do you have Viper?
Roger that. He's still sitting in his car.
Very well. Stand by.

Levy was exhausted. He didn't go home after meeting with Bradford, as he'd been ordered, but had continued to hunt for DeMarco.

The general had said that finding DeMarco was no longer a priority, yet Levy thought it would be prudent to locate the man. But he failed. Again. He had barely slept in the last two days and if he didn't get out of his car in the next minute, he'd fall asleep right where he was sitting.

This is Alpha. Sentry is exiting his vehicle.

This is Bravo. Viper is now exiting his vehicle. Viper is approaching Sentry.

Bravo. Alpha. Execute as briefed.

Roger that.

Levy inserted his key into the lock—and at that instant a bullet smashed into the door, next to his head, shattering the glass. He dropped to the ground and rolled away from the door while simultaneously reaching for his Colt. His reflexes were dulled by fatigue and he fumbled clumsily for the automatic as he tried to pull it from its holster. And he was totally exposed. There was absolutely nothing near the doorway to use for cover. Nothing.

Still rolling on the ground and still struggling to clear his weapon, he saw a man standing in the parking lot holding a silenced semiautomatic pistol in his hand. He couldn't see the man's face clearly because of the lighting, but he could see that the man, at least momentarily, wasn't looking at him. For some reason the man who had just missed his head with a bullet was looking over his shoulder, as if he'd heard someone behind him. Levy thought for an instant that he might be able to return fire, but then the man once again aimed his weapon at him.

John Levy knew he was going to die.

And then he heard the spitting sound of a weapon equipped with a silencer, and the man who'd been about to kill him dropped to the ground.

Who fired the last shot? And who the hell had been trying to kill him?

Levy sat there, his back against the wall of his apartment building, holding his gun now, breathing hard, scanning the parking lot and the surrounding buildings. He couldn't see anyone, but he knew someone was out there.

Finally, he rose to his feet, his gun still in his hand. He was no longer worried about dying, however. The person who fired the last shot obviously didn't want to kill him or he would have done so by now.

He walked over to the man lying on the ground. He knew the man—and he couldn't believe who it was. He didn't understand what was going on.

"Mr. Levy, please holster your weapon." It was a woman speaking, but he couldn't see her.

"Mr. Levy, we don't want to kill you, so please holster your weapon. I'm going to show myself now, but if you raise your weapon you will be shot."

A young woman stepped out from the shadows surrounding the parking lot and stood beneath the cone of light shining down from the streetlamp above her. She wasn't holding a weapon.

"Mr. Levy," she said, "I work for the National Security Agency. You need to come with me."

Alice took Levy to an all-night diner halfway between Washington, D.C. and Fort Meade. Neither she nor Levy said a word while they were driving there. By the time she arrived, Dillon was already in the diner, drinking coffee. He was the only customer in the place. The night cook was out back having a smoke; he had a hundred-dollar bill in his pocket.

Levy sat down at Dillon's table but didn't say anything. He may have been in a state of shock but Dillon doubted that. At this point

Levy was just processing things. Waiting for an opportunity. Alice took a seat several tables away, ready to kill Levy if he attempted to harm Dillon.

"General Bradford tried to have you killed tonight, John," Dillon said. "You do realize that, don't you? And my people saved your life."

Levy still said nothing.

"We've been following you ever since Hopper was killed. Since the night you tried to kill DeMarco."

"So you killed Hopper," Levy said.

"I'm afraid so. He didn't leave us a choice."

"What do you want?" Levy said.

"Don't you want to know why Bradford tried to kill you?"

"The general didn't try to kill me."

"Come on, John. Gilmore was *your* man. The only one who could have given him the green light to kill you was Bradford. You know that."

Levy shook his head. "I don't know how you got to Colonel Gilmore, but you got to him some way. You—"

"I want you to hear something," Dillon said, taking a small digital recorder from his pocket.

Levy said, "If you're planning to play the recording Martin Breed supposedly made, you're wasting your time."

"That's not what's on this recording. This is a recording of DeMarco talking to General Bradford today."

"You're telling me DeMarco snuck a recording device into the chairman's office? Now I know you're lying. DeMarco was checked for bugs before he—"

"John, *please*. I work for the NSA. Do you really believe I couldn't record a conversation in Bradford's office if I set my mind to it? Just listen."

Levy showed no emotion as he listened to DeMarco and Bradford talking.

Dillon hit the STOP button. "Do you understand what DeMarco said, John? He said that you are the only one who can destroy Bradford.

Without your testimony against him, General Breed's recording is insufficient—and Charles Bradford knows this."

Levy just looked at Dillon, and Dillon couldn't help but think that Levy was possibly the saddest-looking man he'd ever met. It was also apparent that in spite of what he'd heard, Levy still didn't believe that Bradford—his mentor, his commanding officer—had tried to have him killed.

"Now I'm going to let you listen to a very short phone call the general made immediately after you left his office today."

Dillon hit the PLAY button on the recorder, and Levy listened to Charles Bradford's words,

Mrs. Cleary, reach out for a Colonel Philip Gilmore. He's stationed at Fort Myer. I want him to meet me in twenty minutes at the chapel at Arlington Cemetery.

"How do I know that's General Bradford speaking?" Levy said. "You may have—"

"John, when Martin Breed told Bradford he was going to expose him, what did Bradford do? It's okay. You don't have to answer that question. You're probably worried that *you're* being recorded right now. So I'll just tell you what he did: He ordered you to kill Martin Breed, a man who had been loyal to Bradford his entire life. And tonight he tried to kill you because now he's afraid *you'll* talk. You know I'm telling you the truth. Just like Martin Breed, you've been completely loyal to Charles Bradford and, just like with Breed, when you became a liability he decided you had to die."

"What do you want?" Levy said.

"I want you to tell the president about the assassinations Charles Bradford ordered. You'll obviously be given immunity"—Dillon knew Levy didn't care about immunity—"and Charles Bradford will be court-martialed. He may go to jail, but whether he does or not, his career will be finished. But what I want to do right now, John, is take you to a safe house. Bradford will try to kill you again."

"And I suppose, if I testify against the general, you'd like me to keep the NSA's role in all this secret?"

"I would very much appreciate that," Dillon said. "No one really needs to know about the transmission we intercepted."

Levy didn't consider Dillon's proposal for even an instant. He stood up. "I'm leaving now. And if you think you can stop me by threatening to kill me, you're wrong. I'm not afraid to die."

"I never thought you were," Dillon said, his voice almost a whisper.

Dillon watched Levy leave the diner before saying, "Alice, offer to drive Mr. Levy back to his apartment. If he refuses and takes a cab, follow him."

"Yes, sir," Alice said.

"And, Alice."

"Yes, sir?"

"Excellent job tonight."

Earlier that day, as soon as Bradford called Colonel Gilmore at Fort Myer, Alice's people began following Gilmore. She had watched Bradford meet Gilmore outside the chapel at Arlington National Cemetery. She'd brought a parabolic mike with her to record their conversation, but Bradford took the colonel inside the chapel to talk to him. And even though Dillon didn't hear what Bradford said to Gilmore, he was positive that Bradford had told him to kill Levy.

Gilmore had waited at Levy's apartment for him to come home, and while he waited, Alice waited, too, with the three agents who had been involved the night Hopper was killed. When Gilmore approached Levy with a drawn weapon, one of Alice's men shot out the window next to Levy's head, which not only startled Gilmore but also gave Levy the impression that Gilmore was the one who had taken the shot. Then Gilmore was killed before he could shoot Levy.

Now all Dillon could do was wait and see if Levy would do as he predicted after reading Levy's file. If he didn't, Dillon might soon find himself in the crosshairs of a sniper's rifle aimed by one of the sentinels who guarded the Unknowns' Tomb. Dillon didn't know exactly what was going to happen next, but he did know one thing for sure: John Levy would never testify against Charles Bradford.

41

Levy parked his car and walked across the damp grass toward the tomb.

It was five A.M. and the only one there was a solitary sentinel. The young man was tall and slender and wore a black coat with light-blue epaulets and dark blue pants with a yellow stripe down the side. The short bayonet on his rifle had been polished until it shone like silver in the dawn light. And the sentinel marched just as John Levy had marched all those years ago. *Exactly* as Levy had marched. The twenty-one slow steps, the twenty-one-second pause before the turn, the click of the heels coming together, the choreographed movement of the rifle shifting to the shoulder farther from the grave.

The sentinel didn't know Levy was watching—he thought he was all alone in the morning mist—and yet he performed the time-honored routine as if the whole world were watching. Levy was so proud of the young soldier—and wished so badly that he could be the one, right now, walking those measured steps on that hallowed ground.

Levy approached the tomb so the guard could see him and saluted. The guard didn't respond, of course, but he must have been surprised to see Levy there at that time of day and must have wondered how he'd gotten into the cemetery. But he didn't stop marching—nor would he, unless Levy attempted to desecrate the grave he protected. Then he'd kill Levy if he had to.

From his position, Levy could see the sentry, the magnificent tomb he guarded, and beyond that row after row of white headstones. There were small American flags near many of the headstones. The top of the Washington Monument was just visible in the distance.

He stood there, in that one spot, never moving, until the sun was above the horizon.

He witnessed a perfect sunrise.

His last sunrise.

"Imagine," Dillon later said to Claire, "that you had devoted your entire life to God. Imagine that you joined a monastery and took vows of silence and chastity and poverty and prayed six times a day, every day, all your adult life, because your belief in God was so strong, your commitment to Him so great. And then one day, in walks an old man and gives you irrefutable proof that God doesn't exist."

Dillon sat with Claire and two of her technicians in the operations room. Through a speaker, he heard Alice.

He's leaving the cemetery.

Fifteen minutes later:

He's entering the Pentagon.

"Claire," Dillon said, "tie into whatever frequency Pentagon security uses for their radios." Claire nodded to one of the technicians.

Ten minutes later the silence in the operations room was shattered:

Red, red, red! I repeat, red! We need medics to the Chairman's office, now! Now!

The man speaking was screaming. Two minutes of silence followed.

Where are those medics, goddammit? Where are they?

They're on the E-ring. They'll be there in another minute. An ambulance is waiting at the entrance.

Forsythe, take Henderson with you and accompany the general.

Roger that. Where are they taking him?

Arlington General.

Four minutes of silence.

Forsythe. Status.

A siren could be heard in the background.

We're three minutes from the hospital, sir.

Two minutes later:

This is Gregory Hamilton.

Hamilton was the Secretary of Defense.

Captain, what the hell happened?

Sir, General Bradford was shot.

I know that! But who shot him?

John Levy, sir.

42

DeMarco had been awake for half an hour. He was sitting in the living room of the farm/safe house in Maryland, sipping coffee, watching the morning news. His unsociable bodyguards were in the kitchen, ignoring him as usual. He was wearing the pants, shirt, and shoes he'd worn to Bradford's office. The suit coat that contained the listening devices had been taken from him—which didn't surprise him—but they also took away the new belt they gave him and insisted he put on his own. This made him wonder if there had been something special about the new belt or if they wanted him to wear his old belt for some particular reason—because it was bugged or had a tracking device installed. His paranoia made him suspect the latter.

The news guy was going on about a tornado that had wiped out a trailer park in Kansas—which made DeMarco think about Dorothy and her red shoes and the Wizard of Oz—but then the newscaster was abruptly replaced in midsentence by Katie Couric, who was sitting behind her desk in the CBS newsroom with a serious expression on her face.

"We have breaking news," Katie said. "The chairman of the Joint Chiefs of Staff, General Charles Bradford, has been shot. All we know at this point is that the general was in his office at the Pentagon when the shooting occurred, and he's been taken to a hospital in Arlington, Virginia."

DeMarco was as stunned as Katie appeared to be. His first thought was: I wonder who shot the bastard? His second thought was: Maybe if he dies, Dillon will let me get back to my life.

For the next ten minutes, all Katie did was demonstrate how little information the network had, but she made the best of it. The station showed an aerial view of the Pentagon, photos of Bradford with the president, photos of Bradford in combat fatigues, including one of him standing next to a bombed-out bunker in Iraq. Katie filled up airtime by talking about Bradford's career and then began to wonder out loud how anyone could penetrate the Pentagon's security and shoot the nation's highest ranking military officer. The picture then cut to a reporter standing in front of a hospital, who told Katie that he didn't know zip and that he and all the other reporters were waiting for somebody to come out and tell them what was going on.

A man in an army uniform walked out of the hospital a moment later and took up a position facing the reporters. He introduced himself as Colonel Andrew somebody and said he was the public affairs officer at the Pentagon. He started off by saying that General Bradford had been shot in the shoulder, and although one of his lungs had been nicked, he was expected to make a full recovery. The reporters immediately started yelling questions, the main one being, Who the hell shot Bradford? The public affairs guy got a funny look on his face, like what he had to say was really painful, and finally answered the mob.

"The general was shot by a man named John Levy. Mr. Levy was a civilian employee at the Pentagon who worked for the Pentagon Force Protection Agency."

Whoa! the reporters exclaimed.

The Pentagon spokesman waited until the uproar died down, then added, "It appears Mr. Levy had some sort of mental breakdown. We don't know, at this point, why he tried to kill the general."

"So where's this guy Levy now?" a reporter demanded. The colonel gave the reporters an irritated look, the look seeming to say, *If you damn people would just shut up, I'd tell you.*

"Mr. Levy is dead. He was shot by a member of General Bradford's security detail."

The reporters started screaming again, but the colonel raised a hand and said, "That's all we know at this point. As other facts become available, you'll be informed."

The television switched back to Couric, who had this wide-eyed, can-you-believe-it look on her face, and then she began repeating for the slow learners everything that the Pentagon spokesman had just told the media.

DeMarco let the noise from the television wash over him. What the hell was going to happen now? He didn't know, but he was certain of one thing: with John Levy dead it was going to be almost impossible to convict Charles Bradford of a crime. Hell, the way things worked, Bradford might even come out ahead on this thing, an assassination attempt being a public relations dream for any high-ranking official.

Charles Bradford's right arm itched where the IV entered a vein near his elbow. He'd been shot twice in Vietnam and this wound was nowhere near as painful as those had been. But maybe the painkillers they used these days were better.

The surgeon had told him that some of the muscles in his shoulder had been severely damaged and it was going to take at least one more surgery to set things right, and after that a lot of physical therapy would be required.

He was a man who had always prided himself on his physical abilities and the thought of being crippled, even for a short time, was depressing. And it wasn't just physical limitations he was concerned about; it was also his image. A general had to appear strong in both mind and body.

He wondered, too, if he was still in shock or if it was because of the drugs, but he felt amazingly calm considering what had just happened.

He had been sitting in his office. He'd arrived at dawn, not being able to sleep, and had been expecting that at any moment Gilmore would call and tell him that John Levy was dead. So when Levy himself opened the door to his office, Bradford was certain his face must have betrayed his astonishment.

The first words out of Levy's mouth were: "Why? You've known me for over twenty years! How could you have ever doubted my loyalty?"

Naturally, he said he didn't know what Levy was talking about. At the same time, he placed his finger on the button beneath his desk.

"You sent Gilmore to kill me last night," Levy said.

"Gilmore? You mean the colonel over at Fort Myer? Why on earth would I have him kill you, for God's sake?"

"I heard you call him."

"You heard me?"

"When DeMarco came to see you, he planted a listening device in your office."

Bradford's heart almost stopped when he heard that.

"I heard DeMarco tell you that they were going to make me testify against you. You should have known I would never do that."

Levy started crying then. Not sobbing, just these fat tears rolling down his long, sad face. "You betrayed me," he said.

"John, you're having some sort of breakdown. It's the stress, the lack of sleep. You know I would never—"

Levy pulled the big Colt from the holster beneath his suit coat and Bradford pressed down frantically on the panic button beneath his desk.

All high-ranking personnel in the Pentagon had a button similar to Bradford's: the Secretary of Defense, the assistant secretary, and each of the joint chiefs. In spite of all the security to prevent armed people from entering the Pentagon, there was always the danger that some employee would go berserk and try to kill his co-workers. That was a too-common occurrence in corporate America, and there was no reason to think the Pentagon was immune to such madness.

Bradford wondered, however, if his security detail would respond in time. He imagined their first reaction would be that he had hit the button accidentally. All he could do was hope that they would perform as they had been trained.

There was no doubt in Bradford's mind that Levy's plan had been to kill him and then kill himself. Thank God that sergeant had been so fast. Levy had just pointed his gun at him when the sergeant burst into the room, his sidearm already in his hand. Of course his gun was in his hand: Bradford had hit the button, which meant his life was in danger.

But Levy hadn't even looked at the sergeant. He was saying, "I loved you more than my own father." And then he fired, but the sergeant fired too, maybe a millisecond before Levy. The sergeant didn't hesitate at all. He saw the threat and he fired, just as he'd been trained to do.

Levy's aim was thrown off by the sergeant's bullet striking his head. He never would have missed otherwise, not standing so close. So instead of the bullet hitting Bradford's heart as Levy had surely intended, he was hit in the shoulder.

It was a miracle he was still alive.

43

"What do we do now?" Claire asked.

"As I see it, we have two options," Dillon said. "We—you and I, my dear—can step forward with what we know. We can testify to some congressional committee, share our recordings with them, and let Congress take it from there. We'll lose our jobs, of course. And our illegal monitoring of American communications traffic will come to a halt, but we'll damage Bradford's reputation enough to at least force him out of the army."

"We can *not* let them disband my division, Dillon. It's vital to preventing another nine/eleven."

"That may be," Dillon said, "but if we expose Charles Bradford, that's what will happen."

"So what's the second option?"

"We do nothing. Life simply goes on as it was before. Bradford may have another John Levy or Martin Breed working for him, but even if he does, I imagine he won't be authorizing any executions anytime soon. He knows we're watching now."

Claire just shook her head.

Dillon stared at her for a moment, then said very quietly, "I'm sorry, Claire, but I don't have all the answers. I think Bradford's won this round and we'll just have to bide our time and look for another opportunity—and hope he doesn't figure out that you and I were the ones helping DeMarco."

"And what about DeMarco?" Claire asked

"He's not going to be a problem. He has no evidence, and he knows what we can do. And I'll threaten him, of course."

"You may be underestimating him, Dillon."

"What are you suggesting? That we murder the man?"

"No, I'm not suggesting that," Claire said. "If we killed DeMarco, we'd be no better than Charles Bradford. I'm just saying, Don't underestimate the guy."

Dillon handed DeMarco his cell phone and the keys to Perry Wallace's truck and said, "You're free to leave, Joe."

"So it's all over," DeMarco said.

"Yes, I'm afraid so."

"And you're not going to expose Bradford, are you?"

"You keep missing the big picture, Joe. I've told you before that exposing Bradford is bad for the country."

"Oh, right. The big picture. Where does my cousin getting murdered fit into the big picture?"

"Joe, I don't have time to debate this with you. And I think you can relax somewhat regarding General Bradford. Now that he knows that other people are aware of his activities, I think he'll exercise some restraint."

"What's gonna restrain him from killing me?" DeMarco said.

"What would be the point? You don't have any evidence and Bradford knows you're just being used by someone else. Killing you won't accomplish anything—or not much, at any rate."

That was really comforting, DeMarco thought.

"Now listen to me carefully, Joe. Some of my colleagues think that leaving you among the living is unwise, but so far I've been able to prevent them from taking any action against you. But if you talk to anyone about any of this. . . . Well, need I say more?"

"No," DeMarco said.

"And you do know, of course, we'll be aware if you talk. You need to keep in mind that every word you say in the future might be overheard. Every call you make might be listened to. Every piece of mail you send may be opened. You need to remember you're dealing with an organization that has at its fingertips technologies you can't even imagine."

DeMarco looked at Dillon for a long moment, then nodded his head.

"I think I'm starting to see the big picture now," he said.

DeMarco was glad that Dillon's people had been kind enough to move Perry Wallace's old pickup from the parking garage at the Days Inn in Crystal City to the safe house in Maryland. Had they not done this, Perry's truck would have been towed away. As things stood now, DeMarco was not looking forward to seeing Perry when he returned the truck, considering how Perry had most likely been grilled by Dillon's agents.

DeMarco turned the key in the ignition, shifted the ancient transmission into first, and took off. He knew that far above his head a satellite was possibly watching him. And somewhere behind him was stone-faced Alice or somebody just like her. And Perry's beat-up Mazda was most likely fitted with a tracking device, and he was almost certain he was wearing listening and tracking devices as well.

He felt like a dog infested with fleas.

He drove a little farther, thoughts buzzing inside his head.

Finally he said to himself, *Fuck the big picture.*

44

"Why's he stopping, Alice?" Claire said.

"He's at that liquor store, the one he went to after he met with Bradford at the Pentagon."

"It would appear that Mr. DeMarco has a drinking problem," Claire said.

"I don't know," Alice said. "He likes his booze, but he doesn't look like an alky to me."

Claire listened to DeMarco's voice through the speaker in the operations room. Alice, parked half a block from the liquor store, was also listening to him via her headset.

Hey. How you doin' today? How 'bout another bottle of Stoli?

Uh, yes, sir.

A couple of minutes passed then*: That'll be twenty-two fifty.*

There you go. And thanks.

And thank you, sir.

"What was that 'and thank you, sir' stuff?" Claire said. "It sounded like DeMarco gave the clerk a big tip or something."

"I don't know what you mean," Alice said.

"I mean that sounded funny. It sounded off," Claire said.

"You want me to do something?"

"No. Just watch his ass. I don't know why, but he's making me nervous. Dillon had better be right about him."

Fifteen minutes elapsed.

"He's stopping again," Alice said.

"Where's he going this time?" Claire said.

"I don't know yet," Alice said. "He just parked the truck. Okay, he's going into an auto parts store."

"What the hell for?" Claire said.

Hey, I need some oil.

The oil's right over there, sir.

Thanks.

Five minutes later.

That'll be twenty-eight fifteen, sir.

"He's heading back to the truck," Alice said.

"Twenty-eight bucks for oil? Does that sound right to you?" Claire said.

"No," Alice said, "but maybe he bought something else."

"What's he doing now?"

"He tossed a bag into the truck and now he's adding oil to the engine. That truck's a piece of shit. It leaked oil all over the garage at the safe house."

Claire didn't say anything.

"He's taking off again," Alice said.

Fifteen minutes later, Alice said, "He's stopped again. He pulled into a loading zone in front of a Starbucks. I guess he wants a latte for the drive home."

Two minutes later, Claire said, "Can you see him?"

"No."

"Get in there, Alice, and see what he's doing. The GPS shows he's not moving, but we can't hear him."

It was five long minutes before Alice reported back.

"Claire, the Starbucks has a back exit that leads to a shopping mall, and I found his clothes in one of the men's rooms. Everything except for his shoes. And there's an empty plastic bag that used to hold a set of coveralls. It looks like he bought the coveralls at that auto shop."

"Son of a bitch!" Claire said. "So we have no devices on him?"

"No," Alice said. She hesitated, then said, "Claire, the Gallery Place metro station is one floor below the mall level. He could be on the metro."

Claire called out to the techs in the operations room. "I want live feed from all of metro's surveillance cameras. Look for a man in coveralls. Start at Gallery Place and expand out from there."

"If he's underground," Alice said, "we can't follow him by satellite until he surfaces again."

"I know that," Claire snapped. "What color were those coveralls?"

"The bag didn't say. Just coveralls."

Shit.

"He's going to be hard to spot in the crowds coming off the subway," Alice said.

"Goddammit, quit telling me things I already know!" Claire screamed.

Claire paced the op room, hovering over her technicians. Ten of them were now looking at surveillance camera images from metro stations trying to spot a man in coveralls. The problem was that from the Gallery Place metro station DeMarco could have gotten on either the Green, Red, or Yellow lines. And one station away was Metro Center, where he could switch to the Orange or Blue lines. He could be headed in any direction, to any place in the District, Virginia, or Maryland—and he could get off at any one of eighty-six metro stations.

But what the hell was he doing? Claire wondered. Where was he running to? Or *who* was he running to?

"Alice," she said.

"Yes?"

"Go back to that liquor store and question the clerk. There was something funny about DeMarco going there."

"Roger that," Alice said.

Fifteen minutes later, Alice called back. "We got a problem," she said. "The clerk at the liquor store is the son of a guy DeMarco works with at the Capitol. When DeMarco went to the store after seeing Bradford, he had the clerk copy the digital recordings to a flash drive."

"Aw, Jesus. Did the clerk listen to the recordings?"

"No."

"Do you believe him?"

"Yeah. He told me the truth."

Claire wondered what Alice had done to the clerk.

"And today," Claire said, "DeMarco went back to the store and got the copy, didn't he?"

"Yes. He's taking the recordings to somebody. Maybe you should focus on the metro stops near the *Post,* and I'll head on over there now. But what do I do if I find him?"

"Tackle him. Taser him. Hit him with your damn car. I don't care. Just get that flash drive."

DeMarco waited as the train approached the next station. He'd switched trains a couple of times to see if he could spot anyone following him, and he thought his tail was clear. They couldn't hear him and they couldn't see him underground with their damn satellites, but he bet they could monitor the surveillance cameras in the stations. Nothing he could do about that.

The station he wanted was coming up next, and once he left the station it was gonna be a foot race.

The metro driver announced the next stop: Union Station.

He put the Nationals baseball cap on his head. He'd paid a kid, one of the metro riders, thirty bucks for the cap. Goddamn thief. The kid could tell he was desperate for the cap.

The train pulled into Union Station. He walked calmly toward the exit, keeping his head down, the bill of the ball cap—he hoped—hiding his face.

"Claire," a tech said, "I think I've got him."

Claire ran over to the tech's monitor. "Where is he?"

"You see that guy?" the tech said. "Coveralls. Ball cap."

"Blow up the picture," Claire said.

The technician did. Claire couldn't see the man's entire face because of the bill of the cap, but she could see his chin. Yeah, that was DeMarco's stubborn chin.

"That's him," she said. "Where is he?"

"Union Station."

Dillon walked into the operations room. Claire had called him as soon as she learned DeMarco had made a copy of the recordings.

"Where the hell's he going?" Claire muttered to herself.

"The Capitol?" Dillon said. "To see a congressman he knows?"

"Then why didn't he get off at the Capitol South Station? That's closer to the House offices."

"Then maybe it's a senator he wants to talk to. The Senate Office Buildings are three blocks from Union Station."

"We have him on the satellite, Claire." It was one of the techs speaking, his little nerd eyes shining. "He's running."

Claire looked up at the screen. Yeah, there he was outside Union Station, running. And he wasn't jogging; he was *sprinting*. Claire bet DeMarco hadn't run that fast since high school.

"Alice," Claire said, "he just came out of Union Station. Do you have anyone near there?"

"I'll be there in two minutes," Alice said.

"Hurry, Alice," Claire said. "Two minutes may be too late."

One of the techs watching the satellite feed said, "He's not going to the Senate Office Buildings. He just ran past them."

Dillon closed his eyes. He knew where DeMarco was going.

"He's going to the Supreme Court," Dillon said. "He figured out who Thomas is."

Alice could see DeMarco ahead of her; he was just starting up the steps of the Supreme Court. She couldn't get any closer to the building in her car because concrete security barriers blocked the street in front of the court.

She stopped the SUV, opened up the tail gate, and took out the rifle. She heard a nearby pedestrian cry out in alarm.

DeMarco was now halfway up the steps.

She aimed at DeMarco through the scope, took a breath, and pulled the trigger.

DeMarco was almost there. He could see U.S. Capitol cops at the top of the stairs looking down at him. He could tell they didn't like the way he looked—some wild-eyed guy running up the steps like a madman. He figured they were going to swarm all over him as soon as he made it to the top of the steps—and that was fine by him.

Then he tripped. He was winded running all the way from Union Station and his left foot hit one of the steps and he pitched forward. At that moment, just as he tripped, he saw a woman coming down the steps topple over. One minute she was walking, and the next second she dropped to the ground like her legs had turned to rubber. He didn't know what had happened to the woman and he didn't have time to find out. He got up and started running again.

"Damn it," Alice muttered. The son of a bitch tripped and she missed him. She figured she had time for one more shot. She aimed again.

As DeMarco passed the fallen woman, he saw the dart sticking out of her chest. A fucking tranquilizer dart. Someone was shooting at him.

But he was almost there now, just a couple more steps to go. And the Capitol Cops were coming right at him, five of them.

DeMarco zigzagged to his left—not to avoid the cops but to throw off the shooter's aim. But the cops thought he was trying to get past them, and one of them pulled out a gun. Oh, shit. The other four cops just kept coming at him but before they reached him, the one in the lead dropped to the ground. There was a dart in his neck.

And then the cops were on him, driving him to the ground, covering him with their bodies.

Thank God.

"How did he figure out that Thomas was Thomas Antonelli?" Claire said.

Dillon stood up. "I don't know," he said, "but he did."

"Where are you going?" Claire said, when she saw Dillon walking slowly toward the door of the operations room.

"Where am I going?" Dillon repeated. "Well, Claire, I think I'm going to jail."

And Dillon was right.

Epilogue

"Okay, Calvin, I'll see your three Marlboros," Clarence Goodman finally said, and tentatively put three Salems down in the center of the card table like they were hundred-dollar chips.

George Aguilera, smiling like he'd already won, immediately added a small can of smoked oysters to a pot which consisted mostly of cigarettes but also a John Grisham paperback and a five-year-old *Playboy*. "I'll call your three and raise you three," Aguilera said.

"Wait a damn minute," Calvin Loring said. "I thought we agreed yesterday that the oysters were worth five cigarettes, not six."

The debate ensued—and Dillon closed his eyes.

In the minimum security section of the Allenwood Federal Correctional Complex at White Deer, Pennsylvania, cigarettes were the gold standard and other commodities for bartering and wagering were based on their value. The value of a cigarette, however, changed periodically, owing to availability of supply and other more esoteric factors. Dillon was thinking about writing an essay on the subject, explaining how the prison economy in black market goods and services was eerily parallel to that of the outside world—there was inflation, price-fixing, insider trading, and market fluctuations due to disasters—although the disasters themselves were unique to prisons, such as lockdowns or retribution from the guards.

Dillon and the three men playing poker with him were dressed identically: blue jeans, white T-shirts, white socks, and plain-toed black lace-up shoes. Dillon's jeans, however, had been tailored by another inmate, a man incarcerated for identity theft but who was quite skillful with needle and thread.

None of his poker-playing pals were violent men. George Aguilera had been the president of a telemarketing company that specialized in bilking old ladies out of their savings. Calvin Loring was a physician who had supplemented his income by supplying OxyContin to teenage addicts via the Internet. Medicaid fraud charges against him were pending. Clarence Goodman had been a hedge fund manager—and the designated fall guy for looting a union pension fund. The depressing part for Dillon was not that he was incarcerated with such people but instead that these three men were the best poker players at Allenwood—and they were uniformly atrocious. None of them, including the hedge fund manager, appeared to have the slightest understanding of the mathematical odds of a particular hand winning or losing. After Dillon had won enough cigarettes to become the Donald Trump of Allenwood, he began cheating. He had always been a good card mechanic and in prison he had plenty of time to practice and become a truly stellar one. He didn't cheat to win, however. When it was his turn to deal, he would give all the players, except for himself, outrageously good hands—four of a kind, flushes, full houses—and then would sit back and watch them go crazy betting against one another. It was one of the things he did to alleviate the perpetual boredom.

Boredom was, in fact, the worst thing about being in prison—although if he had been sent to some other federal facility he might not have been able to say that. He had almost ended up in a maximum security prison in Ohio, where he would have undoubtedly become the plaything of one of the psychotics who resided there. Fortunately, and thanks to information he had obtained while at the NSA, he was able to keep that from happening.

It had all gone pretty much the way he'd expected: DeMarco had delivered the recordings to Justice Antonelli—and Antonelli believed every word he heard. DeMarco had figured out that Thomas Antonelli was the Thomas on Breed's recording when he saw a newspaper photo of Antonelli at General Breed's funeral and the accompanying article that said Antonelli was related to Breed's wife. And then Antonelli did exactly what Dillon had thought he would do: he went immediately to the president and told him that if he didn't clean up this whole NSA/Bradford mess, he was going to go public with everything.

Fortunately, at least from Dillon's perspective, Antonelli was wise enough to realize that the U.S. government couldn't let the entire world know what Charles Bradford had done because no one would believe that Bradford had been acting independently and without the sanction of his government. If Bradford had only killed a few Muslim terrorists, it might have been different, but Bradford had executed members of the Saudi, Pakistani, and Chinese governments—and the president really didn't want to piss off the Chinese. Nor did the president particularly want it known the NSA was—once again—intercepting the communications of U.S. citizens without the required warrants.

The president assigned a special prosecutor—one of the few people in Washington actually capable of keeping a secret. The prosecutor questioned people in camera—meaning that none of his meetings were open to the public—and the records of those meetings were sealed for fifty years. The president figured that whoever was president half a century from now could decide if he or she wanted to declassify this god-awful debacle and let the world of the future know about it.

DeMarco was questioned several times by the prosecutor, and one time he was questioned with Dillon present. The prosecutor wanted to see if Dillon would deny any of DeMarco's accusations—which Dillon didn't. Dillon admitted that he had David Hopper and Colonel Gilmore killed but only to protect the lives of DeMarco and John Levy. He also admitted he planted bugs in Charles Bradford's office and manipulated John Levy to kill Bradford. That is, he freely admitted he did his very best to rid the United States government of Charles Bradford while trying to keep secret everything Bradford had done. In other words, he admitted that he tried to do exactly what the president was now trying to do.

What Dillon refused to do was provide the names of anyone at the NSA who had helped him, and the only people DeMarco could identify were Alice and the three men who guarded him at the farmhouse in Maryland. But DeMarco didn't know anyone's last name, and Alice and the guards had disappeared. The one thing Dillon lied about was that he'd intercepted the transmission of Paul Russo being killed intentionally. He explained, in complex technical language, how the intercept had been inadvertently obtained due to "satellite malfunction."

The president's special prosecutor didn't believe him.

Admiral Fenton Wilcox and his deputy director were fired and a new director was appointed to the NSA. The new director was a bright fellow, a three-star air force general who had previously worked at the agency, and he was told by the president that his first task was to ensure that the NSA was eavesdropping in accordance with all the rules. To assist the general in this task, seventy independent inspectors descended upon Fort Meade to review everything the agency was doing. Naturally, almost all the inspectors were former NSA employees because the new NSA director couldn't find other people with the appropriate security clearance and the technical knowledge to do the review.

After six months of grueling work, the inspectors found a few minor compliance and procedural problems but failed to uncover the true nature of Claire Whiting's secret division. One reason for this was because the day after DeMarco gave the recordings to Justice Antonelli, Claire's personnel all began to perform legitimate—albeit less useful—functions, and the only American communications they intercepted while the inspectors were conducting their review were those permitted by FISA warrants. Claire's ability to hide her true role in Dillon's organization was also made easier by the fact that after Dillon was incarcerated, the new NSA director, deciding he needed to raise the glass ceiling at Fort Meade and have a few more women in high-ranking positions, concluded that Claire was the best person to fill Dillon's former position at the agency.

The president's special prosecutor also questioned the two young soldiers who had killed Paul Russo and the reporter, Robert Hansen. They sat there, shell-shocked, saying how they'd been told by John Levy that the men they had killed were foreign terrorists, and the prosecutor had no doubt the soldiers had been duped by Levy and the late Colonel Gilmore. The soldiers, however, knew nothing regarding Levy's connection to Charles Bradford.

The prosecutor realized that there were probably ten or twenty soldiers out there, present and former members of the Old Guard at Fort Myer, who had committed assassinations under Bradford's orders. He was sure all these dedicated young men had no idea that they had done anything illegal, and he was equally sure they had all been sworn to secrecy. And he was confident that Charles Bradford and Martin Breed had selected only men who could keep a secret. The prosecutor decided—and the president concurred—that it would be in everyone's best interest to probe no deeper into the activities of the Old Guard. Without a Charles Bradford to lead them, the sentinels who guarded the Tomb of the Unknown Soldier would go back to being nothing more than exceptional sentinels.

Charles Bradford, as Dillon had expected, presented the president with an impossible dilemma. There was no direct evidence proving Bradford had ordered Martin Breed to assassinate anyone—and Bradford, when questioned by the prosecutor, denied giving Breed any such orders. Bradford said he may have supported *in principle* what Breed had done, but he would never have acted in such a unilateral, illegal, and dangerous manner. And he noted that, at the end of his life, Martin Breed had been afflicted by a terrible case of brain cancer, and the last time he saw Breed, the man had been unable to distinguish reality from fantasy.

The prosecutor did have in his possession the recording DeMarco had given to Thomas Antonelli, the recording in which Breed admitted to carrying out thirteen assassinations for Charles Bradford. The prosecutor was sure that Breed's admissions on the recording, combined with DeMarco's testimony, would be sufficient to convince any reasonable jury of Charles Bradford's guilt. When he told Bradford this, Bradford's response had been: *So try me.*

Bradford knew the last thing that the president wanted was a public trial or a court-martial. Bradford also knew that when the public heard about who Breed had assassinated—mostly people with known links to terrorists—a large segment of the population would consider Charles Bradford a hero for what he had allegedly done. The rest of the world would, of course, have a different view of his actions—and it was really the rest of the world the president was trying to keep in the dark.

The president considered convening a secret military tribunal; after Bradford was found guilty he would be locked away in a maximum security prison in total isolation. He was afraid if he did this, however, someone on the tribunal, someone sympathetic to Bradford, would talk to the press. Someone always talked to the press. He also considered simply having Bradford killed and wondered if he could do as King Henry II had done with Thomas à

Becket—*Will no one rid me of this troublesome priest?*—and hope that someone on his staff would show some damn initiative for a change. In the end, though, he just couldn't bring himself to do it. He wanted whatever he did with Charles Bradford to have at least the appearance of being legal.

While the president was deliberating, Chief Justice Thomas Antonelli was leaping up and down in his black robes, demanding that the president do something, and do something soon! Antonelli had knowledge that crimes had been committed, and this knowledge weighed heavily upon his conscience. And he pointed out that Bradford hadn't just assassinated foreigners, he'd also killed a number of U.S. citizens, including Paul Russo and a member of the press.

Thomas Antonelli didn't see the big picture either.

Then the president's devious, brilliant, special prosecutor found a solution.

The right of habeas corpus—basically, the constitutional right to be tried before one is imprisoned—had been overturned several times by past presidents via executive order. Lincoln issued an executive order to suspend habeas corpus during the Civil War. Japanese Americans were interned during World War II because of an executive order issued by Roosevelt. In more recent times, executive orders had been issued to suspend habeas corpus in the case of folks like the terrorists in Guantanamo.

Well, okay, the president said. If it was good enough for Lincoln and Roosevelt, it was good enough for him, so he had his special prosecutor write up an executive order saying, in flowery legal language peppered with historical precedents, that it was okay for him to toss a guy into a cell without a trial when the guy had committed extraordinary crimes and when public disclosure of those crimes could do grave harm to the United States. The president figured he might be able to convince Justice Antonelli to play along if he promised to limit his executive order to Charles Bradford and shredded it immediately thereafter. If

Antonelli didn't play along, at some point he would have to admit that he had remained silent while the president struggled with the Bradford dilemma.

Yes, the president liked the idea. There were still a few details to be ironed out, but the basic concept was solid. He'd sign the executive order and then Bradford would be whisked off to a cell by a few extremely tight-lipped folks and be kept in isolation until he died. Exactly where the cell would be and who would do the whisking were a couple of those details that needed to be nailed down. To explain why Bradford had suddenly disappeared, he would appear to die while piloting the Cessna he owned. But then—just when the president was on the cusp of discussing his plan with Justice Antonelli—something happened, something that made Dillon Crane, a lifelong agnostic, reconsider his views regarding the existence of a Divine Being: Charles Bradford was diagnosed with pancreatic cancer. He would be dead in less than a year.

The president summoned Bradford to the Oval Office, showed him the executive order, and gave Bradford a choice: resign immediately and agree to keep his mouth shut or he would go directly from the White House to a special facility in the Blue Ridge Mountains the CIA used for detaining certain folk. Bradford, still in shock from the news of his illness and impending death, took the deal. After he resigned, the president took the precaution of assigning people to monitor all of Bradford's communications to make sure he didn't e-mail his memoirs to a publisher; in a twist of irony, the organization assigned to monitor Bradford was the NSA.

So in the end, except for the fact that Dillon now resided behind bars in White Deer, Pennsylvania, things worked out. The men responsible for the deaths of Paul Russo, Robert Hansen, and several others were all dead or soon would be, and the world at large would never know what Charles Bradford had done.

Dillon's reverie was interrupted by George Aguilera. "Dillon, for God's sake, will you please settle this? How much did we agree the damn oysters are worth?"

Dillon sighed, opened his eyes, and stood up. "Would you gentlemen please excuse me? I'm not feeling very well."

Actually, he'd never felt better in his life. That was one of the positive things about a prison environment: it was extraordinarily healthy. He ate a balanced diet, slept eight hours a night, exercised regularly, and ingested no alcohol. He'd even taken up yoga and was more flexible than he'd been as a teenager.

He walked out into the exercise yard, took a seat on a bench, turned his face toward the sun, closed his eyes—and recommenced designing the villa. He'd already designed the exterior, the great room, the master bedroom, and was now working on the kitchen. He'd committed none of his plans to paper, preferring to keep it all in his head as a mental exercise. Soon, however, he would actually begin constructing the villa on land he'd already purchased in Italy on a cliff overlooking the Mediterranean.

He would be released as soon as Bradford died, although the government hadn't agreed to this yet. He hadn't been convicted of a crime; he had been jailed for contempt, for refusing to tell the special prosecutor who had helped him at the NSA. The reality was, however, that, just like Charles Bradford, no one was quite sure what to do with him, and he'd made it clear to the prosecutor—and the president—that to do anything truly harmful could have grave consequences.

Dillon just *knew* too much. He knew too much about too many operations and about too many people. He and Claire had acquired enough information since 2002 to blackmail a large number of very influential politicians in Washington—Justice Thomas Antonelli and the president's special prosecutor, unfortunately, being exceptions. He also had in his possession, or so he told the prosecutor, a recording of the president having a very interesting phone conversation with a young woman in Miami. He pointed out to the president's lawyer that with all the other problems the president currently had, he certainly didn't need to go down the Bill Clinton trail.

But when Bradford died, he would ask, quite politely, to be released. After Bradford was dead—and after the new NSA director had completed his review to verify that the NSA was squeaky clean—there wasn't much point in keeping Dillon in prison and risking his talking about what he knew. So he'd wait, and after Bradford's funeral he would remind the special prosecutor it would be in everyone's best interest if he were to be given a very quiet, under-the-table, presidential pardon for any crimes he *might* have committed and allowed simply to retire to Italy.

Why Italy he wasn't really sure, but that's where he had decided to build his villa. He could have stayed in the Untied States, but it seemed prudent to put some distance between himself and his homeland. He knew he'd enjoy the Italian climate, food, and wine; he might even be able to find a group of people who could actually play poker. But the truth was that he didn't want to retire. He was afraid that his Italian villa would soon become just another prison and he'd be as bored there as he was now.

He missed the game so. The game the NSA played, the game he'd played all his life—the game he'd never play again.

DeMarco couldn't figure out what to do with his cousin's ashes.

After he finished testifying to the president's special prosecutor about Charles Bradford and Dillon Crane, he called the young pastor at St. James, told him that Paul had a will in a safety deposit box at his bank, the will left about four grand to the church—and if the padre wanted the money, it was *his* problem to figure out how to get it. The only remaining task he had on his plate related to his late cousin was dealing with his ashes—and he was stumped.

He finally called Mary Albertson, the lady who had worked so closely with Paul at the church. She told him there was a spot on the Potomac that Paul always spoke of, a peaceful place shaded by old trees where the river flowed rapidly over a number of large boulders. Mary said Paul used to go there quite often to relax and pray. When she volunteered to go there with him to hold a small service for Paul, DeMarco could have kissed her.

Mary recited a couple of psalms from memory and, as she did, DeMarco thought about his cousin—a quiet, pious man, who had the courage to do something so incredibly dangerous that it cost him his life. As DeMarco released Paul's remains into the current, Mary Albertson sang "Amazing Grace." She had a magnificent voice and almost moved DeMarco to tears.

The president's prosecutor had scared the hell out of DeMarco. He said that if DeMarco lied to him, he was going to throw him in jail. He told him if ever spoke to anybody about Charles Bradford, Dillon Crane, or the true circumstances surrounding the deaths of David Hopper, John Levy, and Paul Russo, he would also throw him in jail. DeMarco didn't know if the prosecutor actually had the authority to make good on these threats, but it didn't matter. It didn't matter because (a) he was terrified of the prosecutor and (b) he had no desire to talk to anyone about what he knew. He couldn't do his job for Mahoney if he was a celebrity witness—nor could he do his job if he was in jail.

Mahoney recovered completely from the infection that almost killed him. DeMarco was relieved by this but not surprised; he had always known John Mahoney couldn't be killed by an army of tiny germs. Mahoney would meet his end one day with a massive heart attack, or the husband of some young woman he was bedding would shoot him through the heart. DeMarco did end up telling Mahoney about Charles Bradford and Dillon Crane in spite of the prosecutor's dire warnings. He did this because Mahoney found out through his vast network of informants that DeMarco had been to the Justice Department several times to meet with an unnamed prosecutor, and Mahoney was afraid DeMarco might be testifying against *him.* So to allay his boss's concerns—and to keep his job—DeMarco eventually told Mahoney what had transpired while Mahoney had been in a coma.

Angela returned home from Afghanistan. She had lost weight and had deep circles under her eyes, as if she hadn't slept for a month. Worse than her appearance, though, she couldn't sleep after she returned to Washington and eventually began to see a CIA psychiatrist twice a week. DeMarco had no idea what she had done for the CIA in Afghanistan or what she had experienced. All he knew was he hated her damn job but she refused to quit.

DeMarco couldn't imagine what it would be like to be responsible for keeping terrorists from attacking the country with nuclear bombs or anthrax or God knows what. And that's what people like Angela and Dillon Crane did. DeMarco didn't like the fact that Dillon had manipulated him and forced him to participate in his plan to bring down Bradford, but he privately thought the country was less safe with Dillon gone. As for monitoring phone calls without warrants, well, he certainly didn't want *his* calls monitored, but when it came to other people, maybe. . . .

Oh, to hell with it. It was too complicated. He cast all thoughts of Dillon Crane out of his head, took a deep breath, exhaled slowly, hit the ball with his pitching wedge—and it landed within ten feet of the cup. Yes! His game had improved dramatically in the last few weeks because half the time when he was supposed to be talking to the president's special prosecutor, he played golf instead. How was Mahoney supposed to know?

Mahoney didn't have a satellite to keep tabs on him.

Alice walked into Dillon's old office. There were no Picassos on the walls, no putter propped in the corner, no expensive topcoat hanging on the coat rack. The office was now as stark and functional as the person who occupied it.

"We picked up something important last night," Alice said.

Smiling slightly, Claire repeated what Dillon had once said to her on a similar occasion. "I'm sure it's important, Alice, or you wouldn't be here. But is it interesting?"

A satellite orbits a blue planet, huge solar panels extended like wings.

Author's Note

The title of this book came from a speech by Abraham Lincoln given in 1858: *A house divided against itself cannot stand.* The "house" in this case is the Department of Defense, with the NSA pitted against the Pentagon and the chairman of the Joint Chiefs.

I speculate in this book that Dillon Crane's bosses at the NSA wouldn't have the technical background to understand what Dillon and Claire were doing. This was just an assumption on my part, but as I was finishing this book, I read *The Shadow Factory* by James Bamford, a work of nonfiction. Mr. Bamford is an expert on the NSA and has written three books on the agency, *The Shadow Factory* being the most recent. In *The Shadow Factory,* Bamford attributes the following quotation to the three-star air force general who was director of the NSA during the controversial warrantless wiretapping program reported by *The New York Times* in 2005: "*I am not a mathematician or a computer scientist and I won't pretend to be one. I will be relying heavily on all of you who are.*" The general has a master's degree in history.

Regarding the NSA's warrantless surveillance program, following is a quotation from one source I used that is consistent with many other sources:

> (The) NSA warrantless surveillance controversy concerns surveillance of persons within the United States incident to the collection of foreign intelligence by the National Security Agency as part of the war on terror. Under this program . . . the NSA [is] authorized by executive order to monitor phone calls, e-mails, Internet activity, text messaging, and other communication involving any party believed by the NSA to be outside the U.S., even if the other end of the communication lies within the U.S., without warrants. The exact scope of the program is not known, but the NSA . . . was provided total unsupervised access to all fiber-optic communications [in] some of the nation's major telecommunication companies.

AN/PRC-150 radios—the radios used by John Levy and the sentinels the night they killed Paul Russo—are indeed encrypted radios used by the military. I have no idea, however, if the NSA can de—encrypt transmissions from these radios. Smarter folks have said probably not—but, hey, this is fiction and I'm still thinking the geniuses at the NSA can probably do just about anything.

Would a lawyer from the Justice Department be able to enter NSA headquarters, be given access to intercepts, and do an audit as Aaron Drexler does in this book? Once again, probably not—and certainly not without a giant fight between the Pentagon and the Justice Department over security issues related to such an audit. In my research, I did find information on audits conducted by the Department of Justice's Inspector General related to government surveillance programs, but these audits were looking more at the FBI than at the NSA.

St. James Church in Falls Church, Virginia, does have a number of tall stained-glass windows depicting various saints, and St. John of God is one of the patron saints of nurses and the dying—but I didn't see a window depicting St. John.

Last—just like DeMarco—I'm rather ambivalent about the NSA monitoring the communications of U.S. citizens to identify terrorist plots. I certainly don't want them listening to *my* phone calls, but I think it may be okay for them to monitor *yours* to keep us safe.

Acknowledgments

I have a lot of people to thank who helped with this book. David Gernert for numerous suggestions to improve the book; the finished novel is significantly better than the first draft, thanks to him. Lance Otis for his insights regarding the NSA. Bob Koch for reading sections of the book and giving me his political perspective on one section. (Those who know Bob and me well will see the irony in this.) Frank Horton for finding ten thousand typos. A huge thanks to Georgia Steffen for coming up with the idea of the sentinels at the Tomb of the Unknown Soldier and to Maureen Harman for passing it on to me. Also Bill Harman and his friend Ken Dietrick for helping me understand how the state of Virginia deals with wills—any errors in the legal stuff in the book are mine and mine alone. My nephew, Dan Smaldore, of whom I'm very proud and who is an Arlington police officer and who answered questions regarding police procedures and jurisdictions. His Honor James Donohue and Bryan Dearinger for questions regarding the Justice Department, and fellow writer Dr. Allen Wyler for medical advice—once again, any errors on the medical stuff are mine alone.

Lastly, everyone at Grove/Atlantic and The Gernert Company.